Praise for *Seeking the American Dream*

"Heidi Thomas's latest novel grips the reader from the first opening sentence, as her nurse-protagonist struggles to face the wretched suffering in war-torn Hamburg during the final days of WWII. From there, her sweeping saga takes her away from Europe's lurching efforts to rebuild, and into the building of her own new life in America. From the perspective of a hard-working, and still bright-eyed young woman, we participate in America's own next chapter." –Mara Purl, best-selling author of the Milford-Haven Novels

"Once again, I open the pages of a Heidi Thomas novel and I'm transported to another time and place. From post WWII Germany to the sometimes-brutal Montana ranch life, Seeking the American Dream explores one woman's journey as she faces impossible odds to live her dream. Ms. Thomas is excellent at period literature. You won't be disappointed."— Brenda Whiteside, Author of The Love and Murder Series

"Seeking the American Dream is such a beautiful, heartwarming book! It was a pleasure to read about Anna's quest for her dream. I didn't just enjoy it, I loved it! Heidi Thomas has a way of building suspense that just kills me. Readers will love it as much as I do." –Carol Buchanan, award-winning author of "The Vigilante Quartet" series

Other Books by Heidi M. Thomas
Cowgirl Dreams series
Cowgirl Drea~~
Follow the D
Dare to Dr

Nonfictic
Cowgirl Up: A History o

Praise for the "Cowgirl Dreams" series

Cowgirl Dreams: "Nettie Brady defies anyone who challenges her right to become a rodeo rider. She'll gladly take the bone-jarring, gut-twisting ride of a wild steer rather than endure the stark boredom of women's work in the 1920s. Needlepoint isn't her thing– horseback riding, working cattle, and, yes, rodeo riding are what her life is all about. But family is important, too, and their disapproval makes for heart-wrenching decisions. Heidi Thomas does a magnificent job of pulling readers into another time, another place. *Cowgirl Dreams* is an exciting read, full of heart and yearnings." —Mary E. Trimble, author of *Rosemount, McClellan's Bluff,* and Spur Award finalist *Tenderfoot*

"...Brings heart, verve and knowledge to her depiction of the intrepid Nettie. A lively look at the ranch women of an almost forgotten West." —Deirdre McNamer, MFA English Professor, University of Montana, *Red Rover, My Russian,* and *One Sweet Quarrel*

Follow the Dream: "I enjoyed this bittersweet novel with its accurate depiction of the lives of cowgirls in 1930s Montana and its tender portrait of a marriage." Mary Clearman Blew, award-winning author of Jackalope Dreams, *All but the Waltz: A Memoir of Five Generations in the Life of a Montana Family,* and *Balsamroot: A Memoir*

"In her poignant tale of Nettie Moser's diligent pursuit of a dream, Heidi Thomas gives a stunning example of what it means to "Cowgirl Up." *Follow the Dream* is a dynamic story of a woman's strength and determination that is sure to inspire as well as entertain.—Sandi Ault, award-winning author of *Wild Sorrow*, in the *WILD* Mystery Series

Dare to Dream: "Finding our place and following our hearts is the moving theme of *Dare to Dream,* a finely-tuned finish to Heidi Thomas's trilogy inspired by the life of her grandmother, an early rodeo-rider. With crisp dialogue and singular scenes we're not only invited into the middle of a western experience of rough stock, riders and generations of ranch tradition, but we're deftly taken into a family drama. This family story takes place beginning in 1941 but it could be happening to families anywhere - and is. Nettie, Jake and Neil struggle to find their place and discover what we all must: life is filled with sorrow and joy: faith, family and friends see us through and give meaning to it all. Nettie, or as Jake calls her, 'Little Gal' will stay in your heart and make you want to re-read the first books just to keep her close. A very satisfying read."—Jane Kirkpatrick, *a New York Times* Bestselling author and WILLA Literary Award winner of *A Flickering Light*

Cowgirl Up: A History of Rodeo Women: The best kind of history lesson; Informative and entertaining. Thomas does a great job of showing the lifestyles of these women in a very male dominated world, and how through hard work and determination they gained the respect of many people not only in the U.S., but throughout the world. You can't help but be impressed with the toughness of these women, who competed even with broken bones and other injuries. An eye-opening look at the world of rodeo, and the accomplishments of these women. –John J. Rust, author of *Arizona's All-Time Baseball Team* and *Fallen Eagle: the Alaska Front.*

A SunCatcher Publications book

Cover Design by Jason McIntyre
www.TheFarthestReaches.com

Library of Congress Cataloguing-in-Publication data is available on file.

ISBN - 978-0-9990663-0-0

Printed in the United States of America

10 9 8 7 6 5 4 3 2 1

Seeking the American Dream
A Novel

Heidi M. Thomas

To Sarah —
Thank you for
"being there"!
Hope you enjoy this —
Heidi M. Thomas

SunCatcher Publications
Chino Valley, Arizona

DEDICATION

I dedicate this book to the memory of my mother, Rosel Engel Gasser, who showed such courage in seeking her dream in America.

ACKNOWLEDGMENTS

I thank God for giving me the writing gene, my family for their continued support and encouragement, the teachers and editors who believed in me, my fellow Women Writing the West members, my former critique groups in Washington who encouraged me when I was just starting out, and my present critique group who has given me such valuable feedback: Sally Bates, Barbara Beck, John J. Rust, and Brenda Whiteside. Thank you to my beta readers, Carol Buchanan and Brenda Whiteside for helping make my work better.

"Go up to the land flowing with milk and honey." Exodus 33:3

CHAPTER ONE

Hamburg, Germany. October, 1944

The smell of death seeped into Anna's nostrils. It clutched at her hair, her clothes, her life.

She paused at the door of the operating room, steeling herself against yet another day of cries and moans, the cloying sweet stench of rotting flesh above the acrid odor of disinfectant. There was only so much sulfa could do to ward off infection. She adjusted her starched white cap, willing herself once again to face the blood and pus, the gaping wounds, the young soldiers' lost limbs, as she had every day for months in this hell that was the surgical ward. Would this war never end? Her skin turned clammy.

Anna saw her fiancé, Dr. Fritz Baumgartner, in the scrub room. He looked up, smiled and blew her a kiss. She mimed catching it and throwing one back. A warm light lifted her heart. What good fortune that he was such a specialized surgeon that he hadn't been called to serve at the front. He was needed at this hospital. For now, at least, they could be together.

How often he had reassured her, "This, too, shall pass. We must believe that God has a purpose for us. We are here to help." His quiet comfort, his faith, her love for him—perhaps it wasn't enough. Her heart darkened again. She hated this war, despised that she couldn't do more for these suffering men.

Anna shook her head. How enthusiastic she'd been five years ago when she'd started her nurse's training as a Red Cross helper. At sixteen, she'd still worn the idealism of the young.

But then a couple of years later, she'd been conscripted for a year in the work camps, where women did the farm labor in place of the men who were at the front. Where women were treated as slaves, as chattels, bearing the brunt of cruel taskmasters' whims. Her back tightened, feeling again the pain of the riding crop as she had stumbled in the pre-dawn darkness to the fields. She shook her head to clear the memories.

But no relief awaited her at the hospital. Every day since she returned from that conscription she'd felt as if her efforts were tiny and feeble. Her shoulders sagged. She felt as ancient as Methuselah.

Anna pulled up her mask, hoping to block the sick sweat, fecal stench, and vomitus, to no avail. She couldn't breathe. She just couldn't face this shift—not yet. She turned away. As if watching herself from above, she found herself running to the end of the long corridor. Past the rooms of groaning young men. Past the Nazi recruiting and anti-spy posters lining the hallway. Past those flyers encouraging blackouts. Past the one depicting a woman plowing the field while her husband fought on the front. *Ja*, Anna had been there, with those women. She'd done her duty, was still doing her duty for *das Vaterland*.

She flung open the outside door, tore off her mask and gulped great draughts of fresh air.

Anna walked fifty yards beyond a low bunker and leaned against the sand-bagged wall. The morning sun warmed her up-thrust face and burned a red haze against her closed lids. She barely heard the incessant drone of warplanes anymore—the sound more like bees buzzing around spring blossoms—when blooming gardens were still part of life. Gradually her breathing returned to normal and her shoulders relaxed a few notches below her ears.

Now, Fräulein Schmidt, enough of this self-pity. She opened her eyes and placed her fists on her hips as if lecturing a first-year apprentice nurse. *You have all of your limbs. Your whole life is ahead of you. It is your duty to care for these boys and be cheerful about it. Now get back to work.* Funny how that voice in her head sounded just like Papa's, always no-nonsense, so stern.

Anna smiled then, a trembling upward curve of her lips, but a smile nonetheless. Cheery. Calm. This is how she must present herself to her patients.

The buzz droned louder, more persistent. Anna blinked and frowned. She squinted into the white-hot sky, now darkening. Planes. Hundreds of planes. Her eyes widened. A piercing whine cut through the hum. Anna screamed. With a deafening roar, her world exploded around her. The concussion catapulted her to the ground. Bricks rained from the sky. She covered her head as best she could with her arms and buried her face in the loamy earth. *Death. Here it comes. Ach, mein Gott, let it be swift.*

***

How long she lay there, Anna could not tell. She needed to breathe. A damp, earthwormy smell clogged her nostrils. She was still alive. She wiggled her fingers, her toes, felt the crisp dried grass on her bare legs. Then she raised her head. Dust and smoke and flame boiled from the huge pile of rubble that had been a two-story hospital only minutes before.

"Fritz!" Anna pushed herself up with her scratched and bleeding arms, then to her knees. Pain ricocheted from the back of her legs to the top of her head. She cried out, then struggled to stand, ignoring the discomfort. *Ach, du lieber Gott.* She put her hands to her head. Her cap was missing, the white pinafore apron covering her blue pinstriped dress smudged with dirt and blood. But she couldn't worry about her injuries right now.

Fritz. Where was Fritz?

She staggered toward the wreckage, terror icing her veins. The nurses. The soldiers. They needed help. She must find them. Anna pulled at the pile of bricks where the door had been, flames sending her into retreat. "Fritz! Liesel! Maria!" She called out her friends' names. "Where are you? Answer me!" She choked on her words. *Nein. Nein.* This couldn't be. The

3

hospital was gone. She saw no one moving around, heard no one. Air raid sirens shrieked above the ringing in her ears. Anna skirted the burning rubble, looking for movement—for bodies. She choked on her sobs. Gone. All gone. She stumbled and went down.

***

Anna awoke to the dank smokiness of a bomb shelter. Someone bathed her forehead. She moaned, struggled to lift her head, to see the hunkered silhouettes crowded in the cellar, no bigger than the bedroom she shared at home with her sister, Elsa.

"There, there. You're safe." A woman supported her shoulders, helped her take a drink of tepid water.

Anna gulped, then choked, remembering. "All...dead?"

The woman nodded. "I'm sorry. It was a magnesium bomb. The hospital burned to the ground. You apparently are the only survivor. You were lucky somehow. Just cuts and bruises."

No one left. Nothing. Anna closed her eyes and sank back on the blanket covering the dirt floor. "*Mein Fritz. Nein, nein.*" A tear leaked from the corner of one eye and spiraled down her cheek toward her ear. She curled into a fetal position, squelched the sob choking her, and willed the dark oblivion to return.

***

The days following the bombing blurred. Anna returned to the hospital wreckage. Hitler Youth in their uniforms and old men in tattered coats searched through the rubble, moving it brick by brick. Anna scrabbled in the ruins, her fingers bleeding. Hope flared when she saw a man, his back to her, standing near a pile of debris. Something familiar about the way he held his shoulders.

Her breath caught. "Fritz."

The man turned toward her, eyebrows raised. No. Not Fritz. Cold emptiness filled her. She staggered backward, dizzy. Anna turned and ran.

And still the air-raid sirens wailed. They screamed day after day, night after night, as first the British and then the Americans relentlessly bombed Hamburg as they had all the German cities for three long years, causing merciless destruction with their "thousand plane raids."

Anna tried to go to bed each night as normal, but she lay tense and awake, straining to hear the sound of the planes. If she dozed, she awoke with a start and a feeling that she'd missed something. When the sirens screamed, she ran again and again through the streets, stumbling through rubble from previous shellings. Planes roared overhead, machine-guns rattled in dog-fights, more bombs convulsed the earth. Panic spread like a wildfire inside as she headed for the bomb shelter—the choking sensation, the pain welling up from the bottom of her stomach, and the suffocating, breathless fear.

In the darkness, Anna felt the cold drafts of others' whispers like buffeting wings: "My husband...my children...our home...what will become of us?"

And every time, her stomach cramped, and she wondered how many of her friends would be still there when she came out again, and how many newly wounded would be brought into hospitals—those few left standing.

CHAPTER TWO

She barely remembered the 300-mile train ride home to Bad Orb—was it days or weeks later? A vague sense of Mutti helping her to bed, tenderly bathing her face, murmuring and humming as though Anna were a baby.

Cuts and bruises healed. But Anna couldn't escape the image of that burning heap of debris in Hamburg. All those wounded men. Her friends on staff. Fritz. Left inside. She curled inward and wrapped her arms around her stomach. It didn't make sense. Because of her weakness, running away that day, she was the only one alive.

Snatches of laughing conversation with Fritz. Their plans to be married, once the war was over. His lingering kisses. The candlelit night he'd proposed. His kind, caring manner as a doctor. And when she did go out of the house his smile transposed itself on the face of every man she saw.

Sleepless nights. The drone of the war planes. The whistle. The whump. The rain of bricks. Smoke and fire. All returned when she finally did fall asleep in the gray light of dawn.

Her nursing supervisor from her apprenticeship at St. Maria Hospital in Bad Orb came to visit. "We need you. You must come back to work. It helps to forget."

How could she go back into a hospital, to see and hear and smell the wounds, the dying, the hopelessness? No, she wouldn't forget. It would be a constant reminder of Fritz, of what she could no longer have.

Before, she had love to give her hope. Hope of a normal life beyond this war. Now, she had nothing to look forward to but more destruction, more fear, more loss.

The images haunted her day and night. There was no escape.

Anna's mother knocked on the bedroom door. "Come. Eat. You must keep up your strength."

"Ja, Mutti." With a sigh, Anna opened the door and allowed herself to be guided down the stairs, through the hall and into the small cozy kitchen, where eight-year-old Karl already sat at the table.

Mutti closed the door behind them and scooped two bland-looking patties from a frying pan onto Karl's and Anna's plates. Then she sat, with a cup of hot water in front of her.

Karl dug into his food and shoveled it in his mouth.

Anna frowned at her mother. "You're not eating?"

"*Nein, nein.* I'm not hungry." Mutti waved away the suggestion.

Anna peered at the plate. A fried turnip patty. Turnips had been the only thing on the menu all week. All at once the fog in her brain lifted. They were running out of food. With Papa and Hans on the Belgian front, and Elsa still in the civilian work corps, they had no income. An arrow of guilt pierced her middle.

"Oh, Mutti. I'm so sorry…" She cut her patty in half, slipped it onto a small plate, and set it in front of her mother despite Mutti's protests. "I just haven't been thinking straight."

Her mother gave a small, sad smile. "*Ach,* 'tis nothing. Tomorrow I'll go into the country and see what I can find. Maybe some potatoes, for a change, *nuh?*"

Anna drew her shoulders back. It was December, for goodness sake. Nothing would be available now. "Well, that's fine, for tomorrow. But it's time I go back to work at the hospital." She drew in a deep, cleansing breath. If nothing else, perhaps she could sneak some food home from there. Yes, that's what she would do.

***

Papa returned in January from the Battle of the Bulge with a leg wound and the news that her brother Hans had been captured. Anna's heart seemed to stop. She turned away from her father, covering her mouth. They might never see him again. Images of her older brother flitted through her mind—tall, strong, handsome, and caring. Her throat thickened. Another loss loomed over her.

Anna joined Mutti in fussing over her father—bringing him hot water to drink, what little food they had to share—as if to fill in the vacant spaces around her heart.

All through March and April Papa sat, listening to the daily reports of the Battle of Berlin, his face wrinkled in pain with the news that the parliament building, the *Reichstag,* had been bombed. Before the end of the battle, the report came that *Fuhrer* Adolf Hitler had committed suicide. A single tear trickled down his cheek. Anna held her breath. *What would this mean for Germany?*

One day in May, Anna came home from the hospital to find her family huddled around the radio. The sonorous tone of the broadcaster came through the static. "Today in Reims, France, General Jodl signed papers of surrender of all German forces to the western Allies..."

As if anesthetized, Anna stood frozen, her mouth open, staring at her parents. The war was over. She should be happy.

Papa covered his face with his hands.

"We lost. The war. All those boys." Mutti dabbed at her eyes with an embroidered handkerchief. "After the sacrifice your papa made for his country. His poor crippled leg. And Hans." Her voice broke. "Where is my boy?"

Anna couldn't think about that loss right now. She couldn't cry or celebrate. All emotion had been drained from her. At least the bombing was over. She and Mutti could take down the blackout curtains.

In the months that followed, Anna found some relief in not having to cower fearfully in the shelters any more. Elsa was home again too, tired and thin from hard physical labor, saying little about her experiences. Everything was rationed—bread, flour, clothing, gas. But food was still scarce. Even if they had the coupons, too often the market had nothing left.

Papa devoured the newspapers Anna brought home from the hospital. "We will rebuild. Our country will soon be well again," he kept repeating as if to convince himself.

But Anna had little faith that Germany could return to normal any time in the near future. Such a waste—of life, of property, of *Heimat*. American soldiers still occupied the western half of the country, Russians the east. It would take so many years and so much effort to clean up the mess. Anna sat heavily in a kitchen chair, a black shadow growing over her heart.

Stories of Jewish death camps spread like wildfire. Mutti put both hands over her heart. "*Nein*. This cannot be true. Hitler rescued our economy, made life good again. We were attacked. These camps—it must have been the Russians."

Anna had heard the rumors, the propaganda. So it must have been true. She pressed her lips together. *Best to never speak of it.*

Mutti wrung her hands, cried, hovered, and jumped whenever Papa spoke. Anna moved through her days, zombie-like. She couldn't stand the thought of more loss. If only she'd been taken in that bombing, too. *Ach, Gott*, how she missed Fritz, his strong presence, his encouragement, his sweet love. Her hopes, her dreams…were gone.

The only thing that kept her going was her job at St. Maria's hospital. It was the sole source of income for her family.

***

Anna bent over to breathe in the scent from Papa's roses. Between two bushes hung silver strands of a broken spider web, buffeted by the July morning breeze. Her heart nearly stopped. In those dangling filaments, she saw her country, her family, her own life, torn apart by war. Then a spider leapt across the chasm, stringing a new bright thread.

She took in a deep breath and walked to the hospital, trying to dredge up her own spirit of renewal.

For a few minutes, Anna stopped to gaze at the quiet streets. The country's rebuilding had begun. But it could be years before the economy would be healthy again. The spider was trying to weave her world back together. The German people were trying. Anna had to try too. But she couldn't conjure a single idea of what her future might hold. Surely not nursing for the rest of her life. She'd had such high hopes for her chosen field when she started at sixteen. She sighed. The war had broken her safety net, left her impotent to make a difference.

Conditions at this hospital were just as deplorable as they had been in Hamburg. Supplies were short, and the situation so hopeless for the still-suffering wounded, she struggled to find ways she could help these poor patients. Anna prayed every night for a miracle to take her away. Working there only reminded her daily, hourly, of her beloved Fritz. She closed her eyes against the sharp pain. Fritz. Gone.

He had told her how he admired her philosophy of taking each day as it came and doing the best she could with it. But it wasn't really, it was more the fear of looking ahead. Death had shattered her hope.

At the hospital, Anna busied herself reviewing paperwork and preparing medications for her day's rounds. A buzzer at the nurses' station startled her. Room 212 was calling. Ah, yes, the American, the practical joker. She rolled her eyes. No doubt trying to get attention again.

A member of the occupation forces, this soldier had fallen from a pile of rubble and broken his leg. Despite being "the enemy," he had helped a German family retrieve any belongings that might have been left intact. He would leave the hospital soon. Although they didn't share a common language, Anna had to admit he was the one bright spot in her work because of his impish sense of humor—giving her weak tea water instead of a urine specimen or dumping his lunch tray into the bedpan.

She bustled into the room, carrying a pitcher of water.

Today he had company. The visitor stood and removed his double-peaked wool dress cap as the soldier in the bed introduced him with hand signals and broken German.

"Anna Schmidt, my . . . *freund* . . . Neil Moser."

Her gaze traveled upward at this more than six-foot-tall G.I. with a crisp dark crewcut and ready smile. At least a foot above her, she focused on gentle hazel eyes behind a pair of bent, taped-up wire-rim glasses. For a heartbeat, her world paused; then she averted her gaze as she greeted him. "*Guten Tag.*" Moser. Hmm. An American with a German name.

Despite a strange, overpowering urge to leave, Anna turned to check the patient's pulse and temperature, and adjusted his leg to a more comfortable position. The visitor's presence tickled at her back. The two young men bantered back and forth in English, laughing easily. Although she understood none of the words, Anna caught the patient's teasing tone as he gestured toward her.

"You'd better behave yourself or you'll get another needle in the rear." She wagged a stern finger at him and mimed the injection. Even though she spoke in German, the young men laughed uproariously.

Anna hurried from the room, her hands trembling and her face uncomfortably hot. Now why would she react like this? It hadn't been that long since ... since she'd lost Fritz. She wasn't interested in any other men. She couldn't be. Especially not an American.

But for the rest of that day she caught herself picturing the tall, slim soldier as he rose to greet her. Even as she drifted off to sleep that night, she couldn't get his eyes out of her mind, that soft, gentle gaze from behind those ridiculous taped-up glasses.

At first, when she returned for her next shift, she couldn't wait to get back to Room 212. But then she found herself avoiding the room, scolding herself for being so eager to meet "him"—Neil Moser—again, yet listening, hoping to hear that buzzer. Finally, she had no choice. She had to give the patient his medication. She stopped in front of the door, steeling herself, then felt like a foolish schoolgirl as she entered and found no one there except the patient. *Good!* she told herself, tending to the soldier's needs in an abrupt business-like fashion. But her shoulders sagged a bit when she left the room.

Later, as Anna bustled from room to room, caught up in the pace of hospital work, changing bedding, giving sponge baths, and carrying linens to the laundry, she heard a buzzer.

"Anna, it's your patient," another nurse called. "Room 212."

Her heartbeat sped up, and once again she chided herself for her reaction. This was ridiculous. She gave the door a brisk shove, intending only to stick her head inside and find out what the American needed.

"What is it?" She stopped in mid-breath as her eyes followed the tall soldier's rise from his chair.

"*Guten Tag,* Fräulein Schmidt. It's nice to see you again," he said in German.

Anna gasped. Where did an American learn to speak such passable German? She stared, speechless. Finally, she squared her shoulders and stood as tall as her five feet, two inches would allow. "*Guten Tag.*"

Then she strode to the bed to check on the patient. He grinned and shook his head at needing anything. Anna frowned. Just trying to get her in here while his friend was visiting, that imp. She gave Neil Moser a curt little nod and left as quickly as she could, mortified to find her face burning.

The next few days, she found herself rushing to work with anticipation. The American came to visit his friend every afternoon without fail. And every day he spoke to her in his soft, polite German. Anna found herself humming, even smiling, as she worked.

One afternoon, he followed her with his slow, easy saunter as she left the room. "I hope you don't think I'm being forward, but..." He took off his cap and shuffled his feet. "But...I wonder if you could... Ah, would you be able to have coffee with me when you're done here?"

Anna recoiled inwardly. German girls who went out with American soldiers had an unsavory reputation. Many of them exchanged "favors" for cigarettes, liquor, or a pair of nylon stockings to use as trading stock for desperately needed food. She had always been careful to avoid such scandal. After all, she still lived with her parents, and despite the hardships of the war, her family had an impeccable image in the small town. A pang of guilt pierced her heart. *Fritz.* She felt as though she were betraying her fiancé.

"I'm sorry," he said after her momentary silence. "I've been presumptuous."

Anna looked up at his earnest face. This young man intrigued her. She would like to find out more about him. After all, it had been a year since Fritz's death. That was a proper mourning period. It wouldn't hurt to have a coffee and talk a bit.

"Yes," she said at last. "I'm off at four o'clock. I will meet you at the Rhineland Café just down the street."

He rewarded her with a soft, sweet smile.

***

The afternoon sun threaded through leaves of the oak trees that lined the street, leaving dappled patterns on the tables. People strolled by the little café, chatting and laughing, as if trying to recapture some normalcy, even though the country was still in chaos and few were working. A few stared at Anna and cast disapproving looks.

Sitting across the sidewalk table from Neil Moser, Anna sipped her ersatz coffee—"real" coffee mixed with roasted grains—and traced the brocaded design in the tablecloth. *He's not saying anything. And I don't know what to say either.* She raised her eyes from under lowered lashes and caught him smiling at her.

"How…?"

"What…?" Both spoke at once, then burst into laughter.

"I'm sorry." Neil looked down at the table. "I'm not very good at this. I haven't known many beautiful young ladies such as you."

Anna blushed and dropped her gaze to her cup. Beautiful? He must be near-sighted. "This war..."

"I know." His face was solemn now. "I'm just glad it's over for your sake. But it's still going on in the South Pacific. My unit just got shipped out a few days ago."

"How is it that you didn't go?"

Neil laughed and pointed to his taped, bent glasses. "Broke these things and couldn't get a new pair in time. I have a new unit and a new assignment because I speak German." He spread his hands and shrugged his shoulders. "So, here I am."

"And how *did* you learn such good German? Are your parents from here?"

"No, but I have relatives in Switzerland. I wanted to be able to communicate with them, so I taught myself by listening to Berlitz records." He lowered his voice sonorously, imitating the deep, precise voice from the recordings. *"Mein Grossvater sitzt in seinem Sessel.* My grandfather sits in an easy chair. *Er raucht eine Pfeife.* He smokes a pipe."

Anna laughed. The sun broke from behind a cloud and shot a ray of inexplicable gladness into her heart.

***

Over the next few weeks, Neil came by the hospital every few days, whenever he could get away from his military duties, and they would go to the coffee shop when Anna got off work. She was beginning to relax around him now and looked forward to their conversations.

He told her of the vast open spaces where he lived in Montana. She couldn't picture endless miles without buildings or roads. "Is it close to New York?" She'd at least heard of that big city, and could compare that idea to Hamburg or Frankfort.

Neil chuckled. "No, it's clear across the country." He drew a makeshift map on the back of an envelope. Montana was about the size of the whole of Germany, he said, and it wasn't even the biggest state.

Anna felt her eyes grow as large as the saucers under their coffee cups. How could it be that big? "What do you do in Montana? Are you a farmer?"

Neil said he and his parents lived on a "ranch" and were "cowboys." Anna tried to fit her mind around that concept, but the words didn't translate well. His mother a cow-boy too? No. She couldn't see it or believe it.

But he was easy going and made her laugh, something she realized she'd been missing for a long time.

They commiserated over the lack of good coffee and sweets. "You should taste my dad's cowboy coffee. So strong you need a knife to cut it." Neil grinned. "And my mother's coffee cake... Mmm."

"Come by 19 Friedrichstrasse tomorrow, and join my family for coffee." Anna blinked, startled, as if someone else had uttered these words. How had that happened?

"I'd be delighted," was his quick response.

Walking home that July evening, Anna took the time to look around her. Bad Orb seemed an oasis in the midst of a country trying to dig itself out from the rubble. The only jobs available for the able-bodied were clearing the debris in cities that had been hit harder than Bad Orb. She pictured the smoking ruins of Hamburg—and the hospital. In contrast, only a few buildings had been destroyed here. Thank God for that.

Young men working amid a pile of debris reminded her of the American patient who'd broken his leg while helping. And, had introduced her to Neil. Anna stopped in mid-stride. *Neil.*

Ach du lieber Gott, what had she done? She had no business inviting this American to her home. What if he turned out just like all those others who wanted personal favors for a chocolate bar? Papa would be so upset. Americans were the enemy. But Neil was so interesting. He didn't seem cruel and heartless, as she'd heard the Russians were. Surely her family would like him.

She resumed an anxious pace. *Now what does Mutti have in the house that we can put on the table?*

Anna finally reached her stuccoed, two-story house that shared a common wall with the neighbor's dwelling and barn. No wide-open spaces here. Farmers returned to their houses in town every evening, as they had since feudal times. She turned up the short walkway, lined with Papa's rosebushes, trudged up the five stone steps, and unlatched the heavy wooden door.

First she went upstairs to change out of her uniform, then came down to the cozy kitchen, where everyone always gathered. The parlor door was kept closed unless they had company.

"*Guten Abend.*" Anna kissed her mother on the cheek, as Mutti stirred the *Suppe* on the cook stove. "I hope you don't mind..." She swallowed. "I've invited a friend for coffee tomorrow."

Mutti beamed. "Oh, how nice, dear."

Anna turned her face away. "He's an American."

Her father rose half out of his chair, momentarily forgetting his leg. "You did what?"

Anna braced herself for the tirade.

Mutti slapped her hands on her thighs. "An American? How could you, after they destroyed our cities, our homes, and killed thousands of innocent Germans? They didn't have to go *that* far to win the war." Her mother's voice rose to an almost hysterical pitch.

"That's right. Look at Dresden. Look at your hospital in Hamburg, for heaven's sake," her father growled, seated again. "And don't you forget, they took your brother prisoner and won't tell us where he is."

"But, Mutti, Papa." Elsa's dark eyes flashed. "Remember, the Americans have all the provisions. It wouldn't hurt to have a friendly one around." Anna's older sister spread her hands and shrugged.

"Yes, that's true." Anna shivered with nervous tension. "He really is a very nice person. And, he speaks German." Her words ended on a hopeful up-note.

16

"The big, powerful *Amis*," Papa muttered with a note of disdain.

Mutti stood by the table, twisting her hands in her apron. "Come, let's eat. We can talk about this later." Supper was a silent ordeal, with tension as thick as the lard they smeared on their bread.

Finally, Papa relented. "Just this once, mind you, and if ... well, if he's not what you say he is, we won't invite him back!"

***

By three o'clock the next afternoon, Mutti had retrieved an embroidered linen tablecloth from the storage trunk hidden in the attic and used the last cup of flour to make a *Pflaumenkuchen* with plums from the tree in their back yard.

"You'd think the American general himself was coming." Elsa smirked as Anna bustled around the tiny kitchen, measuring the roasted grains for "coffee," washing the good china pot.

Anna felt a deep bloom in her cheeks, like her father's favorite roses. She flicked her hand at Elsa. "Shoo, get out of my way. He'll be here any minute."

Anna pulled her eight-year-old brother Karl away from the window as Neil approached the house. She glared at her sister standing at the door. "You, too. Get away from the peephole." Anna wiped her sweaty palms on the skirt of her blue flowered dirndl and awaited his knock.

He doffed his cap in greeting and handed her four Hershey bars. "One for you, your brother, sister, and father." Then a bouquet of wildflowers. "For your mother."

Mutti and Papa were already seated in the parlor when Anna entered with Neil. Papa's eyes frowned over the top of his reading glasses at the tall young American.

Mutti gestured toward a chair. "Come, sit, eat." Already in motion, she waved her hands in an apprehensive mime at the table, where pieces of the plum cake waited on china plates. She poured the thin liquid that passed as coffee into dainty china cups.

Everyone sat. Despite the suspicious stares, Neil seemed relaxed as he sipped his coffee and ate the cake with gusto. "*Sehr gut.* Very good. You must give me this recipe to take back to my mother."

Papa sat upright at Neil's excellent German, his eyes wide. Mutti blushed, ducked her head and allowed a tiny smile.

"So, rich and powerful America, huh? The land of plenty." Papa leaned back in his chair. Anna held her breath. Oh no, was Papa trying to pick a fight? Surely he hadn't already made up his mind to dislike Neil.

Neil stiffened a bit. "Well, not exactly. My parents went through many years of drought and deprivation." He explained how hard his family worked to raise beef to sell.

Anna's stomach growled at the thought of plenty of meat to eat.

Papa merely nodded with a slight raise of one eyebrow.

"More *Kuchen?*" Mutti asked, perhaps to break the tension.

Neil nodded and held out his plate.

Anna's breath jittered inside. She should've warned him to leave enough for Papa to have a second helping. Oh dear. Neil seemed awkward. Where was the charming young man who had won her invitation?

After he had made several more attempts at conversation, Anna glanced at the clock. It was getting late. Surely he didn't plan to stay for supper. They didn't have enough to give him. Fritz would have known instinctively. He would've known to bring gifts of food. *Ach, nein.* Where did that come from? It was unfair to compare the two men. Neil didn't know.

Finally, he unwound his lanky body from the chair, shook Papa's hand, thanked Mama again for the plum cake, and took his leave. "*Auf Wiedersehen.*" His face looked drawn with disappointment.

Her earlier elation plummeted. This had not gone well. She went back into the parlor just in time to hear Papa scoff, "... and merely a couple of chocolate bars.... What does he think we Germans are, whores?"

18

Anna bit back sudden tears, ran upstairs to her bedroom, and flung herself face-down on the bed. *Ach du lieber Gott*, what was she to do now?

***

Anna dragged herself through the next week. Neil didn't come by the hospital. Oh well, it would've been an inappropriate relationship anyway. Her parents would never accept him. He was part of the enemy forces, after all. And he wouldn't be staying in Germany long, either. But she found herself glancing at the clock, thought of laughing with him over afternoon coffee at the Rhineland Café. Whenever she saw an olive-green American uniform, she started, believing for just an instant it might be Neil.

Sunday afternoon, Anna had just sat down with her parents for a cup of weak coffee—no *Kuchen* today—when she heard pounding at the front door. She left the kitchen door open in her rush down the hall and peered out the peephole.

Standing on the front stoop was Neil, his arms laden with packages.

Anna broke into a smile. *He came back!* Her thoughts fluttered like birds in the elms. Oh dear. What would Papa say? Would he even allow Neil to come in? No. Papa didn't have anything to say about this. Neil was her friend. She lifted her chin, stood as tall as she could, and opened the door with a smile. "Welcome."

Neil grinned back at her, a twinkle in his eye. "It's good to see you, pretty lady."

Blushing, Anna escorted him toward the kitchen, where Mutti peeked around the door jamb and Papa sat in royal stoicism.

"I thought you might enjoy a hazelnut torte with your Sunday afternoon coffee." Neil produced the cake with a flourish and set it on the table.

Mutti's eyes were moonlike as she looked at the cake, then cut a glance at the bags Neil had placed on the buffet by the door when he entered. Anna's mouth watered.

"And to go along with the torte, I sneaked some real coffee from our mess hall."

Papa raised his eyebrows.

Mama brewed the coffee and cut generous pieces of the torte. "Eat, my boy," she clucked. "You are so thin." She finally sat and took a sip of the coffee. "Mmm. Pure heaven." She closed her eyes, a look of ecstasy erasing the lines in her face.

Anna inhaled the aroma, then swirled a delicate sip of the brew in her mouth, relishing the robust, dark flavor. She reached a hand out to touch Neil's sleeve. "Thank you so much. This is such a treat."

Neil distributed the items he'd brought—a sack of plump juicy oranges, large firm white potatoes, a chocolate bar for Karl, and to Anna's wonder and delight, a basket of fresh eggs.

"You must come back again soon." Mutti's hands flew to her flushed cheeks, and she let a small giggle escape.

Neil left, and a giddy lightness overtook Anna. Oh, thank God, this was so much more comfortable than last week's visit. Then a pang of guilt pierced her euphoria as she thought of Papa's "whores" remark earlier. Did her parents accept Neil only because of the food he brought?

Papa settled down to a supper feast of eggs and potatoes. He took a big mouthful. "Not bad." Then he concentrated on the newspaper by his plate.

Mutti winked and exchanged grins with Anna, Elsa, and Karl as they dug into their own platefuls.

Neil returned the following Sunday afternoon, bearing more gifts—flour, sugar, salt—and cigarettes to use for barter. He pointed at each item and told Anna the English word. She hesitated, pursed her lips, then tried. "Flo-ow-ah." Her face burned. He had learned German so well—how could she possibly learn English? "Ssshoogah…"

"The words *Zucker* and sugar are almost the same." Neil grinned. "See how easy it is? You'll be speaking English in no time."

A pleased smile formed on her lips, and she joined in his easy laughter.

"Why did you want to learn German?" Mutti asked.

Neil explained about his relatives on his dad's side in Switzerland. "I hope to go meet them while I'm stationed here."

Anna blinked. What a sweet thing to do. Neil was such a nice man. And he had a Swiss family. *Hmm.* His company brought a glow of pleasure to her heart, something she'd never thought she'd feel again.

He continued teaching her English words and phrases as they walked and as they ate and sat companionably in the evenings with the family. And he began to pick up *Orberish,* the dialect the natives of Bad Orb spoke. Now Anna had reason to laugh at *his* fumbled pronunciation.

***

Over the rest of the summer and into the fall, Neil became a fixture at the Schmidts' table. Anna's heartbeat danced faster when she saw him striding up their sidewalk. And his face seemed to light up when he saw her—at home or when he stopped by the hospital. He supplied the family with food, and Anna's parents welcomed him with big smiles. Papa even took him aside and asked if Neil could check into Hans's whereabouts. Neil shook his head doubtfully, but promised he would try.

When he visited, someone—usually Karl—would ask about America. "Tell us about where you live." Anna's young brother sat at Neil's knee, gazing up with rapt attention.

"...I have a horse named Blue, and every spring my mother and father and I round up the cattle... We have hundreds of cows that roam over many acres in Montana."

Listening, Anna felt like Karl, wide-eyed with astonishment. It was hard for her to picture what he talked about. She was accustomed to seeing only a couple of milk cows that came home to the barn every night. She smiled up at Neil. "Oh, how I'd love to travel there and see your ranch and all your cows."

He grinned back at her. "Maybe you can someday."

Anna took a deep breath. *Oh, wouldn't that be an adventure!*

Neil even brought a borrowed violin on occasion and played tunes that made Anna's feet itch to dance. Mutti raised her eyes heavenward. "*Ach.* Such beautiful music."

Anna smiled and daydreamed about dancing with a tall, handsome American soldier.

Elsa sulked in the background as only Anna kept Neil's attention. The cousins all found excuses to come visit when Neil was there, hungry for stories from the "land of milk and honey"—America. And, of course, the food he brought.

Questions spilled out. "Everyone owns a car?"

"Almost." Neil nodded.

"Tell us about these 'supermarkets' in the cities."

Neil could only shrug. "I don't know about those. I've heard there are some in big cities, like New York, but none in Montana."

Papa had finally relaxed his stern demeanor and seemed to enjoy luring Neil into another debate about the workmanship of the 1940s American Packard versus the pre-war Mercedes Benz—"*das Merzedes, naturlich!*" —and which automobile would be better when production started again. "*Nein, nein, the Merzedes will still be better.*" Papa roared his approval.

A fountain of happiness rose inside Anna as she joined in their laughter, the first time she'd really laughed since... She shook her head to clear memories of Fritz. No, she wouldn't allow those to spoil this pleasant time.

Most of all, Anna enjoyed walking with Neil through the woods just a few kilometers from home, where her father had worked as a forester before the war. She gazed up at the tall fir trees. "I hope Papa can come back to work here again. He loved it so."

Neil took her small hand in his big one. Startled, she nearly snatched her hand back. But then a thrill coursed through Anna's body. She relaxed. It felt so natural to hold his hand.

"I can see why he would." He gave her a shy smile. "And I sure enjoy walking through this forest with you."

A bright stream of sunlight slanted through the branches and warmth spread through her. Anna dared not speak for fear of breaking the spell of this small respite from the world. She squeezed his hand and welcomed the answering pressure.

Neil seemed such a shy, quiet, young man, and yet he conveyed a sense of adventure and enthusiasm as he talked to her of the books he had read. They had so much in common. Was he really one of those awful enemy Americans? He seemed so nice.

***

"I can't believe he is so polite," Anna whispered to Elsa as they dressed one morning. "He is not like those others we've heard so much about."

"*Ja*, and Mutti and Papa seem to like him. Even the cousins keep coming to see him," her sister teased. "I don't know, but I think you might have feelings for him."

Anna's neck and face flushed. This couldn't be true. Not after she'd sworn never to love again after losing Fritz. "*Nein, nein*. He is just a friend, an interesting one. I like learning English from him. And he brings good food."

But she couldn't deny the flutter she felt in her stomach when he looked at her and smiled, or the sensation of electricity when he touched her arm. Yes, he might be something special.

"You can't think about it," she told herself, drawing up to her full height and frowning at her image in the mirror as though she were an unruly patient. The war was over now, and the Americans would undoubtedly return to the United States soon. Neil wouldn't stay here. He had to go back to help his parents on the ranch. She would just enjoy his company while she could.

She shook off a tremor of dread and finished dressing to go to the hospital.

***

That evening Anna once again stood before her mirror. Neil was coming by to take her to a concert by the Bad Orb

23

Symphony, its first public performance in a long time. She arranged and rearranged the finger waves in her dark brown hair. Did it look better falling softly around her face or pinned back behind her ears? *Ach, Himmel!* She twirled the skirt of her navy dress—years old, but still serviceable. How she wished she had the gold earrings from her grandmother, but they'd been sold long ago for food. She swiped a soft cloth over her old black pumps and steeled herself. *All right, this will have to do.*

With nerves tingling and breath held, she finally came downstairs into the parlor. Neil stood from the sofa, took off his olive drab cap, and ran a hand over his black brushcut. He gave a low whistle. "You look beautiful."

A flush warmed Anna's neck, but she let out her pent-up breath in relief. *Beautiful.* She lowered her eyes. He made her feel like a princess in a long flowing gown.

"Shall we?" Neil offered his arm, and she clutched it tight as they strolled into the cool evening.

When they walked into the concert hall, an almost-forgotten air of festivity danced from one concert-goer to the next. The war was over, and people were trying to pick up the threads of their lives again. She smiled. Like the courageous spider on Papa's roses.

But Anna couldn't imagine how life would ever be the same. The country was in upheaval. Sons and fathers, husbands and fiancés would never return. *Fritz.* The concerts they had attended... before... She swallowed past a catch in her throat.

There was little food, no money and no jobs. Anna was afraid her employment at the hospital might be short-lived now that no more wounded arrived. Elsa was having trouble finding a job. How was her family going to make it? What was her future going to be?

She tried to lose herself in the music, yet even Beethoven's *Fifth Symphony* failed to distract her for long. Neil reached for her hand. His presence beside her stirred thoughts and feelings like a whisk in a *Kuchen* batter. How did she really feel about this American who had once been part of the faceless enemy? They had killed so many Germans. Fritz, for one.

But Neil was so nice, so polite. Not at all as she'd pictured soldiers to be. Not even like the cruel Germans who ran the work camps. She certainly found herself blushing a lot when he was around. Hoping he would hold her hand with quiet gentleness. Or liking the heat beneath his touch when he put a hand on the small of her back to escort her.

Anna shook her head to rid herself of such disturbing thoughts. *Oh, come now, Anna.* Sure, she liked him, but...it almost felt like she was being unfaithful to Fritz. Still, she wondered what Neil felt for her. He wouldn't be around forever, though. Surely he had a girlfriend back home. She'd never dared to ask.

After the concert, they strolled homeward, arm in arm. It was a cool, but pleasant, October evening, and the crisp smell of wood smoke wafted on the breeze. Leaves crunched underfoot. This was nice. She could grow accustomed to this feeling of closeness, warmth, and possibility.

"I enjoyed the concert." Neil finally spoke after a long silence.

"Yes, it was quite good." Anna gazed at the stars glittering in the night sky. She still wasn't used to his reticence. Was he searching for something to say, or did she sense some hidden discomfort?

"Well..." Neil hesitated and sighed. They walked on a few more steps. He cleared his throat, then blurted, "The outfit is headed for the States in a couple of days. We just got orders last week to ship out." His face crumpled into a hang-dog sadness as he stared down at his feet.

All the breath in Anna's body seemed to lock up in one tiny spot in her chest. *Nein.* It just couldn't be true. Not now. Her hopeful thoughts disintegrated into rubble. Yes, the inevitable had arrived. Sure, she had known he would be leaving one day, but she'd tried to ignore that thought. A cavernous ache filled her. She'd had no inkling how empty she would feel. Finally, dizzy from holding her breath, she exhaled slowly.

"Oh," was all she could manage. She gazed at his somber profile.

"I've enjoyed this time we had together, getting to know you." Neil turned to her, leaned forward, and kissed her lips gently.

She melted into his chest. *Nein. Nein.*

"I'll miss you—and your family. May I write?"

Anna could only give him a short nod. Her body and mind were frozen beyond thought.

CHAPTER THREE

Shut in the room she shared with Elsa, Anna sat composing a letter to Neil in her head, as she had so many times before. Every week that passed with no word from him added to her dismal sadness. Anna sat in the dark, heaviness pushing in on her, making her heartbeat sluggish, like a wind-up gramophone losing power. A relationship with this American was just not meant to be. She tried to shrug it off. *I wasn't really that attracted to him anyway.* It had just been a pleasant distraction from the horrors that were her life at the hospital, that's all.

But as she gazed out the window at the stars, the memory of his kiss tingled on her lips.

Loss. Anna put her hands over her heart. Friends. Innocence. Love. The anguish of losing Fritz rocked her body all over again. *Fritz. Neil.* She compared the two men, their quiet strength and the way they both had made her feel comfortable—and important. Their absence left a bomb-like crater in her core. What kind of future did she have now?

***

Mutti knocked at Anna's bedroom door. "Hermann Zahn is here to see you. Says he'd like to take you to the opera on Saturday."

"Go with him, Anna." Elsa's voice chimed in beside Mutti's. "He's a nice man. You always liked him."

Anna groaned. "*Nein.*" She hadn't seen Hermann for several years, assuming he'd been in the armed forces, too. The Zahns were long-time family friends. Anna and Hermann's sister were the same age, and the five of them had played many games of tag or hide and seek in the vacant field next to the

Schmidts'. Elsa had occasionally dated their older brother when they were teenagers. But to date Hermann? He was just a chubby boy who had never really fit in.

Her mother's voice was insistent. "You can't spend the rest of your life locked up here in your room. At least come downstairs and have some coffee with him."

Anna made a face. But Mutti was probably right. She might never hear from Neil. A cup of coffee with Hermann wouldn't hurt anything. She quickly ran a comb through her dark hair and pinned a brooch to her blouse.

Hermann sat at the kitchen table, already sipping coffee, a wedge of apple cake in front of him. He rose from his chair when he saw Anna. His round ruddy face beamed. "*Guten Tag. Wie geht's?*"

"Good afternoon. I'm fine, thank you. And you?" Anna tried to ignore the sheen of perspiration on his broad forehead, already enhanced by prematurely thinning, nondescript brown hair. The gray wool hunter's jacket failed to cover a substantial round belly.

She pictured Neil's long slim stature, his kind eyes. *Hermann's not really my type.* Anna sighed, then forced a smile. "Another piece of *Apfelkuchen?*"

Hermann pushed his plate away. "No, thank you, but I would be honored to escort you to the opera this weekend. Would you go with me?"

Swallowing her distaste, Anna shrugged inwardly. Mama was probably right. She really should get out more. "All right, I'll go."

***

Hermann held the door of his black Mercedes open for Anna, then took her elbow to guide her into the concert hall. He was the perfect gentleman, almost too polite, though. A bit wooden. Gazing around at the arriving crowd, she suddenly realized she had missed being with people. Just getting out of the house uplifted Anna's spirits more than they had been in several weeks. Her mood soared along with the music of the operetta.

During the program, Hermann kept asking, "Are you comfortable? Are you too warm? Too cool? Would you like something to drink? Anything to eat?"

After the umpteenth time, Anna was ready to stuff her scarf into his mouth. If she could only get through this night, she wouldn't have to put up with him again. "No, Hermann, I'm fine. Let's just enjoy the music."

The next day a dozen roses arrived, with a note: "It was a fabulous evening for me. I hope you enjoyed it as well."

Phffft. Does he think he can buy my affections with flowers? Anna tossed the note into the wastebasket. "Here, Mutti, put these in your room. You enjoy roses."

Mutti raised her eyebrows but took the flowers with a smile.

After a week of staring at the four walls of her room again, Anna's resolve weakened with Hermann's persistent invitations. Maybe she wasn't that attracted to him, but she had enjoyed the opera, getting out, seeing people. There might be some advantage to dating a wealthy man. And there was nothing else to do.

That first evening with Hermann soon became a series of concerts, dinners at restaurants, coffee at Grandmother Zahn's, and flowers—always more flowers.

"Where does he find hothouse roses around here?" Mutti shook her head. "Where does he get his money?" Then she whispered, looking furtively around the room, "He must be dealing in the black market."

A chill ran through Anna. Indeed, flowers seemed such an extravagance amidst a life where the next meal was often in doubt. If he was doing something illegal... She sighed. Why did she keep going out with him? He was just trying to show off his wealth. He was bland. Boring. Stiff. But then again, at least she wasn't sitting in her room, doing nothing.

"Hermann's here." Elsa's voice broke into her thoughts. Anna rolled her eyes—another evening stifling her yawns as he tried to make small talk—and walked down the stairs. She paused before entering the living room, straightened her shoulders, checked her lipstick, and put on a smile. "I'm ready."

***

The weeks passed. Anna dragged through her work days. The hospital was quiet, nurses went back to their normal or even reduced shifts. Anna had been cut to part-time, and she worried about money. Papa wouldn't be able to work for a long time yet. They'd heard nothing more about Hans. Neil had not been able to get any information about him before he left. Anna's stomach churned as she wondered if she'd ever see her brother again. It was up to her and Elsa to support the family—if Elsa could find a job. Even with money, rationing was still in effect and food still scarce.

One evening close to Christmas, she dawdled on her walk home from the hospital, dreading another quiet, lonely night in her room. As she turned into their walkway, she saw Karl waiting on the front stoop. He jumped up and skipped toward Anna as she turned to open the gate to their front yard.

"You got a letter, you got a letter," he chanted, hopping from one foot to the other.

Hope flared. Anna hardly dared breathe. "A letter? From whom?"

"From America!" he shouted.

Anna broke into a run. She snatched the blue tissue envelope and clutched it to her breast as she headed up the stairs to her room. Sitting on her bed, she smoothed the paper and peered at the return address. Then she frowned. What was this? It didn't look like Montana.

She carefully slit the ends of the self-contained tissue envelope.

> *Dear Miss Schmidt,*
>
> *I finally found someone who could write this letter in German for me.*
>
> *I want to thank you for your special, kind care while I was in your hospital. You were the only one who*

treated me as if I were not the enemy. My leg healed well and I am home now, back to work at General Motors, and will be married soon.

I hope that you and my old buddy, Neil, were able to enjoy each other's company. You two seemed suited for each other somehow.

Regards,
James Hogue, (Room 212)

Anna crumpled the letter and jammed it to her mouth as the tears came.

CHAPTER FOUR

Neil paced the deck of the *George Washington*. The pre-WWI German luxury liner, seized as war reparations and now taking its last voyage as a troop transport, slowly churned its way back toward America's east coast. The dark sea was as choppy as his thoughts. He agonized again over his last evening with Anna, as he had so many times since he'd left her. No one else he'd ever known had drawn him out of his shyness the way Anna had. And yet, he had frozen up at the very moment he needed courage. The only picture he had of her was in his mind, and it would not go away. Those blue eyes, the way she looked at him, listened so intently when he talked. Her big open smile and her acceptance of him despite being the "enemy" showed she understood him like no one else. His chest burned inside, a fuzziness clouded his eyes. He was in love with Anna Schmidt! Doggone, he'd been stupid. He should've proposed before he left.

It was just such a shock, getting orders to ship out that fast. "Get the boys home and out of the service," was the message from the brass back home. Neil's unit had received no warning—only the message to get out—now. America was reducing its military strength, the occupation of Germany curtailed.

He gazed into the star-shattered night. It would take three weeks to get to New York. If he wrote a letter of proposal now, aboard ship, maybe he could get it posted in time to get it on another ship back. Yes, that was it; that's what he'd do. But wait...Mom and Dad. How would they take the news? They probably still had their hearts set on him marrying Ruthie Miller, the fluttery redhead from the ranch down the road. No, he couldn't marry Ruthie. He wasn't in love with her. And he couldn't simply ask Anna now and repent to his parents later. They would never understand. They probably still thought of the Germans as the enemy. He'd have to wait until he was furloughed, and plead his case to his parents in person.

Neil scrubbed his fingers through his black crewcut, then slapped the transom railing with both hands. Couldn't this tub move any faster? He turned on his heel and stomped below to his bunk. He could at least write Anna a letter, to let her know he was thinking of her.

***

The borrowed 1938 Ford pickup rocked through the ruts, a cloud of dust rising like a parachute behind the speeding vehicle. The eastern Montana prairie was as arid as ever, the morning heat building already, even in March. Just another couple of miles now and the nearly thousand-mile trip from Ft. Lewis, Washington, would be over.

Home. Neil braked just short of running into the gate that opened into the Moser ranch. He leapt out the door, threw open the barbed wired structure, and lurched the truck through. He jumped out again to close the gate then pulled up in front of the familiar white two-story ranch house.

Home at last. But a mixture of thoughts roiled in his head. What would his parents say about his news? Even if they did approve, was he already too late? It had taken months to get a leave and come home. Maybe he should have written the letter of proposal right away instead of the chatty ones he'd sent. Maybe he should have told his folks about meeting Anna, and his intentions, when he wrote to them. But he'd really wanted to tell them in person. It seemed more respectful that way.

Surely Anna had many suitors. She might even be married by now. He bounced a fist off the steering wheel. Why hadn't he asked her before he left? A hornet's nest of fear buzzed in his chest. *C'mon, Moser. Better go find the folks. Get this over with.*

Then he saw his parents riding in from the north pasture, herding a cow, his dad carrying an apparently early calf. A flash

33

of memory—Mom always on horseback, always a partner to Dad. Neil jumped out of the pickup and ran down the incline toward the corral.

"Neil!" His mother gave a cry, with eyes wide and mouth open. She swung down from her horse and ran toward him, flinging her arms out. "You're home, you're finally home."

Neil embraced Nettie Moser, a tiny, slender woman, wiry as any man from riding the range every day. She stood on tiptoes and planted a kiss on his cheek, then stood back to look him over from head to toe, tears brimming. "I can't believe it. Look at you, so handsome in your uniform. We had no idea you were coming. Oh, it's so good to see you, dear. It's been too long."

An arm still around his mother's shoulders, Neil shook his dad's hand. Jake Moser's blue eyes twinkled, and Neil detected some moisture there. His father pushed the old stained Stetson back on his reddish-blond hair, now streaked with gray. "Well, good to see you, son. We weren't expecting you. How long'd they let you out for—home for good?"

"I'm just here for a weekend visit for now. I'll be discharged from Fort Lewis in a month or so." Neil took a deep breath. "But I came because I have something important to talk to you about."

His mom touched his arm. "C'mon in the house, dear. It's nearly noon. I'll get dinner on."

On the porch the German Shepard, Lad, thumped his tail in greeting. Neil stopped to scratch his ears, then went to his old room to change out of his uniform.

After a hearty venison stew, the Mosers sat around the polished oak dining table, drinking tea from heavy white crockery mugs. The long, narrow ranch kitchen had the same yellow checked curtains and the same blue and gray speckled teakettle on the stove as when he'd left two years ago. The wooden candleholder Neil had carved in grade school for his mom was still on the windowsill. The room felt homey and comfortable, but smaller somehow, even though this was not the house they'd lived in when he was a kid.

34

Neil's mother kept touching his arm as if to make sure he really was there.

Dad leaned back in his chair, smoked, and grinned. "So, ya see much action over there?"

Neil stiffened. This wasn't what he'd come to talk about. "Naw. Not really. I was a transport driver, mostly an errand boy and mechanic."

Mom sighed. "Oh, I'm glad you're home safe. We were so worried." A hopeful smile lit her face.

Neil took a sip of tea. An awkward silence filled the room. He fidgeted with his napkin. "Good prices for calves last fall?"

"Uh, fair to middlin'. Yup. Fair to middlin'. Hopin' for a little better this year." Dad scratched his head.

"Tell us about Europe, dear. Is it pretty?" Mom got up to reheat the kettle for more tea.

Neil shuffled his feet. Okay, he could at least tell them about his travel experiences. His dad kept slipping in questions about the war, but Neil evaded them. How could he describe the devastation, the poverty, the hungry look in the Germans' eyes? How could he tell of interrogating man after man after the surrender, looking for seemingly now-non-existent Nazis. Because he could speak German, this had been his job after he broke his glasses and his unit left for the South Pacific. He'd hated it. Hated the fear he saw in those men's faces. And the arrogance in others'.

All the while the one question he had for them niggled in his mind.

Finally, he pushed his chair back, stood up and paced the length of the kitchen.

"I met a girl in Germany, Anna Schmidt." He searched their faces for approval. "She's beautiful, she's intelligent, she's fun, and I'm going to ask her to marry me."

His mother's eyes widened. She slowly set her cup down. "A German girl? Oh my."

His dad frowned. "But, son, I don't understand. You want to marry one of *them*? You were just over there fighting those Huns—they're the enemy."

"What about Ruthie?" His mother had a stricken look on her face. "She's been waiting for you."

"But I'm not in love with her." Neil turned from his pacing to face his parents. "It's Anna I love. I want to bring her to America. I'll go to college, and later we'll set up a household of our own."

His father grunted in exasperation. "What about this ranch?"

Mom placed her hands flat on the table and stared at him. "We had plans to expand the herd. After all our struggles to get this ranch, we finally have something to build on. We were just waiting for you to come back, honey."

"Who's going to help us run it if you go off to college? You've had plenty of book-learnin' anyway. These colleges just put fool ideas in your head." Jake fumbled in his pocket for his tobacco pouch. "We made sure you went clear through high school. Your mother and I never made it that far, and we've done all right."

"Yeah, you're doing okay now." *What about all those years you struggled, moved from one place to another*, Neil wanted to add, but he couldn't bring himself to say it.

Dad shook tobacco into the cigarette paper, rolled it and sealed the ends with his tongue. "Around here all you need is common sense. Remember the things I taught you. Besides, how you gonna support a wife and maybe kids if you're in school?" His father lit his cigarette, took a long drag and pushed the smoke out forcefully between his teeth.

Neil knew what that meant. He'd seen his father react this way too many times.

"I'll have the G.I. Bill." Neil bit back his anger now. "And I was hoping maybe you'd help me out by letting me put some more of those heifers in my name, since I've been sending you my paychecks."

"Well, dear. This is just so sudden. Such a surprise." His mother sighed. "I—we always thought you and Ruthie would make such an ideal couple. It would be perfect, with their ranch near us."

"I just don't see how we can support you in this tomfool idea." His dad stood abruptly, knocking his chair over, and left the room.

Neil saw the tears in Mom's eyes. They were disappointed in him, ready to fight him on this. They had no understanding—they couldn't have—of how he'd changed. He'd left as a boy two years ago, but they apparently couldn't see that he was now a man. He sighed. *All I thought of back then was music. I had no idea what war was like.*

He swallowed hard and followed his dad out onto the covered porch that ran the length of the house.

"Dad, I..."

"Why couldn't you just come home, like you were plannin'? Marry the neighbor girl and settle down here. Why'd you get some queer idea in your head about college—and some German girl?" He stopped short. "Is she pregnant?"

Neil shook his head and clenched his fists, holding back the angry words that threatened to spew out. "No. How can you think that way? She's not that kind of girl." He grabbed a denim jacket, slammed down the steps, and headed for the barn.

The mealy smell of oats mingled with the familiar perfume of horse sweat as Neil pushed back the big barn door. He surveyed the well-used stalls, the saddles that hung from the beam, the small mound of hay in the corner. He grabbed his bridle and walked beyond the corral into the horse pasture.

A big blue roan nickered a greeting when he saw his old friend. Neil strode forward and leaned his forehead into the horse's mane as he stroked its neck, his tension flowing out onto Blue's strong, muscular body. "You understand, don't you, boy?"

After a few minutes just breathing in strength and calm, Neil put the bridle on and leaped onto the horse's bare back. He urged his roan into a gallop through the thick gray-green sagebrush, down a steep coulee, and over the crest of the low hill. Once they reached the wide bare pasture, he let Blue have his head, urging him on until the horse was lathered. He stopped on a tabletop butte that rose above the rolling prairie and overlooked the Moser ranch. The pastures showed just a faint tinge of green, no early spring rains yet. The air was crisp and clean, spiced with the faint scent of sage. Neil knew the savageness of this windswept, desolate landscape in winter, and its miraculous rejuvenation in spring, color birthing moment by moment as though it were the first days of the Creation.

He loved it here. The wind in his hair gave him a sense of freedom, and under the huge canopy of sky flowed a peace within the miles of nothingness that he had not felt for a long time. The overpopulated countryside in Europe had left him feeling stifled, claustrophobic, and that the war was senseless and destructive.

Would Anna find this country too desolate, too lonely? She was accustomed to town living, people around. Maybe it wouldn't be fair to bring her here, to ask her to give up her family. Oh dear God, this was turning into an impossible nightmare. Maybe he should just forget about Anna, settle down, and marry Ruthie. She was a nice enough girl, good hearted, fun-loving. Anna's smile flashed into his mind: her inviting lips and her sparkling eyes when she laughed. He longed to embrace her voluptuous figure, caress her soft, wavy brown hair.

Neil tried to shake the image away. He couldn't figure his folks' reaction. Mom had always encouraged him in his reading and study, told him he should learn all he could so he could have a better life than they'd had. It had opened his eyes to worlds beyond ranching and rodeo. He'd been pulled by those insatiable urges to read, to study, and to continually learn. He scrubbed a hand over his brush cut. Maybe they were just symptoms of restlessness, of his youth.

Neil never quite felt like he measured up to Dad's expectations, though. Maybe his father didn't feel that Neil was rough and tough enough, that he was a sissy because he'd rather read a book than wrestle a steer or ride a bronc. He swallowed hard. Dad had as much as told him that when Neil wanted to become a pastor.

Maybe this need to become somebody different from his father had been filled by his travels, his war experiences. Ranching was part of his heritage. It was all he knew, except for mechanic work. How else would he support a wife?

When Anna was beside him, as his wife, and they were settled in a house of their own, with a little herd of purebred Herefords—if she was willing—maybe then he'd feel fulfilled. He had to at least ask her. It couldn't wait any longer. He had to do this.

Darkness had swallowed up the horizon when he finally came back to the house.

***

After Neil walked out the door, Nettie covered her mouth with both hands and fought to breathe normally. Her insides had turned to jelly. How could it be? Her son wanted to marry a German. Those people had killed her beloved nephew Gary, left her sister devastated. She still saw the image of a broken, wrung-out Margie. An arrow of loss pierced her heart. So many young Americans dead because of the war. Even Mama's death from pneumonia. The right drugs weren't available—because of that consarned war. She gazed at Neil's high school photo on the wall. She'd almost lost him too. Tears stung her eyes. But he was home now, safe. She wanted him to be happy. But would marrying a foreigner make him happy? She sighed. He was all grown up—so tall and so handsome.

"He's a man now. He needs to be able to make his own decisions." Nettie couldn't believe it was her voice saying that.

"Hmmf." Jake paced, his boots clumping on the wood floor. "If he'd make the right ones…"

"Jake. Don't you remember? You and me? We didn't want the big fancy wedding my mother had planned for me. We wanted to plan our own lives, live them the way we dreamed. We eloped, for heaven's sake."

"Yeah, yeah. Guess I just hoped he'd be more like us."

"He is, honey. He's the best of both of us, and yet he is his own man."

"Oh, for the love of Mike." Jake snorted and paced some more. Finally, he gave a loud sigh, settled onto the creaky leather sofa and opened a newspaper. "I suppose…if it's gonna keep peace in the family."

***

Neil stood on the porch, watching the stars blink above. Was Anna gazing at the sunrise in her sky, thinking of him? He couldn't live in Germany. He needed her here with him. He gritted his teeth, squeaked open the screen door and walked through the kitchen.

Dad, reading his newspaper in the living room by kerosene lantern light, didn't even look up. Mom, in her rocking chair, slowly put her darning into a striped canvas bag by the chair. She looked like she'd been crying. "I'll warm your supper." She put a soft hand on Neil's arm as she passed by him into the kitchen.

Lad thumped his tail from the rag bed in front of the coal-burning stove. Neil knelt to pat the dog. His gaze took in the wood floor polished by many footsteps, the worn leather sofa and the stack of newspapers on the end table. He wanted this for himself. With Anna.

"It really is my life." He spoke after long minutes. "It doesn't matter who I marry, I'm still me. I love Anna. I am going ask her to come to America and marry me. You can't change my mind on that. I'll stay here and help you on the ranch, though. I can always go to college later."

His dad lowered his paper with a long exhale. "All right, son. Your mother and I've been talking. I don't like the idea, but she thinks we should do what makes you happy. If it means that much to you, bring the girl here. We'll help you get a herd of your own started. But, on one condition—we'd like you to wait a year to get married. Make sure she's really the one, that she fits…er…likes it here first."

"What?" Neil stared at his father, unbelieving.

Mom spoke from the kitchen doorway. "This is all such a new idea, honey. You've been gone so long. I guess we figured we'd all pick up where we left off when you..." There was a little hitch in her voice and she stopped a moment. "You're all grown up. Different, somehow." She turned away, and Neil heard her soft words. "My little boy. All grown up."

He studied his scuffed boots. Well, agreeing to this ridiculous condition would at least get Anna to America. Once she was here, there wouldn't be much they could say.

Why was it so hard for parents to give up their kids? They didn't seem to realize he had his own dreams, too, as they'd surely had theirs. He'd certainly heard often enough about how his mother had wanted to be a rodeo star. And hadn't her parents opposed that idea? He reached down to wipe dust from the toe of one boot. *You'd think they'd want to be different with their own kid.* He certainly would be, with his.

"All right, then. I'm going to send for her." He smiled then. Anna. Kids of his own. Neil turned and took the stairs two at a time to his bedroom. He'd write that letter now.

CHAPTER FIVE

The new year, 1946, padded in on stealthy feet. Anna barely noticed. She spent the normally-festive eve in her darkened room. *Neil Moser can just freeze to death in Montana for all I care.* But the memories of his kind hazel eyes, the electricity of his touch, their quiet conversations tortured her. Once again, her heart lay shattered in an empty cavity.

She hadn't admitted to herself, until she got the letter from her former patient, how much she'd been hoping for one from Neil. Hadn't he promised to write? Maybe she should write him a letter. No, the first step should be up to the man. Shouldn't it? Her shoulders slumped.

Work at the hospital was hardly a distraction. After seeing men's intestines hanging out, legs literally rotting off during the war, and the skeletal POWs released afterwards, now patients with influenza and gall bladder trouble didn't faze her. She held off developing any friendships with the other nurses. Somehow, she felt it wasn't worth it, if friends just went away. Or died.

Hermann kept calling on her. She tried to put him off, but his persistence wore her down. And she had to admit she enjoyed his attention, the lavish gifts of silk scarves, flowers and food, and the concerts that brought a bit of excitement to her sad, dull life.

But she felt no spark when he kissed her, no thrill when he held her hand with his moist, pudgy one. He was nice enough, polite enough, she supposed, but … something was missing. There was no sense of excitement or anticipation in seeing him.

He wasn't Neil.

Anna's birthday, February 11, was just another day at the hospital. She spent more time changing bedpans and linens than actually caring for patients. She couldn't help but remember two years ago, when she'd turned twenty. Fritz had beckoned her to follow him into a small supply room. She'd glanced around to see if anyone was watching, wondering if he was about to try to take liberties with her. She enjoyed his kisses, but she'd heard rumors about nurses who went into supply closets with doctors. Instead of a tryst, Fritz had presented her with a whole chicken leg for her dinner. She smiled, remembering his beaming pride. That was the best gift she'd ever received. He wouldn't even take a bite—she'd had to eat the whole thing herself. Anna's mouth watered. It would be wonderful to be able to buy an entire chicken again.

She plodded home through streets where the only vehicles were the Jeeps of the American occupation forces. Why were they still here? If they were here, why wasn't Neil?

When she reached home, she trudged up the stairs to her chilly room without even popping her head into the kitchen, as she usually did. More than ready to take off her heavy oxfords, Anna plunked herself on her bed and heard a crackling beneath her. She moved aside and saw a blue tissue airmail envelope. No, there were two. Her breath caught in her throat. Could they be from America? Anna swallowed, not daring to let herself hope. Oh, yes. Probably that former patient again. She turned the envelopes over. No—both return addresses read "Neil Moser." One was postmarked in November from New York, the other in December from Fort Lewis, Washington—both seriously delayed. Anna gave a little shriek and nearly tore the first one in half, hurrying to read the words written in German.

> *My dear Anna,*
>
> *I'm writing this aboard ship on my way back to the States. It will be several weeks before we arrive, and then, I'm sure, several more weeks until you receive it.*

I'm sorry I had to leave so quickly, and before I had a chance to tell you that I do care for you. I've been thinking of you every day since I left.

I miss our times together, our coffees, our walks. Even dinners with your cousins and all their questions.

Please give your family my regards. I hope your father's leg is healing well.

I will write again soon. And I await your reply.

Sincerely,

Neil

Anna realized she hadn't been breathing. With a gasp of air, she ripped open the second letter. It read much the same—a little more chatty, about the rainy winter weather in Washington state where he was stationed at Fort Lewis. She clutched her baggy uniform dress to her thin body and lay back, daydreaming. If there never had been a war Fritz would still be alive. They might even be married by now. But if the war hadn't happened, she wouldn't have met Neil.

He misses me. He cares for me. He thinks of me every day. Now her breaths came quickly until she was about to hyperventilate. She didn't know whether to laugh or to cry. This was what she'd been waiting for. But a voice in her head mocked—*Surely you didn't think he was going to send for you.* Perhaps she was just fooling herself, thinking there might be a better life somewhere else and that he was her ticket out of Germany. She pictured the acres of grain Neil had described, the slabs of bread and the meat he was probably eating every day in America. For just a moment an ugly specter of resentment hovered, made her clench her fists and shiver.

No. Feeling this way was fruitless. She couldn't change the way things had turned out. But she could write back. She stood, went to the little desk and took out a piece of paper and pen.

Dear Neil...

Mutti called several times to come downstairs for supper—potato pancakes and a dried-apple cake. Anna smiled at her mother. So typical of her to find something special for her birthday. She even smelled a hint of onion in the pancakes. Her mouth watered.

A bouquet of roses stood in lonely splendor on the table. From Hermann, naturally. Anna rolled her eyes.

Elsa twitched her eyebrows. "So. Flowers from one and letters from the other. What did your Neil Moser have to say— in *two* letters?"

Anna tried to remain nonchalant. "Oh, nothing much. Just his trip across the ocean aboard ship. Where he's stationed now. I'm sure he's happy to be back in America again."

Papa looked up from his newspaper and snorted. "*Ja*, out of sight, out of mind."

Anna frowned. Now why did he have to say that? It just was not true.

***

It took Anna days to complete her letter to Neil. She re-read his letters several times a day, studying each word, as if to extract some hidden meaning from the lines. Biting her lip, she wrote, scratched out words, and crumpled her first sheet of paper into a ball. Her breath hitched. That was a waste of paper. She couldn't be doing that. What words could she use that would let him know she cared, that she wanted to see him again? She studied the APO address on his envelope. Should she send it there? What if he was transferred before he got it?

Hermann took her dancing the weekend following her birthday. Tonight, he presented her with "a late birthday gift," an emerald brooch.

Anna's eyes widened. "Oh, but I can't accept this." How could he afford to buy jewelry? It just wasn't right.

"Why not? It suits you. Accents your eyes." His gaze bored into hers. "Besides, I want my girl to have the very best."

His girl? *Nein.* She couldn't keep this façade up any longer. "Hermann, I…I have never gotten over the death of my fiancé. I can't think of anyone else seriously. I mean, I appreciate you

45

taking me out, and I've enjoyed the concerts and dinners, but…"

"Shh-shh-shh." Hermann put a pudgy finger to her lips. "I understand. Just give it time. Let me show you that you can love again."

He wouldn't take the brooch back, so she took it home and hid it in the bottom of her bureau drawer.

Guilt from her little white lie kept Anna awake that night. What had she gotten herself into, and how could she get out of it? She didn't want to hurt his feelings. But she couldn't tell him about Neil. Especially when she really didn't know what Neil intended. *Ach mein Gott.* Such a tangled web.

The gray winter days softened into the first spring buds. She refused Hermann's invitations as often as she could, but at times couldn't find the strength to think up another excuse.

Elsa frowned at her. "What's the matter with you? He's rich. He could take very good care of you." Then she giggled. "And you could throw your leftovers and discarded finery my way."

Anna wrinkled her brow at her sister.

***

Over the next few weeks, Anna wrote several letters to Neil, equally as chatty and non-committal as his. But she didn't receive another one from him. Maybe Papa was right. Maybe he'd decided to forget about her after all, marry some Montana girl. A cowboy-girl? She still couldn't imagine what that might be. But undoubtedly someone more suited to him and his life.

What about her life? Should she accept Hermann's invitations and a proposal if he asked? Elsa was right—he was well off. Never seemed to lack for money or good food. A life like that would be nice after so many years of wondering if the next meal was going to be a single potato, even a half-rotten one. But how he made his money—she'd heard rumors about the black market being run by a tight-knit organization—thefts of cigarettes, artwork, beer, even automobiles that were shipped to France and other countries in return for jewelry, perfume, cash. Anna closed her eyes, suddenly dizzy. Surely he wasn't involved in any of that—his family was in banking. They were respected.

A long, mournful sigh escaped her. Everything about her life felt so heavy, so dark. She couldn't make the simplest decisions. Didn't want to. All she wanted to do was crawl under her feather comforter and hide...and forget...and dream.

***

These lean times made giving up something for Lent superfluous. What more could Anna give up? She hadn't been to Mass in months despite Mutti's disapproving scowls—didn't see any purpose in it anymore. She ignored the soft air of April, the cheerful purple crocuses, and Easter's promise of rebirth. She had nothing to celebrate. There were no lambs for an Easter feast, few eggs to color and hide for children.

Hermann continued to pester her. "Come with me to the Easter Eve bonfire. That'll cheer you up. We'll sing songs." When that didn't elicit a response, he added, "There'll be food."

Anna rolled her eyes. Sure, tempt her with something to eat. "Maybe. We'll see. I might be needed at the hospital for the evening shift." This wasn't so far from the truth. Nurses with husbands and children wanted to have time off to spend with them. Anna could work in their stead. Why not?

On Good Friday the bells of the ancient church tolled the solemn message of Christ's death. Anna couldn't help the tears that welled. She felt the loss of her faith too, as acutely as the loss of Fritz. And Neil. Clouds threatened spring showers as she trudged home after work.

The letter lay in the middle of the kitchen table. Anna stopped in the doorway. Her heartbeat sped up. *Nein.* No reason to get excited. It would just tease her. She turned away, deliberately ignoring the letter and Mutti's raised brows, and clumped upstairs.

Anna sprawled on her bed and covered her eyes with one hand. She inhaled deeply, trying to slow her breathing. *I don't care who the letter is from.* But what if it was from Neil? *I don't care, I don't care, I don't care.* Another breath. Her heartbeat echoed in her ears like a bass drum in an Easter parade.

Elsa clicked open the door. Anna sat upright.

"Don't you want to even know who it's from?" Elsa waved the blue envelope in front of Anna's face.

"*Nein.*" If it wasn't from Neil, then...

"Oh, sure you do." Her sister made a big show of peering at the return address. "Can't quite make it out. Hmmm. Is that an 'N'? Maybe an 'M'. It's from the U.S.A., anyway."

Unable to stop her hand, Anna reached out and snatched the letter away. "All right. Go away now. Leave me be."

Elsa giggled and sashayed out of the room, crooning, "Love, love, love."

CHAPTER SIX

Anna tried to quiet her shaking fingers as she carefully tore the ends of the envelope and read the now-familiar scrawl.

> *My dearest Anna,*
>
> *I hope you received my other two letters. I've been hoping for one from you, but I have the feeling the mail service is quite slow.*
>
> *I've come to realize, over the past few months, how much I love you. I miss our talks, our long walks in the woods, and just laughing together. I'm worthless without you. I'm praying to the Good Lord above that I'm not too late in asking—will you come to the United States and marry me? I know this is a difficult decision to leave your family and your country and come all this way. But I can't stand being apart from you. If you care for me at all and will have me, I will send money for your ticket.*
>
> *All my love,*
>
> *Neil*

Anna gave a sharp cry and hugged the letter to her breast. *Ach, du lieber Gott. You are still up there after all.* Now the tears came, fresh and cleansing as spring showers, to create a fountain of hope within her. To go to America. To marry Neil. He loved her. She had a future.

Anna dried her eyes with her hanky and sat at the little desk to write her reply. She dipped her fountain pen into the ink. *Dearest Neil...*

Then her hand froze. Wait. Did she really want to do this—go to America, a foreign land so many thousands of miles away? If she went, she may never get to come home again. She closed her eyes, picturing Mutti at the stove or the sink, always cooking or cleaning, always caring for her family. Papa sitting at the table, reading his newspaper. Elsa's teasing smile as she wolfed down her chocolate bar, then badgered Anna for some of hers. Karl's little blond head sticking up over the fence, waiting for her to come home. And Hans, tall, sandy-haired and serious. Would she ever see him again?

Anna put down the pen and went to the window, looking down on their narrow cobblestone street, where the neighbors all knew each other, traded daily gossip as they swept their walks, and shared each other's tears and triumphs. In America she would know no one. Maybe they would all hate her.

The questions flitted through her mind like darting swallows. Would she fit in with that cowboy culture? Would she have to ride a horse? She didn't really know that much about Neil or his life. What would he be like without his uniform, in his cowboy clothes, on his "ranch?" *Ach du lieber.*

Anna paced the length of her small room, around the end of her bed, then Elsa's, to the door and back again to the window. And such a huge country. Neil had told her that all of Germany would fit inside Montana, just one state out of forty-eight.

Should she talk to Elsa, ask her advice? She shook her head. Her sister would just tease her more.

Maybe she should say her prayers and get a good night's sleep before she wrote that letter. But she lay awake, thinking of her close-knit family, long after Elsa crept into the room and her soft snores began.

The next few days blurred as Anna walked with her constant companion, doubt. The questions rolled through her mind like the train to Frankfurt. But she had no answers, except the longing in her heart.

Frankfurt. What would Tante Rosa say? She wished she could talk to her favorite aunt. But that was impossible. She lived too far away. Anna didn't even know if Rosa was still in Frankfurt. She pictured her mother's tall, angular sister, always ready with an encouraging word for Anna—"You go to school. Learn a trade. Don't be afraid. Stand up for yourself. Be

50

strong." Anna smiled. She had done that, had learned nursing, had persevered through the hard times.

Then she knew what Tante Rosa would tell her—"Follow your heart."

***

As soon as she mailed the letter, Anna walked outside the Post Office and leaned against the wall. She had done it. The decision was made. No turning back now. *What have I done?* Her sudden fear threatened to cut off her breath. She leaned forward over her knees and forced herself to inhale deeply.

Calm down, Anna. She scolded herself as if she were a reluctant patient. *You've been waiting months for this. It's what you wanted. Now get hold of yourself.*

Neil. Love. America. She did a sudden little schottische step, then looked around with a giggle to see if anyone watched.

Oh dear. Mutti and Papa would be upset. Stifling a worming fear, Anna started home, but before long realized there was a buoyancy to her step she hadn't had in…years. She actually felt happy. With a huge smile, she opened the door into the kitchen, where Mutti was just about to dish up supper. "I have wonderful news."

Papa looked up from his newspaper with a frown. Elsa's eyes widened. Karl gave an expectant smile. Mutti stepped forward. "*Ja, und…?*"

With just a bit of trepidation, Anna took a deep breath. "Neil has asked me to go to America and marry him." She registered Mutti's shocked look and Papa's stone face. "And I just posted my letter back, saying yes. I'm going."

Elsa squealed and rushed to hug her. Karl jumped up and down. "America, America!" Her parents froze in their places.

Mutti put her hands to her cheeks. "*Ach, du lieber…*Go…to America…marry…?" Then she came to hug Anna, bursting into tears. "Oh, my little girl…oh my…"

Finally, the tears and exuberance abated, and Mutti composed herself enough to finish serving supper. Papa still hadn't said a word. Anna sat at the table next to him, heart pounding. *He doesn't approve.* "Well, Papa, are you happy for me?"

He grunted and opened the paper once again, the pages shaking. "I suppose there's nothing I can say that will change your mind. You'll do what you want."

Mutti burst into tears again. Elsa frowned at her father, then reached over to pat Anna's arm. "They'll be all right," she mouthed.

Yes. Her family would survive this. They would have one less mouth to feed, anyway, especially if...when...Hans came home. Anna had her future now, and love. Everything would be just fine.

All she had to do was get her passport—and her tickets—and go.

CHAPTER SEVEN

The next morning Anna walked downtown to apply for her passport at the registration office. Since the occupation, the Americans required all residents to register when they moved in or out of the city. After she'd stood in line for three hours, she triumphantly announced her plans at the clerk's window.

The man shook his head and smirked. "You need to go to the American consulate in Frankfurt to get a visa."

Disappointment welled up. But then she straightened her shoulders. If that's what she needed to do, that's what she'd do. This was just a little inconvenience.

First she had to get permission to take a day off from the hospital. So, it was the following week before she finally boarded the train for the city. Mutti had packed a slice of bread for her lunch. "Remember Tante Rosa lives in Frankfurt, if you have time to go visit her." Then she sent Anna off with a hug and a wistful "*Auf Wiedersehen.*" Anna raised her eyebrows. *Until we meet again.* As though Mutti were already saying good-bye.

Ignoring the other passengers crowding the car with their haunted looks, Anna gazed at the green countryside and smiled at her reflection in the window. She hummed as she leafed through a magazine. But she couldn't concentrate on any of the articles. Before her eyes swam Neil's smiling hazel ones and the words of his letter, "I love you, *mein Liebchen*...will you marry me?"

The street outside the American consulate was packed with armies of wanderers who had lost their homes, people who had fled the bombing and now wanted to return, and Jewish families desperate to get out of the country—an exodus to anywhere. To deal with the crowds, the officials had set up makeshift immigration offices, bare wood structures within the gates.

Anna waited outside in line for hours, the damp spring air chilling her to the bone, a dull throb beginning at the base of her neck. At five o'clock, when she finally moved inside and was now seventh in line, the clerk put up his "Closed" signed and announced, "Sorry, you must return tomorrow."

"No. You can't. Wait!" she called out. "Please. I've come all this way—" But the clerk merely turned and walked away.

Oh no. So close... Anna pressed her palms against the headache at her temples. What was she going to do? If she went home tonight and rode the train back tomorrow, she'd be at the end of a long line again. She had to be here early in the morning, but she couldn't afford a hotel. And she couldn't sleep out on the street. Her shoulders slumped.

But wait. Tante Rosa. With her mind focused on the day's task and going to America, she hadn't even given a thought to Mutti's suggestion to visit. She hadn't seen her favorite aunt since before the war. Mutti received a letter from her last Christmas, or maybe it was the year before. A momentary pang of guilt stopped Anna. *I hope she's still here.*

She hurried through the deserted and dilapidated streets to reach her aunt's apartment before dark. All the shops were closed, and she passed by a Catholic church with a large hole in the roof, but it looked as if it were still being used. Finally, she came to an area of town with several apartment buildings. Now which one was it? With so many buildings gone, it was hard to remember. Too bad she didn't have any way to contact Tante Rosa, to see if she was home. Ah yes. There it was, the one with a now dry and crumbling fountain in the courtyard. Someone had planted cheery red geraniums amidst the rubble—maybe her aunt.

Anna knocked, a nervous flutter in her stomach.

Rosa opened the door. A huge smile warmed her face. "My dear Anna. What a lovely surprise. What are you doing here? Come in, come in. I just made a lentil *Suppe*."

Anna's shoulders relaxed, and she stepped into her aunt's bear hug. Then the older women held her at arm's length. "Let me look at you. My, my, you are so thin. I wish I had more to feed you."

Anna smiled. *It doesn't matter.* Just being with her Tante fed her soul. She looked around the combination kitchen-living room, crowded with dark overstuffed furniture. A blanket hung over the door into Rosa's bedroom, and all other rooms were sealed off, doors stuffed with quilting. No one had money enough to heat an entire house. But a coal fire in the kitchen stove made this room warm and cozy. She felt at home.

"And how is your Mutti?" Rosa dished up a bowl.

Anna told her how her mother had sacrificed and scrounged the countryside to feed her family, all the while keeping her optimistic outlook.

Her aunt sighed. "How I wish we could be closer. I will come visit one day soon."

Anna smiled. "Yes, Mutti would like that. We all would."

The soup was thin and watery, but it warmed Anna's stomach and Tante Rosa's encouragement warmed her heart. "Ja, you must go to your young man in America." She nodded her silvery head. "Follow your heart."

Anna rose before daylight and was among the first in the crowd waiting at the doors of the consulate when it opened. The harried clerk, desk piled high with paperwork, gave her a wrist-high stack of forms to fill out, a list of people from whom she would need letters of reference, and instructions to return when she had it all in order. She looked through them during the train trip home and gulped.

My goodness, this will take a week or more to finish.

In the evening when she walked up to her house, the smell of supper cooking made her stomach contract, and she realized she had not eaten all day. As she opened the front door, she heard a masculine voice from the parlor. "Welcome home."

"Hermann." She had forgotten all about him. The hunger pangs turned sour. Oh, my, what was she going to say?

55

"What is this—your parents told me you've been to Frankfurt?" He smiled with the rictus of forced politeness.

Anna gulped, set down her sheaf of papers, called a greeting to her parents in the kitchen, and turned back to Hermann, sitting in the semi-darkened parlor.

His face grew darker and his body more rigid as he listened to her plans. At first she thought he was going to hit something. Then he visibly relaxed. He leaned back on the sofa and his smile came back, the kind that was probably meant to reassure, but instead made her feel like a hen being watched by a fox. "But my dear, we have had such a good time together. Please reconsider. Be *my* wife. You know I will provide very well for you. Everyone will look up to you. You will have all the money, clothes and servants you want. I can offer you much more than that American." He reached out and took her hand.

His words sounded stilted, like a rehearsed speech. Anna frowned. Had he known about Neil somehow?

The long hours waiting in line, the lack of sleep and proper food were all suddenly too much for Anna. Her determination sagged. Maybe she should stay in Germany. Her life would certainly be a lot easier as Hermann's wife. She wouldn't have to leave her family behind, and he would probably see that they were well cared for too.

Yet, the rumors that he was profiting from the black market... She felt an uneasiness that gave her goose bumps. A good reputation was of utmost importance to her parents. It was not a subject she could ask him about. But she had her own future to consider. What should she do? The thoughts whirled in her head, making her dizzy.

She stared at his round, pasty face, and slipped her hand from his clammy one. "I can't talk to you right now. Please go. I need to rest ... and think."

As he headed to the front door, Anna turned and walked down the hall into the kitchen. Her mother was suddenly busy setting the table and her father became engrossed in his newspaper. Anna rolled her eyes. They'd been eavesdropping on her conversation with Hermann.

"Sit, eat." Her mother pointed to Anna's chair, and dished up a vegetable stew. "I walked miles today and traded my ivory brooch to a farmer for enough vegetables for a few days' meals."

Guilt wormed its way through Anna's chest. Mutti deserved better. Her mother tried so hard. Giving up her beautiful brooch.

But to spend the rest of her life with Hermann. He just wasn't comfortable and easy-going, like Neil. Not nice-looking and genuine, like Neil.

He wasn't Neil.

Papa made throat-clearing noises throughout dinner, but whenever Anna looked at him expectantly, he busied himself with his stew and the paper beside his plate. Finally, he wiped up the last drops of soup with a hunk of bread and sat back. "You know, you could do worse than Hermann Zahn. He has connections, and he would take good care of you."

Mutti wrung the skirt of her apron as though it were full of water. "The cousins have been asking me every day, 'How can she leave us and go to the country of the enemy, where the people hate the Germans?' If you married Hermann…"

Tears blurred Anna's vision. "Please, Mutti, Papa. I know all that. I hate to leave you, but… I couldn't bear to be with Hermann when I love Neil so much!"

They did not speak of Hermann Zahn again.

***

A week later, Anna had what felt like a bushel basket full of applications filled out and was ready to board the train for Frankfurt. The proper pages were certified. She had letters from her nursing supervisor and the hospital administrator, the banker where she kept her account—when she had money— and the police department. Even her school principal, the family priest, her parents, the neighbors, and her best friend. She'd delayed asking each one for this favor, knowing that no one really approved. Finally, with an apologetic blush Anna steeled herself to the task. But to her surprise, they all agreed to help.

Hope gave her a floating sensation as she gazed out of the train windows at the green pastures, the forested hillsides, the Main River that meandered by Frankfurt. She re-read Neil's last letter, soaking up his words. He sounded so excited she was coming to America. Soon she would be with her love, and they would tend cows in their own barn, their own pasture. Neil had talked about the wide, open spaces in America, the great cities where you could buy whatever you wanted, and the large farms that could provide food for entire countries. Anna started a letter to him, full of anticipation.

On this day there were even more lines, each just as long, but she made it to the window as the clerk reached for his "Closed" sign.

Not again! "Oh, *bitte.*" She flung her paperwork on the counter. "Please, I need to catch the train back to Bad Orb tonight." Reluctantly, the clerk took her papers and hurriedly flipped through them. "*Nein,* these are not the right set of forms. We received new ones from the government today. You must fill out these." He handed her a stack twice as high as the one she'd had before.

"But—" Her protest was cut off as the window slammed shut.

Anna's shoulders slumped. In an instant, she felt so very tired. She couldn't face the trip home. She went to her aunt's house and fell into Rosa's arms, sobbing.

"There, there," Tante Rosa comforted. "Come, have some nice warm soup, and we'll talk."

Again, her aunt's compassion and tender care soothed Anna, and she began to feel better. "You must have patience," Rosa counseled. "I believe it is God's will for you to make it to America. I've prayed at Mass for you and your young man every morning since you were here last."

***

58

The year passed into 1947. Anna filled out the required papers. She went back to the immigration offices again and again. Yes, these were the correct forms, but they needed to be filled out in duplicate. No, they were very sorry, but some new forms were needed—please fill these out in triplicate. You'll need this series of vaccinations. Then, because it's been so long since you've received your shots, you'll need another booster. And always the message, you must wait; you must be patient. The months blurred.

She packed. She unpacked. And packed again. Each time, she chose or discarded different items, noticing the wear on the skirts, the scuffs on the shoes, the threadbare sweaters. If she took these things to America, they wouldn't last long. But she had no money to buy anything new, even if she could find something for sale.

Anna's fingers became calloused from writing and her back bent from hunching over the kitchen table for hours on end. Her feet hurt from standing in line and trudging from one office to the next. It became a full-time effort, and one day her supervisor at the hospital called her into the office.

"I realize you are working hard to get your paperwork to go to America, but you are taking too much time from your job." The head nurse shook her head with a rueful expression. "We're having to cut back on nursing staff, anyway, so perhaps…"

Anna gulped. Working less and less, she wasn't providing much for her family anyway. Elsa had a job cleaning at a hotel now, so that would help. She nodded. "Yes. I'd better resign."

She took a deep breath, bit her lip to keep the tears at bay, and walked home in a state of numb disbelief. At home the guilt and weariness overcame her and she threw herself on her bed and cried herself to sleep. What was she doing? Was it worth all this? Perhaps she was just being selfish. She wasn't able to help her family any more.

She continued to write letters to Neil. "Another setback, but I have faith that I will be coming to America soon."

Neil's replies remained full of reassurance and encouragement. "I would come and take you away myself if there were any way I could. I wish we could have been married before I left. Don't give up hope—it will work out. We will be together."

"This 'red tape' is going to reach across the ocean to America all by itself long before *I* get there." Anna searched her sister's dark eyes for solace one night, after yet another long and frustrating trip to Frankfurt.

It was now 1948.

***

One day Anna sat before the desk of a now-familiar American official at the consulate in Frankfurt, nearly in tears. She'd just received another visa application rejection. "Please. I beg of you. Can you find out the reason behind this, so I can make it right?"

The man sighed and ran a hand over his face. "I know this has been a long ordeal for you, as it has for many." He looked at her and his expression softened. "Let me see here." He shuffled through his papers. "You have all the letters from your employers, banks, and so forth... You worked as a nurse..."

"Yes."

"You've not been married to anyone here?"

Anna shook her head. "No."

"You were not a member of the Nazi Party?"

She nearly snorted. "No."

"Affiliations ...? Hmm." He adjusted his glasses and peered at a page. "Do you know a Hermann Zahn?"

Anna frowned. "Hermann? Yes, I know him. He's... a friend... of the family... used to be a neighbor."

The official's eyebrows raised. "Well, apparently, government officials are looking into his background..."

"Background? His family is in banking."

"Says here, possible Party membership."

"What?" Anna sat upright. "What does that have to do with me?"

60

"Apparently you've dated him?"

"Yes, but only for a short time. I haven't seen him in more than a year." A chill ran through her. *Nein*. This couldn't be.

CHAPTER EIGHT

As the train left Frankfurt and all its bureaucracy behind, Anna sat in shocked numbness. Hermann a member of the Nazi Party? This couldn't be true. Surely she would've had some inkling. It had to be only rumor and speculation. Didn't it? But what about all the money he seemed to always have? The fine suits. The gifts he'd given her. The concerts and dinners out. Here she'd been skeptical of him because of the black market, merely a means of survival.

She still couldn't understand what this had to do with her wanting to emigrate. She went out with him only a few times. She didn't have anything to do with what he did or didn't do. And she certainly had never joined the Party, nor had any member of her family. *Ach du lieber.*

"*Schweinhund!*" Papa thundered when Anna returned home to tell her family what had happened.

"Oh you poor dear. Let me make you something to eat." Mutti patted her shoulder and busied herself in the kitchen.

Food was always Mutti's answer to any problem. Anna blinked back a tear. She would miss her mother and her fussing over the family.

Elsa shook her head. "I always knew he was trouble."

Anna's twisted her mouth. *Sure you did.*

The next day Papa went to the bank where Hermann's father was president. Over supper he reported, "Herr Zahn denies his son has had anything to do with illegal activities."

Anna's shoulders slumped. "But what about my papers?"

Papa shrugged. "He said he will look into it. See what he can do to help you."

That night Anna thrashed beneath her feather comforter. It had been against her instincts to accept Hermann's first invitation. Why had she given in? Because she'd been feeling sorry for herself, feeling Fritz's loss so heavily, she'd succumbed to the attention and the food he could offer her. *Ach du lieber.* What a mess she'd gotten herself into. What would she tell Neil now? She might never be able to go to America. Tears cascaded down her cheeks, and she buried her sobs in her pillow.

The weeks went by. Papa visited his former neighbor at the bank almost daily. "Nothing new," he would tell Anna every evening. "Herr Zahn is still looking into it. He's concerned about the family's good reputation. He wants to clear his son's name, as well."

Then one spring evening Hermann was at their door, hat in hand.

"I apologize that you were mixed up in these false accusations. It was all just paperwork confusion. I hope you don't think ill of me." He smiled and held onto her hand. "I wish you all the best in America." Then he turned and was gone.

Anna stood in the doorway, stunned. Maybe Hermann had some redeeming qualities after all.

***

Finally, the day came—two years, three months and twelve days after that first innocent "Yes." The immigration official stamped her papers, Anna received her passport, her alien visa, and her Luftansa airline tickets to Minneapolis and a domestic flight to Miles City, Montana, U.S.A. She would be arriving on November 15, 1948.

With a shriek, Anna ran through the house, clutching the last of the precious papers. "I'm going to America. I'm really going!"

Papa pursed his mouth, nodded, and went back to reading his newspaper. Mutti's eyes instantly shone with tears. "*Ach, mein Liebchen.*" Her voice husky, she kneaded her apron with her fingers, and turned back to the stove.

Elsa chattered away about the "land of milk and honey" as she helped Anna set about packing once more—for the last time. Mutti came in, clutching a dainty rose-strewn china cup and saucer. "This was your grandmother's. Wrap it well. Remember us in America when you sip your coffee from it."

Anna's throat closed. No words came. She laid her cheek against her mother's wet one. They rocked together in a long tight embrace. Then Mutti left the room without another word.

Elsa handed her a hanky. "We'll miss you, sister. But you have a whole new life ahead of you. I'm so happy for you."

Anna wiped her eyes then tucked the lace handkerchief away with the cup and saucer. She put on a smile and turned back to the task at hand. Soon clothing littered the floor of their bedroom in the sisters' frenzy. Everything she'd chosen before seemed wrong now. She was limited to one trunk. That wasn't enough to start her new life. A new life. With Neil. In America.

She could hardly wait.

***

Anna tried to swallow. She stood next to the train that would take her to the airport in Frankfurt and took a long, last look at her family—her mother's round, tear-stained face as she smiled bravely, Elsa's vicarious excitement over what she thought of as her sister's upcoming adventure, and Karl's little mouth puckering at the corners. Even her father blinked rapidly as he shuffled his feet, told her to be careful, and caught her in an uncharacteristic hug. "*Auf Wiedersehen.*"

Until we meet again. The breath caught in her chest. *Will I ever see them again?*

The conductor blew his whistle and called out, "All aboard!"

Anna hesitated. The cousins, aunts and uncles had been upset over Anna "abandoning" her parents, since she and her sister were the family's only source of income. For a moment, guilty tears rose. She let her shoulders slump forward and wondered why she was leaving them, everyone she loved, everything familiar. *Because there is no future in Germany*, she told herself sternly. The war had caused such destruction, so much death, and very little hope for the future. She had lost her job, and Elsa was the one working now. Papa's leg was almost healed, and he would go back to work in the woods soon.

Anna set her shoulders, walked up the steps into her train car, then turned and blew them one last kiss. She was on her way to a new life in a new land, where someone who loved her awaited.

The first leg of the trip—Anna's first experience on an airplane—took her to Shannon, Ireland, to top off the fuel for the flight across the ocean. Anna stood on the tarmac before re-boarding and gazed at the Irish countryside. Raindrops from a recent shower shone on the grass in the sunlight, and the carpeted hills rolled smoothly to the sky. She took in a deep, hopeful breath of the fresh, clean air. Anna had never seen such a brilliant green. It was as if leprechauns had painted a magical backdrop to this fairytale she now lived.

Anna watched the passengers ascend the stairs—harried mothers with young children, a grandfatherly man, plump, rosy-faced Irish, an American soldier with a limp. As the plane took off again from the small airport, a thought struck her. *We're leaving Europe. I wonder where all these people are going. Will we ever come back?* A tearful bubble rose in her throat.

***

Anna stayed awake most of the night as the plane roared across the black ocean below. She thought of the pictures Neil had sent of the tall white ranch house, and wondered what kind of a house she and Neil would have, what the town of Ingomar would be like. A smile formed as she pictured a white picket fence around a little cottage on a tree-lined street. Yes, she had made the right decision. Life in America would be better than what she'd left behind. She could forget the war, the bombings, the blood.

She awoke as the stewardess announced their arrival in Newfoundland with the sun's first rays of early morning light. After just enough time to get off the plane and stretch cramped legs, the flight continued with a breakfast of hard-boiled eggs and rye bread. Next stop: Montreal, then Minneapolis, then Miles City—eighteen hours of flying time from Germany.

In Minnesota, the other passengers bustled off the plane, and Anna gasped as the below-zero air hit her lungs. November in Germany was never like this. Would it be this cold in Montana?

She peered fearfully at all the signs in English, but airline officials helped her through customs, since this was her entry into her new country. After all the time she'd spent standing in lines in Germany, traveling to get her paperwork to go on this trip, this was no worse. No soldiers stood guard. The clerks smiled and nodded as they stamped her passport and visa. They didn't even open her bag.

Another friendly official gave her a hotel voucher and helped her into a taxi, which dropped her off at a multi-storied building downtown. Her eyes traveled up and up, into the sky as her gaze followed the floors to the top.

Inside, the desk clerk jabbered something unintelligible at her. *Oh my.* He spoke so fast, the only words she could understand were "help" and "you." She placed her voucher, passport and plane tickets on the counter and pointed to the time she was to leave the next morning. The clerk nodded. He selected a key from a rack on the wall. "O-KAY." He drew out the syllables and spoke in a loud voice. "YOUR ROOM IS NUMBER TWO-TWO-FIVE." He pointed at the number on the key, then motioned for a bellman.

A hot flush rose up Anna's neck. "Thank you," she replied in English. Tears threatened, but she firmed her mouth and followed the young man to her room.

She sat on the soft bed in a room that must be reserved for queens. Burgundy velvet draped the windows, the bedspread matched the carpet in tones of rose and wine. An easy chair flanked a mahogany writing desk, which held a telephone.

Anna's stomach gurgled. It was past suppertime. But where would she find a place to eat? And if she did go out, she wouldn't be able to place her order. These people spoke so fast and what they said didn't seem to make any sense with the words and phrases she'd learned. She sighed and searched her purse for a package of soda crackers from the plane. She would just go to sleep. Then she wouldn't need to eat.

***

Anna smoothed her hair and looked at her watch for the fifteenth time in ten minutes since the stewardess had announced the upcoming arrival in Miles City. One foot tapped in space as she sat with crossed legs. She fished a mirror from her purse and checked her lipstick again. Would Neil recognize her? It had been so long. Maybe he had changed. Two years was a world apart. Maybe he wouldn't like her anymore. She gulped. What if he weren't there? No air reached her lungs. For a moment, she was afraid she would sob out loud. He said he would meet her, and he surely would. She looked at her watch again.

Anna pressed her forehead to the window as the plane descended. Finally, Miles City, Montana. Below her a mosaic of gray, brown and pale yellow fields showed through a background of snow. It was so flat! She peered at the horizon, yet saw no mountains, no forests, and no towns. Nothing like Germany. A narrow river wound its way from tan mounds that rose in the distance, through the wide prairie, and trickled around a group of low buildings nestled under a sharp cliff.

"Ladies and gentlemen, we are landing in Miles City, the cowboy capital of Montana. Thank you for flying Northwest Airlines."

This was a city? Anna could count all the houses as they banked to approach the short runway atop the cliff overlooking the town. When they landed, she gathered her valise and purse and inched toward the door. The sun shone, but the cold hit her like a chunk of ice slamming into her chest. She could see her breath when she stepped out of the warm plane onto the stairway. Anna paused for a moment as she scanned the small group of strangers waiting just outside the tiny, low terminal building. Her heart beat a staccato tattoo.

There he was, standing head and shoulders above everyone else. A warm river of relief flowed through her. Neil had come. She knew he would.

She started to run toward him, but then slowed to a more sedate walk as she saw two more individuals detaching themselves from the rest. A tall man walked beside Neil, and a slim, boyish-figured woman, no taller than Anna, strode forward, head erect. She was dressed in a suede leather jacket with fringe on the sleeves, a warm chocolate-colored full skirt set off by a bright copper belt and dangling earrings to match. A cowboy hat and high-heeled cowboy boots completed the image.

Anna self-consciously smoothed the wrinkles from her plain brown skirt. Her future mother-in-law. She looked so strong and self-assured. A cowboy-girl.

"Anna." Neil loped across the remaining space between them and gathered her up in a lingering embrace. "I'm so glad to see you, my love," he whispered in German, holding her tight.

Anna couldn't speak for the pure sweet joy that washed over her. So many sensations—Neil's rough denim jacket against her cheek, the soapy smell of his neck, the vise-like yet warm grip of his arms around her.

At last he released her, laughing. Holding her at arm's length, he gazed into her eyes. "I was beginning to think you'd never get here. It's been so long."

She could only smile. *Me too.*

The sound of a throat clearing behind them broke the spell. They turned toward the couple. "Mom, Dad, I'd like you to meet my Anna," Neil said, and in German, "Anna, this is my mama, Nettie, and my papa, Jake."

Anna nodded, extended her hand and said in her best English, "I please to meet you, Mr. *und* Mrs. Moser."

Jake's large calloused paw enveloped hers. His grip was strong, like Neil's. He gave her hand a quick shake, then shoved his hands into his jacket pockets.

Nettie extended a cool slender hand. "Hope you had a comfortable trip."

Anna bit her lower lip, then gave a nervous smile. Neil's mother was like no other woman she'd ever known. What would they have in common? How would Anna talk to her? Mrs. Moser wasn't like Mutti, round and warm, always ready with a hug.

"Let's go pick up your luggage and head for the ranch. It's going to be late by the time we get there." Jake turned abruptly toward the terminal.

Anna's stomach contracted. Neil's parents didn't seem very glad to see her. They acted so aloof. Fear tickled her imagination. She must appear so different. Maybe they would send her back. Could they?

***

Nettie swallowed hard. This girl was not like any of the girls around here—not a ranch girl—certainly not like Ruthie. She wondered what had attracted Neil to her. Well, yes, Anna was a pretty girl with her dark waves and blue eyes. But she couldn't speak English. Nettie couldn't imagine how they would communicate, what they would have to talk about. *I wonder if she's ever ridden a horse.*

A German. They were all terrible killers, Nazis, weren't they? An ache for her nephew Gary who'd been killed in the war pierced her heart. Nettie peered at the girl. She looked so innocent. And scared. *C'mon, Nettie Moser, you would be too, in a foreign country, knowing practically nobody.* She shook off her unsettled feeling, trying to think of how to relate to Anna. Maybe she was like a green colt. *I need to be patient.* Nettie swallowed again.

***

Anna followed them to where the plane was being unloaded, feeling as if she were watching the scene unfold from above. Maybe she was only dreaming. But then Neil encircled her shoulders with one long arm and gave her a squeeze. She looked up into his smiling face. He, at least, seemed happy to see her. He wouldn't send her back. She smiled too.

Anna had only a modest steamer trunk in addition to her small valise. So, in just a few minutes, they were all loaded into a sky-blue 1940 Buick. It didn't take long to leave the "city" behind, and soon they were bouncing along a gravel road. Neil drove skillfully with one hand and reached over to grab Anna's, a broad grin on his face. Not a sound came from the parents in the back seat. Neil talked to her in German about cows and winter pastures, snowfall and buying hay to feed the cattle. "We're passing the Hedges' ranch here. It's about five thousand acres, and the next one over is the Wagner homestead."

The strange words flowed past Anna like the wind past the car, and Neil pointed out the window at more nothingness as far as Anna could see. "What is 'acres'?" she asked. Dizziness overcame her, as if all this space would just swallow her up.

"One hectare equals about two and a half acres," Neil explained.

"Where are the towns? Where does everyone live?" she asked finally, after riding for what seemed like hours without seeing a single house.

"We all live out in the country here, not in town. Our ranches are much bigger than your farms in Germany." Neil nodded out the window. "There aren't many towns, and they are small. We'll be getting to Ingomar soon, and we'll stop for supper before we go on out to the ranch." He reached his arm around her and pulled her closer. "The ranch is eight miles— about fifteen kilometers—from town. And we're eighty miles from Miles City."

Anna nestled into the warmth of his embrace. Finally, she saw a few lights winking in the distance. She couldn't believe they would be from a town. Then, Ingomar, a tiny collection of gray wood buildings, rose from the thickening darkness. The unpainted houses were so low, the roofs not nearly as steep as she was accustomed to seeing. This was no town like she'd ever seen.

With Neil's help, she read aloud the fading signs painted on the two-story facades: "Ingomar Merc," "Bookman's Electric Garage," "J.W. Smith Lumber," "Ingomar Hotel," and finally, as they parked the car, "The Jersey Lilly Cafe & Bar."

"What is 'Jersey Lilly'—a flower? In Montana?"

Neil chuckled. "No. This bar is named after another famous bar in Texas. A man named Judge Roy Bean fell in love with Lilly Langtree, a British actress he never even met. So he named it for her, hoping she'd come there some day."

Anna blinked. How strange. "Did she?"

"No, I don't believe so." Neil helped her out of the car. "But *my* love did." He took her arm and walked her into the building, Nettie and Jake following.

A rush of light and noise and the sharp smell of tobacco and liquor greeted them. Anna's gaze took in the massive mahogany bar that dominated one length of the room, a mirrored wall behind it lined with bottles. The bartender, a stocky man with an eye patch, joked with cowboys sitting on high stools at the bar. Small tables and wrought iron-legged chairs filled the rest of the room. A bit different from the small cozy pubs in Bad Orb.

Amid shouts of "Hello there, Mosers, belly up to the bar," Nettie and Jake joined the group at the bar. With grins and back slaps, they greeted their friends and called to the bartender.

Then the noisy conversation stilled. Anna held back as this crowd of strangers turned from Jake and Nettie toward her. The room seemed to darken, and all she could see were glittering eyes. Cold perspiration trickled from her underarms down her sides. Her head spun. Anna shifted her weight as if to hide behind this tall man beside her.

Neil squeezed her arm and drew her closer. "Everybody, this is my bride-to-be, Anna Schmidt."

The room began to refocus, and she willed herself to smile. "Hello."

"Well, I'll be," said a short bowlegged cowboy.

"Nice filly," rejoined someone else.

"What's he doin', bringin' a Kraut here?" A mutter broke the jovial mood. The rest of the cowboys returned their attention to the glasses in front of them.

Anna froze. *Ach, du lieber Gott, they hate me. I can't stay here.*

***

Neil tensed and drew his lips into a thin line, clenched his fists and took a step forward. *Boy, I'd like to smash that smug face.*

He thought he had overcome the community's reaction. When he first announced he intended to take a German bride more than a year ago, most everybody had been appalled. They'd said similar things to tonight's remarks.

"A Kraut wife? Aren't you afraid she'll kill you some night when you're asleep?" The postmaster had laughed at his own joke.

Neil couldn't believe the man would say such a thing. "Anna is a person, just like you and me."

"Aren't they all Nazis?" sneered the owner of the Mercantile.

"She and her family suffered under the Nazis. Her father was wounded and her brother was taken prisoner, they had very little to eat, and the bombing practically reduced her country to dust." Neil had tried his best to explain.

And from Ruthie, "How *could* you? I thought I was in love with you, but I'm glad I found out about you now. Traitor." Her green eyes blazed, and she tossed her red hair as she turned away.

He had no reply. That remark still stung.

He brushed his hand over his grown-out crew cut, frustrated by their lack of comprehension, small thinking and prejudice. The waiting, all the agonizing, second-guessing his decision—it had all been worth it. Anna was here. He'd known the minute he saw her step off the plane. His world had stopped, and he'd made a vow to never let her go.

She'd have to do the rest now to win them over, with her beautiful smile, her intelligence, and her charm.

Neil let his clenched jaw and fists relax and laughed, a little too loudly. "She's the prettiest gal in all of Europe, and I'm just lucky I corralled her." He turned to his parents. "Dad, Mom, we're going into the cafe. Why don't you order some beer for us?"

***

Anna sat at the table, her knees still shaking. *So, this is my welcome to America.* But then she looked at Neil's sweet, smiling face. *No, he is my welcome.* She smiled back and breathed deeply.

Then the waitress brought thick T-bone steaks of a size she'd never seen, on platters spilling over with fried potatoes and coleslaw. She felt her mouth drop open. Was it a whole cow? It had been so long since she'd eaten like this.

"Mmm, das shteak ist so goot." She tried out her meager English, pointed at the potatoes. "*Was ist das?*" and laughed as she tried the words "French fries." Then she watched, puzzled, as Jake shook an oozy red substance from a bottle onto his potatoes.

"Ketchup." He handed her a potato strip dipped in the red stuff. "Here, taste." It was slightly sweet, tangy and salty all at the same time. She smiled, shaking her head in wonder.

Jake lifted his glass in a toast. "Welcome to America, Anna." The elder Mosers' attitude toward her seemed to have warmed with the beer.

"Yes, we have a room all ready for you at home." Nettie's smile was more generous now.

"Thank you." Anna lifted her glass and drank the watery-tasting brew. Nothing like the good heavy German beer you could almost chew.

But so much food. She leaned over and whispered to Neil. "I can't eat all this. What am I supposed to do?"

"Just leave it. The waitress'll throw it away."

73

Anna sat in stunned silence. The leftovers alone would have fed her family for a week during the war. Surely he remembered the lack of food then.

"Oh." Neil must have noticed her shocked look. "We'll have her wrap it up, and you can eat it tomorrow."

After eating, they all piled into the car again and headed out of town on a rutted, one-lane path that seemed to go on forever. Neil steered around bumps and gunned the car through steep coulees, while Anna hung on to the hand strap and pushed herself back against the seat. *Ach du lieber Gott. What have I gotten myself into? We must be at the end of the earth.*

Late that night, they pulled up in front of the two-story white ranch house. The cold wind flapped the women's skirts, and an early scattering of snow crunched underfoot as the four walked up onto the big open-air front porch. Neil opened the door into the kitchen with a flourish. "This is your new home, Anna. I can't believe you're finally here."

Anna could hardly believe it either. Was she dreaming? All the sights, sounds and experiences of the past few days swirled around her. Then the rush of warmth at seeing Neil again. That certainly was not a dream. She tucked her hand comfortably into his as she entered her new home.

CHAPTER NINE

The evening had floated by like wisps of cloud. Neil still couldn't believe she was actually here. In America. In Montana. In his car, with *him*. How could he be so lucky? He kept breaking into a grin, and he had the sense he was chattering away like a lovesick schoolboy, but he couldn't stop. Once he'd grabbed hold of her hand, he couldn't let go. He sneaked looks over at her, could hardly take his eyes off her to watch the road. He was bringing *his* bride to *his* home. Oh, there was so much to tell her, to show her, to teach her. They would go horseback riding, go for walks, care for the newborn calves. Together they would build a house....

Home at last, Neil showed Anna around and settled her bags and the blue steamer trunk that had belonged to her grandmother into the upstairs guestroom. He spoke to her in German. "I'll fill your water pitcher." He picked up the crockery container from the basin on the dresser.

Anna looked around. "Where is the water closet? Did I miss seeing it?"

"The toilet. Oh, I forgot. I am so sorry." His words jittered over each other. His face felt hot. "We...we don't...have one...in the house. There's a chamber pot under the bed if you need it in the night. But come, I'll show you where the outhouse is."

Anna's eyebrows went up, but she didn't say a word.

Neil led the way outside, a kerosene lantern cutting a swath through the pitch-dark night. About thirty yards from the house, a little wooden shack appeared out of the darkness, approximately five feet square, a half-moon cut-out adorning the door. Neil pulled the latch and aimed the lantern beam at a wooden bench with two holes. Between the holes was a dog-eared Sears & Roebuck catalog. A blanket of snow dusted the whole scene.

Anna shivered and stepped backward. "Thank you for showing me. I … don't need it right now."

Face flaming, Neil escorted her back to the house in silence. What a dummy. He'd forgotten to warn her about having to go outside. This would be a difficult adjustment for her. He would have to remember to help her with every little detail.

***

Anna lay awake on the hard mattress. She punched her lumpy pillow, trying to get comfortable. She missed her fluffy feather bed. Tears rose as she listened to her future in-laws snoring in the next room. She was so alone. Neil slept downstairs in his parents' bedroom—no mistaking the Mosers' intention to keep them apart.

Here she was in America, at last. But that tiny town, those rude people at the bar, that terrible road here to live with strangers. She'd waited so long, traveled so far. Everyone talked so fast. What few English words she thought she knew were lost in an unintelligible barrage of speech. Anna blinked back a tear. *Ach du lieber, what have I done?*

This country was so odd. Not at all as she had imagined. The countryside so barren, so flat. All gray and brown, not a speck of a green tree anywhere, no cities, no people. And this "outhouse." Although similar to what they'd used in the German work camps, it was covered in snow. She pictured herself pinching her nose shut against the smell in summer, brushing the snow off the seat in winter, and jumping at the shock of cold on bare skin. Suddenly she was laughing so hard she had to bury her face in the pillow. No matter. She had seen hardships of a worse kind; she could get used to this inconvenience.

***

The smell of breakfast next morning woke Anna. She dressed quickly and went downstairs. "*Guten...* Ah... Goot morn-ing." The Mosers were already sipping their tea and digging into tall stacks of a flat-looking doughy cake, swimming in syrup. The aroma of fried bacon made her mouth water.

Neil greeted her with a peck on her cheek.

"Did you sleep okay?" Nettie set down her cup.

Anna looked at her blankly.

Neil translated. "*Hast du gut geschlaffen?*"

Anna nodded. "*Ja. Danke.* . .thank you."

Jake merely grunted and took another bite.

"I know you prefer coffee, so I made us some." Neil pulled out her chair and gave her a cup.

Anna breathed in the rich aroma of fresh coffee and took a sip. "*Gut...danke.*"

Nettie set a plate of food in front of her.

"*Pfankuchen,*" Neil explained.

Anna looked at the strange dish. It did remind her a bit of *eierkuchen,* but the German version was fluffier and usually topped with fruit. She took a bite and raised her brows. Delicious.

After breakfast, Anna offered to help Nettie with the dishes, but she shook her head. "You go out with Neil."

Anna looked down at her wool skirt and lace-up medium-heeled shoes and frowned. *I did bring the wrong clothes.* She couldn't go out in the cold and snow like this. "I don't have anything to wear," she said to Neil.

He chuckled. "That's okay. I have something for you." He helped her bundle up in a large pair of denim coveralls, a heavy quilted work coat, and rubber boots over her shoes. How awkward. She waddled beside him like an overstuffed Christmas goose as he led her out to show her the corrals.

Anna felt her eyes grow large as he introduced her to Blue. "He's a giant!" She reached a tentative hand up toward the horse's head. The roan fluttered its nostrils, and she jumped back in fright. She'd never been this close to a horse before.

"He's just getting to know you. He won't bite. Here, hold this cake pellet in your palm. Flat, like this."

The horse gently nuzzled the treat from her hand. "It tickles." She giggled and stroked the soft velvet of his nose. He smelled like musty hay and fresh air, with a tangy hint of manure all at the same time.

"We'll have to get you up on his back one of these days." Neil gave her shoulder a squeeze.

Secretly hoping she'd never have to mount that huge beast, Anna followed Neil to a wagon, already loaded with loose hay.

Jake had just finished harnessing a pair of draft horses to it and now sat on the high bench. "Ready to go feed the cows?"

The wagon jolted over the frozen ruts of a trail leading away from the buildings and out onto the prairie. Anna slitted her eyes against the bright sun that did nothing to warm the air, shivered, and huddled against Neil for warmth. They seemed to cover miles of this desolate country. No farmhouses, no people, no vehicles, only emptiness. Nothing like home.

Finally, ahead, she saw a large congregation of red and white cows watching them approach, their heads up and alert. Suddenly, the lead cow broke into a run toward the wagon, tossing her horns. The herd followed on her heels.

Anna gasped and grabbed onto the wagon seat. Her mind flashed back to the times that as a child she had been given the job of bringing a bucket of feed or water to her uncle's big Holstein milk cows. She had been so afraid she stood back several feet and tossed the contents of the bucket toward their trough, hoping some of it would land inside.

Here again, the terror welled up inside. "There are so many. Won't they run over us, stick us with their horns?"

"No, no. They're just anxious to eat." Neil climbed into the back, grabbed a pitchfork of hay, and threw it over the side as Jake drove the team slowly forward. The cows bellowed and formed a line, each trying to nose its way into the knot of cattle around the forkful of hay. The first animal to reach the hay grabbed a bite, then lumbered off after the wagon, stopping to grab another mouthful at the next pile. Some milled around the wagon, reaching up to pull hay off the load.

This was certainly different from the way the farmers did things back home. She'd had no idea. So many cows. So big. And so pushy. Anna watched in alarmed fascination. "Why don't you keep them in a barn in this cold weather? Won't they freeze?"

Neil chuckled. "You see how many there are? We couldn't build a big enough barn to hold them all. They're not cold. Just look at their heavy coats. They're used to being outside in this climate. Besides, it gets a lot colder than this."

Colder yet? Anna shivered and shook her head in disbelief.

***

About a week and a half later, the day before Thanksgiving Neil told Anna, "You two will be baking pies today." He explained the origin of the holiday and its customs.

Anna started the morning with trepidation, wondering how she would work with Neil's mother without knowing how to talk to her.

Anna liked the idea of getting together with family or neighbors for an occasion of eating and thankfulness. That was German-like. "This is like our *Erntedankfest* at home. But that is a church celebration of the end of the harvest the first Sunday in October."

Neil nodded. "Yes. That is what this is meant to be, too. Giving thanks for the harvest bounty."

But "pie" was not a German dish. Anna was confused. "*Was ist das?*"

Neil thought a moment. "It would be similar to your *pflaumenkuchen*, only the crust is different. You'll see." He grinned. "It's good. You'll like it."

With hand motions and a few words that Anna understood, Nettie showed Anna how to cut lard into a pile of flour, work it into crumbles with her fingers, add just enough water to make the dough stick together, then roll it out into a circle for pie crust. Anna followed Nettie's direction with an eager sense of relief. Cooking was one area women could communicate across language barriers.

Earlier they had boiled a pumpkin, scooped out its insides, and mixed the pulp with fresh cream, sugar and spices. Now Nettie poured the liquid filling into the crust, formed to the shape of the pie pan. Then, she mixed a sauce with cherries from a jar and filled another pan. That one at least looked similar to the plums atop a flat cake crust Anna was accustomed to.

"Pie." She tried the word aloud. "*Ist nicht* 'pie' in Germany."

"No pie in Germany?" Nettie raised her eyebrows. "That's the best part of a holiday meal. Delicious." She tried a German word. "*Gut.*"

Anna smiled and nodded. Nettie seemed to be trying to make her feel a part of this occasion. They put the pies into the coal-fired oven to bake.

A large frozen fowl lay thawing in a dishpan of cold water. "Turkey." Nettie pointed at the bird. "I'll get up at five o'clock tomorrow morning, make the dressing, stuff it and put it in the oven so we can eat at noon."

"From Turkey?"

"No, no. From here. Jake shot it earlier this fall, and I kept it frozen in the ice box until now."

Anna frowned, trying to understand. Her family had served goose or duck at Christmastime. She had never seen a turkey, let alone eaten one. Another different custom.

***

During the night the temperature had turned a little warmer, bringing a gentle skiff of snow. Anna looked out the window at the slate gray sky and shivered. Maybe she'd wear her blue wool dress. It would be warm but somewhat festive. A neighbor family was coming for this Thanksgiving holiday. Her stomach fluttered, wondering if they would be like the rude people in the Jersey Lily. She swallowed and practiced saying

80

"Happy Thanksgiving," hoping she'd be able to understand a few words.

Strange but tantalizing smells arose from the kitchen. She went downstairs to help set the table. Just before noon, an old beat-up Ford sedan pulled up outside the house. The Gibson family stomped the snow off their feet on the porch and trooped in, carrying dishes wrapped in white dishtowels. Neil introduced Anna. "This is Ed and Lucille, and the kids here are Buck, Hoot, Billy, Kelly, Gail and Sandy."

Anna gave a tentative smile. Such strange names.

"Hiya, Anna." Ed's voice boomed, and he reached a huge paw out to engulf her hand in a vigorous shake. All talking at once, the rest of the group laughed and shrieked as they pushed and scuffled to be next to shake Anna's hand.

Inwardly, Anna recoiled from this boisterous display, but kept a smile on her face as each Gibson greeted her, every one a long, skinny, freckle-faced towhead. Lucille took damp cloths off bowls of fruit salad, cranberry sauce, and wheat rolls she'd brought and set them on the table. Without invitation, the clan found chairs, noisily scraping up to the table and looking expectantly toward the oven.

Anna stared. How unmannerly. The children in her family would have stood politely until a grownup told them to sit down. Maybe this was another new American custom.

Nettie chuckled. "Hang on there just a cottonpickin' minute, guys. Let me get the turkey out. Here, Anna, would you give me a hand? Neil, I need the potatoes mashed."

When they'd finally put all the bowls and platters on the table, Neil said grace, and before the "n" of Amen died away, unleashed appetites set upon the feast as though no one had eaten in weeks. Conversation flowed around mouths full of potato, fork loads of turkey punctuated the air. Anna felt as if she'd been lifted into the middle of a hurricane, trying to keep up with who was talking about what.

"Consarned sheepherders can't keep their woolies on their own side of the fence."

"Mrs. Wagner had a wonderful garden this year. Gave us all the cannin' we could keep up with."

"Anna, did you have Thanksgiving in Germany?"

"Did ya get your bulls out on time this year? When'll ya start calvin'?"

"Did you see the bombs? Was it scary? Did you see anybody get killed?"

"So, ya had a few late calves, courtesy of the Mayfield's bull, huh?"

Anna listened and watched with awe, barely able to catch enough words from the staccato conversation to make sense, let alone try to answer any questions. Neil tried to translate for her, but soon, he too, was lost in the patter. So she concentrated on the new and different tastes and thought of all the people back home this spread could feed. How she wished she could send some of it to her family. It had been many years since they'd been able to celebrate a bountiful harvest.

That evening, after Jake and Nettie had gone off to bed, Anna and Neil cuddled on the sofa in front of the stove, nibbling on bits of leftover turkey and pie and finishing a bottle of wine Neil had bought.

"Your Thanksgiving is a nice celebration." She tucked one foot under her and leaned into Neil's side, comfortably speaking in German again. "Before the war, we used to have parades and dancing after the church services. Lots of food, too. Stuffed goose, potato dumplings, green beans..."

"Mmm-hmm." Neil's head rested against the cushion, his eyes nearly closed.

Surely he wouldn't drift off to sleep. This was the first time they'd had alone in days. They hadn't even talked about the wedding, when they would be married and move to a place of their own. Did she dare ask? She stole a glance—so handsome and at peace. Her heart lurched. She had to know. She couldn't wait forever to be his wife, couldn't live in the same house with him indefinitely and not be able to be with him.

"So. When shall we plan for the wedding?" She tickled him under the chin, and his eyes flew open.

He sat upright. "Oh. The wedding. I-I've been meaning to talk to you about that." He scrubbed his hands through his hair. "When the folks gave me their blessing to send for you, they thought it would be best... if we waited a year before marrying. I—"

"What?" Anna nearly dropped her glass. "You didn't tell me that. We've already waited more than two years." Her voice rose as she tried to overcome sudden tears.

Neil rubbed her hand between his. "I know. I know. Don't be upset. I'm sorry. I agreed because... I just wanted to get you over here."

"B-but, don't you want to be married, too?" The room whirled. This was insane. What kind of people were Nettie and Jake, to make them wait? Anna's breath came rapid and shallow. She thought she might faint.

He pressed her hand to his chest. "Yes, *mein Liebchen*, I want to marry you, more than anything. And we will be—soon. Don't worry. Just let me work on the folks. They're gradually warming up to the idea."

Anna frowned. That didn't seem like him, not able to stand up to his parents and do what he wanted. That sounded more like—she recoiled inwardly—Hermann. She looked him straight in the eyes. "But—"

Before she could say any more, he took her into his arms and kissed her with a hunger that convinced Anna he meant what he said.

Soon. She had to believe that. Soon.

***

The Saturday night after Thanksgiving, Anna piled into the Buick with Neil, his violin, and his parents and headed for a big community dance in Ingomar. When they parked at the Grange hall and got out, Anna couldn't help but stare. Cars arrived from every direction and discharged men in coveralls and women in flouncy skirts. Many clutched their work coats around their shoulders, children in tow, and shuffled along in their rubber boots until they could duck into the dance hall out of the cold.

Anna took Neil's arm with a prickle of apprehension as they entered the huge room with so many people milling around. Neil found seats for her and his mother on the wooden benches along the wall. He kissed her on the cheek. "I'm sorry to have to leave you, but I hope you enjoy the music."

Since he was to be part of the band, he made his way up to a bandstand at the far end of the dance floor to tune his violin with a guitar and an accordion player. Jake went off to a stand-up bar in the corner, where he smoked and laughed with the little knot of men there. Nettie and Anna sat on the bench watching the crowd.

Anna jiggled her knee, wondering what was expected of her. She and Nettie found it hard to understand each other, and often sat in uncomfortable silence—together, yet each apparently alone in her thoughts. They had yet to find a common bond, other than Neil, and Anna sensed that Nettie resented her intrusion into the harmony of that relationship.

One of the band members announced "Turkey in the Straw," and they launched into a lively tune. Anna smiled to see Neil sawing away with his bow, "fiddlin'" as he called it. She tapped her foot, watching the other couples twirl around the dance floor. Her thoughts whirled with all the new sights and sounds. *What strange customs these Americans have.* The music was like nothing she'd ever danced to in Germany, although it had a lively beat, and she could understand why people wanted to get out and dance to it.

Someone had strewn the floor with sawdust, and kids chased each other through the hall, sliding along the slick floor, and out the door again. As the evening wore on, the babies and toddlers finally fell asleep on the huge pile of coats in one corner.

Through tune after tune, Anna sat along the wall, enjoying the music, yet feeling as though she were invisible. No one stopped to talk or ask her to dance. She was pleased and impressed with her fiancé's musical talent, but she wished he could be in two places at once, so she could dance with him.

When the band took a break, Nettie went off to find Jake, and Neil joined Anna. "I'm sorry to leave you alone." He encircled her shoulders with his arm. "Let's go get something to drink." He pulled her to her feet and they went to the little bar for a cola. For a few minutes her sense of abandonment left, and she basked in the warmth of his nearness.

As Neil returned to the bandstand to begin another set, he stopped and talked briefly to Jake, glancing back at her. Anna walked back toward her seat, suddenly catching a snippet of conversation off to the side. "... that *German* woman. How could he bring *her* here? She don't belong with us Americans!"

Anna understood just enough of the words to feel a twisting pain inside. Her neck grew hot, but she took a deep breath, and sat down again, trying to smile and look as if she were having fun. But any enjoyment she'd experienced had been spoiled. Should she tell Neil? No, it would only hurt him and maybe make him angry. It was best to just leave it alone. After all, they didn't know her yet. Surely they wouldn't hate her forever.

"Anna, may I have this dance?" Startled, she looked up to see Jake holding out his hand. She stood, and he whisked her out onto the floor with a flourish, and whirled her into a jitterbug. He sent her flying, caught her just in time to bring her back into a spirited two-step, then twirled her around under his arm. The tune was different, and it took her a moment to register the familiar steps, but it was the same as the swing music she'd danced to in Germany.

After the dance, Jake left her at the bench, breathless and laughing. As she was beginning to breathe normally again, Jake and Nettie pulled her up into a threesome, for a schottische. As she began to catch on to their timing, Jake caught her arm in the crook of his, whirled her around then advanced to twirl Nettie. Anna almost forgot about feeling left out.

At midnight, the music stopped and the bow-legged guitar player, dressed in a bright red-checkered shirt, took the microphone. "Now, for all you hungry cowboys, we're gonna have us an auction." He picked up a heart-shaped box, covered in red cloth and white bows. "What'm I bid for this beauty? Some young filly's been cookin' all day to make a lucky guy his supper. Do I hear a dollah, a dollah, a buck, who'll gimme two?"

The musical cadence of his voice mesmerized Anna as she watched young men waving their dollar bills in the air. She turned to Neil. "What is this?"

"I didn't tell you about this part, because I didn't want some other fella to eat supper with *my* girl."

Anna raised her eyebrows and cocked her head.

"The single women bring a lunch, all wrapped up pretty, and who brought which box is kept secret until the auction," Neil explained. "Then the single men bid on the boxes they think their favorite girl brought, and buy a chance to have supper with her—or someone. C'mon, there's fried chicken in the kitchen for the rest of us."

Warmth zinged through her heart. Neil wanted to be with her. She wouldn't have to eat alone.

***

Anna greeted each day with an almost intoxicated anticipation, wondering what new adventure it would hold, knowing it brought her that much closer to being married to Neil. Yet she also felt a simultaneous flutter of apprehension in learning how to live with her future in-laws.

On Sunday afternoons when Neil was finished with chores, he took her out to shoot his .22 rifle at tin cans. At first, she shivered with trepidation at handling the gun, but when she pulled the trigger and heard the plink of the bullet hit the can, and Neil shouted, "Atta girl," her face flushed with pleasure. She turned to him with a big smile. "This is fun. May I do it again?"

One afternoon they went sledding in the marshmallow snow, the heady closeness of their bodies cutting through the cold, their laughter spewing frosty trails through the air. Every so often Neil overturned the sled and they tumbled in the drifts, snow packing inside Anna's collar. "You did that on purpose!" she shrieked.

He wrapped his arms around her and kissed her until her toes tingled. She didn't mind a bit.

Evenings, as Jake and Nettie sat reading on the sofa, Anna and Neil sprawled on pillows around the coal stove with the dog, Lad, Neil helping her with pronunciation and phrasing in English, playfully teasing the words out of her. His soft laughter melted her frustration. Anna came to cherish these times—stolen moments from this harsh, untamed life that Mother Nature had dealt the ranchers of eastern Montana. When they weren't together, anticipation and longing to spend time with Neil built inside Anna like the leaping flames in the stove.

Sometimes she feared they'd never get around to marrying. She didn't know how she could wait a whole year, living like this, with her future in-laws watching every move, judging her. Yearning built inside for a life together with Neil, their own house, maybe their own ranch.

She wondered if she'd ever be able to fit in here. The thought hovered somewhere just behind her, not an overt fear, but a constant presence. How she wished she could talk to Neil about this, but she didn't want to hurt his feelings. It was obvious he loved his parents and they doted on him.

At first, she'd tried to go along with the three of them when they went about their daily work, but soon felt as if she only got in the way. Nettie would give her sidelong glances, and Jake grunted when she fumbled with a gate or spooked a cow in the wrong direction. Fear of making a mistake and looking foolish clouded the joy of being near Neil.

Anna simply found it easier to stay inside, write letters home to Germany, and embroider pillowcases. She tried hard to read English, but trying to decipher words on her own often drove her to toss the book on the floor in frustration.

When Nettie came in from feeding, Anna helped her almost silently prepare the noon meal. Then Nettie went out again to help the men in the afternoons. From the words Anna could understand and Nettie's actions, Anna gathered that most women in the neighborhood were content to stay indoors, running the household, but Nettie much preferred the reins of a horse to the handle of a dust mop.

Anna stacked the plates in the dishpan and put on the kettle to heat water. *Maybe this is where I can be useful.* Since Nettie didn't enjoy everyday household tasks, Anna could clean and cook. Those chores, at least, would help her feel as if she were contributing something to this working family. Then maybe her future mother-in-law wouldn't look at her so disdainfully. She remembered the days in Germany, working at the hospital, providing for her parents, brothers, and sister. She'd been useful then.

The next day, Anna spent the afternoon rearranging the contents of the kitchen cupboards. Humming happily, she put the plates and silverware closer to the table, and poured flour, sugar and salt from their containers into airtight jars. Then she prepared a hearty stew for supper.

When they all came in from chores, Nettie eyed the set table, the stew, bread and butter with a raised eyebrow then sat. "Thank you," she said finally.

Neil grinned and gave her a squeeze. "Looks good."

A warm feeling of accomplishment swept over Anna.

Jake dug into the stew with a grunt and never looked up from his bowl until he'd sopped up the last juice with his bread. "Good. A little heavy for evening. I'll probably have indigestion now." He looked at Nettie. "How about some peppermint tea to settle the stomach?"

"That sounds good." Nettie got up, put the teakettle on the stove and went to the cupboard. She opened the door, reached for the spot where the tea and sugar were usually kept and stopped, her hand in mid-air. "What the...?" She turned with a puzzled look.

"Oh." Anna jumped up and opened another cupboard close to the stove. "Here is tea. And sugar, here." She pointed to the jar on the baking area of the counter. "I clean. I arrange."

Nettie's lips compressed into a tight line. She grabbed the box of tea and slammed it onto the counter.

Anna's neck heated. *Ach nein.* What had she done?

Muttering almost under her breath, "…rearrange … *my* kitchen …" Nettie put everything back the way it had been.

Anna's pride in being able to help out dissipated as suddenly as if she'd been dashed with a bucket of ice water. Her insides trembled. Before angry tears could erupt, Anna turned, ran up the stairs to her room, and crumpled onto the bed. *She hates me. I can't please her.* She buried her face in her pillow and wailed. *Mutti, I want to come home.*

A few minutes later, Neil knocked on her door, entered and sat beside her, rubbing her back. "It's okay, *mein Liebchen.* That was a very nice thing you did for Mom."

"I can't do anything right." Anna turned her face toward him, still gagging on her sobs.

Neil stroked her hair. "No, no. It wasn't wrong. It was just a surprise. She'll see the advantage of how you do things. It'll take her awhile to get used to it. Mom's never liked housework. You're being very helpful, and I thank you for that."

He took her into his arms then, and Anna allowed herself to melt into his soothing warmth.

***

Nettie sat nursing her cup of tea in the darkness of the kitchen. Guilt over her angry reaction curdled her insides. She sipped the tepid liquid. *My stars! It's hard to have another woman in the house, much less one I can't understand.* She'd simply been surprised not to find things where they'd always been, that's all. Anna was just trying to be helpful.

Nettie sighed. She would have to try harder to understand her daughter-in-law.

***

The flare-up between Anna and his mother followed Neil like a dark cloud the next morning as he went about his chores. Gosh, he sure hadn't seen that one coming. What was it with women, anyway? He jabbed the pitchfork into the haystack. He loved his mom and he loved Anna, and he'd assumed they'd love each other. Anna was just trying to be helpful.

Jake climbed up on the stack to help.

Neil paused and scratched his head under his winter cap. "What the heck happened last night between Mom and Anna?"

Jake snorted. "W-e-l-l, son. You'll learn after awhile. Ya just have to let them work it out. You've seen a mother cow with her calf. If you get between them, she'll come at you on the fight, no matter how gentle she usually is."

Neil frowned. Yes, he knew that about cows. But he certainly hadn't thought to compare them to women. He shook his head and pitched another forkful of hay into the wagon.

***

One afternoon a week before Christmas, Neil and Anna drove to Ingomar to pick up the mail and some groceries— flour, sugar, coffee, tea—and tobacco for Jake. It was a cold sunny day, the sapphire sky swept clean of clouds by the west wind. Glad for a couple of hours alone with Neil, Anna felt giddy with his presence. She snuggled close to him as he drove. He held her hand, bringing it to his lips. The feathery kisses sent a shiver through her.

"You want to get a hotel room?" Neil teased.

Anna laughed. "Yes, but I want you to make an honest women of me first." He made her feel so warm, so full of wanting. She didn't know how much longer she could wait. Surely he felt the same way.

The main street was practically deserted, with only a few pickup trucks parked in front of the Jersey Lilly. Hand in hand, they went into the tiny post office cubby-holed next to the Mercantile. Since she'd first arrived, the ruddy-faced postmaster had gradually seemed to warm up to her.

He grinned. "Hey there, you two lovebirds. Got some mail for you."

Anna squealed with delight at the blue tissue envelope. "A letter from home." She tore it open to read. "Papa's leg has healed well and he's back to work... Elsa has a boyfriend. Oooh, it's that Albert. I knew it... *Ach du lieber*—Hans is home!" She looked into Neil's eyes. "Can you believe this? He was in a POW camp right here in Montana." She paused to let the enormity sink in. *He may have been close by all this time.* "Look, it says 'Glasgow'. Do you know it?"

Neil's eyes grew large behind his glasses. "In Montana? Yeah, I know where Glasgow is—up north of here. Well, I'll be..."

Anna read on. "He hoed sugar beets...ah...well-treated, well-fed, gained weight." She felt a moist tingle in her eyes. "They're worried about me. Oh, I wish I could've seen Hans. I wish they all could come here once."

Neil took her in his arms and held her. "They will, someday. They will."

She slid the letter into her purse and looked at the next envelope addressed to her. "Who would be writing me from Washington, D.C.?" Ripping it open, she started to read it. "Here." She handed it to Neil. "I can't understand it."

He took the paper, read it, and gasped. "It has taken all this time to catch up with you." He studied the postmarks on the envelope. "Gosh, they sent it to my first APO at Fort Benning in Georgia, then it went to Fort Lewis." He looked up at her. "The government says your visa expires January 1, and you have to go back to Germany."

"*Nein.*" Anna reeled with the shock. How could this be? It was not possible. It had taken two years to get to America, and in less than a month, they were telling her she had to leave again.

CHAPTER TEN

Anna's legs buckled beneath her. She clutched Neil's arm to steady herself. "What are we going to do? I just got here. I can't go back."

Neil put his arms around her and rubbed her back. "Don't worry, *mein Liebchen*. I won't let them send you back. Let's go into the Merc and see if we can use their telephone to call the immigration office."

Anna's heart nearly beat its way out of her chest as she watched him talk on the phone. Could the officials really force her to go back? How much more red tape would she have to go through? Nothing seemed to go right in this strange new country. Everything was so difficult—just going to the grocery store was a major undertaking. And the weather—so harsh, even life-threatening. And yet, this is where she wanted to be. Here, with Neil. The hollowness in her heart left by war had been filled with her love for him. She didn't want to be apart from him, ever again. Anna clasped her hands over her chest.

Neil hung up the phone with a smile. "They say yes, you can stay in America."

Anna's heart rate slowed, and her tight shoulders relaxed. "*Ach,* thank God."

"But, there's a catch." Neil looked into her eyes.

Her heart tripped again. "What?"

"We have to be married before the end of the year."

Anna furrowed her brow and stared at him blankly. "That's only a little more than a week away. What about your promise to your parents that we would wait for a year?"

Neil shook his head. He stroked her chin with his fingers and tipped her face up. "I never thought I'd be able to keep that promise anyway. And this gives us the perfect excuse." He leaned forward and kissed her.

She melted into his embrace. Oh thank goodness. She knew she couldn't have waited that long, wanting Neil to herself, yet having to live in the same house as his parents.

Then reality struck. "But I'm not ready for a wedding. Who will marry us? And where?"

"Don't worry. We'll find someone. Let's go have coffee and figure this out."

At the Jersey Lilly, they sat with their coffee and apple pie.

"I haven't seen a church here in Ingomar. Do you have a place you go?" Suddenly Anna realized there was so much she didn't know about Neil and his family. She should have asked all these questions during the two years she'd waited.

Neil shook his head. "You were brought up Catholic, weren't you?"

Anna nodded.

"Well then, why don't we go to Miles City and talk to the priest tomorrow?"

"That would be nice." Mass had meant something to her once, before the war. Then, with all the loss and upheaval, she'd fallen away. It might be good to get back to her religious roots.

***

The next day, Father Reilly peered at them over his round, wire-rimmed spectacles. "Well." He rested his elbows on the desk and formed his fingers into a steeple. "This is quite short notice. You would have to receive some Catholic instruction, Neil. And, you will have to sign a document stipulating, in the event of Anna's death, that any children you have will be raised Catholic. We wouldn't be able to have the ceremony until February, at the earliest."

Neil's heart thudded. This was all too much, too sudden. He only wanted to do this out of respect for Anna's religion. He met her eyes and saw the almost imperceptible shake of her head. He stood abruptly, nearly knocking over his chair. "No, that's not acceptable. We must be married by the end of the year."

They walked out, arm in arm. Neil shook his head, disappointment weighing heavy.

"What are we going to do now?" Tears trickled down Anna's cheeks as he helped her into the front seat of the Buick. "We don't have much time. What if...?"

Neil slipped an arm around her shoulders. "We'll figure something out." They drove toward home, silence distancing them, his mind searching for options. He had promised to take care of her, this love of his life, to make sure she didn't have to go back to Germany.

He had a sudden thought. "I know. We'll stop in Forsyth. There's a Lutheran church I used to attend before the war. I even thought for a while of attending seminary. And the folks were married in a Lutheran church—it has some similarities to Catholic, but they're not quite so strict. How would you feel about that?"

Anna nodded through her tears. "Okay."

Reverend Leo Tormaehlen met them at the door of the little, white clapboard church. A stocky man in his late thirties, he had a ready smile and a hint of a German accent. "Hello, Neil, good to see you again." After hearing their experience with the priest, he nodded. "Of course, my children, you are welcome here. Normally, in a larger community, you would need instruction and to join the church, but I'm a bit of an independent out here. I will marry you."

Turning to Anna, he winked, and spoke in German. "Now, Fräulein Schmidt, how did a pretty young lady such as you get together with this cowboy from the middle of nowhere?"

"Because she is a very smart, pretty young Fräulein, and she knew she was getting a real prize," Neil joked, also in German.

The pastor looked at him in surprise, then erupted into laughter. "You speak German. Wonderful. We'll do just great. Come into my office."

They followed him inside the small room and stood as he looked at a calendar on his paper-strewn desk. "Now, about the date. I'm leaving on an extended trip the day after Christmas, so it will be about the end of January before I can schedule a wedding."

Neil grimaced as Anna's fingers bit into his arm. He shook his head. "No. We must be married before the end of the year, or Anna will have to return to Germany. Her visa's about to expire."

Tormaehlen raised bushy eyebrows. "Oh dear." He bent over the calendar again and mumbled as he checked dates. "The only possibility I can see is Christmas Eve, just before the evening church service."

Neil looked at Anna's pooled eyes. "Is that okay?"

She nodded, with a feeble attempt at a smile.

"So the wedding is set for 4 p.m. on Dec. 24, 1948." The pastor grinned at them. "Congratulations."

***

Joy surged through Anna. A Christmas Eve wedding. All this waiting and now it was happening. She'd have to write a letter home right away.

But later that evening, Anna sat at the supper table, fidgeting, as Neil told his parents about their plans, her happiness dampened with nervousness.

"What?" Jake set his cup down with a thump.

"But you kids promised to wait at least a year before you got married." Nettie looked puzzled. "This is a very big commitment. You certainly shouldn't rush into marriage...with your cultural differences, and all."

Neil sighed. "We've already made that commitment. We have no choice, Mom. Anna will be deported. There was some kind of paperwork snafu and the visa expires Dec. 31. You know how long we've waited already." He looked at Anna, his eyes bright. "We love each other, and we're not waiting anymore."

Anna reached for Neil's hand under the table. How fortunate to have him on her side.

Jake mumbled something unintelligible and rolled a cigarette.

"Besides, I remember hearing about how you guys sneaked off and eloped when you had a difference of opinion with Grandma about your wedding." Neil chuckled.

Nettie rolled her eyes. "Yes, we did. You've got us, there." She smiled at Anna. "Well, we need to hurry and make some plans. You don't have a dress, do you?"

"No." Since Anna'd had no money, and there was nothing available in Germany before she came, she had hoped to find something in America.

Nettie stood. "Well, let's you and I run into Forsyth tomorrow and shop for a wedding dress."

Tears sprang to Anna's eyes. Maybe her future mother-in-law didn't dislike her so much after all. "Yes, I would like that."

But in store after store the next day, they found nothing faintly resembling a lacey white wedding dress. Nettie and the sales clerks tried to explain. Ready-made clothing was still scarce in America too, because all production had gone into the war effort for so many years. Anna understood enough English to realize it was probably hopeless.

"If you wanted to make a dress, I think the Mercantile probably has fabric," one clerk suggested.

Nettie laughed. "Not me. I don't sew."

Anna shook her head. She did only handwork. Besides, they didn't have enough time. Finally, footsore and weary, they stopped for coffee.

"I'm sorry." Nettie sighed and set her cowboy hat on the chair next to her. "How important is a white dress?"

Anna swallowed a lump. She'd never thought she'd be married in anything but a traditional wedding dress. But this was turning out to be a not-so-traditional marriage in a land full of not-so-traditional customs. Nettie was trying to help, and Anna did appreciate that. They had been able to put aside their differences for one day in this mutual quest.

Anna shrugged. "It's okay."

Nettie shook her head. "Goodness, my mama so wanted me to have a fancy white wedding gown, and she kept me trussed up for weeks, pinning and tucking and sewing. That just wasn't my style. I got married in a red blouse and gray wool skirt—an outfit I'd worn before, the night Jake proposed." She chuckled.

Anna looked at her mother-in-law, dressed in a trim black wool skirt and jacket, her hair tied under a black and white patterned scarf to protect it from the hat. Anna was accustomed to seeing Nettie in blue denim overalls, but when she went to town, she dressed like a highborn lady. Well, it probably didn't matter that much what Anna wore to be married. The important thing was that she and Neil would be married—soon.

Anna settled on a practical but festive navy mid-calf crepe dress. In a moment of concession to the idea of sewing, Nettie bought garlands of silver sequins to stitch onto the bodice.

The next couple of days turned into a blizzard of preparation, both women sewing sequins, Nettie cleaning and preparing the master bedroom for the newlyweds, Anna vacillating between ecstasy and jitters. The men spent their days outside, avoiding the confusion.

***

"Come, Anna. Let's go over to the parsonage to change our clothes." Nettie's voice behind Anna startled her. She followed her soon-to-be mother-in-law to the pastor's house next door to the church to change out of their winter coveralls and heavy work coats worn against the December cold. Their breath clouded white in the dusk and their boots squeaked on the snow.

Mrs. Tormaehlen greeted them with an effusive hug and the scent of freshly-baked cookies. "You may change in my bedroom. Let me know if there's anything you need."

Anna took the wrapper from her navy-blue wedding dress and slipped the garment over her head. Oh, the wedding she might have had in Germany, before the war. She would have

97

worn a full-length white satin gown, with a long train. Papa would have walked her down the aisle, with Elsa and her cousins as bridesmaids, and the ancient Catholic church, built in the 1600s, would have overflowed with guests. Afterwards, there would have been a feast such as she and Neil couldn't have dreamed of, with dancing and celebrating late into the night. Tears threatened at the corners of her eyes. She blinked them back, smiled and twirled in front of the mirror.

"My, but you look pretty." Nettie reached up to adjust a wave in Anna's soft brown hair. "Let's go get you married."

Impulsively, Anna reached out and hugged her mother-in-law. Nettie squeezed back.

Gratitude nearly closed Anna's throat. "Thank you. For all . . . for Neil."

Nettie nodded. "You make him happy." She touched Anna's arm gently and smiled.

Then they dashed across the snowy yard to the church in their boots, carrying their high heels.

Anna paused in the church doorway, breathing deeply the fresh scent of pine boughs and Christmas tree. The stage was already set up with a nativity scene, ready for the Christmas Eve service and Sunday school program later that night. Candles flickered throughout the room. Anna blinked. So beautiful. Just like the church at home, only smaller.

It seemed to have taken forever to get to this moment, and yet it felt as if it had all happened so quickly. Well, this was it. Anna swallowed hard and stepped forward.

Neil and Jake waited at the altar with the pastor. Anna entered the sanctuary, followed by Nettie and Mrs. Tormaehlen. Anna paused for a heartbeat. No bridesmaids, no flower girl, no church filled with wedding guests. *Ach,* no matter. There was her handsome, loving man, all dressed up in a dark blue wool suit. A good man. She inhaled deeply and smiled, so proud to be marrying him.

Neil's face broke into a broad grin as Anna walked down the aisle. He strode forward to meet her and greeted her with a kiss.

"Now, none of that until *after* the ceremony," Jake teased.

Anna blushed. He actually seemed to have changed his mind about her marrying his son. She smiled at him, and the four of them gathered around the pastor.

"Dearly Beloved, we are gathered here, in the sight of God..." He read in German, then repeated the phrases in English.

Anna's heart tripped a staccato beat as Neil slipped the plain gold band onto her finger.

"Do you take this man...?"

Anna could barely gather enough breath to repeat the vows. She looked up at this tall, dark-haired man beside her. At that moment, she felt a rush of warm happiness she'd never before experienced. No fancy, expensive wedding could replace her man's love. Her heart was full and her thoughts danced in anticipation of their life together.

"I do," she said in English.

"I pronounce you husband and wife." Rev. Tormaehlen lifted his arms with a flourish. "Presenting...Mr. and Mrs. Neil Moser."

The pastor's wife struck the opening chords to Mendelssohn's "Wedding March" on the piano, the notes echoing in the empty sanctuary. Neil leaned forward and gave Anna a deep and lingering kiss that thrilled her down to her toes. The audience of three applauded.

The Mosers hugged each other, laughing, the women crying at the same time. Jake pumped his son's hand. "Congratulations, my boy." The pastor grasped Anna's and Neil's hands. "God bless you both. May you have a long and happy life together."

Anna's heart raced. Married. She had just been married.

Neil glanced at his watch. "Well, not to hurry this along, but it is four-thirty and the courthouse closes at five. No telling if the mail is going to get the papers out on time. So if the Reverend is going to come with us to sign them, I guess we better be on our way."

Neil took Anna by the hand and led her out to the Buick. The cold air shocked her lungs and cut through her flimsy clothing, numbing her skin. She shivered and leaned close to him on the short drive to the courthouse.

There, they presented the wedding certificate, and Neil, Anna and Pastor Tormaehlen signed the papers to be forwarded to the immigration office. The young clerk glanced at the clock. "My, you really are cutting it close, aren't you? Five o'clock on Friday night, and Christmas Eve yet. You're lucky we're still open." She smiled at the couple. "Congratulations, Mr. and Mrs. Moser."

Anna's face warmed. Mrs.... Oh, how nice that sounded. Mrs. Moser, Mrs. Moser, Mrs. Moser. She nearly giggled.

"Boy, that's a relief." Neil sighed as they got back into the car. "Now *nobody's* going to come take you away from me!" Jake and Nettie joined in their laughter.

"Let's get something to eat," Nettie suggested.

Finally, the stomach-knitting tension of the past week rolled away, and Anna realized her stomach was rumbling. "*Ja*, let's eat."

The window of the Cozy Corner Cafe shone with warm light from colored electric bulbs, and Christmas carols warbled from a wind-up phonograph behind the counter. The four Mosers—the only customers—sat in a worn, upholstered booth near the Christmas tree, festooned with popcorn and cranberry strings.

Anna couldn't help but stare at the waitress. Dressed in a white uniform, her nametag proclaimed "Dottie" in large letters surrounded by a miniature wreath. One miniature red Christmas ball adorned one ear and a green one the other. Anna'd never seen such a thing. And this café—not very fancy for a wedding supper. Oh well, what did it matter? She was hungry and she was with Neil—her husband.

"Howdy, folks. I won't be open much longer, but you're in luck. I still have some fresh pork chops from today's special." Dottie waited, pen poised above her pad.

Jake set down his menu without looking at it. "Mmm, that sounds good." The others nodded their assent. "It's these kids' wedding day," he told Dottie, "so make those chops something special. And the meal's on me."

At that moment, Nettie's heart filled with gratitude and warmth for Jake.

The waitress grinned. "Well, certainly. Congratulations, you two."

Neil squeezed Anna's hand under the table, and she couldn't keep the smile off her face. *Mrs. Moser.*

Nettie leaned forward and perused a flyer on the wall. "*The Fuller Brushman* with Red Skelton is showing at the Rialto. That sounds good. Why don't we go to the movies after we eat?"

A movie? Was Nettie joking? Anna glanced at everyone from under lowered lashes. The men were nodding and saying it sounded like a good idea. No, it wasn't a joke then.

A wedding to beat a deadline. Pork chops at a diner. A movie after the wedding. What a different celebration from what Anna had pictured as a young girl. For a moment, disappointment threatened to subdue her happiness. Then she sat up a little straighter. It would be all right. This was all a part of the adventure that formed her new life.

The waitress arrived at the table, balancing plates on both forearms. To Anna, nothing had ever tasted so delicious as these pan-fried pork chops with mashed potatoes and gravy and a side dish of applesauce.

"Happy?" Neil asked.

She nodded, her mouth full, and leaned against his arm.

As they were mopping up the last of the gravy, Dottie came from the kitchen with half an angel food cake, topped with red and green-colored coconut and a silver bell she had taken from the Christmas tree. "Many happy returns."

The food, the lights, the warm camaraderie, and now this festive cake brought moisture to Anna's eyes. It hadn't been the huge family wedding and feast she might have had in Germany during better times. But it couldn't have happened there now, anyway. This was enough for her. A new life. A new family. A new Mrs. Moser.

***

On the fifty-mile drive home after the movie, Anna laughed to herself. Snow crunched under the tires as Neil drove the Buick, hooked to a trailer-load of oats. She had been surprised and a little irritated that morning to see the men hitching up the trailer before they left.

"Well, we need some oats for the horses, and since we're going to town anyway…" Jake had explained.

Anna shook her head. She hadn't been able to stay upset for long. These practical American ranchers—they couldn't go to town *just* to get married.

A skyful of stars sparkled in the clear night. The car's headlights burned a yellow tunnel through the darkness. Anna murmured her contentment, snuggled up against Neil, and closed her eyes. About to doze off, dreaming of babies, kittens, and puppies frolicking about their little white cottage, she was jerked awake by a loud thumping noise. The car and trailer see-sawed across the road. Anna gasped and reached for the hand strap above the window.

Neil wrestled the steering wheel and brought the vehicle to a stop. "We've got a flat."

"Dadgummit," Jake erupted. "And we don't have a spare."

The men stepped out into the night, their breath foggy in the cold, and dug their coveralls out of the trunk. Neil took out a patch kit and went to work on the tire.

"Well, this probably isn't the wedding night you'd planned." Nettie shifted in the back seat.

"No, it's certainly been…unusual." Anna shivered in the front seat, wondering if they were going to be stranded. Just as she pictured her frozen body lying by the road until after the spring thaw, the men jumped back into the car.

"It's fixed." Neil leaned over to give her a peck on the cheek. "We're almost home."

Anna drew in the fresh air of relief and looked at Neil with pride. These Montana cowboys certainly seemed capable of fixing anything.

It was midnight when the Mosers drove up to the house. Nettie and Jake went ahead inside.

"Well, that was some adventure for your wedding day, huh, sweetheart?" Neil picked Anna up in his arms, despite her giggles and protests, and carried her through the doorway. "Welcome home, Mrs. Moser." He gave her a lingering kiss that banished Anna's shivering and warmed her belly all the way to her toes.

In the living room, Jake added coal to the stove and stirred the fire back to life.

"Let's open our Christmas presents." Nettie shed her coat and lit candles throughout the living room.

Open presents? Hmm. Since it was so late, Anna had just assumed Neil's parents would go to bed and let her and Neil have some private time together before… She shivered with nervous anticipation.

"You cold?" Jake rattled the stove door. "Room'll be warmed up directly."

Anna curled her legs under her on the sofa and absorbed the warm glow of the crackling fire and the flickering candles. This was nice, though. She needed a little time to get used to the idea of her wedding night in the same house as her in-laws. A thrill chased through her body. Wedding night—she was married! *Mrs. Moser.*

Neil brought stemmed glasses and opened a bottle of champagne with a pop. "It was nice of Tormaehlens to give us this bottle. This occasion calls for fancy glassware and fancy wine." He poured a glass for each.

"To a long and happy life together." Nettie lifted her glass in a toast and reached over to pat her son's shoulder.

"May all your troubles be little ones." Jake slapped his knee and chuckled.

"*Prosit.*" Neil clinked his glass with Anna's. They sipped, Neil's gaze locking onto Anna's across the crystal stemware.

103

Long after the presents were opened and Nettie and Jake had finally gone upstairs to bed, Anna and Neil snuggled on the floor next to the tree, sipping the last of the champagne and planning their future.

"Maybe I'll go to college and study languages. Or veterinary medicine." Neil held one of her hands in his. "Or we'll get a ranch of our own first and have a passel of kids."

Dreamy with champagne, Anna's fingers caressed the heart-shaped gold earrings that were Neil's Christmas gift to her. Husband, father, teacher or vet—Neil would be good at anything.

She exhaled a long, contented breath and leaned forward to kiss him. He tasted of springtime, of bubbling waterfalls, and hope. "My darling, I am so very happy."

Neil rose, reached a hand out and pulled her to her feet. Anna's knees felt rubbery—from the champagne, the kisses? He led her into the master bedroom his parents had given up for them. Gently and slowly, he helped her undress. She shivered in the cool room as his fingers brushed her skin.

How she had longed for, dreamed of this moment, for the past two years. Yet now that it had arrived, she felt like one of Mosers' skittish horses. But she couldn't run. Didn't want to.

Neil slipped under the covers and drew her in beside him. He encircled her with warm arms. Their lips barely touched, but their bodies molded together. Hands gently brushing, hot moist skin tingling. Anna felt their individual spaces blending into one new and glorious essence.

***

The next morning, Anna awoke to the smell of coffee. She opened her eyes and reached for Neil, but he was already gone. Her skin tingled, remembering the feel of him. Caressing the rumpled sheet on his side, Anna basked in the warm afterglow of love. She stretched and slid slowly out of bed. *I am a married woman. Mrs. Neil Moser.* She held up her left hand with the gold ring shining on her finger. *What more can I ask for?*

Neil was already sitting by the wood stove, holding a steaming cup. He smiled at Anna and encircled her shoulders with his long arm as she snuggled beside him. Ah, this is what she'd waited for.

Outside the window, snow drifted down, adding layer upon layer. After a while, Anna saw Jake wade through the drifts from the barn. Tall and lanky, an older version of Neil, he stepped up onto the front porch and inspected the sky. Then he stomped the snow from his feet and brushed off his shoulders. He stepped out of his boots into the warm kitchen, where the smell of Christmas ham wafted from the oven. "Boy, oh boy. It's deep out there, and still comin' down. The Wagners aren't going to be able to make it for Christmas dinner, for sure."

Christmas Day was a quiet contrast to the Thanksgiving Anna had experienced with the rowdy Gibson family. She took a bite of ham. *I wonder what my family is eating back home.* Her childhood Christmases before the war had always been noisy, happy days, filled with relatives dropping in, and more food than they could ever eat in a day. Her mouth watered, thinking of pastries loaded with whipped cream, chocolate tortes with hazelnuts, the special sweet Christmas bread *Stollen,* and the honey-ginger *Lebkuchen* cookies Papa was so fond of. And there had been lots of presents for all the children's delight. But that was just a fond memory now. Anna hoped Mutti, Papa, Hans, Elsa and Karl had enough to keep from going hungry this year.

For a moment, an overwhelming yearning came over her. She wished she could be with her family during this holiday. Or at least send them some of this bounty. Anna shook off the feeling, and redirected her attention to the conversation at the table.

In the late afternoon, a strong wind began to howl, and no one wanted to venture outside. The Mosers gathered around the stove in the living room. Jake soon snored in his easy chair, Nettie dozed in her rocker, while Anna and Neil snuggled together on the sofa.

It was still snowing and blowing the next morning. Jake stomped around the kitchen. "We got no choice but to go out. Shoulda brought 'em in yesterday when we fed."

Anna touched Neil's arm. "Why do you have to go out?"

"The cows need to be fed every day. We need to bring them in closer to home, too, otherwise we might not be able to get out to feed them for several days. We could lose a bunch of them."

Nettie drummed her fingers on the table. "I should go out and help you."

"No, little gal." Jake's voice rumbled. "You've had years of helping me fight the snowstorms. You deserve to stay inside where it's warm."

Anna watched the men bundle up in layers until they resembled roly-poly snowmen and waddled out to find the hay wagon. A few feet from the house a whirling white curtain swallowed them.

Anna felt her eyes widen with fear. "How will they find their way back?"

"They'll be fine." Nettie busied herself scrubbing the kitchen floor. But Anna noticed that she glanced out the window every few minutes, her shoulders hunched, the lines in her face etched deeper than usual. Her heart softened toward her mother-in-law. *She must be worried, too.*

Noontime came, with no sign of Jake and Neil. Nettie silently dished up bowls of ham and bean soup, but neither had an appetite.

"Where are they?" Anna asked.

"They'll be along. It's only a mile to the pasture." Although Nettie's words were nonchalant, her actions betrayed her concern. With every thump or change in the sound of the wind, both jumped up and ran to the window.

Anna paced from the kitchen to the living room and back, picking up a dish and setting it down again. "*Ach du lieber Gott,* where are they? Please let them be all right," she prayed.

At a quarter past two, the women heard voices and their husbands' lumpy silhouettes materialized on the porch. Nettie gave a cry and ran to the door. "Oh, my gosh, where have you been? We were worried sick."

Anna fell sobbing into Neil's snow-covered arms.

"Now, now, girls. It's okay," Jake said through chattering teeth. "Just took a while to find the cows, that's all. Good thing the team knows the way home."

Neil peeled off his gloves, grimacing as his white fingers came into view.

"Oh dear. Frostbite." Anna hurried to the stove to heat the kettle. She glanced at Jake who was still shuddering uncontrollably, and her nurse's training kicked in. "Get his wet clothes off. I'll warm a blanket in the oven. Put him in our bed and pile on all the covers you can find."

While Nettie ran to get the blankets, Anna poured hot water into a basin, tempered it with cold until it was just lukewarm and stuck Neil's hands into it. "Aah!" he yelped as feeling began to return.

"Keep them soaking," she instructed as she yanked the blanket from the oven and took it into the bedroom to where Nettie was helping Jake get undressed.

Later, when Jake was warmed up and Neil's hands were rosy again, Nettie poured them all tea. She gave Anna a cup, holding her hand around Anna's. "You are a good nurse, Anna. Thank you for helping our men."

Anna smiled at her mother-in-law as Neil wrapped his arms around her. She leaned against Neil's strong chest, relief all mixed up with fear. Oh, what a harsh and dangerous world this Montana was.

The blizzard settled in for several days. Anna shivered as the wind howled. She clung to Neil's arm each morning as he put on his layers to go out and do chores.

"Don't worry, *mein Liebchen*," Neil assured her, "we brought the herd home that first day, so we just have to go to the corrals to feed. And we have that rope strung from the house to the barn to help us find our way."

After Neil and Jake came back from feeding, the four ate dinner together, then spent the rest of the day reading, napping, playing cards, and listening to music.

At first Anna relished the quiet time together with her new husband, even though Jake and Nettie were always nearby. But after two weeks of confinement, with only an occasional frigid trip to the outhouse and to empty the slop bucket, Anna thought she would go crazy. She tossed her book down, prowled the house, stopping to scratch a peephole in the thick frost on the window. "I'm tired of studying English and doing embroidery. Are winters always like this?"

"No, not always." Neil reassured her. "It's always cold and snowy in the winter, but it's usually not this severe. Next winter will probably be warmer, and we may not get much snow at all."

Finally, a day dawned sunny and calm, but with temperatures still well below zero. Anna dressed in warm clothes, tugged and buckled rubber overshoes over her boots. Feeling like a stuffed polar bear, she waddled behind Neil along the path the men had shoveled from the house to the barn. They walked between snowy walls, the tops almost level with Anna's head. On one side of the barn snowdrifts had blown as high as the eaves. The other had been swept clean by the storm. The once-red siding, now bleached and weathered, was starkly exposed. The dazzling whiteness undulated into the vast blue horizon.

Anna stared at the landscape in awe. She turned in a circle. Except for the barn and house, barely showing above the drifts, a column of smoke drifting from the chimney, she could see nothing else.

They found the cattle huddled on the lee side of the barn, corralled by mountains of snow. Neil pitched hay from the top floor to the grateful beasts, and scattered sacks of "cake," pellets made from compressed grains, minerals and molasses.

He shook out the last sack and turned away from Anna. Suddenly he bent and gathered a handful of snow. As he whirled back to face her with a grin, he threw the soft snowball, catching her on the side of the head.

"Aaaah!" she shrieked, then quickly packed her own snowball and gave chase. Soon, they were wrestling in the snow like puppies, laughing breathlessly. Neil ended the contest by pinning Anna's arms down and giving her one of his long, toe-curling kisses. Warmth consumed her body until she thought the snow would melt beneath her.

Later, Anna dozed by the fire, weary but contented.

That night, just as the newlyweds were retiring to their bedroom, Anna heard a terrible racket outside the window. Car horns sounded, kettle lids crashed, lanterns flashed and people shouted in the dark.

Startled, Anna jumped into bed, pulling the covers over her head, reverting to German. "Help! What is it?" Her body shook uncontrollably, the memories of air raids still fresh enough to bring terror.

Neil looked out the window and laughed. "It's just the neighbors. They've come to shivaree us."

"What is shivaree?" Anna poked her head out from under the covers and shivered.

"Come, get dressed. I'll show you."

The house filled with neighbors she'd met a time or two, bringing refreshments, gifts and musical instruments—Paul Wagner with his guitar, Albert Hedges had a fiddle, and Bill Stewart added a harmonica.

Nettie took Anna's arm as she took a tentative step from the bedroom and led her into the living room, Neil following. "It's the old western tradition of celebrating a marriage. They wait till dark when they think you've gone to bed, then surprise you."

Anna held back a bit and looked over her shoulder for Neil. It certainly had surprised her, all right. Scared the daylights out of her. Her knees still felt like jelly.

The men tuned their instruments, and soon the ranch house vibrated with music and laughter.

Anna gradually stopped shaking. The warm camaraderie drew her in. These rough Ingomar ranchers, some of whom had called her a Nazi or misunderstood her English, were actually welcoming her tonight.

This was similar to the German tradition, *Polterabend*, where friends and relatives congregated at the bride's house the night before the wedding, smashing pottery and banging pots to frighten away the *Poltergeists*. She tapped her foot to the music and took another sip of champagne.

Maybe Montana wasn't such a cold, inhospitable land, after all.

CHAPTER ELEVEN

Anna scratched a peephole in the window frost then stuck her numb finger in her mouth. Back home in Germany she'd never had an inkling of what being snowed-in was like, with sub-zero temperatures that never abated, week after long week. Would this never end?

Jake and Neil struggled daily to keep the cows fed and watered. The ice on the reservoir measured thirty-six inches deep, and the men could no longer keep it open with axes. One day they brought the herd of seventy-five home from the pasture to drink at the well. But the shallow well that relied on a windmill for power couldn't pump enough to provide more than one watering, so the next day the men led the cows with the hay wagon to another well about a mile away, then back home the following day. How different from Germany, where the farmers brought their cows home to the barn every night. Of course, there were only a few, not nearly a hundred, like here.

Anna watched the swirling snow. The storm seemed never to let up for even a minute. Although the haystacks were eight to ten feet tall, they soon became invisible under snowdrifts. Neil and Jake dug channels to the stack for a small wagon, pulled by a team of horses. Unable to pitch enough hay onto the wagon to feed the herd in one load, they took one out in the morning and went back with another after dinner at noon.

Anna studied and practiced her English every night with Neil. But when she tried to get her ideas across in this new language, it was as though she were a five-year-old again.

Tension radiated from her mother-in-law, even though Nettie appeared to be pleasant and provided projects to divert them both. Anna figured that Nettie, who was accustomed to being out of doors and riding every day, was growing restless and irritable being cooped up all day. There was only so much cleaning two women could do, and although they both did needlework, neither was satisfied sitting hour after hour every day. For the hundredth time, Anna longed for her close-knit, boisterous family back home. Or at least, a home of her own, with Neil all to herself.

One afternoon, Nettie uncovered an old treadle sewing machine and brought out a box of fabric to patch some of the men's denim overalls. Anna watched, fascinated, for a while. Her *Tante* Louise had been a dressmaker, and Anna had sewed many things by hand, but she had never learned to use a machine. She rummaged through the box and found an envelope with an apron pattern. "Show me?" She lifted it up for Nettie to see.

Nettie hesitated. She looked from the picture of the square apron to Anna. "Well, all right," she said slowly. "I guess we can read the directions."

They picked out a piece of material with bright yellow sunflowers and smoothed it out on the kitchen table. Anna cut the excess tissue paper from around the edges of the pattern while Nettie read the instructions.

"Nap. What is that?" she muttered. "I need a nap."

Anna frowned. What on earth was Nettie talking about? Why would she want to take a nap?

Nettie looked at Anna's puzzled expression. "Just joking. Let's see… Straight grain of fabric… Oh my. Okay, here's a picture. Do it like that." She grimaced and pushed the instruction sheet toward Anna.

Anna laid the pieces of tissue on the fabric and pinned them. The cutting went smoothly, but when it came to the instructions for sewing the pieces together, the project fell apart. Trying to learn to pump the treadle, hold the cloth steady, and sew a straight line all at once, Anna lost control of the process. She couldn't count the number of times she had to rethread the machine and rip out seams. Nettie tried to explain, but Anna couldn't understand.

Nettie finally burst out, "Oh, this is dumb. It just isn't working. Let's give it up."

Anna's own frustration erupted in tears, and she ran for her bedroom, where she resolved never to come out again. This country. This weather. Nettie. *Ach, Gott*, she wanted to go home.

***

When the men came in for supper, Neil took one look at his mother's taut shoulders and thin lips. Anna was nowhere to be seen. "What's wrong, Mom?"

Nettie rolled her eyes. "We tried to…SEW." She spat the word from between gritted teeth and looked at Jake. "You know how much I love to SEW." Then her shoulders crumpled, and she rested her head on Neil's shoulder, tears pooled in her eyes. "Oh, dear. I'm afraid I hurt poor Anna's feelings. I'm sorry, Neil."

With trepidation burning in his stomach, Neil went into their bedroom. Anna lay in the dark, her face buried in the pillow. He sat on the edge of the bed and stroked her back.

"I am just too stupid to learn." She choked out the words. "Your *Mutter* thinks I am a *Dumkopf.*"

Neil rocked her in his arms. Oh, dear Lord. What was he going to do to keep his women happy? Such a big deal over a little sewing. He would never understand the fairer sex. "No, no. That's not true. You are not stupid, and Mom doesn't think so, either."

"*Ja,* she does. She said so."

"She hasn't done much sewing and probably doesn't understand the instructions either. I seem to remember stories about how her mother tried to get her to learn and how much she hated it." Neil chuckled a little. "We just need to study English a little more, and I will help you learn to read a pattern later, okay? I promise."

"I try so hard, but I don't think she likes me. What do I do wrong?"

Neil closed his eyes. *Good grief.* Give him a horse to break any day over this...catfight between women. "You're not doing anything wrong. She likes you. Honest." He patted Anna's back. "Now, dry your eyes, and come eat."

Anna and Nettie skirted each other in embarrassed silence that evening as Neil and Jake sat around the stove, reading. Neither spoke of sewing again—for which Neil was thankful—and eventually they settled into their own activities, usually in separate rooms.

***

Finally, during the first week in February, the snow let up and the temperature rose to an almost-balmy twenty degrees above zero. The atmosphere inside the house warmed as well. Able to go outside again, Nettie smiled more. She and Anna even laughed as they put on their coats and boots and headed out into the sunshine. Neighbors cleared the road with a team-drawn plow so vehicles could pass from the Mosers' ranch all the way into Ingomar.

"We need to go in to Forsyth to sign some more of those immigration papers," Neil said one morning. "And it's getting close to your birthday, so why don't we go to town today and have a nice supper out?"

Anna suddenly felt lighter than she had in weeks. "Could we? Yes, let's go." She dressed carefully in her brown wool tweed suit and even put on heels, carrying the heavy winter ranch garb and boots along.

"My, you look nice." Neil picked her up to keep her feet dry and carried her the few steps through the snow to the Buick, which he had warming in front of the house.

The sun beamed through the windshield, and Anna stretched like a cat. The snowy hills sparkled like gem-studded carpets. "So *schön!*" She caught herself and repeated in English. "So beautiful." For the first time since the snows had held her captive on this isolated ranch, she felt a sense of freedom.

Giddy with sunlight and the prospect of going to town, seeing people, she burst into a German song, "Oh, I love to go a-wandering, my knapsack on my back..." Neil laughed with her, gave her hand a squeeze and hummed along.

The little town bustled with activity. It seemed many ranchers, enjoying a respite from the cold, had the same idea and came into town for a drink, a game of cards, and some much-needed socializing.

Anna's business at the courthouse took only minutes then they walked up the street, stopping to look into shop windows. A furniture store caught Anna's eye. "Oh, look at that dining set. And that baker's cupboard..." She stopped, looking up at Neil, a wistful longing in her heart.

He smiled and took her hand. "We'll have a house of our own one day soon."

They went into the dimly lit, smoke-filled Rancher's Bar and Cafe for an early supper and ordered T-bone steaks with baked potatoes and green beans. Neil lifted his wineglass. "Happy twenty-fifth birthday." He slipped his hand into his coat pocket and drew out a small box.

Anna tore open the wrapping, saw the gold heart-shaped locket, and gasped. She stuck a fingernail into the opening. Inside was their wedding photo, so tiny she could barely make out their faces. "So precious. *Danke schön.* Thank you, my darling." She glanced around to see if anyone was watching, then blew him a kiss across the table.

They emerged from the restaurant hand in hand, gazing into each other's eyes, and stopped short outside the door. The sky had turned an ominous gray, with angry clouds boiling up over the horizon. Anna shivered as an icy gust of wind tore at her hair as if to pluck it out by the roots.

"Oh my gosh, we'd better hurry." Neil grabbed her hand and pulled her into the Buick. Gunning the engine, he turned the car toward home as the first snowflakes began to blow across the road. Soon the snow pelted the windshield, churned by a vicious wind. Anna's buoyant mood of the afternoon deflated.

Anna held tightly to the edge of the seat and stared through the windshield, her gaze held captive by the swirling flakes. Neil drove with skill through the storm, both hands on the wheel, leaning forward to peer through the whiteness.

At the highway turnoff onto the dirt road at Ingomar, Neil shifted into low gear. Nothing happened. He stomped the clutch and tried again. Still nothing. "Darn," he muttered, trying yet again. "The clutch's acting up."

She looked at him, not knowing what that meant. Cold fear tore at her bones. "What will you do?"

"Just sit tight. It'll be okay." Neil reached into the back seat for his coveralls and slipped outside into the storm.

Anna shivered. It seemed that every time they went to town, something happened with the car. *I hope he knows what to do.* She turned to watch Neil out the window, snowflakes swirling around his tall form.

Getting the jack from the trunk, he raised up the car frame. Then he slid into the driver's seat and depressed the clutch. The transmission went into gear. "There. Without the wheels on the ground, it worked. Hold your foot on the brake," he instructed. "Let up as soon as you feel the car drop off the jack." He got out, grabbed the jack, and jumped back into the car as it began to move forward. He grinned. "Got it."

They crept in low gear through gathering darkness and swirling snow. Anna couldn't see where the road ended and the fields began. She hoped Neil knew where they were.

"Yup, there's the gate to the Scotts' pasture. We've only got another mile to go," he said as if he'd read her mind. At that moment, the steering wheel spun in his hands. The car swerved and headed straight into the ditch.

Anna screamed. Plumes of snow flew up over the windshield. The Buick came to a dead stop, up to its hood in a drift.

Neil reached for her. "Are you all right?"

Her voice came back shaky, all English forgotten, "*Ja.* You?"

116

"I'm okay. But I'm afraid we're stuck. It's not so far to the house, though. Here, put on your warm clothes and boots. We'll have to walk."

Anna wrestled the heavy coveralls and parka on in the confines of the car. Since the front was buried in the snow, they climbed over the seat and out through the back door into the night and blizzard.

Neil grabbed a rope from the trunk, tied one end around his waist and the other around Anna. "Okay, follow in my footsteps." He wallowed through the ditch away from the road.

"Where...?" Anna's words whipped away in the wind. She grabbed the rope with both mittened hands and hung on, struggling to keep up. Her fear was as icy as the snow. She had heard Jake and the neighbors tell stories about people lost in snowstorms, their bodies found only yards away from safety. Then, through the eerie light created by the storm, she saw a fence post in front of them, and understood. Neil was following the fence line.

Blowing snow crusted her eyelids, her fingers and toes ached, and Anna soon felt numb. She struggled to lift one heavy boot up after the other. Thankfully, she'd remembered to bring them along. It seemed as if they had walked for hours. Several times she fell, and Neil turned to help her up.

"Just a little ways farther," he encouraged.

"I'm so tired. Can't we stop and rest awhile?"

"No. Just keep on moving. We'll be there soon." Neil took her by the hand and trudged forward.

Just when Anna thought she couldn't take one more step, Neil shouted, "Look, I see a light. We're home."

The two stumbled onto the porch.

Jake yanked open the door. "What happened? Are you all right?"

Nettie grabbed a broom, swept as much of the snow off them as she could, and helped Anna peel her coveralls off. Anna stepped out of the heavy clothes, shivering, and wishing Nettie would wrap her arms around her like Mutti.

"Get the teapot," Nettie instructed Jake.

Wrapped in blankets, Anna and Neil sat by the stove in the living room, sipping the hot tea. Gradually the feeling returned to Anna's limbs and her fingers tingled and itched. "Oh, ow," she muttered through gritted teeth.

"That storm came up so fast, while we were inside having supper." Neil rubbed his own limbs as they thawed. "We had no idea. It was sunny when we went in, and by the time we came out..." He shook his head. "Then the clutch went out at Ingomar. I managed to get it into low gear, but then lost the road by Scott's place where it joins ours and went into the ditch."

Nettie's forehead was pinched. "Oh, we were so worried about you two."

"Good thing we were close to home. I know every inch of that fence from building it." He chuckled, and drew Anna close. "Well, another adventure in the wilds of Montana, huh?"

Anna squeezed her eyes shut. Like a lost child, she yearned for her Mutti. She didn't know if she could survive this new life or if she even belonged here.

***

One morning in mid-March, Anna awoke to the sound of water dripping from the roof. Neil looked out the window, then opened it. "*Liebchen*, come here. Feel the air." A soft breeze blew, the temperature had risen to above freezing, and the snow was melting.

"It's a Chinook," Jake called from the front porch.

Anna turned to Neil with a frown. "What is Shin-uk?"

"It's a word the Indians and fur-traders used. It's come to mean a warm, dry wind," Neil explained. "When it blows, the temperature rises suddenly. The snow melts, and that means it will soon be spring."

Hope blossomed inside Anna, and she hugged Neil. "Oh, I like this Indian wind if it brings us spring."

By the end of the day, it was fifty degrees and the Mosers were up to their ankles in snowmelt in the corrals. Anna struggled to pull her boots out of the muck with each step as she tried to walk. The next morning, Anna heard water rushing through the gullies. Creek beds that Neil said had not seen water in several years ran bank-full.

Anna looked at the flood in awe. "Two days ago, all was snow. Today, all is water."

Now, instead of slogging through deep snow, the men trudged through mud, searching for a clean place to spread hay for the cattle. Anna and Nettie walked out onto the prairie to look for the first signs of green grass. As she walked, Anna's feet became heavier and heavier. She looked down and laughed. She was at least six inches taller with the accumulation of mud on the bottom of her rubber overshoes. "Look, I am Neil."

Nettie lifted her own platform boot, laughing too. "It's called gumbo."

During the next few weeks, the prairie gumbo dried into hard pockets and ridges, strange as a moonscape. But by April the low hills took on a light shade of green. Neil and Anna took daily walks in the late afternoon sunshine, with a gentle, warming breeze, and wispy clouds scattered across the crisp bluebird sky. Anna stopped often to pick a bouquet of sweet, spicy-smelling wildflowers that popped out of the earth, frozen just a few weeks before. It was as though the hand of the Master Gardener had strewn a mixture of seeds over the earth—yellow, blue, white, and pink. In the pasture nearby, the red and white Hereford cows grazed eagerly on the green grass, while newborn calves suckled.

Neil leaned against a fence post. "Now isn't all this worth the wait?"

Anna smiled dreamily, and turned to look into his hazel eyes. "Yes, waiting is worthwhile. And we have something else to wait for now."

Neil raised his eyebrows. "Oh?"

"Yes." She cocked her head to one side and whispered in German, "*Ein Kind. Ein Kleines.*"

Neil stood as motionless as the fencepost and uttered not a single word.

Anna's heart fluttered like a caged bird. Oh dear. What did he think? Didn't he understand? She repeated the words in English. "We will have a baby."

As she waited, the day and its bright hope—the vividness of color, the warbling of the birds, the smell of new grass—all faded. *He's not happy about this.*

Then he reached out a trembling hand and placed it gently on her abdomen. "Oh, *mein Liebchen.*" His voice came in a hoarse whisper. "Our baby."

Her body sagged with relief. The world came flooding back into her senses.

He gathered her into his arms then, and she wept with happiness. Life would be good now.

CHAPTER TWELVE

The springtime of Anna's pregnancy brought quiet joy, heightened senses, a tenderness of feeling. It also brought morning sickness—dizziness, weakness, a wretched feeling that all of her insides would come up and spill out. But later in the day when that would pass, she felt the minute changes within, as if she could watch a rosebud forming, preparing to open its petals. Her head filled with small explosions of scent and color.

Up to now, she'd had nothing of her own—no home, no privacy, no money. But this would be something of her very own, something of hers and Neil's together. Maybe then she wouldn't feel so lonely, wouldn't miss her home and family so much. The life and hope balanced in the secret chamber beneath her hands stilled her restless yearnings for a time.

***

Neil kept breaking into a smile as he fed the horses. It began with a small twitch at the corner of his mouth, then stretched the width of his lips until he felt like a beacon in the dark of night. He stopped to stroke Blue's soft nose. Gentle thoughts of Anna kept singing through his mind—how her face lit up when he came home each day, how much she loved and trusted him by coming to America, how the warm curves of her body felt as they shared a bed.

He walked to the well to check the water. Anna longed for a place of her own, even a little house—he knew that. Maybe it was time to think about doing something besides ranching. Could he still go to college? No, not with a new baby. Rev. Tormaehlen's ruddy, beaming face came to his mind. Neil had once thought of becoming a minister. But again, no. How would he support a wife and child?

Their baby. He felt a great curiosity, protectiveness, and awe all at the same time, toward this new life blossoming inside her. A part of her and a part of him, yet a separate being with its own character and destiny. Would it be a boy, to ride the range with him? Or a girl, to mirror her mother's radiance and beauty?

"You look like the cat that just ate the meadowlark." His dad's voice startled Neil in mid-smile.

"Yeah." Neil nodded, his grin stretching bigger. "Yeah, I guess I am." He put a hand on Dad's shoulder. "We're having a baby."

"Whoa-ho-ho." His dad whooped and clapped Neil on the back. "Congratulations, you ol' sonuvagun, you." He turned and called out. "Hey Nettie, c'mere."

Neil's mom put down her pitchfork and strode to the side of the barn where the men stood. "What do you need, dear?"

"Neil just spilled the beans. We're gonna be grandparents." Dad took off his hat and slapped it against his knee. "Can ya beat that?"

"My goodness." Neil's mom stopped, an astounded look on her face. Then she smiled and reached a tender hand up to stroke Neil's cheek. "My baby. A father now."

Neil saw glistening dewdrops in her eyes. A welling-up of moisture threatened to spill from his own, as he took her small hand in his and nodded.

***

In early June, Jake announced, "It's time to brand. I talked to the Gibsons and Hedges and they'll be over day after tomorrow. Can you gals handle the vittles?"

"Brand? What is this?" Anna asked Neil.

"Ranchers need to mark their cattle so they won't be stolen," he explained. "Every brand is kept on record with the state, so when we sell them, the authorities know the calves actually belong to us."

Early in the morning, while the men rode out to the pasture, Anna and Nettie put a large pot of beans on the stove and a venison roast in the oven. A couple hours later, the sounds of cattle bawling and men shouting and whistling drew them out to the corral.

The day before she'd watched in awe as Neil prepared the syringes, vaccines and antiseptic powders, and sharpened his pocket knife for castration. Now, the herd of cows and calves milled around as the men "cut out the calves," separating them from the mothers. A huge pile of wood fed a fire that kept the branding irons hot, and the day before she'd watched Neil prepare the syringes, vaccines and antiseptic powders, and sharpen his pocket knife for castration.

The awe turned into horror as the men roped each calf, threw it to the ground, and held it while one burned the brand on with the hot iron. The tannic stench of burning hair and hide scorched her nostrils. While the calf was still down, one man gave it a shot of vaccine to prevent blackleg disease, another castrated the bull calves to be sold as steers, and another dehorned others with a special tool that gouged the horn out at the root.

Anna gasped. "They're hurting the poor little babies!"

"They're just scared as much as anything," Nettie said. "It does hurt a little at first, but they're quite resilient, and you'll see them romping around in the grass again in a day or two."

Anna wasn't so sure. She'd been burned on the hot stove a time or two, and that certainly had hurt her. She was doubly skeptical when she heard the calves bleating and saw them struggle. Her nurse's heart went out to these babies, with their crisp white curly heads and their cute frolicking ways.

But by the end of the day, she'd resigned herself that this "barbaric" ritual was necessary. The camaraderie of the neighbor women bringing casseroles and rolls and cakes and cookies warmed her heart, and the Mosers' jubilance at a successful calf crop was contagious. Anna joined in the celebration as Neil brought out his fiddle, and they all sang and danced. Laughter filled the barn.

***

As spring warmed into summer, ranching activities kept Neil, Jake and Nettie busy working outside from first light until dark—moving cows from one pasture to another, cutting, raking and stacking hay. She and Nettie had planted a small garden, but with lack of water and Anna's fatigue, it didn't seem to be flourishing.

Anna leaned against the kitchen wall and glanced at the clock. Oh no. It was almost noon. Nettie and the men would be coming in from haying, wanting dinner any minute, and she hadn't prepared anything yet. Couldn't even think about food. She took a deep breath, steeled herself, and looked into the icebox. The leftover venison roast in its bloody juices stared up at her.

She tried to choke back the bile in her throat and quickly turned away, but before she could make it to the slop bucket on the porch, she retched up the toast and coffee she'd tried earlier. *Ach du lieber*. She reached for a towel to try to clean the floor, but the sour odor made her gag again. Head swimming, she staggered to the sofa in the living room.

"Anna!" Nettie's voice came from the kitchen entry. "Anna? Is dinner ready? The men want to keep haying, so I'll just pack it up and take it—" The voice stopped as Nettie came into the living room. "What's the matter?"

Anna brushed a hand over her sweaty brow. "Too sick... couldn't cook... sorry..."

"What? You didn't cook?" Nettie's voice increased in exasperation. Then she stopped. "Morning sickness still?"

Anna nodded.

"Good heavens. I'd've thought you'd be over that by now. I rode every day for nine months, up till the day before Neil was born." Nettie sighed. "Oh well. Can't be helped. I'll make some sandwiches for the guys." She left the room.

Anna heard her gasp in the kitchen and mutter something about "...mess...housework..." Oh dear. Another failure. She hadn't even been able to clean up her mess. Her mother-in-law must be really angry now.

Anna got up, slunk to her bedroom, and slammed the door on her tears. Why, oh why did her mother-in-law frustrate her so? Surely Nettie understood the nausea in the mornings, the complete lack of energy. Anna could barely drag herself out of bed, much less do all the household chores and get dinner ready for everyone.

She sat, hunched on the bed. Riding the whole nine months ... Well, fine. Anna wouldn't get on a horse in the best of days, much less now that she was pregnant. That woman was just plain crazy.

Early July and it was already so hot. She spread her fingers wide over the small swell of her stomach. Oh, how she'd wanted a baby with Neil, but...

She picked up the blue tissue-paper letter from her mother, full of excitement over Anna's pregnancy and advice about the baby's trousseau. Mutti'd never warned her about this—the awkward, bloated feeling, the nausea, the heat... Of course, Mutti would never know how many times a day Anna had to walk to the stinking outhouse. The bottled-up sobs broke through and wracked her body. This too, the crying— every time anyone spoke to her she automatically heard dislike, mistrust, condescension. Even Neil—her poor husband. He would barely look at her and she would burst into tears. How would she make it through the five months until December when the baby came?

Ach, Mutti, what do I do now? Anna missed her mother so much. The soft round bosom to rest her head on, the plump arms encircling her, the right words to make her feel better. After a while, she dozed.

A soft knock on the door preceded Nettie, carrying a tray with two glasses of iced tea and a plate of cookies. "I made some gingersnaps. They might help soothe your stomach." She set the tray down on the nightstand and sat in a chair nearby.

Anna looked at her mother-in-law through watery eyes. Oh goodness. She'd slept through everything. Nettie must have fixed dinner, then stayed inside to bake cookies. For her. That's what she'd smelled in her dream. She hiccupped. "Thank you."

"I know you're not feeling well. I remember what that's like." Nettie laughed softly. "At first I thought I'd eaten something bad or that I had the flu. I kept throwing up every time I came near food. That really put a crimp in my rodeo plans."

Anna nodded and took a bite of warm cookie, inhaling the spicy aroma. Delicious. She picked up the cold glass and held it to her forehead. This did seem to help. "Were you sick the whole nine months?"

"Oh no. It just lasts a little while. Then you start feeling like a million bucks." Nettie looked dreamily out the window. "There's something about having that little life growing inside you that makes you happy, even if you don't want to be."

"You didn't want …?" Anna looked up at her mother-in-law with puzzlement.

Nettie didn't reply, but rose and took her glass. "Enjoy the cookies. Come out when you feel better. Some clouds came up this afternoon and there's a little breeze on the porch now."

Anna sipped the iced tea. What a different person Nettie was from one time to the next. First, she bit Anna's head off for no reason—well, maybe she did have a reason—they all worked hard and expected meals when they were hungry. But then, the gingersnaps and the understanding words—something Mutti would have done.

Anna stood up and went out to the kitchen, where Nettie washed dishes. She put an arm around her mother-in-law's shoulders and squeezed. "Thank you for the cookies." Picking up a dishtowel, she settled into the familiar, comfortable routine of mothers and daughters everywhere.

***

That night, as Neil undressed to come to bed, Anna brought up the subject she'd worried over like a dog with a bone. "So, will we be able to get a place of our own when the baby comes?"

126

Neil sat on the bed and looked at her, his eyes wide in the moonlight without his glasses. "Uh... yeah... sure... We will."

Hope flared. "When? We have five months till the birth."

He reached for his glasses and polished the lenses on the sheet. "Well... I don't know for sure. I've been working too hard this summer to even look. And... and frankly, honey, we don't have the money for a ranch yet."

"What about just finding a house nearby? You could still work for your dad and save the money."

Neil put on his glasses. "Well, that would be nice. I've thought of that. But there isn't any place within miles that's available. And the old homestead shacks aren't habitable."

Anna's hope sank. Always something delayed their moving on. "Neil, I'm not going to be able to live in the same house with your parents forever." There, she'd said it out loud.

He peered into her face. "No, of course not, *Liebchen*. We'll get a place... but we can't right now."

She gritted her teeth. Would they ever move? She had to know. "How will we get enough money for our own place? We have to ask them for everything as it is. Are we setting something aside?"

Neil swung his legs onto the bed and pulled up the sheet. "Uh... Well, yeah. Sorta. I'm half-owner of the two-year-old heifers, and when we sell their calves in the fall, part of that money will be ours."

Anna bit her lip. So, they weren't even being paid wages. This wasn't much better than being an indentured servant. "How is this so? You are not being paid by the month?"

"No. This is the way it works on ranches. We only get paid once a year, when we sell calves."

This information hit Anna like a kick from a cow. She'd just assumed it was the same as for Papa, who received a regular paycheck for his forester job. But she didn't want to show her ignorance or disappointment. "So, we will have some money of our own soon." She tried to brighten her voice. "And then we can look for a place."

Neil pulled her close to him and stroked her hair. "Yes, *mein Liebchen*. We will."

Long after he'd fallen asleep, she lay awake thinking. It was like pulling teeth from a hen—a phrase she'd heard Jake say many times—to get information from Neil. She'd known he was reticent from the time she'd met him four years ago—heavens, that seemed a lifetime ago—but she hadn't realized how difficult it was going to be to start their own life here in America. She couldn't give up on her dream—a place of her own, for her own family.

What could she do to help make that happen? She wasn't being given an allowance, and Neil wasn't earning a wage. She couldn't work—her nursing education wouldn't meet American requirements, and she certainly couldn't go all the way to Forsyth anyway. She didn't even know how to drive. But they would be getting some money in the fall. So maybe she just needed to be more patient—at least for a while.

The weeks passed, and Anna resigned herself to sharing another winter with the in-laws. Nettie seemed more understanding and even offered to cook until Anna felt better. Gradually the morning sickness stopped, and she regained her energy and enthusiasm for the coming child. Neil brought her wildflower bouquets and waited on her hand and foot the few hours a day he wasn't out working. Anna kept the house spotless, took walks in the sunshine, and grew.

***

Anna sat in the rocking chair in the living room, staring out at the snow-blown silence. The half-knitted multi-hued baby sweater lay in her lap. From the desiccating heat of the summer right into the icebox of winter. Desiccating. That was a good new English word she'd learned the other day. It went well with desolate. Or desperate. Only the end of November, this winter was already threatening to be a repeat of the long miserable one of last year.

Nettie banged open the outside door and stepped into the kitchen, carrying the morning bucket of milk. "The milk's ready to strain," she called. "I'll be out helping the men feed."

Anna sighed. She was sick of doing chores for her in-laws and having next to nothing to show for it. They had received a portion of the calf money in the fall, but prices were down and they still didn't have enough to go out on their own. Sure, in Germany multiple generations of families lived together in one house, but that seemed different somehow. There, it was one big family, with much laughter and good-natured teasing, and when one member was hurting the whole clan was upset. Here… the three Mosers worked together like a well-trained team, but Anna still didn't understand the whole ranching culture. She couldn't compete with that.

She was still the outsider.

At Thanksgiving, she'd tried hard to think of things to be thankful for. She was still glad she had come to America to marry Neil. And at least she only had a few weeks before the baby came. But these last few months, growing large and cumbersome had made her feel even more an intruder in her in-laws' home. The thought of another five or six months of winter confinement in this house with a tiny baby was almost too much to bear. She and Nettie had been getting along a little bit better since the beginning of Anna's pregnancy. But they'd gotten on each other's nerves so badly last winter, and Anna couldn't help feeling that her mother-in-law still didn't approve of her. Oh, how she longed to be back home with her own Mutti—and sister and aunts and cousins—to help her out when the baby came.

She rubbed her distended stomach as the baby kicked vigorously. It would be here soon. An arrow of fear stabbed through her. She remembered that day last February when the car became stuck, and she and Neil had to walk home through the blizzard. She had been so scared. The Tormaehlens had offered to let her stay with them for a few days when her due date came close. But if the baby came early… And if there was another blizzard just when she was ready to go, it was fifty miles to Forsyth. They had no telephone.

Anna twisted her knitting in her hands. Darn it anyway, she wished she and Neil had talked about all this earlier. But he worked so hard. He had many things to worry about, keeping the cows and horses fed, holes chopped in the reservoirs and stock tanks so they could drink. She didn't want to bother him with her worries. Besides, once she got started she might say something unkind about his parents. And that would hurt him.

When Neil came in from his morning chores, he leaned over to kiss her, then frowned. "What is the matter, *Liebchen?* You look upset."

"Oh, nothing. I'm just worried about getting to the hospital when it's time." Anna smiled, although she wanted to shout at him. Didn't he realize how she felt, so far away from the doctor, stores, people—everything—in this inhospitable land.

Neil sighed and sat next to her, one arm around her shoulders. "I told you before, we'll get you there in plenty of time. There's nothing to worry about."

Nothing to worry about. Only being trapped in the middle of nowhere in a blizzard, giving birth. Had he forgotten about the Tormaehlens? She opened her mouth to speak, but stopped.

"In fact, Dad and I are going to plow the road out this afternoon. Tomorrow we will go into Forsyth, and you can accept the Tormaehlens' invitation to stay with them until the baby is born. How does that sound?"

"Oh." Her flame of anger flickered and went out. She burst into tears, then answered Neil's startled look. "Yes, yes, that will be good. I'm all right, just relieved. Will you stay with me there?"

He nodded. "Of course."

Her spirits buoyed, Anna hurried past him into the bedroom with a spurt of new-found energy. Mrs. Tormaehlen was so warm, so comfortable to be with, she actually looked forward to staying there. She set about packing one suitcase with a new nightgown and toiletries for herself and a smaller one with the baby things she had knitted and sewed.

The next morning Anna and Neil climbed into their newly acquired 1935 Ford coupe—reliable transportation they could call their own, Neil had said. Anna wasn't so sure she agreed with that assessment. It was just an old car, as far as she could tell. But Neil was plainly excited about owning a car, so she said little.

The plowed road was hard-packed, and they drove along with ease under the cold, clear skies. The pastor and his wife welcomed Anna into their cozy home. Anna sank into their comfortable midst, chattering with them in German. She wanted to get to know Ursula Tormaehlen better. Anna and Neil attended church services whenever they could get away from the ranch chores, which wasn't often. Anna was drawn to the round, motherly, no-nonsense woman of the old German tradition.

"Everything will be fine," Ursula reassured her. "You're close to the doctor, now." Mrs. Tormaehlen settled her into their spare bedroom, wallpapered with large pink roses. She plumped up extra pillows around Anna and set a cup of hot tea on the nightstand. Anna reached up and hugged the woman. She realized now why she liked her—Ursula reminded her of Mutti.

Neil went home to help with the feeding, but came back in the evening to stay with Anna. The snow had stopped, but the temperature dropped to below zero.

The next morning, Anna sat in the cozy kitchen with a steaming cup of coffee, while Ursula bustled about. "No, no, you cannot help me. You just sit and rest."

Anna luxuriated in being waited on—no more cooking dinner, washing dishes and scrubbing floors for a while. She thumbed through the newspaper, stopping to look in the ad section at ranches for sale. But she didn't see anything that looked promising. She wasn't even sure what they could afford. Darn it, she didn't understand why Neil couldn't talk about these things with her.

After breakfast, the pastor went to his office, and Neil went out to start the car, but the engine refused to turn over. He donned his coveralls and slid under the vehicle on the snow-packed ground. Most of the day he worked on the stubborn machine, coming into the house about every hour to get warm. "Starter's froze up. I have to fix it so I can use the hand crank to start it when it's this cold."

Anna watched her husband shiver. So much for this reliable car. She tightened her lips. He'd spent a good part of their small earnings on this thing.

By suppertime, she heard the engine fire up and saw him jump in to take it for a test drive.

"Should start up easier now," he said when he returned.

Anna certainly hoped so.

***

Anna awoke, feeling disoriented. She looked at the bedside clock. Five a.m. What had awakened her? Wetness crept along the sheets around her, and a sudden cramp wrapped its talons around her middle.

"Neil, wake up. It's time to go to the hospital." She shook his shoulder.

"Huh? What? It's time?" He leaped out of bed, pulled on his clothes, then helped her into a dry nightgown and her warm coat. Muttering a quick prayer, he ran outside to crank the car.

Anna prayed, too. *Ach, du Lieber Gott, please let it start this time.* She held her breath as the old car sputtered and coughed for a moment, but the engine caught and was soon humming contentedly. Neil's work had paid off. Anna let out her breath. *Thank you, Lord.*

Now Neil was all business. He helped Anna into the front seat, tossed the already-packed suitcases into the back, and with breakneck speed, raced along the frozen streets. Beside him, she groaned as another labor pain hit her. *"Ach Gott.* Hurry." *Don't let us slide off the road.*

132

"Hang on, honey, we'll be there soon." He stroked her arm with one hand as he wrestled the vehicle around corners with the other.

***

Neil helped Anna in through the emergency entrance. "Call Dr. Tarbox. The baby is coming," he hollered, worried and excited all at once. A nurse quickly wheeled her away into the depths of the unfamiliar hospital.

"You'll have to stay here in the waiting room, Mr. Moser," the plump nurse at the desk ordered in a no-nonsense tone. "The doctor is on his way."

Neil paced the ancient black and white squares of linoleum, counting the cracks like a thousand expectant fathers before him. Hours went by. The same stern-faced nurse, her hair tightened into a bun beneath a starched white cap, would appear with predictable frequency, reporting, "Nothing yet." Or assuring him, "She's fine."

At noon, he grabbed a sandwich from the cafeteria and returned to the waiting room within minutes. What was taking so long? The pain she must be enduring. How he longed to be by her side, holding her hand, whispering love and reassurances. He slumped on a chair, tried to thumb through a magazine, jumped up again, peered through the door down the hallway.

"Just be patient, Mr. Moser." The nurse's prim voice came from the desk behind him. "Sometimes these things just take a little longer." Her pat answer made him suspicious. Something must be wrong.

Feeling helpless, he settled back in the uncomfortable chair, leaned his head against the thinly padded backrest and closed his eyes. He concentrated on breathing until his tense shoulders gradually loosened.

"Well, well, Mr. Moser. The father-to-be looks pretty relaxed."

The hearty voice startled Neil. He sat upright. A man dressed in black with a white clergy collar sat across from him,

133

smiling, his legs crossed comfortably. Father Reilly. The priest who wouldn't marry them. Dread seized his insides.

"Do you remember me? Father Reilly. I've just been visiting some of my parishioners. I'm glad I found you alone. There's something I wanted to discuss with you." He put out his hand.

"Yes, glad you came." Neil shook hands. "It's been a long labor. I guess I'm pretty nervous." But why was this black-shirted priest really here, talking to Neil, now?

"Of course you are." The priest leaned forward. "You know, I must talk to you about keeping this Catholic girl away from her true church. And I'm concerned about your faith, as well. If there are complications, and something happens to her…"

Neil gritted his teeth. "Father Reilly, we made our choice which church to join. I do not want to hear this." He jumped to his feet, his vision fuzzy with upwelling anger. "How can you talk about her dying now?" His words came in a rush, his heart beat fast and a flush rose into his face. "Nothing is going to happen to my wife, or my baby. I have to ask you to leave. Now."

The priest sputtered, but rose from the chair. At the door, he turned. "I would still like to talk to your wife someday, see if it's really *her* choice…" He stepped outside the hospital before Neil could move toward him.

Neil ground his heels into the linoleum as he paced anew. The nerve of that man accusing him of keeping Anna away from the church, of suggesting that something might happen to her. Especially now, while she was in childbirth. He strode to the desk. "Could I please talk to Dr. Tarbox? Is there something wrong? I need to talk to him, *now.*"

Half an hour later, the doctor walked into the waiting room and pulled off his mask. "Congratulations, Mr. Moser. You have a daughter."

The big round clock on the wall read 10:41 p.m. on December 10, 1949.

134

Neil tried to stand up, but lightheaded, he sat again. "A girl. Is...is Anna all right?"

"Mother and child are both healthy, doing just fine. She had a long, hard labor, but she's a trouper." The doctor shook Neil's hand, then sat beside him. "I know you must be feeling a little disappointment right now..." Neil looked at him in puzzlement. "...That your first child isn't a son." Dr. Tarbox leaned forward. "But you'll have your boy someday. Just keep on trying."

What was this guy saying? Neil shook his head. "Disappointment? Over a daughter? No. Not at all. Why? I'm so thankful my wife and baby are okay. It doesn't matter to me whether it's a girl or a boy. When can I see them?"

The doctor led him to the nursery window. With gut-busting pride, Neil gazed at the tiny, red-faced, pink-wrapped bundle in the crib marked "Baby Girl Moser." Happiness swept through him, like riding at a full gallop in the early spring—full of hope. This was his daughter. How he longed to hold her. Oh, they would have such a time together. He would carry her on his shoulders, teach her to ride, get her a puppy...

"Mr. Moser, you can come in and see your wife now." A nurse interrupted his daydream and led him to Anna's bedside.

Pale, her hair damp and disheveled, she reached for his hand, smiling. "It's a girl," she said. "Our Monica Katarina. Our little gift from heaven."

He leaned over and kissed her. "You are both my gifts from heaven. Thank you." He sat on the edge of the bed. "We'll write a letter to your parents right away. Oh, and I'd better send word out to my folks with the mailman."

On the second day Neil brought his mom and dad in to visit. The proud grandparents peered in awe through the nursery window.

"Isn't she precious?" Nettie breathed.

Jake beamed. "Just like a doll."

As Anna convalesced, Neil came to visit every day with cards, flowers and chocolates. He looked forward to the angelic glow of her face, the soft blue of her eyes as she held their nursing daughter.

***

After Anna had been in the hospital a week, Neil ambled into her room. "Are my girls ready to go home?"

Anna's love soared like a spring bluebird. Her man. The father of her child. She smiled. "Yes, I am more than ready to get out of this bed."

After paying the bill for $100.70, Neil helped Anna and her precious cargo out of the hospital, into the warm Buick he'd borrowed from his parents, and drove them home.

Grandma Nettie met them at the kitchen door. She helped them in, closed the door against the freezing temperatures, and clucked and cooed over the small pink bundle. A hand-lettered sign above the bedroom door declared, "Welcome, Monica."

Nettie smiled at Anna. "Today is my forty-fourth birthday—what a nice present, a granddaughter."

"Well, happy birthday, Nettie. It's a good day for me, too." Anna felt the warm glow of happiness—she had a family all her own now.

Anna settled into bed, admiring the gray wool area rug Neil had purchased and the small oil heater in the corner that warmed the room. At that moment, she felt bathed in contentment, her baby in her arms and her husband by her side. She closed her eyes. A rainbow of warmth and love and happiness played behind her eyelids.

"Did you send the letter to Mutti and Papa?" she asked sleepily.

Neil stroked the silky flax down on Monica's head, his face soft. "Yes, I sent it off before I picked you up. You sleep now. When the two of you wake up, we'll take some pictures and send them, too."

Anna looked down at the wrinkled little face, so peaceful in sleep. Joy coursed through her arms and legs, the top of her head, taking flight. What a miracle. The tiny fingers and toes with perfectly-formed nails. The whorl of hair on the top of her head. The sweet milky smell. Every time the baby awoke, Anna felt as if she was greeting her all over again.

"Oh Mutti, Papa, I wish you could see my little angel." She sighed.

During the ensuing weeks, Monica never wanted for love and attention. As soon as she was awake, it seemed that Nettie was there to pick her up and coo over her. Even Jake wanted to hold her, and Neil helped with diapering. Monica smiled, responding to her family's attention.

Although Anna felt bone-deep weariness, sometimes she longed to care for the baby by herself. Nettie had a different way of doing things. And even though the men were careful and gentle, she held her breath for fear they would drop Monica. This baby was *hers*. At least she was the only one who could feed her.

Anna couldn't believe how every day this little person made a new sound, a new expression. She was a quiet, happy baby, only crying a bit during the night when hunger woke her. Anna would gaze at the tiny face suckling contentedly in the moonlight and feel a fullness in her heart. This must have been what Mutti had felt with her and her brothers and sister.

The day before Christmas, as Anna rocked Monica in a slice of sunlight by the living room window, two cars drove up to the house. Several women got out, carrying packages and dishes of food. Anna peered through the glass. "Who in the world would be coming to visit on such a chilly day?"

"Oh, it's the neighbor women." Nettie went to meet them at the door.

"We've come to give Anna and Monica a baby shower," said Alta Hedges.

Anna remembered her from the Shivaree. Her husband had played the fiddle, like Neil. That had been fun, and she'd felt more acceptance that night. But she hadn't seen much of these neighbors since, just in passing sometimes, in town or driving down the road. They hadn't seemed all that friendly then. And these ladies certainly hadn't come to visit her while she was pregnant.

Of course, there were the distances, bad roads and the demands of ranch life. She greeted her neighbors as if they were old friends. *I don't care if they live twenty miles away, somebody could've come to visit.*

The women oohed and aahed over the baby, each one volunteering to hold her.

Nettie steered Anna back to the rocking chair. "You just sit and open these gifts."

At first, Anna watched with an anxious eye as "strangers" handed the baby around. Releasing her daughter even for a minute felt as if someone had ripped an appendage from Anna herself. But Monica didn't cry, just smiled and gurgled at the women.

Nettie handed Anna a brightly wrapped package. Anna forced herself to smile—after all, they'd gone to this effort. And she was soon caught up in the festivities, as the women chatted, drank coffee, and munched on cookies. Anna murmured over the hand-knit booties and sweaters, caressed the soft cloth diapers and blankets, shook rattles, and laughed at a cuddly teddy bear.

"Thank you so very much. I like—everything." Anna spoke hesitantly, wishing she could express herself better in English. What a nice thing for these women to do.

A seed of pride sprouted. Her daughter brought attention to Anna, too. Perhaps, through Monica, she would become part of this community. Finally, with the baby, she had something in common with these American women. And maybe Nettie would like her better now.

***

After Christmas, blizzard upon blizzard trapped Nettie and Anna inside, exactly as last winter. Anna's elation from the baby shower evaporated in the cold, dry air. It was as if the sense of community she'd felt had been a false hope, had never happened.

Anna heated water on the stove and poured it into a small tub, along with cold water to make it just right, and undressed Monica.

Nettie stopped her pacing and stared out the window at the deep drifts. She turned as Anna was about to immerse her baby. "Did you test the water? Is it too hot?"

"What?" Anna hovered Monica just above the water, her mouth open. "Yes, of course I did. Don't you think I know this?" She regretted the snappish tone of her voice as soon as she uttered the words.

"I'm sorry." Nettie's shoulders slumped, and she sighed. "Of course you do." She gestured out the window. "I should be out there helping the men." She came to Anna's side and touched her arm gently. "Here, I'll hold her head up while you wash."

Anna nodded. Her mother-in-law sure didn't like being cooped up with her and the baby. Her own mood fluctuated just as much. She soared with overwhelming joy and love—for the baby, for Neil, for Nettie, and even Jake. Then she swooped to anxiety, confusion and resentment of anyone else who wanted to care for Monica. And the specter of not having a place of her own hung over her like a dark snow cloud.

Thus, winter passed into spring and the heat of the summer.

***

Anna finished nursing Monica and laid her in the crib for a nap. Though mid-morning, the July heat already threatened to suffocate her. She went into the kitchen where Nettie was taking a break from riding, drinking hot tea. Sweat trickled from Anna's underarms. How could her in-laws stand to consume hot drinks in this weather?

"Makes ya sweat and that cools ya off," Jake always said.

He wore long woolen underwear in the summer for the same reason. Anna couldn't agree. She wanted to feel the breeze, if there was one, on her bare arms and legs. Back home, the mountains would still have a cap of white. She would have taken walks in the moist green forest and picked wild strawberries. Oh, how she craved the cool sweetness of a bowl of strawberries and cream. Dare she ask? Anna reached down inside herself for courage, thinking of how Mutti had scrounged and foraged for food during the war.

"I thought..." Her voice cracked. She swallowed and tried again. "It might be nice to have some fresh fruit on hand. Do you think I could have some money, and we could go into town to buy some?"

Nettie set down her cup and stared blankly, as if Anna had asked for the family fortune. "Well. We just don't have anything extra right now." Her words snapped, crisp as dry twigs. "The hay crop is all dried up. We'll have to buy our supply for next winter. And who knows what we'll get for calves this fall. We can't be spending money on luxuries."

"Luxury? Food isn't a luxury." For a moment Anna forgot herself as anger heated her neck and face. "I know what it's like not to have *any* food." At Nettie's shocked look, her fury died down as suddenly as it had risen.

Her self-confidence curled up inside her like a dried leaf. Turning on her heel, she went into her bedroom, and grabbed the baby from her crib. She left the house without speaking, afraid of the tears that threatened to spill.

Anna shoved the blue baby buggy down the dusty trail. It bumped and swerved over the uneven ground. The wildflowers had already wilted and the grasses turned brown. Her navy polka-dotted housedress clung to her back as the sun beat relentlessly on the scorched prairie. In the buggy, Monica cooed and laughed as she leaned over the side, watching the curly white bum lamb, Blossom, trotting alongside.

The buggy wheel hung up in a gopher hole. "*Toivel.*" She swore in German, lifted it out and steered it between gray-blue sagebrush bushes.

Monica giggled again. Anna smiled, forgetting Nettie's harsh words for a moment. Monica's white-blond hair shone in the sun, her cheeks rosy under the light yellow dotted-swiss bonnet Anna had put on to protect her.

"Laugh all you can, now," Anna muttered, half to herself. "When you grow up there won't be much to smile about."

She turned the buggy onto a path along the crest of a low, rolling maize-colored hill. She felt as though she could walk forever and never see another living soul. Maybe that would be a good idea, just keep going and see where she would end up. Probably no one would miss her anyway.

The land of milk and honey indeed. She snorted aloud and walked faster. The lamb broke into a trot to keep up. Here they were, after almost two years, still living with Neil's parents, still asking them for money whenever they wanted to buy something. And here she was, in the middle of an endless barren prairie, miles from a green tree, the sunny face of a flower, or another human being who even pretended to understand how she felt.

Why didn't Neil speak up and tell his parents what he wanted? He was so strong, so able, but when he was around Jake and Nettie, or a group of other people for that matter, he seemed reserved, drawn into himself. *Ja*, she sure could understand being intimidated by a father. Maybe, like her with Papa, Neil felt he could never measure up to Jake. But surely his wife and child meant enough to him to take some steps on his own.

The picture she'd had of a little white house with a picket fence, roses blooming in the front yard, cows grazing in the green fields, and trees supplying cool shade, now seemed like a childish dream. There probably were no places like that. Not in this part of the country. Everything was dried up and brown and ugly. Nothing like the neat, orderly, green German countryside.

Anna pushed the buggy down through a gully and up the other side. Ahead, a gray weathered shack hunched on the prairie. Its sod roof caved in, it looked to be the remnant of a long-abandoned homestead. Before she spread a blanket on the shady side of the one-room building, Anna checked the ground for rattlesnakes, then took Monica out of the buggy to nurse her. Blossom butted her head against Anna's arm. She pushed the lamb away. "No, this is not for you."

What a country of contrasts. Frigid winters, blistering summers. Cold receptions, warm welcomes. Most of the neighbor women seemed to accept her—as long as she was with Neil or Nettie—but no one ever came just to visit her or invite her to go somewhere. And there were still those who cast sidelong glances at her or pretended they couldn't understand her English.

Anna put the sleeping Monica on the blanket beside her and wrapped her arms over her stomach as if she could quell the pain of those incidents. She was determined not to say anything to Neil. She would have to study harder and practice her pronunciation more. How could *they* understand what it was like to be a stranger in a new country, with different weather, different customs, and a different language? Most of the people here had never been beyond the border of Montana, much less to a foreign country. *Ja,* they believed she was dumb. With this new inner stab of pain, Anna gritted her teeth.

As the afternoon shadows lengthened, she stayed by the sorry little shack that sagged from neglect and harsh winters. "I feel a lot like you," Anna said aloud. She studied the building, trying to imagine living with a dirt floor and a sod roof. How had the woman felt, trying to keep her husband and children fed and clothed, far away from supplies, miles away from anyone? Had the harsh winters and dry summers, or the isolation driven them away?

"I think I understand how you must have felt." Anna spoke to the nameless, faceless woman who had once lived here. "I wish I could have known you."

A horse's nicker and the sound of hooves crunching through the dry weeds roused her from her thoughts.

Neil dismounted Blue. "I was worried about you; you were gone so long."

Anna stood and faced him. "This cannot go on. I cannot live like this any longer. We have been living with your parents for two years, and we are still asking their permission for everything we do. And she refused to let me buy some fresh fruit." The pitch of her voice rose as she blurted her thoughts aloud. "What kind of a life is this? Is this what you want?"

A look of anguish crossed Neil's face. "I'm sorry, *Liebchen*. I've allowed this to go on too long." He gently took her in his arms. "It's not fair to you."

Anna buried her face in his chest and rocked against him. The sobs she'd tried to suppress finally erupted. Neil cradled her against his chest as she let the pain and disappointment pour out.

Finally, with her tears spent, they sat together in silence for a long time. Anna stared across the prairie.

Neil cradled her in one arm and Monica in the other. "It's time to find a place of our own."

"Yes. It is." She heard the snap in her voice, saw his face slacken, and softened. "What about this little house? Could we fix it up?"

He tousled her hair. "No, I don't want my wife and baby living in a broken-down shack with dirt floors." He paused. "I'll go to the PCA in Miles City next week and see if we can qualify for a loan. We'll start looking for a ranch right away."

Relief swept over Anna like a fresh breeze. This meant taking on debt, but having their own place was the most important thing she could think of at this moment. Maybe she would find her white cottage with a picket fence after all.

***

Nettie sat at the kitchen table long after Anna had stormed out, cupping a hand over her mouth, staring at a jelly stain on the oilcloth. The clock on the wall slowly ticked, loud and ominous. Oh, dear Lord, what had she done?

Her shoulders sagged. The worry over drought and hay and uncertainty of ranching hung over her like a thundercloud. She shook her head. *I snapped at that poor girl. I must be a terrible grandmother. All she wanted was some fresh fruit.*

A memory of Neil collapsing with heatstroke after working in the hundred-degree heat when he was about eight years old sent Nettie slumping forward onto the table. *Just like I wasn't a very good mother.*

She choked back a sudden sob. If she drove Anna away, then Neil would go too, and her precious little Monica.

***

While Jake and Nettie didn't appear happy about Neil and Anna's decision, they accepted it without a fight. They could always hire someone to help out if necessary. Anna thought her blow-up with Nettie had perhaps worked for the good. Nettie had apologized, but the two women skirted each other politely after that, using Monica as common ground.

It took another year to find a suitable ranch. Neil and Anna drove all over eastern Montana, and Anna began to feel like it was hopeless. In the meantime, she planted a little garden and carried water, trying tenderly to coax the tiny green sprouts to grow. Although she fought the heat, dust, and bugs, she found a certain solace in the little garden.

Finally, in late summer of 1951, as they drove around the area northwest of the little town of Foster, they stopped at a country store at Horse Creek. The proprietor told them he thought the John Foss place nearby was for sale. Foss had already retired, moved into Billings and was letting a hired hand run the ranch.

With great excitement and trepidation, Anna and Neil stopped by to look at it.

CHAPTER THIRTEEN

Anna's gaze shifted from the huge pile of rusted tin cans beside the front door to the gray, wind-scored boards that covered the outside of the house. She sighed. A million years away from her dream house.

Over the years, Mr. Foss had tacked on three rooms to the original one-room house he built when he homesteaded the place in 1911. The front door sagged on its hinges, the windows were opaque with years of accumulated dirt, and not a blade of grass dared show its head in the dusty yard.

"It's about two thousand acres, with hay bottoms and a couple of grain fields." Neil came from the barn where he'd talked to the hired man. "He says Foss still runs about fifty head of cows and thinks he probably would sell them. It's right about what we can qualify for—and it's only a couple miles from the store and close to the highway." He swept an arm toward the horizon.

Anna had never seen him so excited.

"Do you...?" He stopped and looked at Anna, his eyebrows raised.

She surveyed the gently rolling hills, her eyes lingering on a grove of cottonwood trees Mr. Foss had planted by a dry creek not far from the house. At least there was one spot of green around here. Across the dun-colored prairie she could see the building that housed the post office and grocery store at Horse Creek. People weren't too far away. Could she get excited about this place?

She looked again at the debris-strewn yard. Old boards, tin cans, a three-legged chair, and broken-down machinery littered the landscape. It would be a lot of work. But then, hard work never killed anybody. *I saw worse than this after the war in Germany.* They could clean up this mess and get some paint. Neil was good at working with wood, and she would make new curtains.

"Yes." Anna spoke at last with just a tingle of hope. "I think we should contact Mr. Foss and find out if he's willing to sell."

Neil's grin stretched across his face. "Great. Let's do it."

As they drove home, Monica stood on the seat between them. A year and a half old, she was an energetic, curious toddler, pointing at every object and saying its name. An antelope dashed across the prairie up ahead.

"Antelope," Anna told her.

"Ha-poop," cried the little girl, excited to see a new animal. Neil and Anna laughed. She hugged her daughter, joy singing through her veins.

They stopped at the Jersey Lilly Cafe in Ingomar so Neil could telephone Mr. Foss. Anna sat in the cafe to wait while Neil made the call.

The proprietress brought a high chair for Monica. "Oh, she is growing so fast," she gushed. "You folks goin' to stay for supper?"

"Just coffee, thank you." Anna's scalp tingled in anticipation. This could be their big chance. It wasn't the prettiest place in the world, but they'd seen a lot worse in their search—and for more money, too.

Neil sauntered to the table, bent over and kissed Monica, nuzzled her neck, making her laugh. She banged a spoon on the tray and sang out, "Daddy."

Anna looked up at him. "Well?"

"W-e-l-l." He drew out the word, teasing her. "The answer is yes, he wants to sell. He's asking ten dollars an acre. We can go to Miles City tomorrow and get the paperwork started." He slapped the flat of his hand on the table. His face glowed.

Anna tried to say something, but only a little squeak escaped. She reached out and grabbed his hand and squeezed hard.

146

With the elder Mosers co-signing, the Production Credit Association gave Neil and Anna a fifty thousand dollar loan for the land, Foss's fifty cows, another seventeen head of purebred Hereford stock, and operating expenses.

Neil waved the papers as they walked out of the PCA office. "We're land-owners." He swept Anna off her feet in a bear hug and danced her in a circle on the sidewalk. She hugged him back, giddy with both promise and fear. A ranch of their own. And best of all, it was fifty miles away from Jake and Nettie.

***

Anna took a long look at the accumulated mess around her. Where to begin? Well, from the top, of course. Just like eating hot soup, Mutti always said.

The cobwebs first, then the grime-encrusted windows. That greasy wallpaper would have to be replaced. A picture flashed of her childhood home—the clean streets, immaculate houses, window boxes filled with flowers—and her shoulders sagged. How on earth could she ever make this...this *shack* habitable? Years of bachelor neglect, especially with the hired hand camping out inside, left a house that would not instill pride in a woman.

Thank goodness she'd decided to leave Monica with Nettie until they had the place cleaned up. What a mess. Resolute in her task, Anna tied an old dishtowel around her hair and went for the first bucket of water.

Despite the late summer heat, Neil brought in a bucket of coal for the cook stove and lit a fire to heat the water. While Anna scrubbed, he grabbed a broom and attacked the layers of dead flies, wood chips, coal dust and clumps of dried mud through the house. It was enough to fill a scoop shovel several times. Dust filled Anna's nose and covered her skin. Sweat ran in muddy streaks down Neil's face.

As the day wore on, Anna shoved the pump handle down again and again. Water gushed to fill her pail. She had lost count of the buckets of water they had hauled from the well fifty feet from the house.

But by evening, they had the bedroom walls and floor washed down, and made up the bed that had been left there. Monica's crib would have to go in one corner. Anna had cleaned enough of the kitchen so she and Neil could sit at the table for a supper of cold fried chicken Nettie had sent along. Too tired to stay up much past the meal, they fell into bed. She drifted into an exhausted sleep.

Anna squirmed, then sat upright, scratching her legs furiously. "What is biting me?"

Neil lit a candle.

Bedbugs.

There was no more sleep that night. Anna got up, stoked the fire, brewed coffee and heated water for the next onslaught of cleaning. Neil dragged the mattress outside and set it afire. Watching the blaze, Anna shook her head. Thank goodness Monica hadn't been there.

Later, Neil drove to the Horse Creek Store to see if the Stokleys had a fumigator then the thirty-five miles into the town of Foster to purchase a better mattress and new pillows, so they could sleep.

Anna shuddered every time she thought of the bugs in their bed, and kept hauling buckets. What an unforgiving land this was. First, it's a hundred degrees, then it's fifty below. It floods, then it's all dried up like a desert. There are rattlesnakes to watch out for, mosquitoes that threaten to draw all your blood, dirty old flies, and now bedbugs. Mutti would never believe this.

She set her shoulders. Mutti must never know.

***

Gradually, over the next couple of weeks, the two main rooms were transformed to Anna's liking. She scraped several layers of wallpaper off the kitchen walls and replaced them with a cheery roses-and-teacups design. On her hands and knees with a scrub brush, she removed the strata of dirt and old wax from the worn linoleum, then polished it to the best of her ability. New linoleum would have to wait. She scrubbed, sanded and painted the kitchen cupboards white, and with the paint that was left over, put a new coat on the wooden table that had been left by Mr. Foss. For curtains, she hand-hemmed flowery print material from feed sacks, then made curtains for the bedroom, too, and painted the slatted wallboards a light green.

Anna surveyed the largest room in the house, the living room. Her eyes lingered on the gray wool carpet they had brought from their bedroom at the Ingomar ranch. Other than the two-burner oil stove that took up one corner of the room, the rug was the extent of their furnishings.

Neil checked the oil tank outside and found it contained only a few gallons. "Since we don't have furniture for this room yet, anyway, let's just keep it closed up this winter."

The fourth room was an uninsulated afterthought where seed wheat had been stored. They wouldn't be able to use it for living space, but Anna went in to clean, armed with a broom and shovel. *Will this work ever be done?* As she swept, she caught movement on the floor. Gray, furry, little creatures scurried for a hole in the wall. She screamed and ran outside, with the still-strong memory of the rats that had also sought shelter during the long-ago air raids.

Neil ran from the shop. "What's wrong?"

Anna just pointed. "R-rats." She shivered as if with ague until Neil gathered her into his warm embrace.

"They're just innocent little mice. It's okay, honey. They won't hurt you. But, looks like we'll have to get a cat."

***

Anna stood outside in the bright early-September morning with Monica and studied the squat grey-boarded house. Granted, it wasn't the white two-story she'd dreamed of. But it was hers. Theirs. They'd already made it a home, with new paint on the inside, a vase of wildflowers Neil had picked for her, and cheery curtains at the windows.

The pile of tin cans in front of the doorway was slowly diminishing as Neil shoveled load after load into a wagon, then pulled it with the Ford coupe to a deep coulee a couple of miles from the house. And every time Anna walked to the outhouse or to the corrals, she picked up a handful of discarded bent and rusty nails. The men who'd lived here before apparently threw everything on the ground, wherever they happened to be. Neil would straighten as many as he could to use later. Meanwhile, she didn't want the car tires punctured.

One afternoon, while Neil was out riding to check on the cows, Anna heard a vehicle approach. Through the window she saw a rusted Willys Jeep come to a stop. A short, stocky man lifted a brown gunnysack from the back of the vehicle and came toward the house. Anna stared in astonishment. The man was black from head to foot—his face, his hands, his clothes. As he neared the door, she could see he was covered in grease and soot.

The hair on the back of her neck tingling, she opened the door just a crack. "H-hello. Who are you?"

"Hello there, ma'am." He gave a tiny bow. "My name is James Eichorn, but just call me Jim. I'm your nearest neighbor to the north." His voice was friendly.

Anna brushed wisps of hair from her sweaty forehead. Oh, what was she going to do? She couldn't turn him away—she'd learned that wasn't the "way of the West." But he was so dirty. And of course, smelled as if he hadn't had a bath in a very long time.

Eichorn lifted up the gunnysack and offered it to Anna. "I brought you folks some spuds. I raise the biggest and the best anywhere around."

Spuds? Oh, yes. Potatoes. Neil called them that sometimes. "Why, thank you." She opened the door wider to accept the gift. "Would you like to come in for a cup of coffee?" He seemed harmless enough—she hoped.

"Don't mind if I do." A gap-tooth grin rewarded her offer. He stepped into the porch, took off a battered hat and slapped it on his leg. Dust flew.

Anna recoiled.

"Oops, sorry." He grinned again, hung the hat on a nail in the wall, and followed her into the kitchen.

Anna couldn't tell his age. He was young and old at the same time. Relatively unwrinkled, but with sparse hair and few teeth.

He bent toward Monica. "Well, look at that pretty little gal. What's your name?"

She toddled behind Anna and hid her face in the folds of her mother's skirt.

"This is Monica. She's almost two. A little shy." Anna busied herself measuring coffee grounds and putting water on the stove.

"Well, that's okay. So am I." Eichorn fished a piece of string from one pocket and a greasy washer with a hole in the center from the other. Threading the metal disk onto the string and looping an end around each hand, he twirled it around and around, until the string was wound tight. Then he pulled, in and out, as the string made a high-pitched buzzing sound. The washer was only a blur.

Monica stared from behind Anna, her eyes wide. Finally, she stepped forward, pointing at the whirring disc. "Toy?" She looked up at Anna, then back at it, and giggled. Anna laughed too.

With a sense of relief, Anna heard hoofbeats clopping on the hard earth outside. Good, Neil was back.

Neil strode into the house. "I see we have company." He stopped short as he saw their swarthy visitor entertaining Monica.

"This is our neighbor, Jim Eichorn." Anna gestured toward the man. "He brought us a sack of beautiful potatoes."

The buzzing toy stopped as Eichorn stuck out a grimy hand. "Howdy. Welcome. It's nice to have new neighbors. John Foss and I came here from Nebraska in 1911 and homesteaded together."

"I see." Neil surreptitiously wiped his hand on his pants. "I smell coffee. Would you like to wash up before we have a cup?" He gestured toward the washbasin on a stand in the corner.

Jim stepped to the basin and swished his hands in the water briefly, then wiped them on a towel, talking all the while. "We built this place first, then when he decided to take a bride, I built my house just down the road a ways." He sat at the table, picked up the piece of pound cake Anna had set in front of him and took a big bite, ignoring the fork. "You ever need help around here, just lemme know."

Anna glanced at the once-pink hand towel and back at the filthy man, talking with his mouth full. She hid a smile by taking a sip from her cup. This neighbor could prove entertaining.

***

One by one the neighbors came calling. Charlie and Etta Stokley who owned the store and ran the post office, one evening brought the mail and a two-pound can of coffee. A middle-aged couple with a twelve-year-old daughter, they filled Neil and Anna in on the history of Horse Creek.

"As you can see, we have horses, but there isn't much water around to justify the name." Charley laughed. "But there's a little reservoir up north a ways that never quite goes dry. So, I guess the homesteaders were hoping there'd be enough water to keep their farms going."

Anna thought of the falling-down homestead shack on the Ingomar ranch. Someone'd had hope there once, too.

"It panned out for some." Charley continued. "But for most, it didn't. This whole county used to be much more populated. You'll find remnants of settlements—mostly 'Something-Creeks' or 'Springs'—with nothing left but the name."

"Welcome to Horse Creek." Etta shook Anna's hand as they left. "We'll be seeing you at the store often, I'm sure."

Roger and Genevieve Hunter, who owned the biggest spread in the area, stopped by briefly one afternoon in their shiny new Chevy pickup on their way to their north pasture on the other side of Eichorn's. Both were dressed in new, creased

152

Levis, their boots polished to a high shine. Although she couldn't understand everything they said, Anna immediately sensed their aura of importance in the neighborhood.

Mel and Vickie Thompson, who leased a small place five miles north of the Mosers, came to visit on a Sunday afternoon and brought their little boy who was a year older than Monica. Vickie was a warm, blonde woman who smiled readily. "Oh, I'm so glad you have a little girl about Roy's age. There just aren't any little kids in this neighborhood."

Another Sunday, Tom and Fran McGregor, who lived ten miles south of Horse Creek, visited with their two older children, about eight and ten.

Anna basked in the glow of this new life in their own home, with neighbors who seemed friendly. No one had remarked on her accent and all had brought a welcoming gift of some kind—a hot dish, a plate of cookies, the tin of coffee. This could be more like home. She might like this Horse Creek community.

One morning in late September, Fran and Vickie stopped by. "We're going into Foster to a Missionary club meeting. Would you like to come with us?"

Anna hesitated. "Oh, I don't know. I have so much work to do." A childish, lost feeling came over her with the thought of being around others without Neil.

"Oh, go on in. It'll help you get acquainted," Neil encouraged. "I'm going to be out checking fence today, anyway."

With butterflies ghosting in her chest, Anna gathered up Monica and her doll and got into Fran's green 1950 Chevy sedan. During the thirty-mile drive, Vickie and Fran chattered away in the front seat. Not knowing the people they talked about, Anna soon lost track of the conversation and concentrated on helping Monica dress and undress her doll. Finally, they drove into Foster, the bustling little county seat with a population of three hundred, bigger than Ingomar by a couple hundred.

Fran pulled up outside a large modern house painted white with green grass and a white board fence surrounding it. Hmm. Here was a place that had some similarities to Anna's dream house. Maybe it was possible to have a nice house and yard in this country after all.

A woman with perfectly styled blonde wavy hair, wearing eye make-up and a fine brown silk dress, invited them in. "I'm Nancy Smith." She shook Anna's hand.

"Hello, Mrs. Schmit. Nice to meet you." Anna flushed. Oh why were the s's and th's so hard to say?

"Oh, your accent is so cuuute! Just call me Nancy."

Anna gritted her teeth. Accent. When would people quit noticing her accent? "Cute," indeed.

Nancy ushered them into a large, stylish living room, complete with wall-to-wall carpeting. A see-through fireplace was sandwiched between the kitchen and living room, and Anna admired a chrome chandelier hanging over the dining room table. Several bright-colored cushioned chairs on chrome-plated frames sat next to blonde wood occasional tables. *Goodness, all the latest style.*

The hostess rattled off the names of several other women already seated then added, "Come, your little girl can play with the other children in the bedroom."

At first, Monica sniffled and held on to Anna's skirt, but when an older girl offered her a cookie and a glass of milk, she finally let Anna leave the room.

Anna took a seat on a curved, butter-yellow leather sofa next to Fran. The wall on the opposite side of the room featured a large picture window that commanded a wide view of Nancy's green yard and trees. She raised her eyebrows. *My, this Smith family must have money.*

The women all chattered around her as they sipped coffee from delicate china cups, nibbled on tiny teacakes, and gossiped about the latest "soap opera" on the radio. Anna tried to sit up straight and hold her cup and saucer in the same delicate way the others did. She studied their clothing. The town women seemed to be dressed much more stylishly than those from the country. Her own brown tweed suit she'd brought from Germany was hopelessly out of date. Anna was torn between wanting to be invisible and resentment of not being noticed. It was a mistake to come here.

"So, you're new to the Foster area?" The woman on her right spoke to Anna.

Anna blinked. "*Ja* ... yes, we haff purchased the John Foss ranch at Horse Creek." *Dumpkopf.* Why did she get all tongue-tied and forgetful of English when she was around other women?

"I see." The woman nodded. "Are you Swedish?"

"No. I come from Germany." Anna saw the tiniest flinch around the woman's eyes.

"Oh. German, huh? Did you support Hitler?" The tone of her voice had gone up about half an octave. Before Anna could answer, the woman turned away to whisper to the woman on the other side of her.

Anna's heart felt leaden. Being German still seemed to offend these society ladies. She tried to take a sip of coffee, but could hardly swallow around the lump in her throat. It definitely was a mistake to come. She pictured herself grabbing Monica in her arms and running out of the house. No, of course she couldn't do that.

At last, Nancy rapped a small gavel on the blonde coffee table. "I call this meeting of the United Missionary Society to order. Is there any old business?"

The rigmarole of the meeting lost Anna immediately. This was a waste of time. Why had she let Vickie and Fran talk her into coming? And Neil. He knew how uncomfortable she was in social situations.

"We will finish with the group Bible reading, and then we'll adjourn," Mrs. Smith announced in her perky, businesslike way. "We'll each read two verses. Can we start with you, Fran?" Fran opened her Bible and read.

Then they all turned and looked at Anna. It was her turn. She heard buzzing in her ears. Her heart pounded and her hands shook. "Oh. I...didn't bring..." Her Bible was in German, anyway.

Fran offered her Bible. "Here, you can use mine."

Vickie caught her eye. "It's a pretty difficult passage. I could read it."

Anna took a deep breath of courage and took the book from Fran. "No, I do it." She would prove to these women that she was as smart as they were. Perhaps this would be what bonded them together, the solace in the Word of God. The verses were difficult, with many Old Testament names, but she managed to get through it, stumbling only a few times. Finished, she relaxed her shoulders. There, she'd done it. She smiled with pride.

"Very good," Nancy Smith chirped. "I didn't know you could read...ah...English. Vickie, you're next."

A grimace passed over Vickie's kind face, but she opened her Bible to read.

Anna sat, shell-shocked, as though a bomb had landed right next to her. She couldn't believe this Smith woman would so underestimate her hard-won abilities in English or be so unkind. *Didn't know you could read...* Another instance where someone thought because she didn't speak perfect English she was stupid. Her neck burned, and she knew it had turned a telltale red. She sank back into the soft couch, wishing she could disappear entirely. The rest of the meeting went by in a blur.

As they drove away, Vickie reached into the backseat and touched Anna's arm. "Don't feel bad about what Nancy said. She really didn't mean anything. That's just the way she is. She speaks without thinking first, sometimes."

Anna tried to smile. "It's okay."

But it wasn't. Anna sank into a deep gloom as she relived the meeting over and over on her way home. She hurried to get out of Fran's car and with barely a wave, carried Monica into the house, changed her clothes, and vowed never to go to the missionary meeting again. If that was the way those women showed their Christian charity, then she didn't want any part of them.

Neil came in for supper. "I'm glad to see my girls are back. Did you have a good time?"

Anna averted her eyes. "*Ja, ja*. It was fine." She didn't want to tell Neil about it. It would probably upset him.

"Is something wrong, *mein Liebchen?*"

She shook her head and busied herself at the kitchen counter.

But he kept probing. "Tell me what happened." He draped his long arm around her shoulders and looked into her brimming eyes.

"Those women think I am *ein Dumbkopf*. Because I have accent, they assume I cannot understand or even read." In her anger, she could barely think of the English words. "That *Schmit Frau* with her fancy house and her silk dress thinks she is so much better than me. I'm never going to Foster again." She felt her neck getting hot again.

He closed his eyes, sighed and set his jaw. "To hell with these narrow-minded people. You know, and I know that you are a very intelligent woman. I'll bet none of them could learn a new language as quickly as you have. And none of them have ever had the courage to live anywhere but Foster, Montana." He offered Anna his handkerchief.

She blew her nose and nodded. "That is it. I vill study until I can speak English better than they can. I don't vant to haff accent. Vill you help me?"

"Yes, I will—wuh-will," Neil rounded his lips to form the "w" sound.

"Vill… uh…"

"Here, like this—say 'Oh. Ill'."

Anna pursed her lips. "Oh-ill. Oh-ill, w-will." She smiled. "O-k-a-y."

✳✳✳

As Anna and Neil prepared for the approaching winter, she diligently practiced her "w's" and "v's" and tried not to think of her experience at the Missionary Society meeting. When she declined another invitation, Vickie reached out and squeezed her arm. "I understand. I'll stop by for coffee later this week."

The fall days grew shorter, the nights crisper. Anna cubed, cooked, and canned meat from the deer Neil shot, and vegetables Vickie and Fran gave her from their gardens. She spent long days washing and sterilizing jars and putting up bushels of tomatoes, green beans, peas, and carrots to supplement what she had brought from the garden she'd planted at the Ingomar ranch.

Anna lost count of how many trips she'd made to the musty little root cellar just outside the house to stock the shelves with the multi-hued jars—the green beans, yellow pears, orange carrots and peaches. Wearily, she stood back to admire all the work she'd accomplished. There must be a hundred jars. But she had done it herself. All for her family.

Neil assured her that the jars and the potatoes from Jim Eichorn would not freeze during the winter. Usually people dug a root cellar into a hillside, he explained, but since there were no hills close to the house, Mr. Foss had dug a 6x10-foot hole in the earth, built a wooden frame for a roof and then covered it with a mound of dirt.

Each time Anna unlatched the wooden door, she ducked her head, hoping to avoid the inevitable spider webs laced across the corners, and hoped those horrible mice had not set up housekeeping down there.

Monica was mother's little helper, climbing up on a stool next to Anna, stirring a spoon in a pan. Once, when Anna stepped outside the kitchen door to dump the dishwater, she came back to find Monica shaking generous amounts of spices into the bowl of cake batter she'd left on the kitchen table.

The little girl looked up at Anna with a serious face. "Help Mama cook."

"*Ach.*" Anna covered her mouth with her hand. While aghast at the waste of spices and the cake, Anna couldn't help but laugh to herself.

She chuckled again as she shucked ears of corn, remembering the first summer when she and Nettie had planted a garden. She had looked at her mother-in-law strangely as she laid out packages of corn seeds. "But we have no pigs," Anna protested. "Corn is pig food."

Nettie assured her that this corn was people food, and when Anna tried it for the first time, gnawing the golden kernels from the cob, she had been pleasantly surprised. It would never become her favorite food, but she could tolerate it. Something else Mutti would never believe—living in a bedbug-infested shack with an outhouse and eating pig feed.

No, her family must never hear these details of her life in America. Anna shook her head. But look at what all they had done to make it a home. Oh, how she longed to see Mutti and Papa, to tell them of the happy times with her loving husband and beautiful daughter.

***

The wind began to blow colder as November 1951 approached. Neil ordered a truckload of grain cake pellets and one of hay to supplement the small stack he had already put up that year. He replaced the broken boards on the hay wagon and worked on the old red Case tractor that had come with the ranch, replacing spark plugs and gaskets and changing the oil. It was as dilapidated as everything else. "We'll need it to pull the loads of hay out to the cattle through the snow."

He also chopped up a small pile of old boards that had been scattered around the buildings and hauled a wagonload of coal for the kitchen stove from Foster since wood was scarce in this part of Montana. Then, as the last chore before the winter set in, he caulked around the windows and put up the storm windows he found stored in a granary.

Anna held on to the hope it was going to be one of those "open" winters Neil kept talking about. But the sky stayed gray and blustery.

CHAPTER FOURTEEN

The snow started at Thanksgiving and didn't quit. Three years in a row, and she was beginning to think Neil's "open winter" was a figment of his imagination.

"Only a trick to get me to stay here." She laughed but was only half joking.

In mid-January, the windows frosted thick with whorls and delicate leaf designs as the thermometer plunged to fifty degrees below zero.

Neil scraped a hole in the frost to look out. "If this keeps up, we may run out of coal before we run out of winter."

Anna shivered.

Neil chuckled. "Only joking, honey."

She certainly hoped they wouldn't run out. They'd started the winter with what she thought was a huge pile of coal in the shed next to the root cellar. Every morning, she bundled herself and Monica in long woolen underwear, heavy knitted sweaters, and wool trousers. She had long ago closed off the living room and stuffed rags into the crack under the door. Neil helped her drag the mattress from their bed onto the kitchen floor in front of the stove, and shut the bedroom door, so they heated only one room. The big black cook stove glowed, but kept them warm only when they stayed within a few feet of it.

The three of them huddled together through the night. Anna listened to the wind caterwauling around the house, shaking it with sudden blasts. It was as though the big bad wolf from "The Three Little Pigs" was outside demanding to be let in. Not only might they run low on coal, but the hay supply for the cattle was dwindling. Neil hadn't said much, so she probably shouldn't worry. But she did, anyway. Perhaps the storm would let up soon, and he'd be able to get out and call for a load of feed. *I'm so sick of this cold and snow.* She finally fell asleep, snuggled close to her daughter's warm body.

A few days later the winds abated and the red line in the thermometer rose to three degrees above zero. Neil came in from doing chores. "I'm going to the store to call for a load of hay after a bit. Got your grocery list handy?" He shed his waxed cotton coveralls and felted vest in favor of denim overalls and long underwear under a wool jacket.

"Fifty-three degrees makes quite a difference. It feels almost like spring." He buckled his rubber overshoes over his boots to go back outside.

Anna snorted, but had to admit the weather did feel much warmer. "Before you leave, would you bring in some water to fill the washtub?" Maybe it was time to wash some underwear and overalls before the three of them began to look like Jim Eichorn. She let Monica spread out her toys on the mattress. Neil brought in several buckets of water and filled a tub to heat on the stove. When the water had warmed enough, she threw the clothes in with a cupful of washing powder to let them soak. Soon the windows dripped with steam and the kitchen filled with the smell of wet wool.

Then she lifted the wood-framed washboard down from its peg on the porch. The corrugated metal sheet felt icy cold even in the warm room. Her knuckles reddened and chafed as she rubbed each piece of clothing up and down the grooved surface until it was clean, then rinsed it in a tub of cold water, and wrung it out by hand. Oh, for the electric wringer machine Mutti had at home.

Carrying the clothes in a lightweight wooden apple basket, she waded through the snow to hang the items on the clothesline outside the house. On the way back, she filled the four-foot oblong tin bathtub with snow to melt on the stove. By evening it would be warm enough for all of them to take their baths—Monica first, then Anna, and Neil last. It would be so nice to feel clean again.

As the sun began its early migration into the western horizon, Anna went outside again to collect the clean clothes. They were frozen stiff, although most of the excess water had evaporated in the cold dry air. She stopped for a moment, looking at the laundry.

If Mutti could see her now. In Germany before the war, they'd had machines that did the wash and at least a heated basement where the clothes dried. Mutti had written that life was gradually being restored there.

She pictured her mother wagging a finger. "I *told* you not to go to that God-forsaken land." Her cheeks flamed despite the cold. She would never tell Mutti of their hardships, of Anna's struggle with isolation and the lack of acceptance.

No, Mutti must never know. A tear trickled from the corner of one eye and froze on her cheek. So many things she couldn't share with her own mother.

Anna's gaze shifted to the snowbanks in the yard. The waning sun cast a glow along the horizon, and the edges of the drifts reflected the pink from the sky and melted into lavender shadows below. The air was crisp and clean. As she looked across the miles of sparkling white snow with its unlikely blue and purple accents, Anna pushed the scarf back from her forehead. This was truly beautiful. She'd never seen anything like it.

Anna gathered an armload of the frozen clothes. It was like trying to carry boards stacked haphazardly in her arms. She stumbled through the snow toward the house. A pair of longjohns collapsed and fell from her grasp. When Anna reached down to retrieve them, the rest of her load tumbled into a drift. She tripped over the long stem of a weed and fell headlong. With a face full of snow, she pushed herself to her knees. She looked at the frozen clothes scattered around her and puckered her face to curse. Then a giggle rose from her gut. She sat and laughed aloud at the sheer absurdity of it all. If her sister Elsa could see her now...

When Neil came in later, his freshly laundered denim overalls were standing upright around the kitchen stove, thawing out. He grinned. "Looks like a bunch of old cowboys, huddled around the campfire."

Anna rolled her eyes and gave him a punch on the arm. He grabbed her around the waist and kissed her long and hard, until Monica's voice interrupted. She peered from around a pair of the standing pants. "Peek-a-boo." Anna laughed and hugged her little girl.

After supper that evening Anna sat down at the kitchen table to write a letter home by the light of the kerosene lantern.

Liebe Mutti, she wrote, then paused. No, she couldn't tell her about the day's activities, the way she had to do laundry. But she could describe the beauty of sunshine on the snow, the shadows and colors. She could tell her about the fresh eggs and milk they got every day. And, of course, about Monica. She wrote:

> *Monica is two now and is so inquisitive. She helps me cook and she can sing "Twinkle Twinkle, Little Star" and recite many other nursery rhymes. She is the joy of my life. I wish you could see her. The weather has been cold, but has warmed substantially. I'm looking forward to spring....*

Three days later another blizzard hit.

***

Long snowy days became longer frigid weeks. Between blizzards, Anna wondered if the blinding sun would ever provide warmth again. Four months of bundling in thick layers of warm clothing. Four months of struggling through snowdrifts to feed the cows, a monumental task even with Neil pulling the hay wagon with the big Case. Four months of shivering around the cook stove, trying to conserve coal. Not to mention traipsing through the cold to the outhouse and brushing snow off the seat before sitting down. Sure, they'd had snow in Germany. But nothing like this. Melancholy seeped into her bones like the cold. *Liebe* Mutti. She hadn't seen her family now in three years.

Anna helped Monica dress her doll on the mattress off to one side of the stove. At least they had their own place. And she didn't have to be cooped up with her mother-in-law. Memories of taut silences, split by sharp words, made her shudder. But now, Anna was the one going out to help her husband with the ranch chores. She better appreciated how Nettie must feel, working alongside Jake to accomplish simple tasks made arduous by the weather. Just bundling up Monica and herself every day and leaving the comfort of their warm kitchen was an ordeal. But it left her with a sense of accomplishment.

Finally, the air warmed, the snow melted, and after several more weeks of sloppy mud, spring brought calving season. Anna and Monica drove out every day with Neil to see if any new calves had been born.

The seventeen purebred Herefords were kept in a pasture separate from the fifty mixed breeds they'd bought from Mr. Foss. "Why do we do that?" Anna asked when Neil divided the herd.

"We want to keep the bloodline pure. That usually means more money for the calves. We'll keep some of the bull calves each year. Sell them as two-year-olds for breeding."

Anna nodded. It made sense to plan ahead.

Neil continued. "The way I figure it, having bulls for sale in the spring will add an early income to what we'll get from selling the steers in the fall."

"Okay." Anna liked this idea. They had their own place, their own cattle, and soon would have their own money.

Neil and Anna caught each new purebred calf. While its anxious mother hovered nearby, lowing gently, Anna helped hold the baby while Neil inked its right ear. Then he took the pliers-like tongs, selected numbers made of preformed needles and punched the identification into the skin. Last, he rubbed the ink into the skin, patted the curly head, and let the calf go.

Anna wrote down the number and its mother's name and number in a notebook. Each animal would be registered with the American Hereford Association, which would be important when it came time to sell their young breeder bulls.

When she'd learned how to keep track of the small herd, Anna named every cow. "Oh, that one is a Rosie. She can't be anything else. And that one—Adelheid." A schoolgirl excitement grew with pride of ownership. She recognized every cow now, and knew which calf belonged to her. She felt almost a kinship with these beasts, and the fear she'd had of large cows as a young girl had dissipated with that intimacy. But, she still couldn't get over her fear of horses. They were so big and she never felt in control.

In the evening, Anna showed Neil the book, with its neat columns, names, and numbers. "We have ten babies now, and seven heifers left to calve."

"You sure are a great help. I'm impressed." Neil kissed Anna's neck, which warmed with the pleasure of his compliment.

Keeping the records on the purebreds satisfied Anna's sense of order and detail. She found a joy she would never have guessed, helping her husband. During the three years they'd lived with Neil's parents, she'd always thought Nettie a little odd for wanting to be outside all the time. She'd even decided it was just the way her mother-in-law stayed away from her.

Now Anna understood Nettie's fascination with ranch work a little better. She looked forward to spending time with Neil, driving over the awakening prairie, eager to count the new calves.

The weather continued intermittently dry, then muddy, then windy and dry again, when a mid-April snowstorm punctured the sixty-degree weather. Once the wind and snow let up enough, Neil rode out into the pastures to check for newborns.

With a frown, Anna stared out the kitchen window at the white stuff she had been sure was gone for good a few days before. Why couldn't winter simply be done? She turned back to her bread dough, punched it down with extra force, and sprinkled more white flour over the dough to knead it. Then she formed loaves and set them on the shelf above the cook stove to rise.

At noon Neil came in for dinner. "There were a couple of new calves, but they were up and doing fine. Can you help me feed this afternoon? We'll take the tractor out."

After they'd eaten and bundled up, the three of them headed for the pasture. When they reached the herd, Anna steered the tractor with Monica in her lap, while Neil threw off the hay and the cake to the herd. The temperature had risen a little, but the wind was still chilly.

Anna twisted the wheel as she spotted a dark form under a sagebrush. "Neil, a calf." He jumped off the wagon and ran to check. His shoulders slumped. He shook his head. "We're too late. It's dead."

A choking sensation in her throat caught her by surprise. "Are you sure?" Not even thinking of future money lost, she mourned its lifelessness. A cow stood off from the rest of the herd near the calf, not eating. "The poor mother—she looks so sad."

Neil nodded. "She dropped it in the snow, and it got chilled clear through right away. Didn't get a chance to get up and suck." He sighed. "Must've missed it when I rode out earlier."

The picture of that cow stayed with Anna through the rest of the day and enveloped her in sadness. Neil seemed quieter, too. She pinched her lips together in sympathy. *He blames himself.*

The next afternoon, Neil rode in from the pasture, a dark bundle wrapped in a gunnysack draped over his saddle. He brought the bundle into the house—another newborn calf, its legs stiff with cold.

"What are you doing?" Anna asked as he laid it on the floor next to the stove. A calf in the house? She could hardly believe her eyes.

"Trying to save this one's life." Neil stepped back out onto the porch. "I'll get a box and some more gunny sacks for it to lie on. Would you heat up some milk in one of Monica's bottles?"

The nurse in Anna roused her from her shock at having this animal in her clean kitchen. It already seemed like she could barely keep up with the mud, snowmelt and coal dust. She put milk on the stove to warm and dug in the back of the closet for an old blanket, which she draped over the calf.

Monica stood close by, watching. "Taffy?" She pointed at the calf.

"Yes, honey, it's a baby calfie." Anna poured the milk into a bottle and, just like with her own baby, tested a drop on her wrist.

Monica reached out and put her small hand on the calf's curly white forehead. "Pet taffy?"

Anna put an arm around her daughter. "Nice calfie. So soft." Poor little thing—barely alive. Anna blinked back a tear.

Neil came back in and fixed a bed with the cardboard and sacks. Then he lifted its head and dribbled a few drops of warm milk into its mouth, while stroking its throat. The calf barely moved, but finally swallowed. "Do we have any old wool socks? And I'll need some vinegar…"

Puzzled, Anna again complied with his requests, and watched as he warmed the vinegar, rubbed it on the calf's legs, and wrapped them in the wool socks. "To save them from frostbite," he explained.

Through the rest of the afternoon and evening, Neil and Anna kept the fire stoked, massaged the calf's legs and fed it more milk. Then they went to bed, leaving it asleep by the warm fire.

"Does everyone do this—bring calves into the house?" Anna asked Neil just before dozing off.

"Some do, some don't. Unfortunately, some of the huge ranches allow nature to take its course, then they write off their losses against taxes." He sighed. "Since we're so small and just starting out, we can't afford to let even one die, if we can help it. Each calf means hundreds of dollars." He wrapped his arms around her. "Besides, I can't imagine letting them die."

"I'm glad." Anna smiled as she drifted off to sleep. Her caring, loving husband.

***

"Maaa-aaaa!" A loud bleat and the sound of hard little hooves scrabbling on linoleum woke Anna and Neil at four a.m. Anna sat upright. "Wha—?"

"The calf is up." Neil leaped from the bed and ran into the kitchen. Anna followed. The warmth, nourishment and care had given the baby strength to stand by itself. But the slick linoleum hampered its efforts. It bleated again, looking for its mother.

Anna sniffed. The calf had also relieved itself on the floor. She quickly cleaned up the mess while a bottle heated on the stove. The baby drank eagerly, switching its little tail and butting against her hand. She smiled at the pure white, curly head that contrasted with its dark, reddish brown body. "Isn't she a beauty? Monica calls her 'Taffy'."

Neil chuckled. "Then that's what we'll name her."

As soon as the sky began to lighten, Neil fired up the tractor and hitched up the hay wagon. After he had loaded it with hay and grain cake pellets, he wrapped the calf in sacks and laid it in a hollow in the hay. Anna and Monica climbed aboard to ride with the calf, making sure it didn't try to get up and jump out.

In the pasture, the calf's mother paced the fence, lowing softly as though she had been worried. She met them at the gate, sniffing the wagon. Neil lifted the calf down and pointed it toward the cow. Mama sniffed at it a moment, turned her head as she caught a whiff of the vinegar liniment, and started to walk away.

"Uh-oh. Doesn't she want her own baby?" Anna wanted to jump down from the wagon and help. *Was it all for nothing? Did we doom it by saving its life?*

"It doesn't smell right to her." Neil rattled a shovelful of cake. "Here, Bessie." He emptied it on the ground, and the cow came back to eat. As she bent her head to the grain pellets, the calf trotted up to her side, grabbed a teat in its mouth and began to suck. The cow lifted a hind leg and kicked it away.

"No-no, Bessie, c'mon." Neil spoke in a low soothing voice. He poured out a little more cake. When her attention was redirected, he guided the calf back to her side. As it suckled again, the mother turned her head to watch for a moment, then went back to eating her cake.

"Oh good." Anna laughed. "They're both happy as long as they're eating."

Neil nodded. "Now that she's let it suck, they'll be fine."

***

The flurry of activity and excitement caused by the spring storm finally passed. At last Anna felt like the new season was there to stay. She basked in the return of the sun's warmth and took Monica outside to play. She admired the green that now painted the low rolling hills, and looked forward to the pastures filled with frolicking red and white calves.

One day, Neil cut out four two-year-old heifers from the purebred herd and brought them home into the corral.

Anna was overcome with curiosity. "What will you be doing with them?"

"These heifers are going to have their first calves soon. Sometimes they have a little trouble the first time, so I'll have to help them." Neil walked around the cows, peered at their rear ends, and checked their swelling bags. "This one looks like she might be coming due any day now."

"So, you're a cow doctor, too?"

He chuckled. "No, not really. It's just something ranchers have to do."

Neil put the heifers in the barn at night and set an alarm clock to check on them every two hours. Anna got up with him several times, just to watch. The first two had their calves easily, and the babies were already standing upright and sucking by the time Neil and Anna came to look.

The third had just started labor one night about a week later, so they watched and waited until they saw the nose and the front legs protruding. As the young cow seemed to tire and showed signs of giving up, Neil reached out, grabbed the legs and gave a pull. Another mighty push by the mother, and the calf slithered out in a gush of bloody fluid. Then the cow expelled the amniotic sac.

"*Ach.* That was pretty easy." Almost with a shared sense of accomplishment, Anna watched the baby struggle to its feet and search for its food source, while the cow murmured soft little moos as if to encourage it.

Neil grinned. "Atta boy. That's the way to do it."

The fourth heifer waited, with no signs of imminent motherhood. After watching her for a week, Neil shook his head. "Well, Shortcake, I'm tired of getting up all night long. You're not showing me results."

"Why don't you let me get up tonight and check, so you can get some sleep," Anna offered. "You're so very tired."

Neil eyed the heifer carefully, and finally agreed. "Okay. She doesn't look like she's about to start very soon anyway."

When Anna came out at two a.m., the cow lay on her side, panting and straining. Anna saw a tiny hoof protruding. This looked like trouble. What was she supposed to do? She reached out a tentative hand and pulled on the hoof. It didn't budge. *Ach, nein.* Anna ran to the house to get Neil.

He strode into the barn and took one look. "It's the hind foot—it's coming backwards. Get up, Shortcake. We're gonna help you." He prodded the heifer who lumbered to her feet, then tied a rope around her neck and snubbed it to a post in the corner of the barn. Slathering Vaseline on his hand, he rolled up his sleeves, and reached inside her.

"What do you have to do?" Anna shifted from one foot to the other.

"I'm trying to turn the calf around so it can come headfirst." Sweat rolled from Neil's forehead.

Anna twisted her hands in her skirt. Oh dear. If the head didn't come first, the calf could suffocate.

Neil grunted and tugged. The cow groaned.

"Got it," he said finally. "See that pulley hanging there? That's a calf-puller. Bring it here."

Anna grabbed the chain and pulley device. *How in the world is this going to work?*

He made a loop and held it in his hand as he reached inside again. "I'm going to hook the chains around the calf's front legs, and get it started." When both hooves were out, he took two steel handles, shaped like the top of a shovel handle, and hooked them onto the chains.

"Okay. I need you to hold onto this one, sit down, and brace yourself, like this." Neil shoved his boots against the cow's haunch. "Now pull."

Anna held on to the pulling device, working with her husband to save another life.

"Pull. Harder." Neil spoke softly but emphatically.

Anna thought her arms would jerk out of their sockets. Her breath came in gasps, and she prayed silently. *Please, God, let this calf be okay.*

"All right. Here it comes." Neil's voice held a note of triumph. The calf slid onto the floor of the barn with a soft thud. Neil untied the heifer, and she immediately turned to lick her baby.

This cow has the same maternal instincts as a human mother. Anna remembered how she had felt the first time she had seen Monica. She watched the mother bathe her calf, and soon there came a plaintive bleat, "Maaa."

Anna wanted to clap and cheer, but didn't want to scare the cow and calf. Instead, she grinned widely, turned to Neil and, ignoring the blood and manure on his coveralls, gave him a big hug. "We did it!"

Lying in bed later, Anna was amazed how her childhood terror of her uncle's big Holstein milk cows had been overshadowed by her nurse's instinct—and pride of ownership. These were their calves, and every calf they saved would make that payment to the PCA next fall a bit easier. She'd forgotten her fear.

Anna smiled to herself, feeling a pleasant glow. She'd overcome much in her new life in this new country. Exhausted but satisfied, she snuggled closer to Neil's warm body, and drifted off, still smiling.

***

One morning toward the end of May, Neil drained his coffee cup and stood up from the breakfast table. "It's time to do the branding. I think I'll run over to the Thompsons today and ask if they can help."

This being Anna's fourth season of branding, she was accustomed to the drill. Relatives and neighbors all took turns helping each other. The men brought their horses, and the women would show up later with cakes, salads, and other dishes for the noon meal.

The date was set. Jake and Nettie arrived the night before, and both were up with Neil before dawn. The men from the neighboring ranches arrived with their horses soon after, stood in front of the barn, drank coffee and smoked while Neil and his parents saddled up. The horses' breath sent little clouds of steam into the brisk morning air as they snorted and pawed at the ground, eager to be on their way. A faint apricot watercolor tint washed the clear pearl-gray sky as the riders headed out into the pasture.

Anna put a huge pan of beef ribs in the oven and set a pot of beans with molasses and bacon simmering on top, then mixed a double batch of cornbread to serve to the branding crew at noon. The combined sweet and spicy smells wafted through the kitchen, making Anna's stomach growl.

She glanced at the picture propped on a shelf and had to chuckle. It was from her first branding on the Ingomar ranch. Neil had bought her a purple western-style shirt, with white piping around the yoke, and a pair of brown calfskin cowboy boots. She had dressed the part, including denim overalls. Complete with a gray Stetson borrowed from Nettie, Anna had her picture taken, first up on Blue's back, and then in the corral, holding a calf. She had mailed a copy of the picture home and received a letter from Mutti oohing and aahing over her "cowboy girl" daughter.

That first time she'd been terrified by what she'd considered the "barbaric ritual" of branding.

But now, Anna was over her squeamishness, accustomed to the smell, the noise and the heat, and since this was their own herd, she was interested in how many calves they would sell come fall.

At nine o'clock, she heard the cows lowing as they moved over the hill toward the corrals. She gave the beans a stir, grabbed Monica's hand and headed out to the corral. She took the stub of pencil from the cardboard box that held the vaccine and supplies, and marked the tally on the box flap. Across the top she wrote "Steers," "Bulls," and "Heifers," and made a slash beneath each heading as the calves were branded.

Just before noon, she gave her tally job to Nettie, who gave Monica a hug and nodded at Anna. "Nice looking bunch of calves."

"Thank you." Anna smiled with pride, took Monica's hand, and headed for the house to serve dinner. In the yard, she left Monica to play with Roy Thompson. The neighbor women had brought plenty of delicious salads, Jell-O, cookies, pies and cakes, and sat around the table, drank coffee and visited, occasionally glancing out the window at the children laughing and playing in the dirt on top of the root cellar.

Vickie Thompson stood at the stove and stirred the beans. She turned to Anna. "Smells wonderful. I think everything is about ready."

Anna glowed with pleasure at seeing her friend. The two women usually got together for a cup of coffee at least once a week, and she enjoyed their visits. Still a bit uncomfortable with some of the other women she didn't know as well, she was never sure whether they were making fun of her or not. And she still couldn't feel that Nettie was a friend. They both loved Neil and Monica and that's where their common ground ended.

"Everything looks good." She sent one of the older children to ring a large cowbell hanging by the side of the house. Soon the men lined up on the porch to wash their hands in a bucket of soapy water and trooped into the kitchen to fill their plates. They then took to the shade, ate their grub, and talked of the next ranching job coming up—haying.

By three o'clock, branding was finished, calves were reunited with their mothers, and the riders pushed the herd across the prairie, back to their pasture.

That evening after Monica was in bed, Neil and Anna sat at the kitchen table to look over the tally sheet. "We didn't lose a single calf from the purebreds." Neil had a big grin on his face. "We kept six bulls to sell as breeding stock, we'll sell four steers, and keep the seven heifers to build up the herd."

"That's very good." Anna's fingers floated over the cardboard, as she counted the rest.

From the Foss herd of fifty mixed breeds, there had been one dead calf, and two cows were "dry"—not giving birth. Of the forty-seven calves, Neil and Anna had thirty-three steers and thirteen heifers to sell in the fall. They'd keep eleven for replacement stock.

"If they average four hundred pounds, and if we can get thirty cents..." Anna scribbled numbers on the back of the cardboard tally. "That's a hundred twenty dollars apiece, times fifty—that's six thousand dollars!"

"Atta girl. Way to work those figures." Neil's eyes lit up behind his glasses.

Joy spread through Anna like melted butter. Their hard work was going to pay off. They hadn't endured the cold, the heat, the late nights and early mornings with nothing to show for it.

"I think we're going to do all right our first year in business." Neil threw down the cardboard, grabbed Anna around the waist and belted out a dance tune as he waltzed her around the kitchen. "Come a ty-yi yippee yippee yay..."

Anna whooped and laughed along with him. She might be liking this ranching business after all. If every year were like this, they'd be able to pay off their loan in just a few years.

Increase their herd. Buy a pickup truck. Maybe even paint the house white...

CHAPTER FIFTEEN

Anna turned over the chicken pieces frying in the iron skillet and wiped her forehead with her apron. Golly, it was hot. It must be close to a hundred degrees out, and here she was, stoking the fire and making dinner to take to Neil out in the field. From now on she'd have to cook and bake early in the morning, before the day heated up. She crumbled crisp bacon over the boiled potatoes, chopped an onion, blinking away the burning in her eyes, and added two tablespoons of vinegar for the hot German potato salad Neil had come to like so well.

It was late June 1952, and not a drop of rain had fallen since early April. The young tender wheat shoots already looked stunted and were wilting in the fields.

She had learned that most ranchers in the area did some farming in addition to raising cattle, so they could hedge their bets. If calf prices were down, maybe wheat prices would be up, or vice versa. Very different from Germany. She nodded. A smart thing to do. Fortunately, Anna and Neil had a beautiful calf crop, so even if the grain failed... She sighed. So many "ifs."

Anna transferred the chicken into an aluminum bowl, put the lid on, and packed it into a cardboard box with the potato salad and green peas from the garden. She added plates, silverware, a thermos of coffee and several slices of chocolate cake. She grabbed Monica and her doll, loaded everything into the Ford coupe and headed to the field.

She saw the cloud of dust raised by the big Case even before she drove over the low hill where Neil summer-fallowed. He had explained to her that it was good to let some fields lie dormant for a year between plantings. This way, the soil could reclaim its nutrients from the rain, rotting stalks from last year's crop, and nitrogen from lightning. But, to till those stalks under and to keep the weeds from sucking all the moisture from the ground, he had to plow the fields a couple of times during the summer.

Anna swung the car around so its bulk cast some shade on the hot ground at the edge of the field. As Neil shut down the tractor, she spread out a blanket and set Monica on it. The two-year-old cradled her doll upright in her lap. "Raggedy Ann eat too."

Smiling, Anna, brushed a wayward tendril of hair from the toddler's face. "Okay, we'll all eat."

Neil walked over, gave them each a kiss, and played "dolly" with Monica while Anna dished up a plate for each of them. Then he stretched his long legs out on the blanket. "How's your day going, sweetheart?"

Anna shook her head. "Fine. It's just so hot. I wish for a *schwimbad.*"

Neil chuckled. "Yeah, a swim would feel good right about now. You know, I'm going to be done with these fields by tomorrow, and it'll be a while before haying starts." He took a mouthful of potato salad. "I saw a poster at the store about a dance at Ross on Saturday. We've been working pretty hard all spring. How'd you like to go?"

Dancing. Oh, that might be fun. Anna looked up at Neil's eager face. But…people. Would they ignore her or whisper about her there, as they had at the dances at Ingomar or the missionary society meeting? And Neil would probably be playing the fiddle all night, leaving her sitting along the wall by herself. Anna's eyes went to the plate on her lap, and she stabbed at her peas.

"Don't you want to go? Are you worried about Monica? We can take her along. Everybody brings their kids. It'll be fun. We deserve a break." His brow furrowed, Neil leaned forward, peering into her downturned face. "I promise I won't play all night long. I'm not much of a dancer, but I'll give it a try. And, the people are very nice. Mel and Vickie will probably be there, too. It really will be fun."

"Okay. You're right. We need to do something besides work. Let's go." Anna smiled and reached out for her husband's hand, but the tightness in her chest remained.

***

The road snaked sharply downward through scrubby pine trees, tawny square buttes like tables rising above the dust plume behind them. Neil shifted into low gear and pumped the brake as they wove their way around yet another horseshoe corner.

"Where on earth are we going? I didn't know such rough country existed." Anna braced her feet against the floorboards and held tight to Monica in her lap. A tight turn jolted her against the door. After one glimpse of the steep embankment off to her side, she couldn't look again. Her stomach felt a little queasy, and she hoped Monica wouldn't get carsick.

"This is called the Missouri Breaks. The river carved these deep chasms in the countryside over millions of years." Neil drove skillfully, accelerating and braking at just the right moments on the narrow, curving dirt road.

"And we've driven for an hour and a half over this terrible road, just to dance?" Anna was incredulous. "How do people get out when it rains?"

"They pretty much stay till it dries out. But we haven't had any moisture since April, so I think it's pretty unlikely today." Neil laughed, looking at the clear sky, now turning rusty as the sun sank lower to the horizon.

When the Mosers drove up to the squatty log building nestled among a few scrub pines, a dozen cars were already parked around it. Through the open doors and windows, Anna heard the musicians tuning their instruments inside. Outside, a knot of young men passed around a bottle of Wild Turkey whiskey as they stood admiring a brand new 1952 Ford.

"Evenin' folks," Mel Thompson called out. "Vickie's already inside, gossipin' with the ladies, Anna. Hey, Neil, come take a look at this new car."

The green Fairlane shone in the dusky evening light, its fenders curving gently. Someone had opened the hood. "Look at this. She's got an aluminum engine."

One of the men poked his head underneath. "What a beaut."

Another chimed in. "Whose car is this?"

Anna's eyes lingered on the velvety upholstered seats that invited comfort for long trips over bumpy roads.

"It's mine." A cultured voice startled her, and she turned to see a suit-clad banker-type man grinning at the group. A thin woman wearing a fur stole clung to his arm.

Anna took a deep breath. For just a moment she'd had a flash of her post-war date Hermann from Germany with his fine clothes, and the old fears clutched at her insides with icy fingers. She shrank back from the group.

"Let's go in and check out the music." Neil pulled Anna close with an arm around her waist and steered her toward the cabin.

She melted into his embrace. He always seemed to know when she needed extra bolstering.

A babble of voices rose above the honky-tonk piano, accompanied by the hum of a generator behind the building. Electric lights blazed inside, and a few couples were already dancing to "Twilight Time" as Anna and Neil entered. A man and woman harmonized, "Heavenly shades of night are falling… It's twilight time…"

The guitar player looked up from replacing a broken string. "Hey, Neil, bring your fiddle? Come join us."

Neil waved at him. "I will, later." He turned to Anna and squeezed her still-shaking hand. "Are you okay? Do you want to go home?"

She gave a nervous laugh. "No, of course not. I was just startled. I thought I'd seen someone from my past, a neighbor I didn't like much. Go ahead, get your fiddle and play. I'll be fine."

"No, I'm going to dance with my beautiful bride first." Catching sight of Vickie Thompson with her little Roy and a group of kids playing in the corner, he led Anna and Monica over to them.

Vickie beamed. "Hi there, Mosers, glad to see you. C'mon Monica, you can play with Roy." Anna smiled back at Vickie and at the children, pleased that Monica wasn't so shy as long as Roy was around.

Neil swept Anna onto the floor as the musicians changed the tempo to "Mockin' Bird Hill."

The rest of the evening passed in a blur. Mel Thompson asked her to dance, then a series of men she didn't even know. Her cheeks felt flushed from the activity and the attention. Maybe she was being accepted after all. Or, maybe they just didn't know who she was. After all, it seemed customary for the men to ask everyone to dance. Oh well, she wouldn't worry about that tonight. She was actually having a good time.

When the band broke for midnight supper, Neil and Anna stepped outside for some fresh air. "Looks like you've been having fun." He smiled as he leaned toward her lips. Still feeling the thrill to the bottom of her toes when he kissed her, she held him tightly. A sudden rumble broke them apart.

Neil looked up. "My land, it's thunder. I can't believe it." A crack of lightning opened the darkness of the northern sky. Then came another rumble a few moments later.

"We'd better head for home." Neil sprinted for the log cabin, Anna close behind. Monica was asleep on a pile of blankets with several other little ones. Neil snatched her up.

"It might rain," Anna called to Vickie. "We're going home."

"Nah, it won't rain." Mel Thompson spoke up. "It'll just be a dry thunderstorm, if anything. You can spend the night here, if it does." His words were followed by a chorus of protests from the other men. Nobody else seemed ready to leave the party.

But Neil and Anna said hurried good-byes and bundled Monica into the car.

For a long time after their old car began the climb out of the river basin, they didn't hear or see any more signs of a storm. "Maybe it was just a false alarm," Neil admitted. "But then, we needed to get home anyway. We'll avoid the last minute rush of drunken traffic out of there." As soon as he spoke, a jagged spear knifed the sky, followed immediately by a bomb-blast of thunder.

Monica awoke, shrieking. Anna instinctively curled her upper body around her daughter. Her heart pounded. It was only thunder. Would she never get over the fear from the war? Those long years of explosions and running for shelter with sirens wailing seemed etched forever in the fabric of her being.

The thunderstorm intensified as they drove, the air charged with electricity, but no rain. The hair on Anna's arms prickled as though it, too, were electrified.

Lightning zigged, and a thunderclap followed close behind. Anna held her breath.

Even Neil ducked his head. "Oof, that was close."

She tightened her arms around Monica and leaned back into the seat.

As they approached within ten miles of the ranch, yet another huge bolt of lightning crashed into the earth along the horizon. Anna thought she saw flames flicker in the distance.

"Prairie fire." Neil punched the accelerator to the floor. Then, nothing, just the blackness of the night sky.

Anna breathed a small sigh of relief. Maybe it had been a reflection of the lightning strike against the clouds.

A sudden gust of wind stirred the stillness in the air, and dust swirled in the headlights. Then flames leaped again from the same spot. Anna gasped. In minutes the hillside glowed and smoke rose as the dried grass caught and the fire spread.

"Is it…it isn't our place, is it?" Anna couldn't breathe with the fear that gripped her.

"It won't come our way." Neil's voice was firm with conviction, but his knuckles turned white around the wheel.

As Anna peered into the darkness lit by the fire, she had the feeling it was moving in the same direction as their place.

"What if it does?"

"Can't tell yet, but it is close," Neil muttered through his teeth. He drove like a madman, the Ford's engine screaming in high gear. The rolling hills north of their house were silhouetted in the firelight. Neil swerved onto the road that led to the Hunters' ranch house.

Neil pounded on the door, shouting. After long minutes, Roger Hunter opened the door, pulling a suspender over his shoulder, his sparse hair spiking up in disarray.

Anna fidgeted in the car. *Please hurry, Neil.* What would happen to their house? The hay? *Ach du lieber Gott.* The cows and their calves—oh no, they couldn't let them be burned.

"Prairie fire to the north." Neil yelled to his neighbor even as he ran back to the car. When Hunter saw the glow, he sprinted out the door toward a flatbed truck with a thousand-gallon water tank on the back. The neighbors all had small tanks ready, just in case, but Hunter's was the largest.

Neil careened toward home. The wind blew in full force now, changing direction, whipping from the east, then pushing the fire from the north. As they turned down the lane to their house, Anna saw vehicle lights approaching on the county road from the west. Other neighbors had seen the fire, too.

It was only a half-mile from their house. Anna heard the flames crackle. Her nose closed and her eyes watered from the astringent smoke.

"I'm going to get the tractor and plow a firebreak." Neil jumped out of the car. "You'll have to carry buckets of water and wet down the roof, in case it heads this way."

Anna ran to the house, carrying Monica who now screamed in fright. "Honey, it's okay." Anna tried to control her quavering voice. "Here, you can lie down in Mama's bed and look at these books. I have to go to the well and get some water. You stay right here."

"No, Mommy. You stay." Monica sobbed and clutched at Anna's neck.

"Honey, you're all right. Mommy will be right back. Look at the book. It's your favorite, see? *Three Little Pigs.*" She tucked the blanket around her daughter's shoulders. *Oh, please stay put. Dear Lord, watch over her.*

Anna grabbed the drinking bucket from the kitchen cupboard and ran out into the wind. Her skirts whipped around her legs and her hair lashed her face. She pumped a bucketful of water. Now, where was the ladder? She scuttled toward the house, crablike, grasping the heavy bucket in both hands, water sloshing down her dress. It would take forever to wet down the roof. She had to find a faster way. *What do I do?* Anna looked wildly around and focused on the galvanized bathtub. She pulled it around the side of the house and ran to the granary, where she found the ladder and an armload of gunnysacks. She dragged the ladder to the house, then went back for the sacks. Throwing them into the tub, she dumped the bucket of water on top and ran for another.

The fire thrust intense orange, hungry fingers high against the inky sky and rode the crest of the hill on the other side of the county road. Anna's eyes stung from the smoke haze. Her throat ached. Vehicles with their tanks of water in the back sprayed the flames. Someone had joined Neil with another tractor, plowing a firebreak. The men looked like black stick figures silhouetted in the wavering glow that lit the sky like a sunrise. The heat flushed Anna's face.

She grasped several soaked gunnysacks, climbed the ladder, and spread them over the roof. Between trips, she ran into the house to make sure Monica stayed put, terrified she would wander outside to find her mommy. The little girl whimpered, but lay in the big bed, wide-eyed, holding a book to her chest. It was as if she sensed the danger and knew this was a safe place.

"Good girl. Just stay there, Mama is right outside."

One eye on the fire, Anna climbed up and down the ladder, her pink dancing dress now stained and wet. Then she felt the wind on her face and watched in horror as it switched

183

direction. As if sprouting glowing wings, the fire jumped the road. Now it was headed their way.

"*Ach du Lieber.*" Anna slid down the ladder, missing several rungs. She ran inside, scooped up Monica and raced to the Ford. The engine ground, but wouldn't start. Anna pumped the gas pedal furiously, praying out loud, "*Jesus, Maria und Joseph, hilf mir.*" The engine was flooded. She got out and turned the crank. Nothing. Sweat poured down her back.

Then she remembered something she'd seen Neil do. The coupe was parked on a slight incline. She shifted it into neutral, and panting like an old dog, ran around to the back of the car. Anna pushed with all her strength. Her feet slid in the dust. Then she dashed to the driver's side as the car began to roll.

Anna grabbed the door and jumped inside, then shifted the transmission into low gear. She held her breath as the momentum forced the engine to turn over. After a few reluctant coughs and sputters, it caught. She pushed the choke in and pumped the accelerator until the motor began to run smoother.

Visions of the burning hospital in Hamburg blurred Anna's eyes. She floorboarded the gas pedal until the old car jounced across the prairie. Monica's wails synchronized with the roaring engine.

Anna stopped the car on a hill about a mile to the east of the fire, hands nearly paralyzed on the steering wheel. Her whole body shook. She sat, eyes closed, taking deep ragged breaths until she could collect herself. Then she took Monica in her arms and got out of the car, patting her daughter's back and murmuring to her.

From the safety of their perch, they watched the men struggle to turn the fire. Just as they started another fire line, the wind gave a violent push and the fire jumped over. Men beat at the burning brush and grass with wet gunnysacks, trying to contain the spread. The wildfire twisted and turned, a living entity, consuming the dry prairie grasses.

Anna twisted her ruined skirt in one fist. This couldn't be happening. Would they lose their pastureland and their house, too?

CHAPTER SIXTEEN

Anna wanted to scream in her helplessness. Those few men couldn't fight this terrible force of nature. Tears cascaded down her cheeks. All the hard work she and Neil had done, the cold winter, the calves they had saved and nurtured, the hay they'd stacked—all could be gone in a matter of minutes. She hugged Monica tighter against her chest.

Neil and the other tractor driver drove around the fire to plow yet another firebreak. The flames seemed to reach out for them. Jack rabbits scurried from under the sagebrush.

Anna could barely breathe. *Ach, Liebchen*, be careful. *Dear Lord in heaven, please protect him, keep us all safe.*

Roger Hunter drove his tank truck alongside the swath the men plowed, wetting down the grass.

The flames reached the firebreak and finding no dry fuel to consume, veered to the west and as suddenly as it had come from the north, it roared up and over the hill—away from the ranch. Anna felt a few raindrops mingle with the tears on her face and ran laughing back to the car.

Anna watched for another hour, half-afraid the wind would turn again and bring the fire back. The rain pattered on the car roof intermittently at first and then came down in earnest. She breathed deeply.

Their home was safe.

Anna drove down the hill to the house to fix sandwiches for the men. It looked as if it would still be a long night ahead. Stopping the car in front of their squatty little house, she felt humbled. And very thankful for this miserable homestead shack that had become their home. She leaned her head on the steering wheel. "Thank you, Lord."

"That fire went on for twenty-five miles before the rain finally smothered it." Neil heaped his plate with venison, potatoes and gravy at noon the next day. "Acres and acres of pasture and farmland." He shook his head. "Looks like a huge blackened highway across the prairie. At least it only burned a few acres of ours." His face glowed, victorious.

Anna reached out and tousled his still-wet hair. What an ordeal. After chasing the fire all night, he'd come home as black as Jim Eichorn. She'd quickly heated water for a bath and threw his sooty clothes into a large copper pot on the stove to boil.

"I'm so thankful no one's house burned. I was so scared when that fire jumped your firebreak and headed toward us. I didn't know what to do." Anna's neck still knotted with tension. If this never happened again, it would be too soon.

"I was pretty worried about you girls, too. But you did all the right things—thinking of the gunnysacks, and remembering how to start the car." Neil took her hand and gave it a squeeze. "I'm so proud of you."

Anna's shoulders settled a bit. She flushed with his compliment. Yes, she could be proud that she had been able to figure out solutions under such extreme circumstances.

"It's one of those things we have to live with, out here on the prairie. Thank God it doesn't happen very often. I'm glad you and Monica are all right. Boy, what an exciting night, with the dance, then the fire…" He swallowed the last bit of orange marmalade on a buttermilk biscuit, drained his coffee cup and stood. "Well, I told Jim Eichorn I'd go help him vaccinate some of his cows today. Want to come along?"

***

Eichorn's place was only a mile away, but this was the first time Anna had seen it. The unpainted house seemed to meander from one room to another as each had been tacked on. Chickens wandered in and out of one door, and Jim emerged from another with a large, square pan.

"C'mon in." He banged the pan against the side of the house to loosen the final layer of the last meal. "I was just about to make a new batcha biscuits."

Anna stepped from the sunlight into the dark single room that was Eichorn's bachelor nest. Her first impression of the place, just as when she had first seen him, was the ever-present black. To her right sat a black cast-iron cook stove, where a large blackened kettle bubbled over, water sizzling onto the heated top. Beside the stove stood a soot-encrusted cupboard, and next to that a matching table. A filthy dishtowel hung from a nail on the wall. To her left, Anna saw a jumble of dark bedclothes on a cot in the corner, and a single dirty window that did very little toward letting in light. She heard the chickens cackling from the next room.

"Yeah, built on all these rooms for a woman," Eichorn grumbled. "Turned out she wanted an engagement ring. A diamond. Can ya beat that? Told her t' fergit that idea."

She watched in silent fascination as the old man dumped a mound of flour into the pan he'd just cleaned by beating it on the wall outside. He sprinkled an indeterminate amount of baking soda on top, broke in several eggs, added water to the mess, and stirred it into a batter.

"Okay, we're all set for supper. Anna, would you mind taking the biscuits out of the oven when they's done? C'mon, Neil, let's go take care of the cows."

Neil grinned and winked at Anna over his shoulder as he went out the door. She stood in the center of all that dirt, not wanting to let loose of Monica's hand, just staring. Surely Neil wouldn't want to stay here and eat. She reached toward the grimy towel, thinking to clean the table, but stopped. Smearing dirt over dirt wouldn't do a bit of good.

"Monica, don't touch anything." Gingerly, she stepped to the stove, lifted the lid on the pot and recoiled from the musty odor. It was a pumpkin—a whole one—with a scum of mold floating on top of the water. "Let's go outside and wait until the 'biscuits' are done."

A little later, she went back inside, her lips pressed tight against her teeth, trying not to breathe too deeply of the must and dust and smell of stale grease. Anna opened the oven door and took out the biscuits. She set the pan on the cupboard and tested the contents by pressing a finger down on top. Hard as a rock.

She stepped outside again. "Come, honey, let's go watch Daddy and Jim."

The men quickly finished vaccinating about ten cows, and Anna's shoulders sagged with relief when Neil declined Eichorn's invitation to supper. "Thanks, Jim, but it's still early, and we had a big dinner. Some other time, huh?"

"Sure." Jim smiled his gap-toothed grin and stepped into the henhouse next to the corral. He came out with a big brown egg. "I need a little something after all that work, though." He stuck his thumb into the end of the egg, threw back his head and drank its contents. Anna's stomach lurched. She picked up Monica and turned toward the car. The little girl looked at her wide-eyed. "Mommy, can I have one, too?"

***

Anna went outside to greet Nettie and Jake when they drove in for a visit one evening. Monica was already asleep, and Neil still tinkered with the old Ford.

Jake stepped from the blue Buick. "What's wrong with the ol' girl?"

"I think she's on her last legs." Neil tipped his hat back and scratched his head. "But I don't know how we can afford another car our first year in business."

"Y'know, we don't really need a big car, just the two of us." Jake leaned against the Buick. "And you guys could use the extra room, with Monica growin' so fast an' all, so why don't you take this one?"

"Gosh, hate to take your car." Neil hesitated.

Go ahead, take it. Anna silently urged from the doorway.

"Nah." Jake took out his tobacco and papers. "We got the Jeep to get us where we want to go. We don't need two vehicles."

"Well, that'd sure help." Neil reached forward to shake his dad's hand. "Thanks."

Anna breathed a sigh of relief. *Yes, thank you, Lord.* She'd hated that old Ford ever since it wouldn't start just before she went into labor with Monica.

Before retiring for the night, the Mosers sat around the kitchen table, drinking wine Jake had brought and playing with the Border collie pup intended as a present for Monica. "Monica sure is sound asleep," said Nettie. "She didn't even wake up when the puppy barked."

It was six o'clock when Anna awoke the next morning. She looked over at Monica's bed—empty. She usually wasn't up this early. Alarmed, Anna jumped up and ran out to look for her. The little girl stood in the dusty yard, a big straw hat on her blond curls, her white nightgown swirling around her bare feet. The puppy her grandparents had brought was jumping at a stick she held. It snatched the piece of wood in its tiny teeth and shook it, growling. Monica giggled aloud, a musical sound that seemed to come from the bottom of her toes.

Oh yes, the dog. Anna smiled, filled with love watching her two-year-old daughter with her first puppy.

Nettie joined Anna on the porch.

"Nice morning." Anna brushed the hair from her eyes.

"Yes, it is."

"Was that mattress in the living room comfortable enough for you?"

"Oh, sure. It was fine." Nettie smiled, her face softening. "Thank you. You've done so much work on this place. It looks great."

Relief flooded Anna. Maybe her mother-in-law would be more accepting now. She watched her daughter awhile. Monica seemed to be their only common bond, besides Neil. "Thank you for the puppy. Monica sure seems to be enjoying it."

Nettie chuckled. "Yeah. They're pretty cute together."

"G'amma! See my doggie." Monica ran toward them, her hat flying off behind her. The pup followed her, yipping.

"What did you name him?" Nettie asked.

"Jackie," declared Monica.

Anna smiled. "Grandma brought you that puppy. Can you say thank you?"

"T'ank you, G'amma."

Nettie picked her up, singing, "I love you, a bushel and a peck, a bushel and a peck..."

"An'a hugga hugga neck," Monica finished, and flung her arms around her grandma, giving her a big kiss.

A great cascade of love flooded Anna's heart until she thought it might burst.

***

"We're goin' on into Billings today for the big bull auction," Jake announced at breakfast. "The 'boys' are goin' to be there, and we're all campin' at Margie and Glenn's tonight."

Margie Tester was Nettie's older sister, and the "boys" were her three younger bachelor brothers. Anna had met them once before at the Ingomar ranch. Ben, Chuck and Ed Brady, though in their early forties, had never married. They'd been nicknamed "the boys" when they were young and it had stuck.

Jake sat back in his chair. "Why don't you guys ride in with us?"

Monica started to climb out of her high chair. "Go in G'ampa's car!"

Anna slumped in her chair, hoping to become invisible. That's the way she felt, anyway, during these big group events. She might as well not be there. Oh, well, nothing she could do; she knew they would all go. Besides, she did like the "boys". When she'd first met the three bowlegged cowboys, they'd politely removed their hats, inclined their heads and greeted her, "Howdy, ma'am."

That simple welcome had completely won her over.

***

An air of festivity, along with the pungent odor of manure, permeated the late summer crowd at the Billings Auction Yard. A greasy odor from the café near the stands wafted through on an occasional breeze. The covered bleacher seats surrounding the arena were nearly filled already, with men and women dressed in their finest. The men all sported brightly colored western-style shirts, tight denim pants, cowboy boots and new, unstained hats. Anna smiled, thinking of the dirty, sweat-stained hats Neil and Jake usually wore. *Probably the only time these fancy hats are worn.* Although Anna felt out of place in her light blue paisley shirtwaist dress, she was probably a lot cooler than those women dressed in their long-sleeved shirts and denims.

The Brady "boys" welcomed her. Ben doffed his hat and Chuck shook her hand. Ed, the youngest, smiled. "So, this is your first auction, huh? Well, c'mon, let's find us some seats. We'll show ya how it works."

The Mosers and the Bradys filed into seats at the front of the stands surrounding the arena. Off to one side, pens held the red and white Hereford bulls Anna was familiar with, as well as others she hadn't seen before. "What are those big black ones?"

"They're black Angus from Scotland." Neil put an arm around her.

"We're gonna try and buy one of them," said Ed. "Thinkin' about cross breedin' with the Herefords. Hear they throw good, heavy calves."

A man wearing a large gray cowboy hat stepped up to the podium, grabbed a megaphone and pounded a gavel. "La-dees and Gen-tle-men, welcome to the third annual Billings Auction Yards bull sale. Now, if you cowhands will bring out the first one, we'll get this here auction started."

A couple of horsemen herded a group of bulls into the arena, and singled out one for sale. The auctioneer began his rhythmic chant. "Aaaand, who'll gimme five for this first fine specimen? Five-hunnerd-dollah-dollah, five-hunnerd-who'll-gimme-six...?" As he pointed at raised hands in the audience, the price began to climb. "Sold! For one thousand dollahs, to the gentleman in the second row over theeere."

Monica stood on the bench seat beside Anna, her mouth slightly open, her big blue eyes riveted on the auctioneer. She barely moved, watching his choreographed arm movements, captured by his sing-song cadence. Anna was mesmerized as well. She was surprised to find that she actually enjoyed herself. But how could the auctioneer tell who was bidding? She certainly wasn't able to keep up with the flash of hands or head nods.

Ben began bidding on a big, black, menacing-looking bull. It snorted and pawed the ground as the mounted cowboy tried to herd him around the ring.

"Got lotsa spirit," Ed said. "He's a beaut. He's gonna make a great sire."

Anna was caught up in the excitement as Ben bid against a white-haired rancher across the ring.

"Eight hunnerd." Ben touched his hat brim.

"Eight-fifty." The white-haired man waved his hat.

"Nine hunnerd."

"One thousand!"

Anna held her breath. Could the boys afford to go higher? Neil had taught her that having a good bull was so important in the cattle business. It determined calf size and quality, which in turn determined the price.

"Eleven hunnerd." Ben yelled.

"Eleven-fifty."

"Twelve," shouted Ben at the top of his lungs, the cords in his neck bulging. The sudden silence hung, palpable, over the ring. The bull snorted.

"Twelve hunnerd, going once... going twice... SOLD. To Mr. Brady there."

The crowd erupted in applause, as Ben wiped his forehead with his handkerchief. "Whew." Chuck clapped his brother on the back. "That was a close one."

Anna's adrenaline rush left her feeling as though she had been in a race. The mad dashes for the bomb shelter flashed through her mind. She shook off the chill and sat back to watch the next round of bidding.

"A-l-l right, folks. This fine Hereford has some purebred blood in his background. Let's start 'im out at seven-fifty..."

Before the auctioneer could get much farther into his spiel, a short bow-legged cowboy jumped from his seat just down the row from Anna and waved.

The auctioneer pointed at the man. "Sebben an'a half, sebben an'a half, how 'bout eight?"

A tall lanky farmer dressed in striped coveralls leaped from his bench near the first bidder. "Eight," he bellowed.

Ed leaned close to Anna and Neil. "Uh-oh. It's George against Hank. They got a feud agoin' now."

"Eight-fifty." The little cowboy danced around like a banty rooster.

"We got eight an'a half...eight—"

Before the auctioneer could finish, the farmer rose to his feet again. "NINE hundred."

Back and forth, on their feet now, the two men shouted their increasing bids, hardly allowing the auctioneer to get a word in edgewise. Nine-fifty, a thousand. Then they stopped.

The auctioneer took up his patter. "One thousand, we gotta thousand from George. Whatd'ya say, Hank, can you best 'im? One thousand, do I hear eleven hunnerd?"

The little cowboy stood silent for a moment, his feet planted wide, glaring at the farmer who just grinned back.

"Going once... Going twice..."

"Why, you gol-durned mule-headed sonuva..." The cowboy rushed forward and planted a fist alongside the taller man's jaw.

"Oh my." Anna gasped and pulled Monica into her lap. Her glance met Nettie's, also wide-eyed.

The farmer reeled backward, but like a rattlesnake, recovered with a roundhouse of his own. Then the two men were down on the ground just a few feet away, wrestling in the dust, throwing wild punches and yelling obscenities. The auctioneer bellowed. The crowd cheered.

Anna held Monica tighter. Neil turned his body to shield them.

194

Finally, a group of men got the fighters separated and led them out of the ring.

"Aaand, for your entertainment, ladees and gentlemen…" The auctioneer tried to make light of the fracas. "Sold. To George—for one thousand. Let's take a little break now." Jeers, cheers, and laughter followed his pronouncement.

Anna stood, her knees shaking. "Goodness. Does this kind of thing happen often at auctions?"

"Naw." Chuck put a big hand on her shoulder. "Don't be scared, ma'am. It's just George and Hank. They don't get along so good."

Anna raised her eyebrows. Oh, really? She'd never have guessed.

"C'mon, let's go over to the café for a cup of coffee and a piece of pie." Nettie spoke up.

Anna nodded. That sounded like a much safer proposition.

Leaving the boys after coffee to complete their transaction and arrange for shipping the bull, the Mosers drove to the Testers where they all gathered around a huge dining table. As if watching from outside, Anna watched the raucous family celebration that lasted well into the night.

"I couldn't believe you got such a good deal on that bull, Ben…"

"Did you see Hank and George?"

"That reminds me of the time…"

The clink of beer glasses, laughter, and good-natured teasing seemed warmly familiar, like something her big family would have done. Back home she would have been in the midst of the celebration. Here, Margie and Nettie held that place of honor. But maybe that's the way it should be. It was their family. She didn't have to just sit back and feel sorry for herself.

Anna took a swig of beer and turned to Ben. "I'm glad you didn't have to fight that man to get your bull."

Ben grinned. "Aw shucks, he'd a never stood a chance."

The room erupted in laughter. For just a moment, Anna froze, afraid she'd said something wrong and they were laughing at her. But as the "boys" clinked their glasses and guffawed, she joined in.

Later, after bedding Monica down with the other children, she and Neil lay under the stars in sleeping bags in Margie and Glenn's back yard.

"That auction certainly was exciting. Especially that fight." She snuggled against her husband. "I've never seen anything like it."

He chuckled. "Yeah. Thank goodness that's not an everyday occurrence. But the auction's not my favorite way of doing it. Too much pressure. Some people really enjoy it, though. It'll be a lot easier, the way we'll sell bulls, spring after next. The buyers will come to us, take their time to look them over and pick the best ones. That's more the way *I* like it."

Anna snuggled into her bedroll. She would like it that way too. This had been a fun day though. More like she was a part of the "family."

***

Anna picked up the heavy flatiron from the cook stove, wet her finger with the tip of her tongue, and tested its surface. The little sizzle told her it was hot enough. Then she ran the iron over a pair of Neil's heavy denim overalls. After some of the heat had dissipated, she picked one of his shirts out of the basketful of clothes she had sprinkled with water earlier and rolled to keep damp. She brushed wisps of hair from her sweaty forehead. It was another hot, dry morning, and Neil had gone out to the fields to see if the hay was ready to cut. Monica played with her dolls on the floor nearby.

Anna had hung up the last of her pressed housedresses and started to measure out some coffee grounds when she heard a vehicle drive up. It wasn't the sputtering backfire of Jim Eichorn's Jeep. She frowned. Besides, it was a little early for him to show up. He usually came just before suppertime.

Jackie barked. Monica jumped up and dropped her doll. "Somebody here."

Anna took her daughter by the hand and peered out the door. A slim, red-haired man, his face creased in a leathery smile, walked beside a woman attired in men's striped coveralls and work boots, laces flapping.

"Hello?" Anna called. Gosh, this woman was dressed like she was ready to work in the field.

"*Guten Tag*, are you Anna, *aus Deutschland*?" asked the woman in German.

Startled, Anna forgot the appropriate response.

"Hi. I'm Jack Sparks, and this here's my wife, Gertie. She's from Germany. We live north of Foster. We heard there was another German girl around here."

"*Ach, ja?*" Anna regained her composure. "Come in. This is my daughter, Monica."

The woman bent down to greet the little girl who tried to hide behind Anna. "So pretty. This is your dolly?" Gertie picked up the doll from the floor and held it out.

Monica nodded and stepped forward. "Raggedy Ann."

"How old are you?"

Monica held up two fingers, then stuck them in her mouth.

"Please, sit down. I was just about to make coffee." Anna scooped the pile of ironed shirts off the kitchen table, put them in the bedroom, and set the teakettle on to boil. Suddenly the questions tumbled out. "Where are you from? How long have you been here? How did you meet?"

Gertie answered in German and soon the two were chattering happily. Although Anna found the other woman difficult to understand, between her hometown dialect and the smattering of twisted English she threw in, for the first time in years Anna could talk to another woman in her native tongue.

Anna learned that Jack had been a member of the occupation forces as well, had met Gertie while she was tending bar in Stuttgart, and brought her back to the States.

With a bemused smile, Jack tilted his kitchen chair back on its legs, and worked a toothpick with the corner of his mouth.

When Neil came in, Anna's face was flushed. She was smiling and nearly babbling as she introduced Jack and Gertie. "They manage the Benny Binion ranch up north."

197

Neil shook Jack's hand. "He the guy who owns the casino in Las Vegas?"

Jack nodded. "Yeah, the Horseshoe Club."

"*Ja,* we jus' hollered a load of *Kuh's nach* Billings." Gertie spoke in a raspy cigarette voice, mangling both languages.

"Uh, we had to take in a bunch of old dries," Jack interpreted. "So, this is the old Foss homestead, huh? Pretty nice place." The men wandered outside to talk cattle, while the women continued to exchange histories.

Anna was almost giddy, like a young girl before the war. "Are you finding it difficult to be accepted here? Do people make fun of your accent?"

Gertie guffawed. "*Ja, ja.* I don't care what they think. If they don't like me they can go to—" She broke off when she noticed Monica hovering nearby.

Hmm. Anna smiled. Here was a woman who spoke worse English than Anna did, and she didn't even care. How could that be?

Jack stuck his head just inside the kitchen door. "C'mon, woman, we gotta hit the road."

Anna glanced at the clock. Almost noon. "Won't you stay for dinner?"

"*Ach, nein, danke.* We haff to get back."

"We'll see you folks. Maybe at a dance in Foster this summer," Jack offered.

Anna waved as they drove away and stood watching until they were out of sight before she went back inside.

She hummed as she prepared dinner. Mixing mashed potatoes with flour, eggs, breadcrumbs and onion, she dropped the potato dumplings into boiling water. The Sauerbraten beef brisket had marinated in vinegar and spices for three days, and was now roasting in the oven. *A woman from home.* It would've been nice if they'd stayed to eat. Despite Gertie's coarse language and manner, and the fact that they would probably never have been friends at home, Anna felt a kinship. She grinned. *Better than nothing.*

Neil took a seat at the kitchen table. "Well, what a nice surprise that was. Jack's a good guy. Did you like Gertie?"

Anna set dinner on the table and put Monica in her high chair. She couldn't keep the smile off her face. "Oh yes. She speaks funny, but it's so nice to talk to someone else from home."

"We'll have to get together with them again sometime."

Anna could hardly wait. She was already thinking of things to tell Gertie the next time they met, even though that might not be very soon. They lived at least thirty miles away. Too bad they didn't have a child Monica's age. At least there was a possibility of a woman friend who would understand her. Not like that Smith woman in Foster.

She slid onto her chair with a sigh and remembered where Neil had been. "Oh yes. How does the hay look?"

His face darkened. "We've got grasshoppers. I'm going to have to get out there and cut first thing in the morning before they eat it all. But I'm afraid we might lose our grain crop. It's not ready to harvest yet."

Anna's breath caught in her throat and her euphoria melted. "What do you mean?" There were a few grasshoppers every year, whirring suddenly from underfoot as she walked through the dry grass.

"Thousands of 'em. Happens every once in awhile. We get a real infestation."

"*Ach, nein.*" Grasshoppers. Like the locusts in the Bible. Yet another peril in this harsh land. Quite a first year on their own ranch—a tough winter, hard work, floods, then fire. Finally, the rains came to give the grain and grass a much-needed boost, and it had looked like they were going to have a good crop. But now the grasshoppers were here to destroy it. All that hard work...

CHAPTER SEVENTEEN

Ugh. Anna shuddered as she stared out the kitchen window. Grasshoppers swarmed like a moving pea-green carpet, devouring everything in their path.

"Outside? Play?" Monica's plaintive voice came from behind her.

"No, no, honey. Not today. Look. Grasshoppers." She certainly wouldn't let Monica go outside to play. When Neil drove, they rose in a cloud all around the car, and he had to turn on the windshield wipers to see. "It's a bug blizzard," he told Anna with a wry chuckle.

She dreaded going outside, but she needed to get a bucket of water, go to the outhouse, and gather the eggs. After she settled Monica down for a nap, she grabbed a broom and stepped out. Insect bodies crunched underfoot with every step she took. They swarmed, their wings chattering like a million rattlesnakes.

"Oh, you devils, you." A fury rose within her. "How dare you eat my grass, my flowers." She raised the broom above her head and brought it down to the ground with all her might. Whack! In a frenzy, Anna struck again and again. Grasshoppers flew in every direction. "I hate you. I hate you."

"Whoa, whoa." Neil's voice carried over the whirring and whacking commotion. He caught her by the arm. "*Liebchen,* stop."

Her breath came in gasps. Sweat rolled down her forehead. "Wha—?" Anna focused her eyes on her husband.

Neil encircled her with his arms. "It's okay, honey. I know they upset you. But you can't kill them all with a broom." He drew his head back and looked into her face with a smile.

Ach du lieber. She'd gone a little mad. Anna let herself relax in his arms. Then she smiled back. "Yes, but it sure was satisfying to try." They laughed together, then Anna gathered the eggs, and walked to the outhouse while Neil pumped water.

Days later, when the 'hoppers were gone, Anna's garden was a bare plot. With a leaden heart she found the rose bushes she had planted with so much hope in the spring were nothing but twigs. The wheat and barley fields were only stubble, and the pastures bare dirt in wide swathes where the swarms had passed. A hellish sight, almost as bad as the prairie that had been burned.

Anna lay awake at night, wondering if they would get enough money this fall to last through the next year. But at least she could feel thankful for the calf crop.

Summer waned, and with some grass left on parts of the ranch and extra hay Neil bought, the calves flourished. Prices were good that fall of '52, and Neil and Anna were able to buy replacement hay, seed for next year's crops, and still make their payment to the PCA.

***

Finally, an "open" winter. With little snow and warmer temperatures, Anna and Neil could relax a bit and enjoy pleasant winter days not having to fight for daily survival. She could handle *this* kind of winter.

Neil found an old Singer treadle sewing machine the Fosses had left up in the granary rafters. He hoisted it down with a winch, wiped the dirt off the oak cabinet, cleaned and oiled the mechanism. It still worked.

"It's beautiful." Anna ran a hand over the gilded scrollwork painted onto the black machine head. She and Neil squeezed it into a corner of their little bedroom, under the north window. During the winter afternoons, after they'd done their feeding and chores, Neil sat down with Anna and they pored over patterns she'd collected before her disastrous sewing experience with Nettie. Now, maybe she could make clothes for Monica and a new dress or two for herself. She cut out the thin tissue pieces, ironed them flat, then laid out the pieces on the kitchen table first one way, then another.

Anna pinned one piece to the fabric, fumbled, and ripped the fragile paper. "Darn it." She stood back, hands on her hips. "This is supposed to be a sleeve. It doesn't look like a sleeve."

Neil read the directions. "Who writes this stuff anyway? Nobody could figure this out."

She shook her head with a rueful smile, remembering the fiasco when she and Nettie had tried to sew. And Anna had thought it was because she was dumb.

With Neil's help and interpretation, Anna tried again and again. She pricked her fingers with pins, sewed seams, and ripped them out. Finally, when the first attempt at a simple skirt for Monica was finished, she threw it on the floor in disgust. "Everything is crooked. It looks like Monica made it."

"Well, it's only your first try." Neil tried to console her. "You know, when I first started playing the violin, my teacher would give me one scale or phrase and told me to play it a hundred times."

Anna laughed. "Yes. Practice makes perfect, *ja*? But we can't afford to buy that much material for me to make one hundred mistakes."

"The next one will be better, I know it will." Neil took out the pattern. "Let's try it again. I'll help you."

Gradually, as Anna practiced, she became more comfortable with the patterns and the sewing machine. She cut dresses for Monica out of her old full skirts. For her own housedresses, she used the colorful printed flour sack material—now discontinued—that she had saved the past couple of years. She hung her latest creation on a hanger and stood back to admire the dress. This was more like it. Now, she felt like she could accomplish something. And, she didn't have to walk around in the same old clothes all the time.

As the days lengthened into spring, she and Neil worked in their yard, cleaning up winter debris and raking dead grass, while Monica and Jackie chased each other around the house. Anna watched her daughter shriek and giggle with her pup.

She's growing so fast. Just three, she was already as tall as Roy Thompson who was a year older.

Neil surveyed the house. "We should probably think about putting some siding over these boards. It would make the house last longer."

Anna's hopes soared. "That would be so nice." Oh, maybe she could have her white house after all.

"We've got a little calf money left over after making our loan payment. I think it would be a wise investment." Neil gave a resolute nod. "Let's go in to Lewistown tomorrow and see what we can find."

The next morning Anna dressed in her brown tweed suit and put a gingham dress on Monica, but took along winter coats, coveralls, and blankets, just in case. Her excitement and anticipation seemed to help the 110 miles pass more quickly than usual.

It was nearly noon when they arrived in the little town nestled in the Snowy Mountains. "Let's have a hamburger at the Woolworth's lunch counter," Neil suggested.

Anna led Monica by the hand through the "dime store," gazing at the knick-knacks and gee-gaws on the shelves as they passed. Woolworth's had everything from hairpins and ribbons to fabric and clothing. It had been a long time since anything cost only a dime, though.

She sat on a red plastic stool next to Neil, with Monica on her lap.

The waitress handed them each a stained menu. "Coffee?"

"*Ja*, please." Anna flushed. Oops, she'd forgotten again and lapsed into German. Just one word, thankfully. She breathed a sigh of relief.

The waitress raised her eyebrows, then filled two coffee cups. "Whatcha gonna have?" She snapped her gum, pencil poised above her notepad.

"Vat is your Zoup today?" Anna asked. Oh, why did she always forget the correct pronunciation when she was out among people?

"We-have-TURKEY-NOODLE-soup." The young girl raised her voice and spoke slowly, rounding her lips in an exaggerated manner.

Anna's mood deflated. *Here we go again.* As if she were deaf. Just like when she first landed in America. "Fine. I'll have the soup, thank you." She spoke deliberately, making sure her "s" hissed and her "th" didn't sound like a "t".

She felt Neil tense beside her, saw his jaw clench. She stiffened too. *Oh, please don't say anything. I don't want to cause a scene.* But he took a breath, reached behind, and rubbed her back. "I'll have a hamburger deluxe and a vanilla shake." He looked at Anna. "I'll share with Monica."

Anna nodded. Maybe if she just stayed home, she wouldn't always have to go through this humiliation.

The waitress brought their food. The soup was tasty, hot and thick with home-made noodles. After eating, Anna felt better. *Nothing like good soup for what ails you.*

At the lumberyard, Anna and Neil, carrying Monica, wandered around, looking at the siding options. It quickly became clear they couldn't afford the nice bright white stuff. Anna gazed at it with longing.

"Sorry, honey. Maybe in a few years." Neil pointed to another display. "This is going to be in our price range. Finally, they picked out an inexpensive, asbestos siding that looked like tan bricks.

So much for her dream—at least for now. Maybe they could whitewash it someday. She had to hang on to the hope that their situation would gradually get better. They'd already done very well their first year in ranching. Anna straightened her shoulders.

Over the next few days, working together, she and Neil soon had the old gray boards covered.

When they finished, Anna stepped back and surveyed the new look. Well, it wasn't her white cottage with a picket fence and roses blooming in the front yard, but it certainly was an improvement.

Anna planted rose bushes again, hoping the grasshoppers wouldn't return, and spread some field grass seed in a small area around the house. If the rain continued, at least the house would be surrounded by a bit of green.

The spring had been beautiful, cool and rainy, so when the sun did shine, the countryside popped into bloom. It was the greenest she'd ever seen it here in America, and for the first time in five years, she felt hope and contentment. With less cold and snow during the winter, the cows had stayed fat and were able to give good nourishment to the calves they carried. They'd had another good calf crop this spring, and so far the grain and hay looked lush and thick. This was why she'd come to America—the land of milk and honey. She grinned. And love, of course.

In the evenings, they sat at the kitchen table. Anna read aloud by kerosene lantern light to perfect her English pronunciation. That waitress in Lewistown still irked her. It happened all too frequently whenever they went to town. And the incident at the Missionary Society meeting in Foster last year still stung.

Anna was determined to speak perfect English. Not like Gertie Sparks. The woman's lack of concern for the way she spoke appalled Anna. While she did enjoy getting together with another woman from Germany occasionally, she couldn't quite relate to Gertie on her level.

"You have to tell me when I pronounce something wrong," she often reminded Neil.

Perusing the *Foster Tribune* one evening, she came across an announcement that a circuit judge, who doubled as an immigration officer, would appear at the courthouse once a month for any trials, marriages, citizenship transfers, and other court-related business.

Anna stared at the page. Citizenship. A spark of desire leaped inside. Yes, it was time. Maybe people would accept her then. She'd be one of them. An American.

She looked over at Neil, bent over a European history book. "I think I'd like to study for my citizenship test."

Her husband looked up, his glasses reflecting the lamplight. He reached out and took her hand in both of his. "That would make me very proud."

The next day Anna sent for the application and study book to prepare for the questions the immigration officer would be asking to test her knowledge of the English language and U.S. history.

Every evening she pored over the book then asked Neil to quiz her. "What is the term for a U.S. senator and how many are there?"

Anna closed her eyes. *Senator or representative. Which was which?* "Oh, for heaven's sake. I can't remember all this! I'll never get it! I won't be able to become a citizen!" she wailed.

"No, honey. You're doing so well. They won't be asking all these questions anyway," Neil reassured her and reviewed the correct answers.

She continued to study late into the nights. After the harvest, she made an appointment to see the judge for the naturalization process the next time he came to Foster.

It was a crisp fall day, the sun warming the air gradually as it climbed the sky, the leaves on the cottonwood trees by the creek just beginning to show a touch of yellow. Anna took her hair out of pin curls and brushed it carefully into waves. She dressed in her brown tweed wool suit with her grandmother's brooch at the neck of her white blouse. Her fingers fumbled with the clasp, and she had to stop, take a deep breath and look at herself in the mirror.

"Stop being so nervous." She spoke out loud to her image wavering in the mirror. "You've studied hard. You know all the material. You'll do just fine."

Neil cast an admiring glance at her as she and Monica climbed into the car. "The judge won't be able to help but grant citizenship to such a beautiful lady. He won't even have to ask you any questions."

Anna laughed and relaxed against the seat.

The courtroom was dark and cool as they entered and took seats in front of the judge's raised desk. The room was nearly empty, but Mel and Vickie Thompson had come to vouch for Anna's identity, and a few clerks from the rest of the courthouse filtered in to watch the proceedings. The judge—tall and broad-shouldered—emerged from the back room and arranged his black robes as he sat in the wooden swivel chair.

Anna gulped, her mind filled with memories of German authorities smashing her hopes to immigrate to America.

With a stern face, the judge riffled through some papers, then rapped his gavel twice, and called out, "Mrs. Anna Moser, please come forward."

For a moment, Anna was afraid her legs wouldn't carry her as far as that huge desk. A heel wobbled and she paused, swallowing hard. Neil put his hand on her arm and squeezed. She willed herself to move forward.

Monica stood upright on the bench seat as Anna went forward. "Mommy," she whimpered.

"I have a few questions for you, Mrs. Moser," the judge announced in a loud voice. "Do you understand English?"

Anna nodded and drew in a mass of stale air.

The judge continued. "What are the colors of our flag?"

"What is the fourth of July?"

"What is Independence Day?"

Anna heard Monica whimper and steeled herself not to listen. She didn't want to miss the answer to any of the questions

The judge glanced over at Monica and smiled sympathetically at Anna. "You're doing well. Let's go on. Who is our president today?"

"What are the duties of the Supreme Court?"

Neil heard Anna's soft voice, answering each question perfectly. He grinned, his lungs expanding. *I knew she could do it.*

Monica trembled beside him and reached forward. "Mommy." A tear rolled down her cheek.

"Sshh." Neil put his arm around her. The judge's voice became a loud sing-song cadence as he questioned Anna.

"No. No." Monica screamed. "They're going to sell Mommy!"

Neil picked her up to take her out of the courtroom. She grabbed hold of the arm of the wooden bench and hung on, but the armrest came along with her as he carried her out.

Neil murmured to Monica and patted her back as he walked her up and down the hall, trying not to telegraph his nervousness to his daughter.

"Sell Mommy?" she whimpered.

"No, no, sweetie. This isn't like the auction with the animals. Mommy is fine. She's just talking to the nice man. We'll go home soon and Mommy will come with us, okay?" Finally able to calm Monica's fears, Neil took her back into the courtroom.

Judge Williams was still asking Anna questions.

"Whose rights are guaranteed by the Constitution and the Bill of Rights?"

"What is the most important right granted to U.S. citizens?"

When Anna had answered the last question, the judge boomed, "Congratulations, Mrs. Moser. You're the only person I've ever seen who answered all the questions correctly. Let's continue on with the swearing-in ceremony right now. Mr. Moser, you may come forward and stand next to your wife if you'd like."

Grinning, barely able to keep himself from cheering, Neil carried Monica, now also smiling, to the front and stood beside his wife.

"Raise your right hand and repeat after me the Oath of Allegiance to the United States of America. 'I hereby declare, on oath… I absolutely and entirely renounce and abjure…all allegiance and fidelity…to any foreign prince, potentate, state or sovereignty…of whom or which I have heretofore been a subject or citizen'…"

Anna repeated the phrases in a clear, strong voice, pronouncing the difficult words with ease.

Pride filled Neil's soul. Look at what his wife had done. She was so brave. To move all the way to America—for him. To learn the language so well. And now to adopt his country as hers. He blinked rapidly behind his glasses.

"Welcome, Anna Rose Schmidt Moser, you are now a naturalized citizen of the United States of America." The judge beamed.

Neil applauded. Monica clapped her hands too, and reached for Anna who took her daughter into her arms. The rest of the small audience joined in, then crowded around Anna to shake her hand.

"I am an American." Pride made her voice husky.

Over a celebratory dinner at the Rancher's Café, Anna asked, "What happened with Monica at the courthouse?"

"She apparently associated the ceremony with what she saw at the auction last spring." Neil laughed. "She thought you were going to be sold. The judge did sound a little like that auctioneer."

Anna hugged her daughter. "No, honey, people don't get sold, like the cows do. I'm still here with you." She blinked back tears and looked into Neil's eyes. "It's over." She sat a little taller. "I did it!"

***

In late October, four-year-old Monica grew listless and fussy. She didn't want to play with her toys or sing the usual long ballads she made up while following Mommy around the house. Puzzled, Anna felt her daughter's forehead. "No wonder. It's burning up."

Monica wailed and brushed her hands through her hair. "My head is burning?"

"No, no, honey. I just meant your forehead is very warm. You have a fever." She smoothed back the little girl's hair. "You might have the flu. Come, I'll give you some medicine." Anna gave her half an aspirin, applied hot compresses to her chest and put her to bed.

All afternoon, she kept going into the bedroom to check on Monica, who slept feverishly. What could it be? Her child had been so healthy, hardly even had colds. She tried to remember ailments and remedies from her nursing days.

When Neil came in for supper, Anna relayed her worries. "I can't figure out where we have been that she would be exposed to something. You were at the store today—did you hear if anyone around here is sick?"

He shrugged and sat at the kitchen table. "No. These germs just float around sometimes. I'm sure she'll be fine in a day or two."

But after several days, Monica felt no better. She cried and refused to walk. "My leg hurts, Mommy."

Fear swept through Anna like a prairie fire. She called Neil in from the barn. "I don't know what to do anymore. This is not just the flu. Why can't she walk? We need to take her to the doctor."

Neil furrowed his brow and peered at his daughter, lying in bed, not moving. "Yes, we'd better take her in to Foster." He wrapped her in a blanket and carried her to the car.

At the hospital, kindly, gray-haired Doctor Farnam took Monica's temperature and listened to her heart. She whimpered as he examined her left leg. He held up a fistful of lollipops. "Here you go, dear; which color would you like?"

She chose orange and immediately stuck it in her mouth, tears still trickling down her cheeks.

The doctor stretched and massaged the leg, looked down her throat, and listened to her heart, all the while keeping up a gentle banter to soothe her fears.

Anna kneaded her fingers. Maybe they should've brought Monica in sooner.

After a while he turned from the examining table. "Well, Anna, Neil … I don't know what to tell you. I think it's just a virus, but I'd like to keep her here in the hospital a couple of days for some more tests and observation."

Anna gasped and covered her mouth with her hands to keep from crying out. Her baby in the hospital. *Ach, du lieber Gott*, what could this be? Her glance flew to Neil's face.

He put an arm around her, and with the other, drew Monica off the table onto his lap. "We'd better let the doctor keep an eye on her, see what he can figure out. You'll be able to stay here with her. It'll be all right."

The rest of the day Anna helped the nurses keep moist heat packs on Monica's leg. She lay there so listless and occasionally awoke whimpering with pain. At nearly midnight, Anna still sat beside her daughter's bed, watching her sleep. *Poor little one.* What more could she do to help? She couldn't remember seeing anything like this during her nursing career. She closed her eyes, picturing her nurse's textbook, comparing her daughter's symptoms to what she had learned. Nothing came to mind.

Maybe it was just growing pains. But what if she had some terrible disease and died?

Anna apparently was not one of those women who easily conceived, like Kathleen McKinnon in Foster who'd also been married five years and already had four children. Monica could be her only child. A shiver passed through her body. Anna couldn't bear to think of it any more. She leaned on the bed and buried her face in the blanket next to her daughter.

Over the next two days, Monica was poked for blood draws, wheeled off for x-rays, and prodded so much that she screamed as soon as a nurse came into the room. Her leg continued to hurt, and she still couldn't walk on it.

Dr. Farnam shook his head. "I'm sorry. After all the tests, I'm no closer to knowing what's wrong. Near as I can tell, it's simply a virus that'll have to run its course. I don't think it's anything to worry about. But I think I'll go ahead and put a cast on that leg. Maybe immobilizing it will cut down on the pain."

Neil came in the evening to take Monica and Anna home. The plaster cast helped, strangely enough. Monica could walk, stiff-legged, and she rested the cast on the back of her tricycle to push it around like a scooter.

Anna watched her every minute and felt her forehead often. She was afraid Monica would fall or that her fever would come back. She fretted her daughter wouldn't be able walk again after the cast came off. Anna's fears kept her awake at night.

Gradually, Monica regained her spunky spirit and soon followed Anna around, telling stories again. After a month, when the cast came off, she regained her walking skills quickly. Then Anna could take a deep breath and feel some relief.

Only when the little girl played too hard and became overtired, did her leg begin to hurt again. Anna and Neil gently massaged the limb, put hot towels on it, and sang her to sleep.

***

"Y'know," Charley Stokley reached into the warren of boxes for the Mosers' mail at the Horse Creek Store, "I heard the Dougherty girl—they live 'way down along the river—had polio a while back. She was purty sick, left her with a deformed foot."

"Hmm. That's too bad." Neil sorted absently through a keg of nails. Anna barely paid attention as she gathered up a few cleaning supplies and added a can of ground coffee to her basket. She glanced at the withered produce—good thing she had her garden and canned vegetables—before taking her selections to the counter.

"Yup. Lotsa weird sickness in the world." Charley wrote each item on a receipt pad to put on their charge account.

On the trip home Monica sang in the back seat, munched on Cracker Jacks and studied the three-dimensional picture that was the prize in the box. Anna frowned. Charley's remark niggled at her brain. She looked over at Neil. "Do you think it's possible that Monica had this polio?"

Neil jerked his head toward her. "What?" He turned his attention back to the road. "I-I sure don't know. Do you?"

Anna tried to remember what she had learned in nurse's training. Her head throbbed. "The only thing I remember about it is paralysis and seeing pictures of people's heads

212

sticking out of 'iron lungs'." Machines the size of a small car pushed and pulled on their chests, breathing for them. Most of those people died. Her eyes burned with tears. "Wasn't the American president, Franklin Delano Roosevelt, in a wheelchair because of polio?"

Neil furrowed his brow. "Yeah, that's right, he was. And I remember reading in *LIFE* magazine something about swimming pools in the large cities being closed to prevent the spread."

Anna swallowed hard. It couldn't be. "Monica wasn't around anyone with polio. She wasn't paralyzed. She wasn't deformed. She had severe leg pain."

"I know." Neil nodded. "I don't think it was polio. It doesn't make any sense."

But throughout the weeks, the thought kept returning like a homing pigeon: What if the disease had been polio? What if it came back? What if Monica did end up crippled?

One evening after Monica had gone to bed, they sat sipping wine in front of the oil burner in the living room, still a rare treat for them in the winter. The Christmas tree was decorated in the corner, but Anna didn't feel especially festive. "I keep having these dreams that Monica died of polio. They make me so afraid." She dipped her head and stared at her hands twisting in her lap. "And I haven't been able to give you more children… "

"Oh, sweetheart, that is the least of my worries." Neil encircled her shoulders with an arm. "She's okay now. We just have to thank God it didn't happen that way, and enjoy our little girl."

CHAPTER EIGHTEEN

Anna puttered in the kitchen, baking a chocolate cake, and putting a roast and potatoes in the oven for their noon meal. February 11, 1955—Anna's thirty-first birthday. Neil had told her to take the morning off from helping him feed. She spent the time pinning up her hair and dressing in her one good outfit, the brown tweed suit. Her mouth turned up at the corners as she felt the stirrings of new life inside her. She wanted this day to be special.

Five-year-old Monica sat at the kitchen table, drawing pictures. "How do you spell 'Daddy'? Show me how to make a "D'. How do you spell 'run'?" She asked about each word, as she wrote a little story to go with her illustrations. "See, Mommy. This is you, baking a cake for your birthday, an' this is Daddy, feeding the cows, an' here's me and my doggie running in the snow."

Anna leaned over to look. "That's very good, honey. Look at that. You're making your letters so nice. You'll have to show Daddy when he comes in."

Anna swirled a whipped cream frosting on the cake. She set out the good china with miniature pink and blue flowers entwined around the edges. The set Neil had bought before their wedding. Her face flushed with happiness.

At noon Neil burst through the door, carrying the mail. "Boy, it smells good in here." He stopped, cocked his head to one side as his eyes traveled from her waved hair to her high heels. "Oooh, don't you look nice. Happy birthday, sweetheart." He whipped an envelope from behind his back, presenting Anna with a card and a small package. "And ... the mail ..." He waved the familiar blue airmail envelope.

"*Ach*, a letter from home." Anna sat at the table and ripped it open, tears trickling down to her smile.

"What'sa matter, Mommy? Why are you crying?" Monica hurried over to her mother and lay her head in Anna's lap.

"It's okay, sweetie. I'm just happy, because I got a letter from *Oma*, and your daddy brought me a card and a present." The wave of homesickness every time she had a letter from Germany still amazed her. Anna stroked Monica's blonde curls as she read the birthday card and letter. Hans's little girl, Uli, the same age as Monica, was already in Kindergarten. How Anna wished her daughter had the same opportunity. Mutti and Papa were well, thank the Lord. She smiled a secret little smile. She would have some happy news to write back.

Anna folded the tissue paper, then stood up to put dinner on the table.

Neil poured dark beef gravy onto the mashed potatoes and cut into his roast. He took a bite and chewed slowly. "Mmmm. This is delicious. I'm sorry you had to cook your own birthday dinner, though."

"That's all right," Anna smiled. "I wanted everything to be just right, because I have some very special news…"

Neil lifted his gaze from his food. "Yes?"

She lowered her eyelids and felt a flush begin at the base of her neck. "We're going to have another baby."

Neil dropped his fork and leaped up from his chair, almost pulling the embroidered linen tablecloth with him. He ran around the table to Anna, encircled her with his arms, and gave her a tender kiss. "Wow. That *is* special. Happy birthday, my darling."

"What? What?" Monica gave her parents a puzzled look.

Anna leaned over to tousle Monica's blonde hair. "You're going to get a little baby brother or sister."

Monica's blue eyes grew round. "I am? Oh goody. Can I have a sister?"

***

Spring seemed brighter, greener, the bursting colors of the prairie infused with a golden glow in Anna's mind. She pored over baby clothes in the catalogs and sent for her garden seeds. She sang as she planted her garden and a half-acre of potatoes along the edge of a field near the house. She once again planted roses, to replace the ones that had been winter-killed.

This time, they'll bloom, she promised herself.

With each new calf she recorded in their logbook, Anna smiled at Neil, feeling a miniature flutter inside her belly.

"Good girl, little Rosebud." She watched a young cow licking her new baby. "I know you're going to be a good mother."

One early-summer afternoon, Anna looked out the window to see Mel and Vickie Thompson drive up. A wave of happiness washed over her. Of all the neighbor women, she felt the most comfortable with Vickie. A down-to-earth, no-nonsense woman, she had never slighted Anna's accent or her struggles to better her English, and she had always been encouraging. Best of all, little Roy and Monica loved playing together. There were no other children their age in the neighborhood. Vickie was also excited about Anna's pregnancy. She, like Anna, wasn't able to easily conceive. The two women had discussed the social stigma of not having large families.

Anna made fresh coffee and served oatmeal raisin cookies as the two couples sat outdoors on the shady north side of the house. The field grass she had planted had survived and created a pleasant lawn.

Roy and Monica romped in the grass. After a few minutes, he marched over to the adults and announced, "I'm gonna marry Little Monica. Is that okay, Big Monica?" Everyone laughed.

"Of course, my dear." Anna gave the kids each a cookie, and they ran off again.

"Aaah, this is nice." Vickie sighed. "I never could get anything to grow by our house. I've really enjoyed these Sunday afternoon visits at your house, Anna. They've always been a treat for us."

"Yes, and when this baby is born, Roy and Monica will have one more to play with." Anna looked into her neighbor's face to see tears pooling in her eyes. Oh-oh, maybe she shouldn't have mentioned the baby. "What's wrong, Vickie?"

Vickie caught her breath and shook her head, unable to speak. Mel leaned forward. "We're going to move away soon. Roy will be ready for school this fall, and there isn't any here for him to attend. We've found a little place to lease near Big Timber, between Billings and Bozeman."

A dark cloud passed over Anna's cheery thoughts. Sure. The only woman in the neighborhood she'd thought might become a close friend... And the only child around for miles Monica could play with... *Himmel*. Was there only to be disappointment in this God-forsaken place? Every time things seemed to be going well... Had she done something so terrible in her life that she was destined to be punished whenever she was happy? She felt herself withdrawing from the little group, as though she were on the outside, watching herself go through the motions of pouring coffee, passing the plate of cookies. She didn't recall much of what they'd talked about during the rest of the Thompson's visit.

That evening, after a quiet supper, Neil looked over Monica's story-drawings. "The Thompsons moving does bring up the question, what are we going to do next year, when Monica's ready for school?"

She shrugged. "I don't know. We certainly can't drive thirty miles into Foster twice every day, or fifty miles to Wynona—clear in the next county." The irritation flashed like lightning in her brain. Why had Neil even brought up the subject right now?

"I wish we'd moved someplace closer to a town." With a swish of her skirts, Anna stomped into the bedroom and closed the door with a thump.

***

Neil put resin on his bow, then sat, silently fingering the strings on the violin. He knew pregnancy was hard on women,

217

and he thought he could understand the disappointment of losing their neighbors. But what could he do to make it different? He was at a loss. He didn't know what to say to her, or what to do next. It was probably best to leave her alone for a while.

"Daddy, play 'Pop! Goes the Weasel'." Monica's eager voice broke into his introspection. She loved this song, especially when he plucked the string at the word "pop."

He began to play and sing, "...Round and round the cobbler's bench, the monkey chased the weasel... Pop! Goes the weasel."

Monica danced around his chair; the string plunked, and she burst forth with her high-pitched giggle. "Play it again, Daddy!"

He grinned and blinked back a tear. How he adored his little girl. He wanted to keep her wound tight around his heart, never let her go. How could he protect her from the bruises of life, the ones that seemed to plague her mother?

Neil watched Monica dance and chase the dog Jackie around his chair, her curls bouncing. She had recently started to follow him around everywhere. She "helped" him with chores, rode on the tractor, and every evening, when he milked the cow, Monica brought her little tin cup for a squirt of fresh warm milk. He chuckled. She loved her milk.

He found, almost to his surprise, how much he enjoyed her company. Yes, that doctor had been dead wrong—Neil didn't need a son to feel like a man.

"Again, Daddy." Monica grinned up at him.

"Okay. Here goes. 'Round and round the cobbler's bench...'"

Apparently unable to stay away from the music and laughter, Anna finally came out of the bedroom. She put an arm around each of them. "Sorry. I'm just so disappointed that Monica is losing her playmate."

Neil kissed her and patted her rounded stomach. "Don't worry. Soon there will be a built-in playmate for her."

CHAPTER NINETEEN

When the time came for Neil to go into the fields to cut hay, he moved the equipment to the leased acreage on what had originally been the Tucori homestead, about ten miles south of the highway. Last summer Anna drove the tractor and raked up the loose hay after it had been cut. Although this year she was too far along in her pregnancy to help, she and Monica went along.

She spread a blanket in the shade of the old house abandoned by the homesteaders. As always, her curiosity was aroused by the remnants of the early settlers. This house, boarded up now with the porch sagging, looked like it had been well built, not just another sod hut. In fact, Neil had told her that Jake and Nettie had lived there briefly before settling on their ranch at Ingomar.

Anna leaned back on the blanket, imagining the homesteaders working hard on their land and building this house. What had made them leave? Perhaps it was the drought and hard times of the 1930s. Nettie had told her how often they'd had to move to find grass for their horses—twenty-some years ago. That must have been hard.

"Read to me, Mommy." Monica put down her coloring book and scooted up close. Anna picked up her book, a biography of Dale Evans, rodeo and movie queen, and read aloud of Dale and Roy Rogers and his famous palomino, Trigger.

Monica sat, spellbound. "Can I have a palomino horse, Mommy?"

"Not till you're a little older, honey."

Monica took the book and gazed at the pictures. "Can I learn to read, too?"

Anna looked at her daughter thoughtfully. "Yes, you'll learn to read soon." At least she hoped so.

When Neil shut down his mower and joined them in the shade for dinner, Anna again brought up the question. "What *are* we going to do about school? She wants to learn to read so bad."

Neil looked at the coltish little girl poring over the book, more interested in it than in eating. "Well, I guess we'll have to find some books and start teaching her ourselves."

Anna did a double-take. Wow. She still didn't feel that confident about her own English. Could she teach her daughter to read? She might teach her the wrong accent and pronunciation. If there never were a school in the neighborhood, she would have to help her get through all eight grades. The idea loomed like a huge brick wall before her.

"Let's go in to Foster, talk to the superintendent of schools," Neil suggested one evening after reading Monica to sleep.

"That's a good idea." Anna hung up the dishtowel and put away the dishpans. Another fall had arrived with no school, and Monica would be six in December.

The next day they drove the thirty miles to Foster to visit with the county superintendent. She was sympathetic. "There's that empty schoolhouse near Horse Creek, just no kids in your neck of the woods to start classes."

"What should we do?" Anna asked. "We can't drive into town every day. Monica is so eager to learn to read." Beside her, Monica nodded, eyes shining bright with anticipation.

The woman pushed her glasses up on her nose. "I know. There are a number of families in the county that are in a similar situation. I can give you a recommendation for some pre-primer readers, and you can at least get her started now. She's still a little young yet, so I'm not too worried about her getting behind. Then, by next year, if there's still no possibility of a school in your area, I can help you with books for other subjects."

"Thank you." Neil stood and put on his hat. "You've been very helpful."

The superintendent gave him a sheet of paper. "You can order the 'Mac and Muff' series from this address, but in the meantime, if you want to check the first book out of the library, you could get her started right away."

"Oh, goody." Monica fidgeted while Anna and Neil said their good-byes. They left the office and walked down the dusty street to the tiny library, up the stairs above the drugstore. When she walked into the room filled with wall-to-wall books, Monica stopped and gasped. "Oh, Mommy, Daddy. Look."

Neil grinned. "Yeah. Isn't it wonderful? Look, here are the children's books."

Monica ran over, grabbed several books off the shelf, and sank to the floor to pore over them. Anna and Neil talked to the librarian about checking out the readers. "Are there some books you'd like to take home?" Neil asked Monica.

"Oh. Can I?" She looked up, her eyes wide. "Can I take them all?"

The librarian chuckled. "I know the feeling."

"You can pick out four. We can take them for a month, then bring them back and get some more," Neil explained.

The Mosers went home armed with books. The next day they went to the abandoned schoolhouse to borrow a little school desk, and started teaching Monica to read.

Anna and Monica had "school" every morning. Since Monica already knew her letters—at five she had begged until Neil showed her the ABCs—she caught onto words with just a little prompting. "Mac. Muff. See Mac run. See Muff run." She giggled. "Mommy, I can read." Whenever Neil came into the house, she rushed up to him with her book. "Daddy, let me read to you."

Pride filled Anna like water rushing into a newly dug well. Her daughter was learning to read and write and Anna was teaching her—in English. She could do it. Such a short time ago she hadn't known enough of the language to read these simple children's books. Monica already knew her numbers and how to count, so perhaps it wouldn't be so difficult to teach her other subjects if Anna needed to. Neil was good in history and world events, so he could help there. In the meantime, she would pray that somehow a school would open.

One morning after "school" was done, Anna went out to check on her daughter's whereabouts. Monica sat at a wooden crate inside the old coal shed outside the house. She had dragged in several large pieces of cardboard for a clean "floor," and had a stack of papers and several newly sharpened pencils on her "desk."

Anna poked her head inside the low door. "What are you doing?"

"I'm writing," Monica replied with a serious nod. "Writing books."

"That's wonderful, honey." With a big smile, Anna headed to the garden to get carrots and potatoes for dinner. She sighed as she waddled, and rested her hands on her large abdomen. The baby was supposed to have been due the first week of September, and the end of the month quickly approached.

"Have patience," the doctor kept telling her at her checkups in Foster. "The baby will show up when it's ready."

She brushed the hair out of her eyes. This child showed no signs of making an appearance. Well, on with life. She might as well go out this afternoon after dinner and get those potatoes dug out there on that half-acre. Maybe the activity would get things started.

Anna put her foot on the shovel giving it a push, stabbing into the hard ground, then turned the dirt to expose the red "earth apples." She bent, barely able to reach the ground. Spreading her stance wider to give her belly room, she tried again, picked up the potatoes and put them into a gunnysack. Monica helped for a while, then went off to play in the dirt, building mountains and rivers. The sun was hot and penetrating, still warming the early fall days like summer.

Up and down. Anna dug and stooped, picked up potatoes, and dropped them into the bag. Up and down. She wiped the sweat from her face with a corner of her apron and wished for her old, slender self again under the voluminous maternity housedress.

About five o'clock, she heard the Buick engine rev as Neil drove up, coming from the south acreage where he had been raking straw in the harvested fields.

"Good heavens, honey, stop that right now." He jumped from the Buick. "You shouldn't be digging potatoes in your condition." He took Anna by the arm and helped her into the car, then loaded the potato sacks into the trunk. "C'mon, Monica, let's go home."

Neil made Anna lie down while he prepared a supper of cold roast beef on homemade wheat bread. "I am a little tired," she admitted. "I think I'll rest awhile, eat later." She fell asleep while Neil and Monica ate and cleaned up the kitchen. She awoke in darkness and sat straight up with a cry of pain. Neil charged into the bedroom.

"It's time, isn't it?" He combed a hand through his thick hair.

"It worked." Anna groaned. "Digging the potatoes started my labor. The baby is coming."

The thirty-five miles to Foster seemed to take forever. The headlights slashed the dark narrow highway as Neil pushed the accelerator to the floorboard. "Come on, old girl, you can go faster," he urged, as if the Buick could hear him.

Anna groaned and panted each time the hot, piercing pains hit. *Ach du lieber.* How could she have forgotten how much it hurt? The car hit a pothole, and she let out a cry.

"How're you holding up?" With a grimace that mimicked her own, Neil glanced over at her.

"Can't we...go...faster? Water...broke." She panted wildly now.

Monica whimpered in the back seat. "Mommy, are you sick?"

"Mommy's okay, honey. We're taking her to the hospital, so she can have the baby. You'll have your little sister or brother soon!"

Just when Anna thought someone surely must have given a yank at one end to stretch the road out longer, she saw the shadow of the hill at the edge of town. As they crested the rise, the few twinkling lights of Foster were the most welcome sight she'd ever seen.

The threesome stumbled through the front doors of the hospital, Neil holding Monica's hand and the other arm around Anna who clutched at her wet skirt in embarrassment.

"We're here," Neil called out. Sweat beaded on his forehead.

Doc Farnum got up from behind the reception desk, and hurried forward. "That was a quick trip." He and a nurse helped Anna into a wheelchair. "When you called from the Horse Creek store, I figured it would be an hour till you'd be here. The way you talked, I hoped you wouldn't have to stop along the way to deliver the baby yourself." He chuckled and patted Anna's shoulder. "Come along, hon. We'll give you something for those pains." He wheeled her down the hall to the delivery room.

***

Neil and Monica settled themselves on the lightly padded green plastic chairs in the waiting room. Monica found the "Little Golden" children's storybooks and was soon engrossed. The hospital was quiet, but now and then, they heard a baby cry. Monica would look up at her dad with a question in her eyes. "Not yet, honey. I don't think that's our baby. The doctor will come out and tell us when it's born."

Neil remembered the interminable wait in the Forsyth hospital when Monica was born. He shook his head, thinking of that priest who had accused him of keeping Anna away from her true faith and brought up the possibility of her dying. The nerve. He still felt incredulous anger whenever he thought of it. He was glad they had started going to the Tormaehlens' church

224

in Forsyth after that. They were such wonderful people, and the pastor had really helped Neil understand his own faith and why he'd been drawn so close to God despite little church upbringing.

Now that he and Anna lived at Horse Creek, they hardly ever saw the Tormaehlens and couldn't even attend church often. The nearest one was thirty miles away in Foster or in Wynona, fifty miles away. But they made the drive whenever they could get away from ranching chores.

Neil closed his eyes and prayed. "Please, Lord, let Anna come through this all right. It doesn't matter if it's a girl or a boy, just let them both be healthy."

He'd hardly opened his eyes again when the tall doctor came striding down the hallway. "Congratulations, it's a boy," Doc Farnum shouted before he was even halfway to the waiting room.

"Oh." Neil's throat tightened, and he couldn't speak. He blinked and swallowed twice, tightly gripping the doctor's proffered hand. "A boy." He broke into a grin, then a chortle, and leaned over to swing Monica up into his arms. "You have a baby brother. Let's go see him."

"A brother? Oh, goody." She jumped down and skipped down the hall ahead of Neil.

The doctor led them to Anna's room, where she lay with the tiny boy at her breast. "It's a boy. Just like I thought." She smiled. "Our Kevin Neil."

Monica slept all the way home that night. In the early morning, Neil felt a little hand pat his shoulder. "Daddy, wake up. Where's Mommy? Where's Kevin?"

Neil opened one eye, yawned and stretched. "They need to stay in the hospital for a few days, so Mommy can rest and the doctor can keep an eye on your little brother. We'll go back in to see them this afternoon."

"Okay." Monica hurried outside to say a happy good morning to Jackie. The dog jumped and yipped with pleasure at seeing her. Neil and Monica spent the morning doing chores—milking the cow, feeding the chickens, and filling the tank for the horses. Afterwards, Neil mixed an egg into a bowl of raw hamburger, sprinkled it with salt and pepper, shaped it into patties and fried them for lunch.

"Oh, yum, hankabers." Monica chortled. "You're a good cooker, Daddy."

Love and pride swelled Neil's heart. He gave her blonde pigtail a playful tug.

On the drive into town, Monica was quiet for some time. Then she launched into a series of questions, "How do babies get born? Is it like the calfies when they come out of the cow's stomach? Will Kevin be able to come home soon? When will I be able to play with him? Can he talk?"

Neil tried his best to answer what he could, but finally he just chuckled and patted his daughter's arm. "You'll see, honey."

They stood at the window of the nursery, watching Kevin sleep. There was one other baby in the bassinet next to him. "Baby Boy McKinnon," the McKinnons' fifth child.

"Kevin's so little, Daddy."

"But he's bigger than the other baby." Neil compared the two. *All that curly black hair—like me.*

Monica rose on tiptoes. "He's so cute. I like him."

Neil's throat tightened, and he drew his daughter close as he gazed at his son.

***

Kevin's shrill cry split the quiet darkness. Anna swung her feet over the side of the bed, took one step to the crib and lifted the baby into her arms. Neil groaned behind her, and Monica whimpered in her bed as their sleep was disturbed once again.

Anna tiptoed into the kitchen to change her son's diaper. Then she sat in the rocking chair by the still-warm cook stove and unbuttoned her nightgown to let Kevin nurse. She looked down at the soft, dark curls and crooned a German lullaby. *"Schlaf, Herzenssöhnchen. Mein Liebling bist du..."* Sleep, son of my heart. You are my love.

As she rocked and held the tiny bundle in her arms, a rush of love filled her heart. Had her mother felt this way about her? A tiny shot of regret pierced her bubble of joy. Anna had been away from her mother almost seven years now. She couldn't even fathom how she would feel if her children moved so far away, not knowing if she'd ever see them again.

Anna brushed a tendril of dark hair back from Kevin's forehead. Had childbirth been difficult for Mutti? Was she happy, having four children? How Anna wished she could sit over a cup of coffee and ask her mother these questions, share this happiness with her.

Her son suckled, emitting small, satisfied grunts until he gradually fell asleep at her breast. She lifted him to her shoulder and patted his back to burp him. Maybe she could take a trip back home to Germany soon to share her children with her mother.

Anna hugged Kevin tight, closed her eyes and inhaled his soft, baby smell. She sat for a long time before she went back to the bedroom, reluctant to release him from her arms.

The next morning Neil yawned as he sat at the table. "Kevin was awake a lot last night, wasn't he?"

Anna nodded and rubbed the sleep from her eyes.

"I think we need more than two rooms to live in, now that there are four of us." Neil poured milk over his oatmeal and sprinkled it with brown sugar. "What would you think if we remodeled that storage room into a kitchen? Then we could make this room into a bedroom for the kids."

"Oh. Yes, that would make a nice big kitchen. It would be wonderful." Anna looked at her husband with excitement. Then she paused as she dished up Monica's cereal. "But, can we afford it?" Where could she cut corners to save more money? And, this would probably mean putting off a trip to Germany. But, they really did need the extra room. All four of them crowded into one bedroom was a little much.

Neil yawned and ate another spoonful of oatmeal. "If I do all the work myself, I can save a lot of money. Besides, calf prices are up this fall. Ed and Tom have been talking to this big buyer who is interested in buying a lot of calves from this area. I'll call him from the store today. Want to come along?"

Anna nodded. Poor Neil—he worked so hard and then to be kept awake half the night. No wonder he had dark circles under his eyes.

At the Horse Creek Store, the proprietors Charlie and Etta Stokley greeted them warmly. The creaky floorboards smelled of linseed oil. The electric light from the generator barely touched the haphazard clutter on the shelves, in the corners, and on every surface.

"Just heard some interestin' news." Charlie leaned against the counter. "The Rural Electric Association out of Miles City wants to come out here with electricity. There'll be a community meeting here at the store next week, to see if everybody wants to sign up."

Anna looked at Neil with raised eyebrows. No more pumping up the hissing gas lanterns to keep their harsh light going. With the flick of a switch, she could go from one room to another after dark, without lighting another lantern, or taking the one that was lit from her little family gathered around the kitchen table, reading. Just like she'd been able to do back home.

Neil smiled back at her. "That'd be great." He turned to Charlie. "Anybody mention any numbers yet?"

The storekeeper shook his greying head. "Nope. But I know the ranchers near Miles sure seem happy with the REA Co-op."

Neil went to use the telephone while Anna showed off Kevin to Etta. The older woman cooed and chuckled over the baby, then squatted down beside Monica. "Here, honey, have a peppermint stick. Do you like having a little brother?"

Monica eyed the candy, but hid behind Anna. She put her hand on her daughter's shoulder. Her little girl was still so shy. "Go ahead, you can have it. Tell Mrs. Stokley how you've been helping me take care of Kevin."

"You've been helping your mommy with the baby?"

Monica nodded and reached out for the treat. "I get to hold him sometimes, an' watch him if Mommy goes outside a minute." She smiled then, and her face shone with pride.

"Well, you're getting to be such a big girl—six, now, huh?" Etta put her hands on her knees, pushed herself slowly upright, and turned to Anna. "Are you still planning to teach her at home?"

"I don't know what we're going to do." Anna shifted Kevin to her other hip. Now with a baby, she found it harder than ever to keep up with Monica's voracious appetite for learning. "She's reading already. I guess we'll try with other subjects next fall."

As they piled back into the car, Neil grinned. "This buyer is definitely interested in our calves. Says he saw them from the highway, and they look to be the biggest and best in the neighborhood. He's coming out from Billings tomorrow."

***

During the next few weeks, Anna's head spun as if she'd been caught up in one of those pesky dust devils that whipped through the yard, catching up the dust and sending tumbleweeds spiraling into the air. The electric co-op presented a plan for putting in power lines. The calf-buyer visited with high praise for their Herefords and an offer that was two cents a pound higher than he'd given the neighbors.

Neil was ecstatic. "Can you believe it? That gives us plenty to make our loan payment, sign up for electricity, and get materials for the remodeling." His feet shuffled into a jig. He swung Monica onto his shoulders, whirled around the tiny kitchen, ducking so he wouldn't bump her head on the sloped ceiling. "Get us some paper and a pencil, Anna. Let's make some plans."

She rummaged in a drawer for a pencil, anticipation running through her like a spring snowmelt. A new kitchen. A bedroom of their own. After all these years of "making do." She could hardly believe it.

They sat up late that evening, sketching and talking. "We could put a window here and the door there…" Neil drew, discarded, and redrew floor plans.

"Yes, but let's think where a sink could go, when we get running water someday," Anna put in. "Maybe here, under this window."

"And I'll build cupboards all around here." Neil drew more lines on the paper then jumped up to go into the bare storage room to measure.

"Here could be another window, with the table under it, and we could cut another door here, to go into the living room…" Anna smiled. She could already see red and white gingham curtains blowing in the breeze. "And there will be plenty of room in the old kitchen for the kids' beds. Then we could build a closet in our room and I could move my sewing machine back in, and…"

***

In the fall, the buyer came, loaded up the calves, and left Neil and Anna a nice fat check. "Wooee!" Neil whooped. "Now we can start work on the house."

Anna grinned and hugged him. "Let's have a glass of wine to celebrate."

Through the late winter afternoons and evenings, after Neil had finished feeding cows and doing chores, he worked on the new kitchen. He stripped the boards from the walls. Anna gave Monica several books and asked her to keep an eye on Kevin while he napped. Then she helped clean out the sawdust and old newspapers that had served as insulating material, and they replaced them with modern insulation.

Up went the Sheetrock. A frustrating learning process followed that came with taping the corners, smoothing the edges with drywall mud, and sanding, more sanding, and then sanding some more. After redoing one strip for what seemed like the umpteenth time, Anna wiped her dusty, sweaty face and gave an exasperated groan. Maybe it would never get done. She sighed. *And maybe I'll never get back to Germany.*

Neil studied books and diagrams and strung wire for the electrical switches and outlets. The REA had already been out to put up poles and lines to the ranch. On one of their trips to Lewistown, he found some beautiful knotty pine boards on sale to build kitchen cabinets, and he and Anna picked out reddish clay-colored vinyl tiles for the floor.

One evening, as Neil lay the tiles, Jim Eichorn dropped by for supper, as he often did. Much to Neil's chagrin, he clomped across the floor adhesive with his muddy rubber overshoes, surveying the project. "Whoever invented this stuff oughta be shot." He pulled his boot free of the sticky mess. "What're you goin' to all this trouble for, anyhow? The kitchen ya got is perfectly good. Why, me and John got along jist fine, the both of us, fer years in there."

Neil looked at the gooey tracks and for the first time since he'd met their gregarious neighbor, he was ready to bust his chops. Of all the nerve. Now he'd have to scrape up the adhesive and start over again.

But he bit his tongue, stood, and handed Jim a rag. "Here, if you'd like to clean off your boots, we could go in and have a cup of coffee."

***

The children were in bed, and Anna stood in front of the door that led to the new kitchen with her eyes closed. The door creaked as it opened, and she heard a faint click. Neil led her across the threshold. "Now, open your eyes."

Anna drew in a sharp gasp of breath, and her eyes felt as though they would pop out of her head. Even though she'd been working alongside Neil to get this room ready, he'd not let her come in the last couple of days while he put on the finishing touches. "Oh my goodness."

Electric light bathed the white walls and the soft clay-colored floor. The red and white checked curtains she'd made draped the windows perfectly, the pine cabinets glowed, and the countertops were covered with a bright, red-patterned linoleum. A shiny white electric stove—no more hauling dirty coal to cook and heat with. And the electric refrigerator—no more oily smell of kerosene to deal with.

Her gaze came to rest on the kitchen table, her throat tightened, and her heart thumped in her chest. Neil had draped the table with a white linen cloth and a single, lighted candle in the center. Two champagne glasses sparkled in the light.

"Oh, Neil, it's beautiful. So modern." Tears welled up. She drew him close in a warm, happy embrace. "Thank you, my darling. It's just wonderful."

He squeezed her back, and with a big grin, leaned down to give her a lingering kiss.

When they disengaged, she walked to the stove and ran her hands over the smooth white porcelain surface. Turning a knob, she watched the burner slowly glow red and passed her hand close to feel its heat. "What a miracle, electricity."

Neil merely stood by, watching her and grinning.

Next, she opened the cupboard doors one by one, inhaling the pungent pine smell, and moved to the side opposite the electric stove, where the large white electric refrigerator gleamed. "Oh, Neil, I can't believe this has happened. I'm so happy. I love you so."

Those amenities Anna had taken for granted in Germany had finally come to her Montana home. She thought she'd gotten used to the way they lived, lighting gas and kerosene lanterns, pouring coal into the cook stove and dumping the ashes, the frustrating job of ironing with a flatiron where heat couldn't be regulated, sometimes scorching shirts. But now that she had electricity...how much easier life would be.

But would she ever make it back to Germany to visit her family?

CHAPTER TWENTY

Anna smoothed Monica's red and green plaid skirt and straightened the bow on her blouse for at least the third time.

"Hurry, Mommy, I don't want to be late." Monica started for the door, but Anna called her back and once more brushed her little girl's golden ringlets around her finger.

Monica shuffled her feet and wriggled under her mother's hands. "I've been waiting so long for my first day of school, Mommy. I'm going to read 'real' books and write stories." She stopped suddenly, looking up at Anna. "But will I be able to drink my milk at school?"

"Sure you will, honey. I put some in the thermos with your lunch." Anna picked up the blue and yellow "Dale Evans and Roy Rogers" lunchbox from the counter and handed it to her daughter. She walked her out to the car, where Neil waited, and kissed the top of Monica's head. "Have a good day, honey."

Anna blinked back tears as she watched them drive away. It was what they had wanted—a school in the neighborhood— but why did she feel so reluctant to let Monica go? It was only a mile and a half away, not as if she were going across the ocean.

Just three months earlier, Bill and Emily Mitchell, a couple with six children—three of them school age—had moved onto a ranch about ten miles from Horse Creek. Now, they could justify a school. The men in the neighborhood formed a school board, to which Neil was elected. Then, while the search for a teacher began, everyone worked together on the abandoned schoolhouse to repair, clean, paint, oil the wood floors, and convert a cloakroom into a small "teacherage" for the teacher to live in. The single room would hold a cot, a cupboard/dresser and a hotplate.

Anna had been dreading the task of trying to teach Monica all the subjects at home. She still didn't feel as if she knew enough to be a teacher. And she worried about how it would affect Monica's future—if she would be far behind other students when she did go to a regular school. Although Neil was constantly studying something of his own, he wouldn't always be available to help.

So, a part of her was pleased there would be a school for Monica and other children to play with. But oh, how she missed her already. She offered a little prayer for protection and for her daughter's happiness in school.

Her little girl was growing up too fast. Groping in her pocket for a handkerchief, she went back into the house to dress Kevin, now almost a year old. She dabbed at her eyes. Her son played on the living room floor with a toy tractor, making sound effects with his lips. He caught on so fast—it seemed he instinctively knew what a tractor was for.

Anna picked him up and hugged him close. "Well, at least I still have you around all day, my little farmer boy."

For the rest of the day, she busied herself cleaning furiously and baking cookies for Monica when she came home. At twenty minutes to three, Neil stuck his head in the door. "Want to come along to pick up Monica?"

"Yes!" A tingle of excitement ran through her, and she smiled. "Let me check Kevin's diaper, and we'll be right out."

They sat in the aging Buick outside the white clapboard, one-room schoolhouse. "How do you suppose it went?" Anna twisted the edge of Kevin's blanket. "Do you think she was okay?"

Neil patted her shoulder, all the while peering through the windshield at the school door. "I'm sure she was fine."

Then the door burst open, and the four students exploded out, waving papers, giggling, shoving and shouting. The Mitchells' Chevy pickup raised a cloud of dust as Mrs. Mitchell arrived, her kids piled in, and off they roared. Anna frowned. So much for friendly new neighbors.

"Daddy, Mommy. Look what I did." Monica ran to the car window with the pictures she had drawn and colored. "An' come in. I want to show you what we made."

Inside the tiny schoolroom four little desks sat facing the blackboards, which took up most of two walls. A large crock of drinking water stood on a bench in one corner and an oil-burning heater took up the other.

The teacher, Mrs. Elizabeth Dallas, from somewhere north of Foster, rose from behind her desk, piled with books and papers. At age sixty, she still radiated energy and enthusiasm. Her wiry gray curls quivered as she strode toward them, her hand out. "Hello, Mosers. You've got one bright daughter, here."

Anna was taken aback by the teacher's forthrightness. "Why, thank you, Mrs. Dallas."

"Just call me Dallas," was the reply. "That's what I told the kids." She grinned, lifting her false teeth from her gums with her tongue, moving them around in her mouth and back into place again. "Here, see what she's been doing. She's already 'way ahead with her reading skills, and she told me the darndest stories. Says she wants to be a writer when she grows up."

"Mommy, look at the little house we made," Monica called from the corner. "An' look, I wrote my name on the chalkboard and yours and Daddy's and Kevin's."

Anna studied the neat printing on the board and admired the little cardboard box house. "Good work, honey."

Monica chattered all the way home. "We played games, and Lila, she's the oldest, she's ten, she helped me. Ben, he's nine, an'... I don't know if I like him, he teases me. An' Eddie is the same grade as me... " she paused a second and looked up at Anna with rounded eyes, "but...but he doesn't know his colors yet. And he doesn't know how to read, or write his name."

After hurriedly changing her clothes, Monica munched on her cookie at the kitchen table, and took a big swig of milk. "I didn't really miss my milk at school. I had some in my lunch, but then we were so busy I didn't even 'member till I got home." She jumped down from the chair. "Can I go practice my writing now, Mommy?"

"Of course, honey. I'm so proud of you." Anna turned to smile at Neil, who poured their coffee into dainty china cups. "I'm so glad she likes school. I hope that one little boy doesn't cause her any problems."

"She'll be fine. I'm just glad to see that she didn't let her shyness overcome her. I was a little worried about that. When I took her in this morning, she kind of hung back a little bit, although I could tell she was very excited. But Mrs. ...er...Dallas took her right under her wing and assured me she'd be okay. I think we've found us a good teacher there."

***

Jake and Nettie arrived on a crisp, snowy Christmas Eve to see Monica's first Christmas program, and Monica hardly let them get a word in edgewise. "Gramma, you should see my teacher roll her teeth around in her mouth. She is so funny....

"Gramma, c'mere, I'll show you my books. I can read....

"Gramma, look't our tree. See the lights. Isn't it pretty? I helped decorate it. The one at school, too....

"Grampa, show me the trick with the mouse!"

"You'll have to sit down here for a minute, then." Jake tied two knots for ears in the corner of his red bandanna, rolled it up, and placed it in the crook of his arm. "Oh, such a nice little mouse." He stroked the handkerchief creature with one hand, while he surreptitiously gave it a nudge with the other. It jumped off his arm toward Monica, who shrieked with laughter.

"Do it again, Grampa."

And so it went, nonstop, until it was time to go to the evening program.

"Let's get you dressed now, honey." Anna interrupted the game. "That must have been about the fiftieth time you've done that today." She chuckled at Jake.

"That's okay, for my little gal."

236

Nettie joined in. "She sure is excited about school. I remember Neil was, too."

"Yup. She's a chip off the ol' block." Jake folded the handkerchief and stuck it back in his pocket.

The schoolhouse gave off a warm glow in the snowy field as the Mosers drove up. Bright lights shone from the windows between tinsel garlands, and handmade snowflakes covered the glass. Inside, neighbors were gathering, filling up the benches Charley Stokley and Neil had brought in earlier that day. A record player blared Christmas music, and Dallas directed the room like an orchestra. "Mrs. Hunter, come sit up front, so you can hear... Hello, McGregors, come on in... Ah, here come the Mosers... Come, Monica, come back here and get your costume on."

Anna fidgeted on the bench and sent up a little prayer that Monica wouldn't forget her lines. Nettie gave her an encouraging smile, as if she'd read Anna's mind.

The four students put on a skit based on the poem "Twas the Night Before Christmas." Monica stood straight and tall and recited her lines perfectly. To Anna, she shone like the reflection of a hundred Christmas bulbs. She breathed a big sigh of relief and couldn't stop smiling. Afterwards, everyone stood to visit and enjoy Christmas cookies and coffee.

Nettie gave Monica a hug. "You were the best one of all."

Jake nodded. "Yup. Good job."

"Your daughter is quite the little actress," remarked Emily Mitchell.

Anna, holding Kevin on her hip, glanced at Neil, not quite sure if Emily had paid a compliment or was being facetious. "Yes, she certainly got into the spirit of things. They all did. It was very nice."

Just then "Santa" arrived coincidentally with the absence of Bill Mitchell, and the children all rushed forward to receive their small gifts.

Back at home, packages beckoned from beneath the tree as the multicolored electric lights blinked. "Can we open them now?" Monica danced around the living room, swirling her blue taffeta dress Anna had made. "See, Gramma. Look at me." She twirled again. Nettie laughed, grabbed Monica by the arms and spun with her.

Anna brought out trays laden with slices of *stollen*, decorated sugar cookies, date and nut bars, and chocolate rum balls. "I think we're about ready for that. Monica, you can pick one package to open first."

While Monica busied herself tearing the paper, Neil poured wine and lifted his glass to Anna. "Happy eighth anniversary, my darling." He took out a tiny package wrapped in white sparkly tissue paper and topped with a gold bow.

Anna felt her eyes grow wide as she carefully tore the paper from the small box, and she breathed a soft "oh" as she took out gold earrings shaped like rosebuds with a diamond chip in their centers. She smiled and shook her head. "You're too much. Thank you, sweetheart. They're beautiful."

"Ooh, look at that. How nice." Nettie touched her own ear and jabbed Jake with an elbow.

"Yeah, isn't our boy quite the romantic?" He winked at Neil and Anna.

For the rest of the evening Anna delighted in the ritual. Everyone shared in the anticipation as one person at a time took a package and oh-so-slowly and carefully opened it, slicing through the cellophane tape, saving the paper and bows for future use. Anna loved this delicious delay, savoring each gift opened. She was nearly as giddy as Monica had been, thinking of the box from home, back beneath the tree.

Nettie unwrapped the red sweater Anna had knitted. "Wow. This is lovely. Hand-made?" She held it up to her chest and stroked the wool. "This will be so nice and warm."

Anna smiled with pleasure. Nettie genuinely seemed to like it.

With great exaggeration, Jake inhaled the scent from the package of pipe tobacco from Neil and Anna. "Mmmm, smells good." He winked at Nettie, who wrinkled her nose at the pipe habit he'd acquired recently.

And they all enjoyed the squeals of delight from Monica and Kevin as they opened their packages. Monica cradled a new doll, tried out a coloring book and crayons, and gazed at books, one of fairy tales and another about horses. Kevin ripped paper and chortled when Neil put him inside a cardboard box. A new toy truck and a bunch of plastic farm animals didn't hold his attention as long as the box did.

"Hush," said Anna suddenly. "Did you hear something?" They all stopped what they were doing and leaned forward in silence.

"I don't hear anything," Jake answered.

"I thought I heard sleigh bells." Anna peered through the window.

Monica leaped up from the floor, dropping her book. "Santa!" She ran to the kitchen door and out onto the porch where a red-painted sled sat, loaded with several more packages. "He was here." Wonder softened her voice. She searched the night sky for a sign of the sleigh and eight tiny reindeer.

"Well, let's bring these in, and see what Santa left." Neil stepped out into the frosty air to lift the sled and its load inside.

When the flurry of paper and ribbons and happy shrieks had died down, Anna caught Neil's eye. He bent his tall frame way beneath the tree to bring out the large box, still wrapped in brown paper and twine.

This was what Anna had been waiting for as eagerly as Monica had been for Santa—the package from Germany. For her, the best was last. Anna unwrapped a crisp dress shirt for Neil, sweaters for both kids, tiny Lederhosen for Kevin.

Nettie held up the miniature leather shorts. "Aren't these the cutest little things."

Anna opened the molasses *Lebkuchen* and rich, creamy German chocolate and shared with everyone.

"Mmm." Even Jake seemed impressed with the smooth taste.

Anna stroked the delicate, hand-embroidered tablecloths and sighed over a cut crystal vase, a set of stainless spoons. Oh, this was *Weinachten* at home all over again. Tears slipped over her cheeks as she read the cards enclosed. How she missed Mutti and Papa, Hans, Karl and Else and the crowds of cousins, nieces and nephews. Would she ever return to Germany?

***

Spring came early, hot and dry. Neil trudged into the kitchen and sat down heavily at the table. Anna glanced at the clock. Only eleven, not time for dinner, yet. "Something wrong?" She looked into his face, pale under the darkening springtime tan.

"I feel so tired. I almost fell asleep on the tractor. Thought maybe I'd better come in for a cup of coffee."

Anna took out the electric percolator they'd gotten from Nettie and Jake for Christmas and measured out the grounds. She dipped water from the bucket and plugged in the pot. Turning to Neil, she was shocked to see him with his head on his arms, snoring softly. She felt his forehead. Did it feel slightly warm? He'd been working awfully hard of late, trying to get the crops in and the summer-fallowing done—maybe he hadn't been sleeping well. She roused him with a steaming cup of coffee, which he drank quickly, holding it out for a refill.

"Y'know, I think I'm going to lie down for a little while."

Anna tried to wake him for dinner, but Neil merely groaned and rolled over. By late afternoon, she was pacing the kitchen with worry. She went into the bedroom and shook his shoulder. "Honey, wake up. Are you sick?"

His eyes inched open. "No'm fine," he mumbled, letting them fall shut again. Anna stuck a thermometer under his tongue and felt his pulse. That seemed okay. This was the strangest thing. Neil was normally full of energy. No matter how hard he worked, he usually took only a fifteen or twenty-minute nap after dinner before heading out again. She'd never seen him like this. She took out the thermometer. 102. Yes, he had a fever. Oh dear, how could her man be sick? She sighed. Probably only the flu. Thankfully that wasn't as serious

240

anymore as when Nettie was young and lost a baby sister to the illness. Well, better let him get some rest. She pulled a blanket over him and went back to the kitchen.

Neil slept almost constantly for several days. With growing worries, Anna hesitantly left Monica to watch Kevin as she struggled to do chores. She'd never learned how to milk, so she let the calf have free access to suckle to its heart's content. But that meant no fresh milk for the kids.

She awakened Neil to give him aspirin and water and tried to get him to eat. He wasn't hungry. Anna bathed his forehead with a cool cloth. "Should we go in to see Doc Farnum?" Neil shook his head. He only wanted to sleep.

Then, one morning, he awoke, feeling better. He came out to the kitchen, dressed and ready to go back out to the field.

"Are you sure you feel up to it?" Anna felt his forehead. It did feel cooler.

"Oh yeah. I needed a little rest, that's all." Neil smiled and gave her a peck on the cheek as he headed out the door.

He didn't show up at noon. Anna kept looking at the clock every few minutes. She waited. 12:15, then 12:30. Neil was late for dinner. That wasn't like him. She gathered Monica and Kevin, put them in the car and drove out to the field. As she approached, she saw that the tractor was stopped, but she couldn't spot Neil. Panic pierced her. She steered the Buick through the plowed ruts, fearful he'd fallen off the tractor. She pictured his mangled, bleeding body under the blades of the plow, and bit her tongue to keep from crying out.

But the tractor wasn't running, and he wasn't pinned under the plow. She slammed on the parking brake and leaped out the door, running around to the far side of the machinery. There he was, lying on the ground, in the shade, asleep.

"Neil. Wake up, honey. What's wrong?" Anna scanned his body for injuries, finding none.

He grunted and sat up sleepily. "Jus' got s'tired, had t'lie down."

"I'm taking you to the doctor." She helped him into the back seat of the car, and with the kids in the front and Neil asleep again in the back seat, sped for town.

In Doc Farnum's office, Anna sat on the edge of her chair, Kevin on her lap, Neil nodding beside her, and Monica hiding behind them. She was still afraid of the doctor from her experience with her leg pain.

He puffed on his pipe and studied his notes on the desk in front of him. "Well, it looks like it's just a virus. Although, if it was the flu, he should've been over it by now. With that sore throat and enlarged lymph glands in his neck... " He puffed again, thoughtfully. "Let me write you a prescription for some penicillin. It's probably a streptococcus...."

For weeks Neil continued to sleep, waking up only when Anna forced him to eat a little soup or toasted bread. He complained of headaches. "My back is killing me, too. Wonder if I wrenched it somehow?" Every once in a while, he would wake up as if normal, and try to go out to do some work. But within a few hours, he was back in the house, headed for bed, or Anna would go out and find him asleep somewhere.

The ranch work was falling behind. She did what she could around home, caring for the chickens, feeding the milk cow and horses, and occasionally drove to the pasture to check the cattle. Should she ask Jake and Nettie to come and help? No, surely Neil would get better any day now.

Anna pored over her medical textbooks. Fever, fatigue, sore throat, loss of appetite, muscle aches... It could be some kind of bacterial or protozoal infection...but the penicillin should be helping more. Doc had mentioned a virus.

"*Ach, nein.*" She clamped her hands over her mouth as she cried out involuntarily. It couldn't be polio, could it? The memory of Fred Fowler, a man from church in Wynona, flashed into her mind. They'd visited him in the hospital, where he lay in an iron lung a couple of years ago. He had died shortly after that.

"Monica, I have to go to the store and make a telephone call. Kevin is taking his nap. Wake up Daddy, if you need help." Anna ran out the door.

She paced up and down the aisles at the store, waiting for Doc Farnum to return her call, trying not to let on to Charley Stokley that she was scared out of her mind. The storekeeper tried to engage her in gossipy conversation, and entice her with a "special" on overripe bananas. Anna shook her head and continued to pace. When the phone rang, she jumped and nearly collapsed on the spot.

"Yes, doctor. I'm just so worried. I had a terrible thought." She turned her back to Stokley and stepped as far from the door as possible, trying to speak in a low voice so he wouldn't hear. "Do you think it could be polio?"

"Well, now..." The doctor paused. Anna could almost see him sucking on his pipe. "I had given that some consideration myself, after you brought him in, because the symptoms are similar in some ways. But, I really don't think so. I mean, it's been several weeks, and he hasn't had any leg weakness or breathing problems. By the way, there is a vaccine available now that's been tested and found effective against polio. It's going to be available to all the children in the county...let's see, here it is, yes, it'll be administered in the high school gymnasium on August 15, before school starts for the year.

"Anyway, back to Neil..." Anna heard him tap his pipe into a glass ashtray. "No, there's something else I've been hearing about—Mononucleosis—also known as the 'kissing disease.' It is contagious, so I'd recommend, ah, no physical contact, and keep the kids away as much as possible. But..." The doctor paused again as he relit the pipe. "There doesn't seem to be anything we can give him, other than the penicillin for the sore throat. We'll simply have to let it run its course."

Nearly paralyzed with fear, Anna drove home. What on earth would she do without Neil running the ranch? She clenched her hands on the steering wheel. This disease, whatever it might be—could it possibly take him from her? *Ach, lieber Gott,* that would be too much to bear.

243

Anna had to stop the car. She bowed her head and prayed. No. God would never give her more than she could handle. She had to cling to that thought.

CHAPTER TWENTY-ONE

It was nearly midnight. Anna pored over their bank account, scribbling numbers on a piece of paper. Neil had been sick for so long. It was the end of June 1957. The crops were late getting planted and the fallow fields were nothing but weeds. She had checked fences after the winter snowdrifts had leaned their bulk on the wires, causing them to sag, and in some places, break. But there had been no one to fix the breaks. The calves hadn't been branded yet either. All she could do was drive out through the pasture and make sure the cows were all there and looking healthy. Finally, a week ago, she'd called Jake and Nettie to get a recommendation for a hired hand. They had sent Hoot Gibson, a member of the wild family she remembered meeting her first Thanksgiving in America.

She rubbed her eyes. No matter how she worked the figures, it wasn't going to come out right. Because the crops were being planted so late, there may not be any grain to sell. Calf prices had been a bit low last year, so they had already planned to tighten their belts this year to pay the mortgage. Now, she had to pay a hired man, too. "Dear Lord," she prayed. "What will we do?"

She couldn't sleep, and wandered from room to room, sitting on each of the kids' beds, watching them sleep. She brushed a lock of golden hair from Monica's face, and gently took Kevin's thumb out of his mouth. She looked in on Neil, too. He was so tired all the time—he should be improving by now.

The questions roared through her head. What if Neil didn't get well? What if he couldn't ever work again? How could she take care of her family? Yes, she worked on the ranch, right alongside her husband, but she didn't have the knowledge that he did, nor the physical strength. She didn't know how to overhaul an engine, or pull a well, or change the oil in the Buick. That old car ran on borrowed time with Neil's pampering, as it was.

She couldn't go to the PCA and ask for an additional loan. That would be too embarrassing. They would most likely say no, anyway. She dismissed that thought immediately. And she wasn't about to ask Jake and Nettie for help. They would think she was weak, couldn't handle things on the ranch. Anna went back to the kitchen and put water on for coffee. She didn't know how to economize any further. Their bill at the store was already small. She made all of her and Monica's clothes; she raised a big garden, and canned all the vegetables and fruits they needed to carry them through the winter. Neil usually shot a deer or an antelope for their meat supply, but he might not be able to this fall. She shook her head. She couldn't shoot an animal.

Anna was so tired, she could hardly think straight, but she couldn't go to bed. She knew as soon as she did, her eyes would pop wide open, and the questions would come again, around and around and around, faster and faster. She rested her head on her arms and tasted the warm salt tears that had collected at the corners of her mouth.

She awoke with a jolt, her arms numb. She shook them by her sides, until they tingled. What had she just dreamed? She frowned, concentrating, trying to recapture the thought. Hermann. She'd dreamed about her old boyfriend in Germany. Why on earth...?

"Oh, my gosh," she breathed. "Hermann's a banker. Does that mean I should go to a bank?" She paced again, looked out the window at the faint light along the eastern horizon and muttered to herself.

But the more she fought the idea, the more it took hold. She had no choice. But she wouldn't tell Neil—couldn't burden him with this worry.

"I have to go into Wynona today," she told Neil when she woke him for breakfast. "Can you keep an eye on the kids? I'll be back as soon as I can." Neil didn't even question her. He merely nodded and went back to sleep. She could only hope he woke up often enough to watch Monica and Kevin. She gave Monica instructions to wake Daddy if she needed help, and drove off.

***

Anna stepped into the bank official's office, her hands cold and shaky. The tall man, dressed impeccably in a dark suit, rose from his plush chair and stepped around his huge mahogany desk, a hand outstretched. She put on a smile.

"Jeremy Morgan. Nice to see you, Mrs. Moser." He smiled with an air of self-satisfaction, a gold tooth glinting, and pointed to a chair. "Please, sit. What can I do to help you today?"

Anna took a deep breath. She wouldn't allow her voice to shake. "Thank you for seeing me, Mr. Morgan. My husband has been ill, and I have had to hire someone to work the ranch, and I need to pay him. But calf prices don't look very promising again this year, and... "

"You need a little loan to get you through the year." Morgan finished the sentence for her. He steepled his fingers and gazed at her.

Anna's neck grew hot and she held her breath. *He's going to say no.*

"I know your in-laws." He studied the paperwork she'd brought. "Well, looks like you've kept up your other loan payments pretty well. I think we can make some arrangements."

Anna was able to breathe more normally again.

The banker took some papers from his desk drawer. "Tell me what you need, and I'll write it up now. Normally, we'd need Neil's signature as well, but since I know the family, I'll waive that requirement. We'll make it a short-term loan, and you can pay it back after you've sold your calves and crops this fall."

Each time she signed her name on the umpteen pages, Anna asked herself if she was doing the right thing. But no other ideas came to mind.

She drove home with a feeling of foreboding. She had expected to feel relieved to have solved the problem, but instead, apprehension made the hairs on her arms stand up. *Well, what's done is done.* Best just to work as hard as she could and somehow get through this.

Arriving home, Anna breathed easier to find Neil in the living room, reading to the kids.

***

Monica loved school. She came home every day and gushed about what she had learned. "Look, Mommy, I'm writing stories."

Anna was so grateful for the little school. Today, Dallas had given Monica pictures that she'd cut out of old books and magazines and asked her to write sentences about them. Sometimes the students played "Old Maid" with cards the teacher had made with vocabulary words on them, and they played "Parcheesi" to learn to count and add the numbers on the dice. Dallas made every subject a game, and Monica was hungry to learn. After she got home from school and had a snack, she would go off to read her books or practice her writing.

The only negative note Anna heard was when Monica talked about recess. "Ben wouldn't let me have my turn at the swing," she'd say. Or "Eddie pushed me so hard I fell down when we were playing tag." Sometimes, she'd break into tears. "Nobody wanted to play with me today." Anna worried, but didn't know what to do. After all, the other kids in school were from the same family. They would naturally stick together. It would work itself out, she hoped.

Kevin was nearly two, toddling around, getting into pots and pans in the cupboards or going outside and finding the nearest mud puddle or cowpie to play in. Watching out for him took a lot of her energy, while overseeing Hoot's work, and cooking for everyone.

Hoot was a hard worker. His parents had been big fans of the late cowboy movie star, Hoot Gibson, and had named their eldest after him. She liked him—his red nose, his bow-legged gait, his sense of humor. He spent long hours on the tractor, trying to catch up in the fields. On a rainy day, he went out to fix fence and check the cattle.

He was still a bit of a wild man, though. Anna chuckled and shook her head. Hoot had to go into town every Saturday night and get "tanked up" as the cowboys called it. He often ended up in a bar fight—usually defending his unlikely name—and dragged himself back to the ranch late Sunday afternoon, looking worse for wear. But she was thankful to have him. Neil didn't seem to be getting much better, and even though Anna now felt more comfortable with her in-laws, she refused to show her in-laws any sign of weakness by asking their help. She sighed. *If I go to them, it might spoil things between us.*

***

The big cattle truck drove away with the last of the calves, and shipping was done for another year. Anna breathed a weary sigh. A blustery November day, the first storm of the season threatened in the heavy, gray clouds that gathered in the west. She looked at the check the buyer had given them, and whispered a prayer. It was pretty small, despite the healthy, stocky calves they'd produced. She'd have to do some figuring, but it didn't look like it would cover the mortgage payment *and* the loan from the Wynona bank.

Neil sat at the kitchen table, drinking coffee. He had been feeling a little better recently, had negotiated the calf price, and today helped Anna supervise loading the calves. But he'd lost so much weight from his already lanky frame.

She dropped the check on the table and plopped into a chair. "I don't know. We didn't have much of a hay crop, so we'll probably need to buy hay this winter. And we'd better keep Hoot on for awhile, anyway, until you're stronger."

Neil reached for her hand. "I'm so sorry you've had to shoulder the burden all these months, honey. I just don't know what got into me, sleeping all the time. It's crazy. But I feel like this is going to be the end of it, now."

"I hope so. Doc Farnum seems to think it's this mononucleosis and that you will get better." Anna traced the pattern on the oilcloth with her fingernail. "I have to tell you something." She swallowed hard. "I went to Wynona this summer and took out a loan at the bank."

Neil grimaced, but said nothing.

She looked down at the tablecloth again, unable to meet his gaze. "And it is supposed to be paid back this fall. But I don't know if we can." She blinked. "I guess I'll have to go talk to the banker again and see if we can get an extension."

"Oh, honey, I was so out of it, I didn't even know…" Neil shook his head and rubbed his face with his hands. "The PCA would've given us additional operating capital. I know they would have. Damn."

Anna's face crumpled and tears brimmed in her eyes.

He looked at her and drew her close. "I'm sorry. You did what you thought was best. It's all right. We'll figure something out."

***

Anna sat in the waiting area outside Morgan's office. She'd been there an hour, and he hadn't shown up yet. She crossed and uncrossed her legs, swinging her foot nervously. Picking up a magazine, she tried to read an article about how to be the perfect housewife, but tossed it down again in frustration. Finally, a secretary walked toward her. "I'm sorry, Mrs. Moser. I just received a call from Mr. Morgan. He's been detained and won't be coming back to the bank today."

Anna's shoulders slumped. She had spent days working up the courage to come talk to him, and now… "Please tell him I need to speak with him as soon as possible."

On the way home, Anna stopped at the store to pick up the mail. Tucked in between the *Ladies Home Journal* and the *Foster Tribune* was an envelope from the State Bank of Wynona. With trembling fingers, she ripped it open to read:

> *Dear Mr. and Mrs. Moser,*
>
> *This is to inform you that your loan of $1,000.00 initiated in June 1957 with State Bank of Wynona is now considered past due.*
>
> *Unless payment is received by December 31, 1957, foreclosure proceedings on your ranch at Horse Creek will be initiated.*
>
> *Sincerely,*
> *Jeremy Morgan, President*

Foreclosure. Anna gasped and clutched at her throat. Two months to pay. That man said he knew the Moser family and trusted them. He was supposed to be a friend. Her chest tightened, and her heart pounded like fists on a bass drum. She closed her eyes and slumped in the car seat, filled with despair. She had really done it—gotten them into such deep trouble they might lose the ranch. *Idiot!* She pounded the steering wheel.

What could she do now? Her nurse's training and experience didn't fit American certification standards, so she couldn't get work as a nurse. Besides, she'd have to drive at least thirty miles to Foster every day.

Could she take in laundry from the neighbors? No, probably not. There weren't enough people in the neighborhood, anyway. Mending. Maybe…or cleaning their houses… The ideas flitted through her mind like fireflies, each winking out just as quickly. She drove home slowly, dreading Neil's reaction.

Anna slammed the kitchen door. Monica sat with Kevin in the living room, reading him a story. Her tension softened. "Thank you, honey, for watching your brother."

Neil came out of the bedroom, hitching up his pants, rubbing sleep from his eyes. "Hi, hon. Any luck with Morgan?"

She couldn't answer. The lump in her throat closed off her speech. Anna shook her head and with trembling hands, gave him the letter.

"What?" Neil looked up from the page. "What is this? Didn't you explain it to him? Did he tell you why?"

"He wasn't there." Anna choked on her words. "I waited for over an hour, and he never showed up. This was in the mail when I got back." She sniffed and blinked. "Oh, Neil, I've ruined everything. I made a big mistake, and we are going to lose the ranch." The torrent broke loose, and she collapsed onto the table in heaving sobs.

Neil leaned over, put his arms around her, and rested his head on her back. He patted her back, holding her until her wailing quieted. "It's okay," he kept repeating softly.

Monica spoke from the doorway. "What's the matter, Mommy?"

Anna sat up and fumbled in her pocket for a hanky. "Everything is fine, honey, just some money worries. Go back and read to Kevin some more."

She turned back to Neil. "What are we going to do?"

"It will work out." Neil held her trembling hand between his. "Don't worry about it, *Liebchen*. You did the best you could."

He rubbed a hand over his eyes. "I should have told you that Ed Roberts' brother, George, was foreclosed by Wynona Bank last year. And I heard that it happened to Phil Maund down on the river, too. It sounds like this is a pattern with Morgan. It's not you at all. It's that greedy banker. Maybe we should ask Dad and Mom for a loan."

"No." Anna shook her head violently. "We can't do that. We'd only be admitting that we've failed. They would blame me."

She took a deep breath. "What if we drive in to Miles City tomorrow and talk to the people at the PCA. Maybe they'll help us out. Isn't that what they're there for?"

Neil nodded. "Good idea, honey. Let's give it a try."

Anna stood and walked to the refrigerator to start supper. *If we get out of this and by some miracle get the ranch paid off, I'll never again go into debt.*

CHAPTER TWENTY-TWO

Anna paced the PCA lobby, while Neil nodded in a chair, and the kids played in the corner with toys and books they'd brought. This endless waiting for bankers to decide their fate... She sighed and picked up an informational pamphlet to read:

> The Production Credit Association was created in 1916 by Congress to give a dependable source of credit to farmers and ranchers. Actually a cooperative, the borrowers are also members and stockholders. When the cooperative realizes a profit, the stockholders also receive a dividend. It was a godsend to the agriculture community during the dustbowl and Great Depression of the thirties. Without the help of the PCA, many would have lost their homesteads....

Well, it was twenty-some years since the Depression. Anna lifted her eyes heavenward. The PCA had better be an answer to prayer for her and Neil, as well. Without the organization, they wouldn't have been able to buy the ranch in the first place, and without borrowing operating capital, they wouldn't have been able to hang on to it for long. Surely the cooperative wouldn't drop them now.

"Mr. and Mrs. Moser, come on in." Their loan officer, Jim Dunbar, smiled and gestured them into his office.

Anna followed Neil with jelly-knees and took a seat.

"What can I do for you folks today?"

Neil didn't answer, but simply leaned back in his chair. Anna peered at him. He looked a bit pale. She drew deep inside for the courage to speak. "Well, s-sir. Neil has been sick for several months—the doctor doesn't know exactly what's wrong. I-I had to have help with the ranch, so I hired someone. I needed money, so I went to a...a banker in Wynona for a small loan."

Dunbar's eyebrows arched and he leaned back in his chair.

Ach. She was rambling. *He thinks I'm stupid. An idiot. Straighten up, Anna Moser.* She sat upright, squared her shoulders and continued. "Anyway, the calf prices and crops were not good this fall, and when I returned to the bank, this...person would not talk to me. I—we received the news by mail that the Wynona Bank will be foreclosing on our ranch if we don't pay them back." She handed him the letter.

"Hmm." The loan officer read the letter, then opened their file and studied the papers.

Anna's stomach curled in on itself. Neil looked wan, about to pass out. *Ach du lieber, how am I going to handle much more of this?*

"Well, you folks have done very well the past four years. Always made your payment on time. But this other loan... It's going to be a little tricky... I'll need a few days to look into the matter and take it up with the Board." Dunbar stood and put out his hand to shake Neil's, then Anna's. "I'll get back to you as soon as I can."

After a cup of coffee and a piece of pumpkin pie at the Ranchers Cafe, Neil's color returned and he perked up enough to drive.

"Let me know if you get tired and want me to drive." Anna got into the passenger seat. This illness of his—it seemed to ebb and flow like the shifting shadows of the clouds across the continuous sky.

As the grayed prairie passed by, Anna watched a hawk suddenly swoop from out of nowhere to attack a smaller bird.

"What do you think they'll do? Do you think they'll help us?" She fidgeted in her seat and twisted a hanky.

Neil merely shrugged.

Why didn't he have a reaction? "Don't you care?" The shrill note in her voice made her immediately ashamed.

He sighed deeply and his shoulders seemed to collapse. "Of course I do. I'm just tired, that's all. It'll be all right."

The hundred-twenty miles back home passed in endless silence.

***

Neil was late. Anna had been sitting at her sewing machine for the last hour, glancing out the window every few minutes, watching for his arrival. He had driven to Miles City in the early afternoon to talk to the PCA and to the train station to pick up Jim Eichorn, who had been back to Nebraska for his cousin's funeral.

Neil seemed to be recovering, although he still wasn't able to work as long and hard as before. Strenuous activity exhausted him quickly. And somewhere along the way, his back pain had become chronic. Anna felt worn out, too, running the ranch and overseeing the hired man all those months, and worrying—constantly worrying about the money. They'd finally had to let Hoot go.

She had a deep down cold fear the PCA would say no. It had been three weeks since she and Neil were there. What would they do if the answer was negative?

Anna slumped over the pair of Neil's denim pants she was patching for the third time, trying to get a few months more wear out of them. How could she go on like this? She wished she had someone to talk to—she wasn't comfortable talking heart-to-heart with Gertie Sparks or any of the neighbor women. She missed her family. The feeling of isolation seeped into her pores and filled her with emptiness.

This fall would be ten years since she had come to America, looking for love and a better life. Well, she'd had the love. But sometimes even that was a strain. She and Neil had begun to argue—over money and how to run the ranch to make it profitable. Since his illness, his ambition and interest in the business had seemed to wane. She constantly had to force decisions on him, little ones, like when they should move the cows to their summer or winter pasture. Or if they should fix fence today. She rested her head in her hands. She was so tired.

The sound of the Buick's engine brought her upright.

"Daddy's home." Monica ran to the living room window, her book forgotten. Waving his toy truck, Kevin toddled to the door. "Daddy, Daddy!"

As she opened the door, Anna stopped short. A man stood next to Neil, a stocky, older fellow, dressed in what looked like new clothes—a tan long-sleeved shirt, brown corduroy pants and soft tan leather boots. There was something vaguely familiar about him.

"Who's that?" Monica hid behind Anna.

"Look who I brought home." Neil had a twinkle in his eyes. The man grinned a familiar gap-toothed smile and waved.

"Jim." Anna couldn't believe the change. Clean shaven, his face glowed pink, and his balding head shone. Even his fingernails seemed to sparkle. "My, you look ten years younger. So, how was your train ride? And the visit with your family?"

"Bah. Long." Jim waved a hand in disgust. "First thing my brother did was put me in a bathtub. Practically wouldn't let me out the whole time I was there. Made me spend good money on these silly duds—where the heck 'm I gonna wear these things?" He grumbled on about his relatives and living in the city and the crazy traffic.

Neil grinned behind Jim and mouthed, "PCA said yes." He gave her a little wink.

Anna drew in a sharp breath and clutched her chest. *Ach, thank you, Lord.* She smiled and hastily set about fixing sandwiches. After they had eaten and Neil took Jim home, they sat at the kitchen table. "Dunbar at the PCA said he didn't think your contract with Morgan was fully legal, because I didn't sign it. He's looking into it further."

"Oh my. Boy, what I almost got us into!" Anna's shoulders relaxed.

Neil changed the subject, chuckling over their neighbor's transformation. "Well, in spite of his complaining, Jim is

257

thinking about selling his place and moving back to Nebraska. Says he isn't getting any younger, and the work is getting harder. I think he does miss his family." Neil doodled on the back of an envelope. "This would be an opportunity for us to buy some more land…"

Anna recoiled. "How are we going to do that?" Her words erupted. "We'd have to ask for even more money. We just got out of trouble. We can barely make the payments we've got." She softened a bit as she looked at his tired face. "Besides, you're still not feeling well. How would you be able to handle all the extra work?" Their debt scare was far from over. They still had a long way to go before the ranch was paid off, and because of the low calf and grain prices, they would probably have to borrow even more from the PCA, simply to get by.

Neil nodded, dejected. "I'm letting you down. Instead of a better life, I'm only giving you more problems." He passed his hands over his eyes and sighed. "Oh, I almost forgot…" He headed out to the car, hefted a large box from the trunk, and carried it inside.

"I brought you a surprise." From the box, he lifted a record player, a Patti Page album and one of German folk songs. "One of those new stereophonic phonographs."

Anna looked at the machine, then at Neil. "We can't afford this. When will we have enough money to go to Germany? Jim Eichorn isn't the only one who misses his family." She ran into the bedroom and slammed the door.

Anna pulled the curtains shut and lay on the bed, her hopes and dreams trapped inside the darkened room with her. Always something took any extra money she managed to save—illness, parts to keep the equipment running, an emergency trip to the vet. Germany might as well be on the moon, for all the chance she had of getting there. *Ach, du lieber Gott, will I never get to see Mutti and Papa again?*

For weeks she went through the motions of caring for the children. She barely spoke to Neil when he was around, and came out of the bedroom only to cook meals, hardly eating anything herself. The nightmares were back, the very real, terror-inspiring dreams—running from the bombs...running and running, gasping for breath, but never quite making it to the bomb shelter...

Neil stayed out in the fields or worked in the shop, and when he came into the house, he tiptoed around as though not to trigger a storm. No longer did they sit at the kitchen table talking companionably after Monica and Kevin had gone to bed. Anna knew her feelings were irrational, but she couldn't shake the terrible dread that she would never go home again.

Even the kids sensed the tension. Kevin ran through the house, jumping off the couch and chairs like a hyper puppy. As Monica left for school one morning, Anna overheard her whisper to Kevin, "If Mommy and Daddy start yelling at each other, tell them you have a real bad owie on your leg."

Anna's heart melted in a puddle of guilt. Oh dear, what had she done to her children?

One evening, Neil caught Anna's arm as she was about to leave the kitchen after cleaning up the supper dishes. "Stay tonight," he pleaded. "I want to talk to you."

Anna sat down without a word, staring at the floor.

Neil rubbed his big hands together nervously. "Honey, I know things haven't been easy for you these past ten years. It's been a struggle, especially when I was sick. But I'm back to normal now, and Doc says he can't find any signs of the virus." He drew a long breath. "I went to visit Fred and Marie Steiner today. They offered us enough money so you and the kids can go back to Germany for a visit, and in return, I will plant and harvest their crops for them this summer."

Anna's head came up sharply, her eyes wide with disbelief. He would do extra work for the neighbors—for her? Guilt chewed at her heart. She opened her lips, but nothing came out. Then she covered her mouth with her hands and tears cascaded over them. "Oh, Neil... I... *Ach*... Go home?" Her breath came in gasps. She didn't know what to say. "B-but I can't leave... Your health..."

Neil moved around the table and took her in his arms. "Yes, honey. You need to go home. I'll be just fine here."

Anna swallowed past the lump in her throat as she hugged Neil one last time before boarding the train in Billings. Blinking back tears, she took the kids to their seats. The train whistle hooted, and the car lurched. Anna barely noticed as it slowly moved past the stockyards, a picture of the dejected, hang-dog look on Neil's face seared into her mind.

Mercifully, her attention was diverted away from that sadness, as Kevin jumped in and out of his seat, looking out the window, then trying to run down the narrow aisle. Other passengers simply smiled or said, "He's an active one" when she apologized for what seemed like the tenth time. He finally wound down from the excitement of his first train ride and fell asleep. As usual, Monica's nose was glued to a book. Anna leaned back against the train seat and closed her eyes.

At last, she was on her way home—to Germany. Bad Orb must have changed since the war. Oh, to see her Mutti and Papa and all the relatives again. Her heart filled with nervous apprehension, wondering how they had changed and what the town had done to rebuild. But then a shoulder-load of guilt about leaving Neil alone deflated her excitement. *I hope this isn't a mistake.* She could only pray he wouldn't get sick again.

But, to be going home... For just a moment she allowed herself to feel a delicious, tingly sensation of excitement before drifting off into a light sleep.

During the three days it took to reach Chicago, Anna got very little sleep. Between keeping a firm grip on her purse with one hand and another on Kevin, who was given to running up and down the aisle, she wouldn't allow herself to relax. The kids loved going up into the Vista Dome—the upper viewing car—where they could watch the countryside slide by.

By the time they boarded the propjet airplane in Chicago, Anna wished they were already in Frankfurt.

Monica came back from visiting the tiny lavatory. "Mommy, I just heard those people talking over there—they're going to visit Oma, too. How do they know her?"

Anna chuckled. "They have their own Oma. That's the German word for Gramma."

Monica flushed. "Oh. I thought that was her name." She picked up her book again.

The twenty-four-hour flight went to Montreal, over Newfoundland, to Shannon, Ireland, and then Dusseldorf, before landing in Frankfurt. At first, the kids were starry-eyed with wonder at the clouds outside the window and being served meals on a tray. "This is better than Woolworth's," Monica said. But after the newness wore off, Kevin fidgeted again and cried because he couldn't get up and run around like he had on the train. Anna's rear was sore from sitting, her arms weak from holding Kevin back, and her eyes gritty from lack of sleep.

Hans and Karl waited at the gate, big grins on their faces. Anna gave a little cry and rushed into their arms.

"And how are you?" Karl squatted down to greet Monica in German.

"So, you are Monica," said Hans, also in German.

Monica smiled shyly and whispered, "*Guten Tag, Onkel Karl, Onkel Hans.*"

Soon Anna relaxed in the back seat of brother-in-law Albert's BMW, chattering away with her brothers on the thirty miles to Bad Orb. She gazed out the window at the large buildings in Frankfurt, the lush green countryside, and the lovely homes as they approached her hometown. "Wow, everything looks so prosperous now. It's hard to tell there was ever a war here," she marveled.

"*Ja*, we have worked hard as a country to rebuild," Hans said, "and to make things better than they were before."

Anna held her breath as they drove up *Friedrichstrasse* and parked in front of the two-story, red-roofed stucco house. It looked virtually the same. Suddenly the front stoop filled with smiling, waving Schmidts.

Her heart fluttered. "Oh look, Monica, there is Tante Elsa *und* Onkel Albert; and there, standing in front of them are your

261

cousins Roswita and Elfrieda, and there's my sweet Tante Rosa, and oh…" The crowd parted, and there they were, her mother now a stout, gray-haired woman on the arm of a slight, older gentleman.

Tears filled Anna's eyes and her heart felt so full of love and happiness she thought her chest would explode. "Mutti! Papa!" She swung the car door open and ran.

Her mother's moon-face beamed. Her hands flew to her mouth, and she stopped on the sidewalk, as if unable to continue. "*Ach, du lieber Gott, mein liebes Kind.*"

Anna swept into her mother's arms for a big hug. Her heartbeat melded with Mutti's, and their tears mingled on smiling cheeks. "I've waited so long for this," Anna cried. Home, at last.

Monica was introduced to her cousin Uli, Hans and Erna's daughter, who was also eight years old. Soon the girls played with dolls Anna had brought from America.

Over *Schwartzwälderkirchtorte*—a rich, dark chocolate cake with cherry filling—and strong, black coffee, the group attempted to catch up on ten years' worth of news. Everyone chattered at once, asking questions, relating anecdotes, punctuating the air with their forks. The cake didn't survive the gathering.

For the first time in years, Anna felt relaxed. She didn't feel like she had to be on guard, watching everything she said and how she said it. She was among the familiar; she was one of them. They all accepted her here, and they all loved her. She slept soundly, without nightmares. In a couple of weeks, she felt more rested than she had in a long time.

Every afternoon, her sister, one of the cousins or her sister-in-law took Anna and the kids on an outing—to walk in the lush green woods that were kept immaculately groomed from debris; to climb the *Wart Turm*, the thirty-foot-tall white stone tower that had kept watch above the town for centuries, or to the park to pet the miniature deer. Kevin toddled up to the tiny, spotted animals. "Touch?" Anna's heart filled with happiness.

Uli and Monica went to *das Schwimmbad* nearly every day to swim, and the girls played with the neighborhood kids in the vacant field next to the house. Monica seemed to be picking up enough German to get along just fine. When her cousin's one-month summer vacation was over in mid-July, Monica went to school with her every day. Anna was amazed at what the German schools were teaching, compared to American schools—Uli was already learning simple algebra in third grade. Monica might be better off, going to school here. Even though she was a "foreigner," the other kids here didn't make fun of her or exclude her from their play.

With the scars of war nearly healed, the once-starving economy had grown fat, as had the people. Germans, who had been without food for so long, now considered rich, heavy eating a sign of prosperity. Anna's sister Elsa's once-svelte figure was now round, and everyone urged the slender Anna to eat more.

"*Ess!*" Oma ladled out another bowlful of lentil *suppe* with plump sausages.

"*Hast du hunger?*" she asked, after Anna returned from a walk in the park, which included a stop at an outdoor cafe specializing in rich, cream-laden *Tortes*.

Am I hungry? No! Anna groaned. At this rate, she'd be as big as a milk cow by the time she got home.

Not only did Oma take pride in feeding her charges, but she also delighted in her grandchildren. Monica could understand quite a bit of what she said, but Oma had to adapt her own speech to communicate with Kevin. "Haffta go?" she learned to ask when she babysat the two-year-old in the afternoons. The modern bathroom in Oma's house, which featured an overhead water tank and a pull cord to flush, fascinated Kevin. The little boy wandered into the room whenever the door was left open and repeatedly pulled the chain.

"Yours must be different," Mutti remarked.

"*Ja*, it's different," Anna said simply, thinking, if Mutti only knew *how* different. She smiled and winked at Monica. Anna had cautioned her not to tell they had an outdoor toilet.

Anna showed pictures of the cows in the wide, open pastures under the "Big Sky," and of their machinery—the tractor, plow, and combine.

"No pictures of your house?" Elsa asked.

"*Ach, nein.*" Anna waved her hand vaguely. "They're all the same." She envisioned her squat little brown-sided shack.

Mutti must never know.

Germany seemed so prosperous now, and her family had all the modern amenities Anna could only dream of…someday. They seemed to have plenty of money and painted a rosy future for their children. The women didn't have to work, they had the finest clothes and furnishings, and had time to go on shopping excursions or just have coffee with friends. She found herself wondering what life would be like here—if she were to stay. If she'd be able to go back to nursing. If she'd really be happier here.

But after two months, the daily checking-in by the relatives and their well-meaning advice was a bit wearing. Was the neighbor's gossip at Horse Creek really that much worse?

And, nearly every day, a letter came from Neil. "I miss you so much, I can hardly stand it. I know I haven't given you an easy life here, but I love you and the kids so much. I can't wait to see you again."

Anna sighed. So much was missing from their life in the States. But they did have love. Was it enough?

***

Neil steered the tractor around the field, back and forth, up and down, 'round and 'round. Anna and the kids had been gone three months. He had spent the entire summer riding the back of this noisy, gasoline-eating beast, putting in his own crops and the Steiners' and then harvesting them both. It had given him too much time to think, to miss his family. He had

264

finally resorted to memorizing Bible verses as he drove the endless furrows.

Every morning he awoke with a feeling of dread, and every night he went to bed with a sense of impending doom. He sat, brooding in the dusk, forgetting to turn on the lights, no longer obsessed with the books he usually read and studied.

Neil leaned forward against the steering wheel, his head in his hands. He'd loved Anna since he first laid eyes on her in that hospital room in Bad Orb. He'd tried so hard, but he'd made a miserable life for her. First, he took her away from her family and her native country. Then he'd plopped her down here in the middle of nowhere, where everyone was prejudiced against Germans. They had nothing but hardships ever since— droughts; floods; long, cold winters; hot, dry summers. Every time she even thought of buying herself a new dress, there was something else that came first—sickness, machinery break- down, a cow needing a vet. They'd had such dreams... Maybe she would be better off, staying in Germany.

**

In the darkening gloom, he sat, looking at the stars that also shone over Germany. A sudden, discernible pause in the rhythm of his heartbeat. A cold sweat dappled his forehead. *What if she doesn't come back?* The terror of this thought left him paralyzed. He couldn't think of life without her....

**

Across the Atlantic, Anna sat up late at night, staring out into the dark streets from the second-story bedroom. Could Neil move to Germany? The country was still divided into East and West Germany by the Wall, and the political atmosphere was still volatile with the Soviets' threat of nuclear dominance. If there were another war, their children would be in the midst of it.

No, she was sure Neil would not be happy here. America had more to offer. He knew how everything worked there. Farming was so different—German farmers came home to their house in town every night. Too many people to suit Neil. Here, he would be as out of place as a steer at a garden party. Of course, she felt just as displaced in America. But she'd made the choice to move there and took the vow, "for better or for worse."

What good were all those fine things her family had in Germany—the expensive clothes and furniture, the Mercedes? They still bickered amongst themselves. They still worried about their future—would the men continue earning enough to keep them in the style to which they'd become accustomed?

And she wasn't sure she wanted her kids to grow up with this materialistic philosophy. She appreciated the rewards of hard work. Life struggles were basically the same everywhere, even though at times, things did appear to be better elsewhere. But without love, all that was left was the struggle. At least Anna had someone to share it with.

Yes, she missed him, too. She belonged with her husband on the ranch at Horse Creek.

Anna turned on the electric lamp, took out pen and paper and began to write.

Dearest Neil...

CHAPTER TWENTY-THREE

Neil grinned, and pushed the gas pedal harder. The 120 miles to the Miles City train depot had never seemed so far. His family would be home today. He couldn't help but break into snatches of song, "It's a most unusual day..." pounding out the rhythm on the steering wheel.

He pulled up at the depot just as the train rounded the bend and slowly coasted to a stop. His heart beat like galloping hooves, and his hands were sweating as he got out of the car and waited for the passengers to disembark. Neil watched young men get off the train. Families, a lone woman or two met waiting relatives or friends. But where were Anna and Monica and Kevin? They would be on this train, wouldn't they? Surely Anna hadn't changed her mind. A chill ran up his spine.

There! There they were, his beautiful Anna, with an overnight bag in her hand and Kevin balanced on one hip. Neil swallowed. *Oh, he's grown so much—that's right, he'll be three in a couple of weeks.* Monica followed behind, carrying another small case and a large shopping bag. *So has she. She's turning into a young lady already at almost nine.*

Neil gave a shout and waved.

Anna looked in his direction with a big smile.

"Daddy." Monica's face lit up. She ran to him first, wrapping her arms around his waist. Anna followed close behind.

He leaned forward to crush them all in a long, hard hug. "Oh, I'm so happy you're home," he said over and over.

Finally, Kevin squirmed and whimpered.

"Daddy, you're squishing us." Monica's muffled voice came from his side.

"Oh yeah, I suppose I am. I just want to hug you to pieces." He released them and looked into Anna's twinkling blue eyes. "Welcome home, my darling. I've missed you more than life itself." Their lips met for a deep, lingering kiss.

***

Anna could barely speak past the thickening in her throat. "I missed you, too." She melted into Neil's arms and returned his kiss. Her weary body softened against him in relief. She'd never been so glad to reach the end of their long journey and to see her husband waiting. She almost fell to her knees to kiss the ground, but thought better of it.

Neil put their luggage in the trunk and they all climbed in the car. Kevin hung back, a little shy, but Monica chattered away about her cousin and *Schwimbaad* and school and learning German, until Anna finally gave her a book.

"Still my bookworm." Neil grinned. "How's everybody back in Bad Orb?"

"Oh, they're all very well. Mutti and Papa are a little older, grayer." Anna shook her head. "Germany has changed so much. Everything has been rebuilt—you wouldn't recognize the streets—and everyone is prospering. But they all seemed so materialistic—even my sister and brothers. They all have to have the finest and the best." She paused. "I realized, despite working so hard, we really have a good life here. There is more to life than possessions."

"Well, I'm sure glad you're back." Neil reached over and took her hand in his. She smiled at him, warmth running through her.

As Neil drove up to their house, Monica leaned over the back seat. "We have company."

Anna looked up from tending to a squirming Kevin and saw several vehicles parked in front. She drew in a sharp breath. *Oh no. I just wanted to come home and have a peaceful evening with my family.* She'd had enough company and visiting the past three months. *Oh well.* Stepping out of the car, she forced herself to smile at Neil who was grinning like the Cheshire cat.

He put an arm around her and led her into the house.

"Surprise!"

"Welcome home!"

A living room full of neighbors shouted and applauded. A large banner strung across the room also proclaimed their welcome, and the kitchen table was adorned with a huge cake, platters of meat and cheese, crackers and bread.

Etta Stokely greeted Anna with a hug. "Welcome back, Anna." She turned to the kids. "Look at Monica and Kevin—my gosh, you've both grown."

Charlie Stokley boomed, "It's about time you got home, Mrs. Moser. Poor ol' Neil's just been wastin' away to nothin'."

Tom and Fran McGregor, Fred and Marie Steiner, then Roger and Genevieve Hunter also enveloped them in warm hugs.

Nettie and Jake emerged from the shadows then with big grins. "We're so glad you're home." Nettie kissed Anna's cheek, and she hugged her mother-in-law hard. Even Jake wrapped his arms around her. "He missed you so much," he whispered in her ear.

The old emptiness inside Anna filled with gratitude. She tried to say something in return, but her throat had closed off. She could only nod, blinking back tears.

After all the greetings and hugs and chatter, Tom grabbed his guitar. "C'mon, Neil, get your fiddle and let's have some music."

The women made Anna sit while they served the food. She laughed as her neighbors cracked jokes, she tapped her toes to the music, and finally pushed her plate away. "My, you're as bad as my mother, with all the food."

Anna couldn't stop smiling. Germany and her family wasn't the only place for warm camaraderie, laughter, and sharing. Here, in this out-of-the way place in Montana, it lived and thrived. These were good people.

Finally, one by one, the couples left with more shouts of "Welcome back" and hugs.

Anna smiled at Fran, the last to leave. "Thank you," she said simply, tears filling her eyes.

All those years she'd thought her neighbors didn't like her. But perhaps the lack of friendship was the result of her own fear, and maybe it was the miles everyone had to travel to be together rather than the women's feelings toward her. Today, she was a part of the community.

Later that night Anna curled up in her warm, comfortable bed next to Neil. "What a lovely homecoming. It reminded me of our Shivaree after we were married."

He nodded, his eyes shining. "I'm so happy you're here. I missed you so terribly."

Anna nestled against his chest. "I missed you too." She *had* missed him. The happy realization washed over her. Yes, she still loved her husband. He was her life now, this was her home. It had been wonderful to see her family in Germany after ten long years, but she had her own family.

Horse Creek, Montana, United States of America. *This is where I belong.*

If you enjoyed this book, please leave a review on Amazon or Goodreads or let me know through www.heidimthomas.com

Coming Soon

Look for the next novel in the "American Dreams" series, *Finding True Home*. Follow Anna Moser as she raises a family, continues to face prejudice, endures the hardships of life on an eastern Montana ranch and a life-threatening disease.

ABOUT THE AUTHOR

Heidi M. Thomas grew up on a working ranch in eastern Montana, riding and gathering cattle for branding and shipping. Her parents taught her a love of books, and her grandmother rode bucking stock in rodeos. She followed her dream of writing, with a journalism degree from the University of Montana. Heidi is the author of the award-winning "Cowgirl Dreams" novel series and *Cowgirl Up: A History of Rodeo Women*. She makes her home in North-Central Arizona.